DAMAGE CONTROL

DAMAGE CONTROL

AMY J. FETZER

BRAVA

KENSINGTON PUBLISHING CORP.
www.kensingtonbooks.com

9|10

BRAVA BOOKS are published by

Kensington Publishing Corp.
119 West 40th Street
New York, NY 10018

All Kensington titles, imprints, and distributed lines are available at special quantity discounts for bulk purchases for sales promotion, premiums, fund-raising, educational, or institutional use.

Special book excerpts or customized printings can also be created to fit specific needs. For details, write or phone the office of the Kensington Special Sales Manager: Kensington Publishing Corp., 119 West 40th Street, New York, NY 10018. Attn. Special Sales Department. Phone: 1-800-221-2647.

Brava and the B logo are Reg. U.S. Pat. & TM Off.

ISBN-13: 978-0-7582-3139-0
ISBN-10: 0-7582-3139-3

First Kensington Trade Paperback Printing: August 2010

10 9 8 7 6 5 4 3 2 1

Printed in the United States of America

This novel is dedicated
with much love to my niece,
Angela Marie Tusa

PROLOGUE

U.S. Arctic Research Commission
Above the Arctic Circle

Dr. Walt Arnold took slow breaths to keep from freezing his lungs. At thirty below, he was accustomed to the staggering temperatures, but it was hard to regulate his breathing when he was lifting sixty pounds of pipe and ice. He wrapped the core sample in plastic, then, with his assistant, levered it onto the transport, its metal shell intact. The temperatures were in their favor to keep the core sample from relaxing, as well as maintaining the chemical isotopes in prime condition.

His team took care of transporting the sample to storage as he returned to the drilling. He adjusted the next length of pipe, clamped the coupling, then glanced at the generator chugging to drive the pipe farther into the ice. The half dozen random samples would help correlate the data from the deeper drills. He watched the meter feed change in slow increments. Nearly three hundred meters. It was the deepest he'd attempted on this patch, and he was eager for data. His report wasn't due for a year, but making the funding stretch took hunks of time he needed for the study.

When the core met the next mark, he twisted, the wind pushing the fur of his parka as he waved a wide arc. His assistants jogged across the ice and he warned them again about exerting themselves unnecessarily. They brought it up, the sample laid out in sections. Overstuffed with down and thermal protection, his colleagues rushed to contain it in the storage trenches dug into the ice to keep the sample from relaxing or their measurements for chemical isotopes would be screwed to hell.

The drill continued and out of the corner of his eye, Walt watched the progress on the computer screen. The nonfreezing drill fluid flowed smoothly and he could kiss the scientist who'd perfected it. Pipes locked in the ice meant abandoning valuable equipment. The crew transported the next length into storage below one degree to maintain the specimen. The rest gathered around the equipment housed over the site with a windscreen that would protect them, yet not change the temperature of the core samples. Walt ached for hot coffee.

Suddenly the core shot another twenty-eight feet and he rushed to shut it down. *Shit shit shit.* Not good, he thought, his gaze jumping between monitors. A pipe had come loose, he thought, yet the readings were fine. There wasn't a damn thing wrong with the equipment. That meant there was a gap. An air pocket in the glacier. His brows knit, his heartbeat jumping a little. The core depths so far were a sample of the climate eight hundred years earlier, give or take a hundred.

"All stop, pull up the last sample."

It was useless anyway. The inconsistent drill would change the atmospheric readings of gas bubbles if the core relaxed and lost its deep ice compression. Holes under pressure were usually deformed. The technician went back to securing the steel pipes. Walt switched on the geothermal radar, lowering the amplifier, then waited for the recalibration. The picture of the ice throbbed back to the screen, loading slowly. He didn't see anything in the first half that shouldn't be there. The feed showed an eerie green of solid glacier ice. Then it darkened, a definite shape molding from the radar pulse. Bedrock already? Or perhaps a climate buoy. Thousands of those were getting trapped, yet never this far below the ice floe.

A graduate student moved alongside him, peering in. "There's something in there."

Walt didn't respond, waiting the last few seconds for the pixels to clarify. "Yes, Mister Ticcone. There definitely is."

ONE

Southern Chechnya
A year later

The sound was like a cracking knuckle.

A single pop of a vertebrae, and Sebastian hesitated. Then his gaze fell on the little girl, maybe twelve, lying on the dirt floor, raped to death, and he easily applied quick pressure to her killer's neck. Three successive pops filled the aging farmhouse before the bastard softened in his grip.

He let the body slide to the ground. Sebastian remained still, movement and sound suddenly amplified. A fist hitting flesh, then the grunts of a struggle. Footsteps, the rapid pad of escape. The glow of a bonfire through bleary glass. A shadow flashed beyond, and as if slapped, he strode to the mattress, ripped off the faded blanket, then floated it down over the child.

"Be at peace, *ma petite*," he murmured, then turned away. The poor thing had been dead for hours. Sick bastard.

Armed, he moved through the musty house, ignoring the smoke-stained portrait except to count off the family members he knew were dead. He'd found the parents first when he'd entered the farmhouse through the bedroom window. It didn't take a genius to know they'd suffered. At the door, he hung back, checked his bearings before he slid along the wall to the right. A uniformed body lay a few yards from him, illuminated by the bonfire that had drawn them here. With the screams. He spotted Max on the other side of the barn near the tree line. He was moving fast, a body left in his wake. Not a shot fired. Excellent. This farmhouse wasn't their objective; that was the abandoned prison that lay a quarter mile north along the Argun River. They'd just killed the night shift. Someone *would* be coming for them.

"Report," Sebastian whispered through the Personal Role Radio. The icy air frosted his breath.

"*One ghosted,*" Max replied as if he were standing right next to him. "*You* don't *want to know what he was doing. No escapees.*"

"*Two more in the woods,*" Sam added. "*With a moonshine still.*"

The family money machine, he thought. Food was scarce here, but booze was like black market currency.

"*Lots of prints leading north, no sign of unfriendlies,*" Riley said and Sebastian spotted him near the barn, feeding something to a rangy dog. "*Wish we had sat thermals.*"

A wider spread of thermal imaging needed a satellite link and that could be tracked. They were silent, only PRRs and handheld equipment. Any more and they might as well send up a location flare. "You know that means sponging off Company, right." No one spoke, painfully aware of what that had cost them before. Cost *him*, he thought. "Regroup, tree line."

They needed to make up the time and Sebastian surveyed the terrain before he sprinted to the fire, then a few yards beyond into the woods. Tucked in the trees, he knelt and turned, aiming the short rifle and covering Sam's and Riley's approach. He was the only one wearing a video recorder and switched it back on, then flinched when Max slid up beside him, silent and very deadly.

"It's creepy how you do that sometimes," he said, his breath puffing with frost.

Max looked almost hurt. "You need a hearing aid, old man." Then he flashed a grin. "Time to rock?"

"C'mon, cousin." Sebastian rolled around and launched into the forest, running fifty yards, then dropped to one knee to cover Max's approach. Then Sam's as he shot past him in a blur. Riley took his position as Sebastian ran the next leg. They covered the quarter mile in under four minutes, aware the opportunity to rescue their target was narrowing by the second. D-1 was shattering several international laws just being anywhere in an occupied country. Diplomatic channels were just a pissing contest between each side and no one admitted to holding Vince Mills. Someone was very good at keeping secrets. Hell, the team had to HALO jump from thirty-five thousand feet to get inside the country and were likely already on someone's radar. He just hoped it wasn't the Russians.

He slowed his approach. The dark outline of the prison was blacker against the night sky. A pale cool mist wove around the treetops, reaching out to the prison walls. The penal complex was massive, the yards overgrown as if the land was trying to smother its ugliness. Recent reports said vehicles had left five hours ago and had not returned. Ten guards patrolled the place; five were growing cold on the ground.

"Last intel reports the target on the lower floor, northeast corner." Beside him, Max followed the GPS tracking on the phone used to threaten, to negotiate for the life of Vince Mills, underwater sonar engineer. It was their only link inside enemy lines. Why he was taken was still a mystery, but it didn't matter. He needed rescuing. If he was still alive. Russians weren't known for their mercy. But seizing an American businessman on his vacation in front of his young family stirred up tension across the region. It should have brought tons of help, but no government would lend aid to locate the hostage inside Chechnya. It was stepping into a war zone. Moscow claimed no knowledge, and even U.S. intel said information was sketchy and that a rescue was too dicey. That pissed him off and D-1's Ops commander, Safia Troy, squeezed her old contacts for proof of life. That got them a vague location, enough to triangulate the cell phone used to demand a ransom. Mills had been moved twice already. Oh yeah, the enemy knew they were coming.

Sebastian pulled the strip of black nylon covering Mills's picture encased in plastic. He'd memorized every detail, the expanse of his jaw, the nose that had been broken more than once. Yet the image locked in his mind was Mills's daughter as she pushed a well-loved stuffed rabbit into his hand and begged him to give it to her daddy so he wouldn't be afraid. It was tucked in his leg pocket. Breaking a promise to a three-year-old was not in the cards, and he patted it for luck, then motioned to keep the chatter down.

He didn't have to signal. The team understood the plan: surround, assault, then search and destroy. He liked things simple. Sebastian raced to the southeast corner and kept hidden near a cluster of barren trees, covering Riley as he climbed and secured his sniper position. A moment later, a pinecone hit his shoulder and he spun, searched, then aimed to the treetops. Riley signaled that he didn't see any guards on the rooftops, and no movement from his vantage point. Sebastian headed right, hidden in the winter-stripped woods, widening his path to the north corner. No sign of movement this close made his Scooby senses jump. Granted, it was below thirty degrees, but the kidnappers hadn't been slack till now. He tugged the black balaclava up over his mouth and sprinted to the corner. Ducked low, he crawled forward and looked in the window. The room was empty except for a chair. So much for timely intel. Satellite hadn't given them much beyond some trucks leaving the area several hours ago.

He inched to the next window, spying inside. Vacant. He proceeded to the next, the glass dirty gray and crossed with wires. He backed away, wedging himself near a bush. "Negative target, east side. Shit. Negative anything."

"Same northwest. No patrols either."

That made the skin on his neck prickle. "So . . . they've either moved him again or it's a trap." They'd organized in

Georgia less than eight hours ago. Even Interpol didn't know they were here yet.

"*Yeah. So. Not the first time. GPS is still active but fading,*" Max said. Max and Sam were west of his position.

Sebastian ordered the assault. Low and tucked, he ran to the side of the structure, foliage catching on his boots. He rushed to the only door on this side, and when it opened, his hackles jumped to a whole new level. *Rut-roh.* He slipped inside and dropped to one knee. The light tucked beneath the MP5 rifle barrel illuminated the tight corridor; the laser sight pierced the beam. The ceiling had fallen, the debris coated with the rippling sling of mud. He spotted shell casings, an empty boot on its side. He moved forward, turning a corner, and at least intel was right about the rows of cells lining a wide corridor. There was a decayed body in one, still locked in, still chained to the wall. The body was missing a foot, the exposed bone sawed cleanly. *I found your boot.*

Mills's chance of survival was looking slim, and he pushed on, searching the cells till he reached the end of the wide bay. A broad flight of stairs lay in the center, rising to the second level of cells. He caught the flicker of light and aimed.

"Outlaw, your twenty?"

"*Second deck, north end,*" Sam said.

"Copy that." Sebastian continued to the northwest corner. The cell door was open, a single chair inside the narrow space, to the right of it a battery, corroded and linked to some nasty-looking devices. What the hell did a sonar designer have that was worth torture? Those things looked like dental tools. He backed out, nearly tripping over a body lying against the left wall behind the open door. He spotted Russian insignia first, then he searched the dead soldier, coming back with a pistol, ammo, and a crushed pack of cigarettes. No ID. While the smokes were wet, the pistol was in perfect condition, oiled and clean. It had been *in* the holster. He pocketed the weapon, then brushed back the wool skullcap, and a second before he noticed the blood still bright, he saw the two bullet holes in the back of the head. The guy's face was just *gone*.

"Be advised, one guard dead, execution style. He's fresh. No ID."

"Found two, same-same, Russian Army uniform, no ID," Max said. *"East side, no target."*

"Could intel be that bad?" he said to no one, then found a third body outside a heavy steel door, a key broken off in the lock. He switched night vision to thermal briefly, but nothing registered. He didn't have time to investigate further. Not till they located their target. Not with executed guards littering the place. He stripped the corpse of gear, noticing several tattoos, yet found nothing else. Not even a match-book. Yet a thin, half-smoked cigar lay near the boot. The skin was cool, but not cold. Very fresh. Within the last three hours.

He quickly turned away, searching the ground for foot-prints, and found several. He followed one set, heavier than the others, another beside it, dragged. The prints led him far-ther into the center of the prison. He passed a dining area, rows of tables with bench seats attached, and for an instant, it looked like a school. The kitchen was exposed, pots stacked on metal shelves, coated with a layer of frosted dirt. The footprints directed him to a staircase in the far southern corner. They curved down to a black hole of nothingness.

"D-1 regroup, my twenty. There's a basement." Of sorts. From his position, he could see the chisel marks where it had been carved out of the rock.

"Roger that," came from his teammates. Riley was still parked in a tree.

Sebastian waited for the team before he moved down the metal staircase, the iron anchors screeching as it swayed. He shone his light below and saw the glassy surface of water. "A cistern?" He descended the steep staircase that forced him to turn sideways.

"More like a sewer. Christ, that smells," Sam said behind him.

Max remained topside, covering them. "GPS says we're within twenty-five feet. About two minutes ago. Battery's toast."

"Thermal?"

"Negative. No reading through all that rock."

"I'm gonna be really pissed if they tossed the phone down here." At the bottom steps, Sebastian's boots filled with icy water and he shivered and cursed, then moved carefully. "Low bulkhead," he warned, ducking. Water sloshed over his boots as he advanced in an uncomfortable hunch. The floor was fairly even, but his shoulder scraped the tunnel wall as he followed the water. No current, the surface motionless till he disturbed it. He wedged himself around a curve and the area opened wider. A lot wider. Water seeped down the walls, dripped from ten feet above, one plop at a time.

Beneath it was their target.

Vince Mills was strapped to a stool in the center of the pool. His legs were secured and underwater to his ankles, but his chin rested on his chest. Despite the freezing cold, he wasn't moving. Not promising, Sebastian thought, and leading with the rifle barrel, he inspected his surroundings in a narrowing circle. Mills's clothing matched his wife's description, though muddy, his shirt torn at the shoulder. But that's where it ended. Last seen with a ponytail of dark hair, Mills's head was shaved clean and sported several cuts. A couple were still glossy with fresh blood. At least he hoped it was fresh. The guy hadn't moved a fraction, yet Sebastian felt every hard shiver working up his own body. His toes were already numb.

He motioned to Sam and they covered the circumference, then in his peripheral, he saw Mills's fingers twitch. "Vince Mills, your wife sent us."

A sound came, strangled, desperate. Mills kept his head down.

"He's alive." Always a plus, he thought, exchanging a smile with Sam and moving to face Mills. He knelt, inspecting, then started to reach for his bonds and froze. Wires. Everywhere. "Be advised. We have explosives."

"Well, that just stole the joy," Max said.

Sebastian shouldered his rifle, then slipped off his pack and, with a penlight, followed the leads. He lifted the baggy shirt a fraction. Now that's a big party favor. Slim tubes of C-4 were molded to Mills's rib cage, his skin the only thing separating him from enough explosives to blow the entire prison into kibble. The phone was wired into it. And from the look of it, the fading battery wouldn't matter. There's a secondary power source, he thought, and through his night vision goggles, he studied the water, not daring to disturb it till he was certain the guy's feet weren't wired as well. He followed the trail of wires that led to Mills's mouth.

"Christ," Sam said, peering in. "That's just unholy."

Sebastian agreed as he studied the device, calculating the detonation range, the safe distance from this much blasting material. "Executed guards, no ID, this bomb was meant to erase any trail."

"Roger that," Sam whispered into the PRR so Mills wouldn't hear. "But why make ransom demands in Greece, then end up here? For a sonar engineer?"

"I'm hoping he'll answer that later."

A strained sound came from Mills. "Stay calm," Sebastian said almost absently, examining the bomb he admitted was a work of art. Wires running in five directions and no way to tell if any were dummies. Methodically, he traced each one, marking on his hand where they led and the color. Getting this off without detonation was going to be a bitch. He moved around to face Mills, ducking to meet his gaze. Watery blue eyes stared back.

"Blink once for yes, two for no. Understand?"

One blink.

"It's motion sensitive."

One blink.

"Blasting material in your mouth?"

Two blinks. No.

"The timer?"

One blink.

Crap. Disarming when he couldn't see the timer was a problem. He moved around the stool, inspecting beneath and doing it quickly. Whoever set this wasn't far away. Trained to ignore the outside world right about now, Sebastian couldn't ignore Mills. His nose was running, his breathing fast. In below freezing weather, he was sweating. Sebastian could almost smell his terror.

He leaned in to say, "Don't give up, Vince. We'll get you out of this." He pulled out the stuffed rabbit and wedged it on his lap. Mills seemed to melt right then.

The device was sensitive to Mills's movements, yet he didn't find any liquid motion sensors. If it was in his mouth, they were screwed. He slid behind Mills and with his knife, sliced open the shirt. Well, that's a mess, he thought, removing his pack to pull out a small battery with wire leads and some tools. He searched the device for a secondary rig and power source. When he found it, he realized it had a double pull. With the phone, one detonation would set off the first layer, another the second. He stripped the wires with tender care and clamped them, rerouting the circuit so the secondary device wouldn't trigger. Then from the first charge, he removed the plunge detonator. There were four. The process was slow enough that Mills passed out. Sam whispered him back awake. Any quick motion and it was curtains for the good guys.

Then Mills screamed behind the tape, trembling.

Sebastian lurched to look. Red lights shined though the guy's teeth. Oh shit. Quickly, Sebastian removed another lead, working to his mouth where he could see the red glow. Someone liked theatrics, he decided as he clamped off power to the wires near the mouth, then pulled at the duct tape. Mills fought him and Sebastian grabbed his shoulders, shouting to be still. The timer was still going. He sprayed canned Freon, freezing the tape, and it lifted off. Out of Mills's mouth came a bar timer, blinking.

Twenty-seven seconds. The numbers ticked off fast.

"Christ, Christ," Mills muttered, spat, and Sam kept spraying Freon, freezing the leveling charge and delaying detonation a few seconds while Sebastian rerouted, shifted clamps, then carefully pulled the last metal rod from the C-4. Five . . . four . . . oh hell. He grabbed his cutters and severed the blue wire.

The clock stopped. He let out a tight breath, was still for a moment, then worked the C-4 vest off Mills. He'd passed out again.

"Stand down, bomb disarmed."

"That's good, because we have headlights," Riley said. *"A convoy on the road, moving fast."*

That bomb was supposed to go off minutes ago. The bad guys were coming to learn why it hadn't. "Roger that." He inclined his head to Sam. "Secure the exit." Sam spun and went topside.

Sebastian disassembled the device. Transporting a rig this big wasn't possible. He reworked the detonator, then grabbed the bunny and jammed it in his leg pocket before he helped Mills to his feet. He was lethargic and Sebastian shook him, turning his face so he'd look him in the eye. "Vince? Focus, friend."

Mills blinked several times before his eyes quit rolling.

"You're going home." Mills's strained expression softened. "It's going to be a fast ride. Are you injured?"

Mills cleared his throat a couple times. "I can walk." He took a step and his knees gave. "Just can't feel my feet so much."

Sebastian helped him through the tunnel to the stairs. "Outlaw, my twenty, A-sap!" Rapid footsteps, and Sam appeared at the top of the staircase, sidling down to reach Mills.

Sam threw a dirty jacket over him. "I know it stinks, but it's warm." Glossy blood coated the back.

"Can't smell any worse . . . th-than me," Mills said as they helped him up the staircase. The guy winced with each step and he'd bet his feet were frostbitten. No telling how long he was in the basement sitting in icy water. Some impressive willpower not to shiver and set the bomb off.

"Finn, report." No answer. "Finn!"

"I'm on the ground." Harsh breathing as Riley said, *"Bug out. The Russians are coming."*

"Rendezvous secondary LZ. We have the package. Drac?"

"Mills wasn't the only hostage," Max said.

"A regular party here. Finn, Outlaw is coming your way with the package." Then to Sam he said, "Get him to the LZ, he's the priority."

"Roger that. Just don't go all heroic," Sam said and the tall Texan hefted Mills, nearly dragging him along as Sebastian turned in the opposite direction.

He heard a single gunshot and found Max in front of the metal door, the lock smoking. The body of a guard blocked the door, and he grabbed the collar and waistband, moving it aside. The corpse still gripped a smoke. He took low position, kneeling, and Max swung the door open. The suction of air swished in dirt and leaves. Max and Sebastian flanked the door as they shined lights inside. The room was used for storage, shelves toppled, canned food rusted and bent with pressure. A few had exploded. A table with two chairs sat in the corner near the door, trash surrounding it. Then his light fell on a figure, bare to the waist, arms outstretched and anchored to the wall with chains and some medieval-looking shackles. The prisoner could neither stand nor sit. His skin looked blue. Sebastian covered the perimeter, then approached, shining his light close enough to blind him. The guy's head lolled to the side.

"It would be a great day . . . if you're Chechen rebels."

Sebastian pulled the Velcro square covering the U.S. flag on his sleeve. The guy sank back, muttering something he didn't get.

"Who are you?" Max was behind him, his laser sight on the guy's forehead.

"Beckham, Mitch, Major, 364-71—"

"I know you." Max moved a step closer. "Sorta. He helped us in Singapore with Vaghn. He's Deep Six."

Sebastian had heard the name, but on that Op, he was pinned under twenty feet of rubble and contemplating his life as it tried to pass him by.

"Glad to know so I'm popular." Shivering violently, Beckham struggled to stand as Sebastian worked over the rusty iron cuffs and released him. The guy groaned as he lowered his arms. His trousers were filthy and blood splattered, and his bare chest showed he knew those electrified dental instruments well. His face wasn't in great shape either and Sebastian was surprised the guy could see through those swollen eyes. He didn't have time to wonder how Beckham got here and handed him a weapon. Beckham racked the slide, then crossed to a pile of clothing and rummaged. He pulled on a jacket, not bothering to zip it completely, then followed them. He hesitated beside the body of his guard, scowling down at it.

"What's the LZ?"

"The valley. We're outted. Trucks on the road. Double time." They ran through the prison, taking the stairs to the ground floor, and paused at the rear door. The major staggered a couple times, reaching for the wall for support. Max handed him a PowerBar from his leg pocket. Beckham ate it so fast he thought he'd devoured the wrapper.

"Thanks," he gasped. "I know you guys didn't come for me, so what gives?"

"Hostage rescue. Your turn."

Beckham didn't respond, expressionless. That CIA stare.

Sebastian scoffed. "You need a better class of friends to trust, cousin. Watch your six." He rushed out the doors.

"*Come south, straight line to my twenty,*" Sam said. "*Double time! Company has arrived and are ready to engage!*"

Sebastian saw Sam's signal, a brief flash of red light, and ordered Beckham and Max to hit the trail. "That's not the LZ, Outlaw."

"Never leave a buddy behind to clean up."

Sebastian ran toward Sam's signal and slipped behind a tree, the others scrambling over piles of jagged boulders. A couple feet away beside Sam, Vince Mills shivered uncontrollably, wrapped in rags, but his injured feet would slow them down. Sebastian ordered Sam and Riley to the secondary landing zone. "Take Company boy with you." In moments, the four disappeared into the dark.

Max never took his aim off their trail.

"Get base on the wire," he said to Max. Max pulled the commlink from his pack, and hailed Dragon One's Ops commander, confirming they had the package.

Safia didn't waste time. *"Chopper lifting off. Find some cover, I have a UAV on radar, approaching one mile north."*

A drone. The Russians were pulling out the stops today. "Secondary LZ. I repeat. Secondary LZ. Come locked and loaded," Sebastian said into the radio as he ran tandem with Max. Their breath frosted the air, leaving a path, and behind him, he heard the heavy pound of footsteps, shouts he couldn't translate. Suddenly he stopped, then headed back the way they'd come for a few yards.

"Coonass, what the hell are you doing?" Max said, running.

"Buying us some time! Keep moving!" Sebastian dropped to the ground and through night vision saw men enter the prison, uniformed, orderly. He recognized the tactics. The lack of an explosion had brought them back, and he decided to give them what they asked for. He hit the jerry-rigged detonator and didn't stay to watch, tearing off the NVGs as he bolted. He felt the blast shove him forward, nearly off his feet, and he staggered, gained footing, then ran like hell.

"That was pretty," Max said through the PRR.

"Crowd-pleasers." Sebastian glanced back, then rushed right as brick and stone hailed down. Screams mixed with the explosion, and he saw one man go flying along with pieces of iron. Then he spotted the gray-bellied drone and searched for cover. There was none, the barren land bleak with ice. They ran. Sebastian didn't need a guide. He'd memorized the terrain and he splashed through a creek between jagged rocks as he fixed the commlink in his ear and hailed Base again.

"*The chopper is in the air. You'll have about three minutes after it passes into Chechnya airspace. I'm tracking you thermal. Two hundred yards to the valley LZ.*"

Sebastian was a pilot. Getting in and out of the narrow valley would be a fight with air currents. "Negative, he needs to land farther out."

"*No time.*"

"Negative, Base, he'll never make it out of the valley!"

To prove his point, the wind slid like a fast-moving river in the crevasse and it started to snow. Then he heard the *thip-thip* of bullets zipping through the trees. A couple hit the rock over his head.

"Incoming!" He dropped to the ground and rolled to his stomach, then fired, pulling on his NVGs between shots. The forest beyond filled with movement. Uniformed troops walked without restriction, without taking cover. He dropped one man and the others kept moving. Robotic. Jesus. Then he hit the trigger and the small charges he'd left behind destroyed men and trees. He jumped to his feet and ran, his ears perked to the sound of the chopper, the blades beating the air softly. Stealth mode, he knew, sloshing through a stream, climbing over rocks to the LZ.

"*Chopper, your one o'clock,*" Sam said, tucked under an outcropping of rock with the others and spying through night vision.

Sebastian scanned the sky and spotted the black chopper, guns a'ready. Dawn was coming too fast. Then over his commlink, he heard, "*Oh shit, we've got MiGs.*"

"Repeat last?"

"*A MiG is in the air. Mach 2, ETA two minutes.*"

Sebastian was out of options. "Tell Mustang to follow the smoke."

He pulled the ring and tossed the canister into the only clearing big enough for the chopper to land. Green smoke curled in the pre-dawn light. The MiG would spot it, but the chopper had to get in fast and not waste time searching for them. The scream of the approaching jet grew closer. The chopper traveled low in the rocky valley, hopping on air currents and nearly falling out of the sky. Then it stabilized and lowered. The blades beat back the scrub trees, kicked up a flurry of snow. The team rushed forward, Mills limping, and Sam hefted him in a fireman's carry, running as the helicopter hovered over the ground. Logan hung on the skids, giving Killian commands as he reached for the first man. Riley and Beckham aboard, Sam pitched Mills inside, then turned to cover them as the valley filled with troops. The MiG shot overhead and turned back to take aim. The troops opened up on them, laying a steady stream of gunfire, and advancing quickly.

Sebastian gave it back, unloading his MP5 as he and Max climbed in. "We're in! Lift off!" Max hung on the edge, manned the machine gun, and plowed the road, but the MiG was coming for them. Sebastian shouted, "Go, go!"

The chopper rose swiftly, then curled left, back toward the incoming MiG. Sebastian grabbed a headset, shoved it on, and said, "Mustang, are you insane? Get across the border!" They had to be far from the MiG's path; the jet wash would toss them.

"You really need to cut down on the caffeine, honey."

Sebastian looked at Sam, then lurched around the pilot's seat. Viva was flying.

"We are so going to have a long talk when we get home." Sam shed his pack and weapons, then slid into the copilot's seat and pulled on the helmet. "Give me control."

"Don't go all *guy* on me now, baby." She pulled back on the stick and the chopper rose swiftly, the force driving them into the deck. Then it shot forward, zigzagging the edge of the valley before climbing over the Caucasus Mountains. A wind shear jostled the craft. Sam held the stick with her and brought them higher. The mist surrounded them, the snow-covered peaks only feet below.

"Viva, go postal!" Sebastian saw the MiG rocketing toward them, armed with R-73 missiles.

Then it fired.

"Incoming!! Incoming!"

The missile sped toward them, dead on the target. They crested the mountaintop, then Viva sent the chopper sharply downward into Daryal Gorge, across the border into Georgian airspace. But it wasn't over.

"It's heat seeking!"

"Launching countermeasures." Sam hit a switch and the flaming tubes tumbled, the missile falling toward it. Viva banked it right, but one countermeasure failed, and the missile turned to chase the hotter target.

"Release countermeasures again!" he shouted.

"I can't. It won't open!"

Sebastian grabbed two flares off the wall rack, ignited them, then threw. "Go turbo! Now!" The chopper rocketed with the speed of a Black Hawk. He grabbed on and looked back as the flares tumbled to earth. The missile chased, slamming into the mountainside a second later. Fire blossomed, expanded in a rolling orange cloud. Flames and debris flattened trees, tumbled shale rock. The sight faded as they flew farther into South Ossetia Georgia.

But the MiG wasn't giving up. Over the radio, the Georgian military warned the fighter jet to turn back immediately or be shot down. Pissed, Sebastian threw back the door and aimed the .50-caliber machine gun at the pilot. He fired off a hundred rounds just to get his attention, and the jet banked, returning to Chechen airspace. He sank to the chopper floor, breathing hard. Helluva day. He shut the door.

"Remind me to spank you for that, Viva," Sam said into the quiet of headphones.

"Ohh honey, promise?"

Sam groaned, and Sebastian chuckled. Poor guy. Yet he

understood Viva's need for a little thrill seeking. She'd miscarried a month earlier and wasn't one to sit around and sulk. Like him, she needed the adrenaline push. Though how she conned Killian into trading places was a story he wanted to hear. The man had gone soft. It was scary.

Then he noticed Beckham frowning at Riley. "You're Safia's guy."

"Better. Her husband." Riley grinned.

Beckham looked a little crestfallen. "Tell her I said congratulations."

"You can." Riley cracked open a bottle of water and drank. "She's at the other end of this Op."

Beckham smirked. "Figures."

Viva flew at a more sedate speed as Logan worked over Mills, cracking a heat pack and covering his feet. His toes were blue. Beckham waved off medical care, looking back the way they'd come for a moment, then sank into a corner and closed his eyes. Sebastian noticed his clothing was along the lines of Armani and not Black Ops, but he really didn't want to know why Beckham was here. He's too deep in the nasty secrets, he thought, resting against the hatch, then noticed Mills pushing away the oxygen mask. They couldn't hear Mills over the chopper engine, and Sebastian lurched for headphones, held Mills's hands down, then pushed them on. He plugged him in.

"Vince! Chill buddy, you're safe. Let the doc work on you." Sebastian dug in his leg pocket and pushed the stuffed rabbit that needed a bath into Mills's hands. He clutched it, but was insistent, nearly in Sebastian's face.

"No! You don't understand. You have to warn my wife!"

"Warn her for what? You'll see her in thirty minutes or so."

"It wasn't me they wanted. It was her."

"Shit."

Sam immediately hailed Safia with the warning. Mills didn't settle down till Safia assured him his family was protected. He sank back and allowed Logan to treat him, yet squeezed the rabbit over and over. His anxiousness was as clear as his fear.

"Are you saying this kidnapping was a mistake?"

"Had to be," Mills said. "They asked for codes, over and over. It was the only English I heard. After being hooked up to a battery, I gave the calibration codes, but that wasn't good enough." He passed a hand over the back of his head, gentler on the burns and cuts. "Guys. I'm small potatoes, and any codes I have are useless except to get into my bank accounts. And they're empty till I get paid for the sonar."

He was right about the funds. D1 was here on conscience alone. "Why do you think the target was your wife?"

"She was the intelligence in the family. For three years, she monitored satellite transmissions in the North Atlantic. Eastern Europe."

Russia, China, definitely Chechnya, he thought and could pinpoint about a dozen listening stations, but that wasn't current. Yet the posts were the same. A remote location free of interference, minimally stocked, high security, in small confines as the techs listened for those key words. About as exciting as a submarine sonar technician, depending on the clearance level.

"Anything she could get at—if she could remember an old authorization code, which she can't—would be outdated," Mills said, looking confused. "She just gathered, no analyzing. The right codes would get you into the archives, except you'd have to access the storage server."

"And that would be where?" God, he dreaded this, hoping the kidnapping was simple, uncomplicated greed.

Mills looked a little shocked by the question. "Langley. It was a CIA listening post."

Sebastian glanced at the team. They were all thinking the same thing. If Mills's wife was CIA, former or otherwise, then why weren't they here with them? He swung around to stare directly at Beckham.

The major stared back. "Not connected."

Sebastian didn't believe it. The spy network was a powerful entity and he'd been on the receiving end of personal agendas run amok before. "Transmissions are Delta classified."

Beckham glanced at the team, then settled back, talking with his eyes closed. "Yes, and the U.S. along with about a dozen other countries intercept millions all over the world. We listen, they listen." He shrugged. "If it wasn't anything substantial, it was relayed to the correct agency."

Bullshit. Sebastian didn't trust Beckham's word any more than he trusted the CIA. "You owe us, Beckham," he warned. "Don't think I won't call in this marker."

Beckham scoffed to himself, eyes still closed. "You can try."

Sebastian glanced, caught Max and Riley scowling at Beckham. He waved it off. A pot of gumbo they didn't need to taste, he thought and got comfortable as the chopper swept farther into Georgia, heading for the landing strip surrounded by her troops. Got to love those guys. They were the first to help them, which was more than he could say about the United States. Yet he couldn't take his gaze off Mills as Logan injected him and checked his other wounds.

A kidnapping mistake. Not hardly. Not with troops and a MiG climbing up their ass. The kidnappers had transported Mills from Greece to Chechnya without raising a single flag. If it weren't for Safia and some Chechen rebels, they'd have never located the little geek. Information on this simply did not exist. A tight, small network, he reasoned, yet with the Russians, the possibilities he could immediately list were staggering. The least was selling weapons to unfriendlies like Iran. There was power behind this, enough that they'd risked returning to assure the trail was obliterated.

Enough to get a MiG in the air in seconds.

Yet as far as he could tell, for all the destruction that just rained down on them, the kidnappers didn't gain a damn thing.

*   *   *

Two hours later, Sebastian was reasonably warm in the conference room at a Georgian military base in Tskhinvali. A dented metal tray with a bottle of vodka and glasses rested on the long table, untouched. Beckham was glaringly absent.

Sam and Viva had their heads together on a ratty sofa; Logan leaned against the corner wall, on the phone. A few feet away at a small desk, Riley was finishing his summary for D-1's records. Max tapped him, handing him a wrapped sandwich, and Sebastian wondered where he'd found food.

"Oh, you have skills, buddy." He ate, inching closer to the heater blasting warmth into the room.

The confiscated weapons were turned over to the Georgians as well as a copy of his video to their intelligence. While they hadn't done more than provide airspace and a safe haven, without it, there was no rescue. Vince Mills would be dead. In the rear of the stark room, Sebastian finished off the sandwich and enjoyed the sight of Vince, clean, treated, and in a wheelchair, surrounded by his family. His youngest, Lily, had given Sebastian one of the sweetest hugs for keeping his promise, and he decided, yeah, it was all worth it. But it wasn't over.

"Ya know what I think?" Max mulled aloud. "I think the guards were executed by their boss. Maybe two, three hours before we got there. The ones at the farm? Their tracks came from the prison. Bad guys would have gone after them if we didn't."

Sebastian had a lot of deaths on his conscience, but not those. "They were covering the trail. But the guards weren't the kidnappers, they were hired guns. Did you notice the tats?"

"I didn't look that close."

"Russian prison tattoos on the knuckles. So everyone knows and you never forget. One on the throat," he gestured behind his ear, "was *krasnaya mafiya*. Forget which region, though."

Max's feature tightened. "You're saying the soldiers weren't Russian Army."

"At one time maybe."

"What I don't get is why stick around to watch it go off? The bad guys were near enough to haul ass when it didn't."

"Assurances." And thank Freon spray for delaying the charge, Sebastian thought, because even he couldn't disarm fast enough to beat that clock. "The timer rigged to the phone battery feels like a show of arrogance. We tracked it, but the bomb had a secondary power source. There wouldn't have been anything left to sift." He smiled when Lily pushed aside her older brother, nearly knocking him on his rear.

"They have the sonar," Max said.

Sebastian still wondered about that. Riley had questioned Mills about the design and learned it needed codes to calibrate. Faced with his death, he gave them up because it wasn't worth keeping them secret. His government contract was with the U.S. Navy, but not deep classified. Mills could build another, and Sebastian would bet that in a year or two, it'd sell to salvage and treasure hunters across the globe. Before the kidnapping, Mills had settled his family in a hotel and was to fly to England, deliver the sonar, and return to his vacation. They took him outside the hotel in front of his kids. Anna Mills had pulled some old CIA strings, he realized now, and got smacked by the State Department. They didn't believe it was anything beyond kidnapping a foreigner for money, and stepped out of the picture when the kidnappers failed to show. That's when Dragon One stepped in. Local police and the embassy in Greece were too slow for Anna Mills. But one telling factor about all this was the lack of news media coverage, not even a hint.

Suddenly the door opened and Vasili Something-he-couldn't-pronounce, the Georgian Ministry of Defense attaché, entered first, holding the door wide. Safia marched in, pulling off her earphones and crossing the room. Behind her was a slender man in an Italian suit.

"He's got government flunky written all over him," Sebastian said quietly. Riley left his chair and went to his wife. Logan moved in, closing his phone. Viva and Sam joined them.

"They've taken it all," Safia said.

His gaze flicked to the Suit. "Company?"

She shook her head. "Department of Defense. They confiscated everything we have. We'll be lucky to get take off with our clothes and the damn chopper now." She plowed her fingers through her hair. "He says they're yanking our international business license, and that's it, we're off the map." She leaned into Riley. "Just when I thought I was done with these people."

Sebastian's first concern was their debt to the Georgians. "They take the intel we gave Vasili?"

"No, I don't think they know about it," she said quietly. "But they have ours."

Over her head, Sebastian watched the Suit talk with Mills, smile kindly, welcoming him. Mills was pleased with whatever the guy said, but Vasili looked embarrassed, like a punished child. He didn't doubt that the Suit threatened withdrawal of U.S. support in their fight against Russia if he didn't cooperate. Political bastards didn't need to be in this now. Not when they turned their backs after the failed ransom drop. Sebastian had the sneaking suspicion they'd just been used.

Then Suit crossed to them and Dragon One closed ranks.

"You don't have any authority to shut us down," Sebastian said.

Suit gave a derisive smirk. "National security says otherwise. American military killing Russian troops in Chechnya? Even your clout at the Pentagon won't help you out of this."

"So you were watching. That how it goes now?" He folded his arms. "Americans in trouble and you sit your ass on the sidelines and throw money at it. Dragon One is private hire, civilians."

"I see highly trained U.S. military, mercenaries," Suit clarified, "interfering with national security abroad."

"Bullshit. Your man was already there. Captive. Why?" Suit's blank stare was too familiar, and he took a step closer. If he could shake information out of this lightweight, he'd have thrown him to the floor by now. "What's the real threat here, cousin?"

"You don't need to know." The Suit withdrew a black billfold and flipped it open. Office of the Secretary of Defense.

He was wrong. It really was over.

TWO

Heilongjiang Province, Manchuria, China
Midnight

Olivia fixed the spring-loaded camming device in the crack and pulled the mechanism down, too aware that hanging on a cliff with the river below wasn't exactly the best acoustics for silence. The SLCD gripped the rock. She'd come this far, she wasn't taking chances without securing herself. Olivia looked below to the one-hundred-foot drop into the Songhua River. Bad move. She pressed her forehead to the cold rock, gripping her lines till the vertigo slid back.

"You *said* you could do this," she muttered as she threaded the loop and clipped, careful not to back-clip the carabiner, then tugged the rope tight. She reached for the fissure, fingers gripping, then she searched for footing. Ten feet maybe, and she'd be on the ruins. The shielded neon green digital on her wrist told her she'd already taken twenty minutes to reach the top. She hoped there were answers up there and she hoisted herself another foot, working her way slowly. The crescent moon gave off enough light to make this a little easier, especially with night vision goggles. She reached, slipped, then searched again, finally getting more footholds, and the last few feet went fast. On top, she shucked her gear pack, set up her escape, then headed toward the dig. She moved in short spurts, able to see pika and something slithery in the dark. NVGs rocked.

She moved slowly down the stone steps chipped into the mountainside past the remnants of the palace watchtower barely discernible except for the north corner. The blocks were huge; limestone, she decided. The rain had eaten away at the tops. She hurried to the archaeological dig recently excavated and kept under wraps like most information from China. She paused to switch the lens to thermal imaging. It showed the hidden sensors, and as she neared, the goggles offered the blurred glow of a couple squads of Chinese troops antsy enough to shoot first, talk later.

She switched back to NV, going still when she heard a rustle in the jungle to her left, then saw something slide over the edge of the ground and into the excavation. It reminded her of when her brother's pet iguana escaped his tank and ended up in the bathtub—with Mom already in it. She followed the lizard thing, pacing lightly down the excavation steps and onto the wood platform that surrounded it. The dig was impressive, stretching three city blocks and only half revealed. Over all of it was a tarp harnessed with miles of scaffolding and shielding it from satellite. Or she wouldn't be risking her neck right now. But she knew what the Chinese had and wished they'd just *shared*.

She paused in a narrow corridor that went off in three directions, then headed toward her target, the carved sarcophagus on the platform in the center. The ruling khan of the region in the Manchu era was little known, an afterthought of history. No one expected to find anything significant. Obviously a lie or it wouldn't be under tight security. Her path widened, a couple canisters illuminating the rows of tall urns flanked by stone warriors. They appeared to be cast from humans. Even facial creases showed. Creepy. She approached the stone tomb and terra-cotta soldiers loomed over her shoulder as she knelt along its head. The indentations of the carvings showed in curves and hollows.

She snapped on a penlight and followed the row of characters and symbols. Her breath caught. It *is* here. Her heart pounded, the realization that she was looking at something no one had for a thousand years hitting her, and a giggle bubbled inside her. She swallowed it back. *Focus.* She brushed at the dirt, exposing the markings further, then slipped out two sealed bags. She removed frail paper and charcoal, then placed it over the carving and rubbed. With all our technology, this was the best we had for tactile imagery, she thought as she adjusted it for the next section. She folded it neatly, replaced the paper in watertight sleeves, then back inside her load-bearing vest. With a hand scanner, she swept the neon blue light over the length and width of the entire coffin, then she photographed it through the night vision goggles. One-stop spying, she thought and, just for fun, took a couple shots of the urns and warriors, but didn't have time for much else. Stooped, she circled the coffin, its domed top chiseled with the likeness of the local khan who'd commissioned this shrine of a tomb. A little guy, she thought, and couldn't resist running her gloved hand over the magnificent artwork, the intricately chiseled symbols. She knelt, examining one in particular, when she heard the echo of soft whispers, one deep, and she rushed along the walls of the dig site, heading for the steps carved into the dirt. Her neoprene boots kept her wrapped in silence as she slid along the wall, looking for some cover.

The voices neared, then suddenly stopped. She looked back over her shoulder and spotted a couple locked together like teenagers, mauling each other. They'll set off the alarms, she thought and rushed up the steps, then slid into the bushes and waited, the night vision doing its thing in clear bright greens. The couple unlocked and rushed farther into the dig. *Stop, stop, the sensors are near the statues . . .* The alarm tripped and she groaned, then took off toward the water in a hard run. Behind her, she heard shouts. The place was waking up and she had to reach the cliff before the searchlights came on. She glanced back, the weight of the goggles straining her neck. The first floodlight shimmered to life and she looked away or be blinded. She booked, crawling under gnarled roots, then scrambled over stones that had once been the defense tower.

She caught the scent of cigarette smoke and lurched back under the cover of bushes. An instant later, a hand clamped on her shoulder. Olivia rose in a spin, knocking his hand off, her foot smacking the soldier in the stomach. The guy staggered and she ran. The troop shouted and it was probably good she didn't understand Chinese all that well. Because that sounded like stop or I'll sho—a bullet chipped past her shoulder, the crack echoing. The exploding burn came a second later and she covered her arm as she veered, spotting her equipment up ahead. She yanked the NVGs to her throat, her arm screaming in protest as she pulled on her pack, then ducked under the matte black frame. She slipped her arms into the harness, then pulled it through her legs and secured the links. Pounding footsteps and shouts thrummed behind her. Another bullet plinked off a rock somewhere to her right as she lifted the frame, running, yet couldn't help muttering "OhGodohGodohGod" as she jumped off the hundred-foot cliff. She did a free fall that drove panic through her blood, the river nearing. *Oh hell.* She stretched and the black-winged paraglider caught the wind and sailed. For a few yards, she dangled from the harness, relieved, then she swung her legs back into the guide and adjusted the NVGs into place. Tears burned behind the night visions as she tugged lead lines, maneuvering the glider along the river. Her arm throbbed. Blood drained inside her sleeve. *I'll catch hell for that.*

A mile downriver, she spotted the foam of water when the boat engine started and the craft sped away from its cover on the shore. She was ahead of it and nosed down, aiming for the flat deck roof, and the man standing on it as she closed in. She released her legs and lowered. A foot above, she collapsed the compact wings, her feet touched, and Cruz lurched out to stop her momentum. They toppled a bit, hugging like dancers. Her hip hit the railing. The wind snapped at the nylon wings with the sound of a cracking whip, and she popped the harness clips. Cruz gathered the frame more carefully than she ever did as he took it below. Olivia covered her wound and looked back at the mountain, to the dig just beyond the cliffs. Like a halo, the sky glowed with light and she gave herself a mental pat on the back, then gingerly swung down off the roof and dropped onto the pilothouse deck. She pulled off the NVGs, then the black balaclava, and shook out her hair.

The tall man at the helm glanced her way, nodded approvingly, then went back to driving the speedboat disguised as a fishing trawler.

Cruz knelt near the wing frame, staring at his bloody hands, then to her. "You're hit?"

She uncovered the slice in her upper arm that ruined the skin suit. "Yeah, it doesn't hurt much though."

"It will." Cruz grabbed the medical kit and she let him push her into a seat. "We have people for this, you know."

"God, you're a real killjoy. Wouldn't you want to touch something a thousand years old?"

"Not at the risk of a bullet in the back. You saw the troops. They were bored silly, itching for action."

She waved that off. "They got it. They'll be talking about it for a week."

The captain twisted, scowling. "So you weren't undetected?"

She made a face, showed her bloody palm. "Duh. I didn't set off the alarms. I wasn't the only one in the dig getting jiggy in the dark either." She waited for that to sink in. It took a minute. Men were slow. He conceded with a nod.

"Take that off," Cruz said. He had his medi-pack laid out like a pro.

"What—no date first?" He wasn't amused. But then, she wasn't his type. She pulled off the load-bearing vest, then unzipped the skin suit, glad she didn't have to take a plunge in the Songua River. It was a sewer and ice cold. She worked the stretchy black fabric off her shoulders, the cool air heavenly on her damp skin as she stripped down to bike shorts and a sports bra. Her ego took a dive when neither man paid her a scrap of attention.

Cruz made her sit again, then gently grasped her elbow.

She finally looked at the fleshy part of her arm. "Need stitches?"

"Let me clean it up first," he said testily. "Told you to wear that dragon skin."

Dragon Skin was the newest R&D prototype in bullet-proof protection. But for her, it had one big drawback. "You try climbing up a cliff face wearing thirty extra pounds." She winced as he injected the area with Novocain.

"Work out more. Learn to carry it."

This from a man she could flatten with one punch? "I work out enough." She liked to eat all the wrong things. It was a trade-off.

He had a threaded needle poised, the other hand rubbing the anesthetic in. "It was stupid not to at least take a weapon. You knew they were armed."

"My goal was no collateral damage," she said it loud enough so the captain heard.

Captain looked back, his eyes narrow. "You were it. Sometimes it's your life or theirs, ya know."

"This wasn't one of those times." She'd fired at targets, not people. "Ow! Careful, I sign your paychecks."

Cruz took another stitch, looking angrier, and she thought he was worried, but then, she was bleeding. Hard to ignore. He was probably worried about having to go find her if she didn't return. Cruz DeGama was usually more interested in his research than in making an effort to care about much beyond his rabbit-hole life. Pinching a little too tight, he put a couple more stitches in the wound.

"How did you get that scar?" He nodded to the check-mark-shaped scar on her upper arm, then covered the spot just below it with gauze.

"Mountain climbing with my oldest brother, Matt."

"Did they ever *not* take you along?" He wrapped a dull beige wrap around the wound.

"Yeah, on dates. One of them always got stuck being the babysitter." She shivered. "None are qualified, trust me." Her brothers once stuffed her barely two-year-old self in a backpack like a papoose and took her to a Guns N' Roses concert. No, not even close to responsible then. She thanked Cruz, then pulled on a pair of jeans and a baggy T-shirt advertising tours of the Great Wall. Gathering up the medical debris as Cruz repacked the kit, she bypassed the filthy wastebasket tied to the pilothouse wall with a rag and some nails, and bagged the debris, stuffing it in her pack. No evidence left behind.

Cruz went back to the small drop-down table, hunched over his computer, tracking everything around them in case they were followed. He'd load up the video and scans aboard the aircraft. Olivia knelt by the glider frame, popped the piping apart, wiped off splatters of blood, then secured it with Velcro in the small, neat bundle. She loved the toys, just not the training required to use them. Sitting, she pulled the rubbing from her LBV but didn't unseal it. She wasn't exactly set up to examine it and couldn't risk the wind tearing the paper. Besides, she was hot, sweaty, and had been in these clothes for so long she could smell herself, but the trawler didn't have a bathroom where she could clean up. Apparently hanging over the side was the mode for local fishermen. Not an option, she thought, secreting the rubbing inside the duffel's false bottom. Picking up the NVGs, she moved to the rear of the boat. She sighted in. No one followed. Barely a glimmer of light came from the villages on the river's edge, the haze of pollution blocking the view more than the lack of electricity.

Her adrenaline rush had calmed by the time they reached the docks near Jaimusi, a good two hours later. Hauling black gear bags, the three boarded the light plane on a deserted airstrip, then left Manchuria China behind. They'd have to make a refueling stop somewhere near Shanghai, though South Korea would have been easier. They risked attention with landing anyway, and she prayed they could bribe their way out of an inspection. The pilot never came out of the cockpit before takeoff and by the time they reached altitude, the boat captain was asleep. She envied his casual, no-stress attitude. Nothing was exciting to him and she almost wished she knew his real name, then decided he was a little too scary for any kind of relationship. Handsome, but scary.

Olivia dozed and didn't realize how deeply till the plane touched down again. She rubbed her face, then stood to gather her bags. Captain slung a worn olive green pack on one shoulder, paused at the hatch, and looked back. She went still, anticipating she didn't know what.

"Not too shabby for a scientist." That came with a small reluctant smile.

She felt incredibly rewarded. "Thank you, Captain." He left the plane. She wouldn't see him till his specific skills were needed again.

She and Cruz left one aircraft and boarded a sleek little Gulfstream V that was cool with air-conditioning and the aroma of food. She wasn't hungry till now, always the case, but whatever was cooking made her mouth water. She stowed her gear bags, found a seat, and planted her butt in it with no intention of moving or talking till they were in a noncommunist country. Across the wide aisle, Cruz dropped into the sofa, stretching out. The engines revved, the jet taxied. Her patience wore out, and she yanked the duffel's false bottom and removed the rubbing, then grabbed a notebook and pen before she sat again.

"The light is lousy in here," Cruz said.

"I know, I have to look though. Once we're at cruising speed, load up the video and scans. I need a better view."

"Mind if we eat first?" He sniffed dramatically.

"Yes. We aren't in secure territory yet."

"Man, you need a nap."

"Behave or I'll cut off your Starbucks." That settled him in the chair, and she unfolded the rubbing, drawing the notepad close as she searched for that one kanji character. She found it, duplicating it in a sketch before returning the rubbing to its protective sleeve and hiding place. She studied it, her Chinese minimal, and deciphering the language of characters wasn't much better. But she'd seen this symbol before.

Di nèny er.

The changeling.

Moscow, Russia

His watery eyes followed her as she walked to the bar and poured three fingers of Stoli. She spilled a drop and dabbed it, turning toward the man in the padded chair as she sucked her fingertip. The old man quivered with excitement, shifting in the chair. She could see his erection swell and glanced away, smiling only inside her soul, enjoying manipulating him. He was as foolish as the others, believing her uneducated and desperate. Whoring for the wealthy. It was a keen advantage, for she went unnoticed, a person not worthy of attention. Molenko and his ex-KGB comrades spoke freely, ignoring her even when they lusted after her. All she did was listen and watch.

Tonight, it would end.

She crossed to him, handing over the drink. He guzzled half, letting out a long heavy breath as if it took great effort to do just that. Fool. She stopped in front of him, her knees to his, then she inched her skirt higher as she straddled his broad thighs. He muttered vulgar encouragement as she spread his heavy black robe, exposing the soft, plump flesh thickening his middle. The old man repulsed her and reminded her of her purpose. It had been clear for three years. This man had given it to her—and taken so much. He set the drink aside, then put his ham-fisted hands on her hips and pulled her nearer. His erection pushed against her, and she smiled, kissed his forehead, then his eyelids, his cheek. He tried to take her mouth and she pushed his face away, her eyes warning him.

"Surely just one kiss, little beauty."

She didn't speak, shaking her head, her blond hair grazing his chest. That foul mouth would never touch hers. He cupped her breasts through her garments and she made appropriate noises, tipping her head back. She rocked on him and his impatient touch bruised. He opened her blouse, pushed her bra down, and lifted out her breasts like an eager teen. He nuzzled his face between them almost violently, then bit her nipple.

She shoved him back, slapped his face.

He scowled. "You dare much, little one."

She said nothing. He didn't deserve an answer. She smiled coyly, rising up, her breasts in his face. He groped her body, trying to enter her, and she rocked as if excited for him, wrapping her arms around his head.

"For you, Papa," she whispered.

"Huh?" He tried to look at her, but she held him tightly, bearing her weight down. With one swift, strong move, she twisted violently and heard his neck break. His hands fell away, and she remained still for a second, reveling in one more victory, then backed off and righted her clothing. She fished in his robe pocket for the keys she'd seen earlier. He was rarely without them.

She crossed to the wet bar, a French design, probably two hundred years old, and she slipped behind it. It joined the other pieces in the richly appointed apartment filled with such antiques, the stolen relics of families and countries. He knew enough secrets to be kept in lavish existence while her countrymen begged for bread on the streets. She knelt on the floor, opened the lower cabinet, and removed the bottles of liquor, then drew the safe forward. It had taken her months to learn of it, then spending days with this pig for the opportunity to search. He checked it nearly every day and it spoke of his paranoia and guilt. Her hands shook slightly as she tried the keys. None of them fit.

"Bastard," she muttered, tossing them aside, then grasping her handbag from atop the bar. She knelt again, removing a black pouch, then from it she withdrew the plastic explosive. It was a tiny amount, the size of a coin, and she rolled it to a thin strip no wider than a toothpick, then wrapped it around the lock as antiquated as the man. She inserted the fuse and ignited it, then scrambled to the other side of the bar, listening to the long hiss and a pop. She crawled around, smiling when the lock fell to the floor with a thump. She waved away the acrid smell, then opened the safe, pulling out the stacks of files turned yellow with age. She searched for the one she needed, pausing a moment to read the secrets of the Kremlin. *This* was his blackmail, his leverage to force more money for his lifestyle. For his silence. From the file, something slid free and she held it toward the light. It was a two-gig flash drive. She slid the file into her bag, then returned the rest, wiping off her prints with a cloth soaked in ammonia. The odor wrinkled her nose. She closed the safe, pushing it back, and returned the liquor bottles to disguise it.

Shouldering her bag, she moved around the room, obliterating her presence, and searched for more cameras she might have missed. Near the door, she stopped, inserting the flash drive into her Web phone and watching it load. She lifted it to her ear, and heard the wav file play.

Her heart wrenched in her chest, and she stopped it, unable to hear more.

Positioning the strap across her body, she walked to the door, and opened it a fraction. She spied his guard slumped in a chair near the front door. She slipped out, walking down the hall. At her approach, he stirred awake and gave her a lecherous smirk.

"My turn now, baby?" he said, cupping his crotch.

She scoffed, tipping her chin up. "You are not rich enough to even touch me." She strode out the door. He smacked her butt as she passed, called her a stupid whore. At the base of the wide steps, she turned back, drawing her weapon. When he saw the long-nosed pistol, he scrambled for his own gun. She fired first, the suppressor silencing his death and exploding the back of his head over the antique Prussian drapes.

The Surrey Auction House
Chertsey, Surrey, United Kingdom

Noble Sheppard let out a breath when the Weller auctioneer slammed his gavel down and ended the bidding. The fifteenth-century ship's log was his. While the archaeological provenance was doubtful, its contents were not. He looked across the room at his competition and received a gracious nod at the acquisition. He didn't think it was sincere. His only opposition had tried to pressure him to back out before the bidding began—with a nice bit of cash, of course—but he couldn't be swayed. The bidding war marked the end of a long search, and a sizable negative to his accounts. He hoped he hadn't paid a fortune for too little a prize. While the ship's log was authentic, a thorough examination was refused. The document was on vellum, remarkably preserved, yet too frail to be handled by the bidders. Each page had a plastic sheath to protect it.

He walked to the cashier and signed the credit, shook hands with the auction house staff, then gathered his precious purchase. He cast them a last smile as he left the brownstone, then paused outside the door to slip the linen-wrapped book into his leather satchel. *Finally.* He adjusted the strap across his chest, then stepped out from under the awning and walked down Guildford Street. Turn-of-the-century replica lamps shined yellow light on the damp road.

A gentle fog grew from the pavement, and he suddenly longed for his shop and the smell of old books. Living abroad and traveling was more of a burden than a pleasure. Perhaps he was just getting old, and God forbid he turn into a crotchety old fart like his father. That man never enjoyed life.

Turning right, he walked briskly, the humid night air a familiar comfort. An array of compact cars drove past, slipping into spaces they shouldn't. An occasional horn blast made him glance in the direction. For all its innovation and culture, Europe failed with routing traffic around its history, he thought, then took his life in his hands as he stepped off the curb and dodged between cars to the other side. He'd walked less than a block when he felt someone close behind, but a glance in a window reflection showed a nearly vacant avenue except for a few straggler cars and a couple across the lane, rushing into a pub. He continued, eager to examine his artifact in private. The ship's log was over six hundred years old, Portuguese, and priceless only to a few. But he knew he held one more key to unlocking the legend.

Traffic thinned alongside him as a shiny black sedan pulled away from the curb. The car kept to the edge of the street, wedging traffic to a near standstill, and Noble smelled the exhaust, felt its warmth. The fog pearled higher. He passed shops closed for the night, his footsteps crisp on the pavement and increasing toward his hotel two blocks away. He should have taken a cab, he thought, and in his peripheral saw a man step out of a doorway and from across the street, walk abreast of him. It made him aware of his surroundings, the lack of people, the light between traffic signals dim and shadowy, yet Noble kept his pace even, searching ahead. The area brightened outside a small movie theater. The show had started, the lobby empty except for a young blond woman behind the snack counter cleaning up. He took a few steps past, then suddenly turned back to look at the movie poster. In the glass, he watched his back, and considered himself fortunate to know the tactic.

The man across the street slowed, then turned back a step and searched the ground for something that was not there. Noble remained where he was, his stomach tightening as the fellow looked in his direction. He wasn't fooled. The other buyer had pressed him for nearly two weeks now, each occasion a little more forceful, a little more desperate. He hadn't a clue why they wanted this particular ship's log. It held little information or value to anyone, really. Nor was it much of a relic. Noble needed only two pages for his research.

The man noticed him watching and straightened, then turned in the opposite direction, into the dark. Noble hurried down the next block, and near the end of Guildford Street, he spied the monument marking London Street and strode quickly, eager for the safety offered in lights and people in the Crown Hotel.

The Tudor hotel was unpretentious luxury. Hoping Matterson was on duty, he glanced at his watch, calculating London time. He was several yards away from the entrance when a man stepped in front of him. Noble jerked back, excusing himself and made to go around, thinking he'd have soup tonight, that wonderful leek and chicken he'd had his first night at the Black Cherry Fayre. But the man stepped with him, and Noble frowned a second before he recognized him as the fellow who'd trailed him from across the avenue.

Panic rocketed up his spine as Noble stared into cool blue eyes. "Dear God, you people are persistent. I said no." He stepped around him, but the fellow moved as well. "Don't be a child." He stepped back and was about to cross the road when the man grasped his satchel strap and he caught the gleam of a knife blade. In a loud voice, Noble shouted, "Help! Mugger!"

People turned, focused, the doorman hurrying toward him, a scarred billy club materializing from somewhere inside his coat. It was the distraction he needed and he yanked the satchel strap, shoved off his attacker, and with the crowd's approach, the man immediately turned away, rushing onto Church Walk and into the dark. Noble hastened to the hotel, grabbing his champion's shoulder.

"Bless you, friend," he said, then stepped through the doors and into the hotel lobby. A bit of calm settled through him with the scent of lavender and beeswax, and he searched the small lobby, then aimed to the far left corner, and the concierge behind a carved desk. Matterson. He dug in his satchel, gripped the log, and weaved between furniture groupings and late-night guests, trying not to bring notice. He stopped in front of the desk and Matterson immediately looked up.

"An envelope, please. Large, sturdy." He glanced over his shoulder, saw a figure in the dimly lit hall leading to the bar, immobile, watching.

"Certainly, Mr. Sheppard." Matterson slid back from the desk, then handed him an overnight express messenger pack. Noble searched his pockets for a pen. One appeared, Matterson's smile behind it.

"Thank you, Douglas." He addressed it. "A smaller envelope, please, and paper." Matterson accommodated and Noble wrote, his script faltering for a moment with indecision, then he quickly finished and slid the paper inside, giving it a lick to close it. Keeping his back to the hall, he pulled the satchel forward, digging, bypassing the ship's log for his most prized possession. He took a breath before he pulled out the broad book, then discreetly tucked it into the pack with the note. He pressed the self-seal and wrote across the seam. He nudged it toward Matterson. "Immediately, if you please."

Matterson frowned, nodded, accepting slowly. "Is everything all right, sir?"

He chanced a look back over his shoulder. The hall was empty. "I hope so."

He ordered dinner sent to his room, then strode to the elevator and rode the lift to his floor. He hurried to unlock his door and feel a little safer. He sealed himself inside, falling back against the polished wood and letting his satchel drop off his shoulder. He should have bid online or by proxy, but he'd wanted the log in his hands, to feel and read it. That was his downfall. His insatiable need to read history penned by those who lived it. He pushed off, removing his jacket and hanging it neatly in the closet. He was closing the door when he realized his room had been ransacked.

Nor was he alone.

He rushed for the exit, throwing it open. The blue-eyed man stood on the other side and with a hand to his chest, shoved him back in.

"Don't be a child," he mocked, accented, Slavic.

"It was a legal transaction. You couldn't afford the bid. You must live with that."

"I don't plan on it." He shut the door, then pushed Noble toward the center. He bumped the man behind him.

Noble looked around. His suitcases were upended, the linings cut. He possessed what they wanted, so why destroy his belongings? "Who are you people? What is the meaning of all this?"

The second man slid a gun from inside his jacket, the barrel long and narrow. "You are smart, it will come to you."

Noble retreated a step. Guns? Over an antique?

The blue-eyed man swept up the satchel, but his pleased expression fell when he upended Noble's case on the table and scattered his belongings. Disappointment rose to anger in those cold blue eyes as he lifted out the ship's log, rewrapped the linen, then immediately deposited it in a dark gray pack along with his Web phone. "Where is the diary?"

How did they know of the— Was the bidding against him all a ruse? And to what end? Because he couldn't think of a single reason why they pestered him for the ship's log unless they knew the truth. These were not unintelligent men, he realized, and he understood their true target. It did not matter. He'd been entrusted with the translation and could not reveal even having possession of it. He said nothing.

The blue-eyed man sighed heavily. "This could all have been much easier, Sheppard."

He knew his name? "You have the ship's log, now go."

"I'm afraid that is unacceptable."

The man circled the hotel room, one last inspection, and Noble wondered if he could reach the door before they shot him. Clearly, they didn't come to leave empty-handed. "I don't know anything about a diary."

"If that's so . . ." From behind his back, he withdrew a long knife. Lamplight showed blood on the black blade. "Then you're no use to us." He neared. "Are you?"

THREE

The Craw Daddy
New Orleans

Sebastian smoothed the cloth over the polished wood bar, laid out cocktail napkins, then with a little drama, set the tall Hurricane drinks in front of the two young women.

"Oh-my-God." The petite blonde looked from the broad glass to him and back.

"Go slow, darlin'," he said. "That's a lot of liquor for a speck like you."

"I'll have to drink all of it then, since no one has called me a speck since I was a baby."

Her partner-in-crime glanced at him, then her friend, and leaned into say, "Girl. Are you flirting?"

Sebastian laughed. The blonde shrugged and sipped while her pal drained half the potent drink in seconds. He stepped back, winking at the brunette with far too many tattoos for one so young. "Careful, your virtue's at risk now."

She giggled. "No men, just a girl's night."

"Never pass up an advantage staring you in the face, I say, but she's right," the blonde said. "It was a pinky swear." She threw him an apologetic smile as she left the stool. The girls jiggled and bounced through the crowded bar, searching for a prospect to break that "no men" oath.

Sebastian leaned back against the counter, watching the

crowd. The joint was jumping. He'd dragged a pair of street entertainers in for a session before the mike. They were jazzing the crowd and he loved seeing all those smiles. Servers moved quickly between the tables, and Jasmine caught his eye, then nodded at two college kids a little too drunk too early.

He glanced at his watch. No clocks in his place. The Craw Daddy closed when the crowds thinned and in New Orleans, that was somewhere around three A.M. He heard the order-up ringer and went to the kitchen. Grabbing a tray, he slid on the heaping plates before he turned back into the crowd to deliver it. Jasmine rushed to take it from him and he shook his head. The tray was massive and he held it above the crowd, working his way to the rear.

She popped out a tray stand. "You look like you could use a drink. You doing okay?"

He set the tray down and let her take over. "Stop asking me that. I'm fine."

"We're related, it's my right to annoy you. " Before he could say anything, his sister focused on the customers, laid a plate of steaming crawfish and a pot of warm butter in front of a man. "Hi. I'm Jasmine. Y'all's first time to N'Orleans?"

Sebastian went back to the bar, cleared the empties, mixed a half dozen cocktails, then started refilling the ice chests. His newest employee, Pip, a young Filipino, nudged him out of the way.

"Go stir something, Mr. Fontenòt, you get impatient again."

"*Are* getting impatient," he corrected, backing away. "But very good."

Pip beamed. They had a pact. Pip had a work visa, but Sebastian insisted he improve his English and work toward citizenship. That the compact man could cook like a pro and mixed a mean martini worked in his favor, but being a martial arts expert made him handy when the crowds got wild. And they always did.

But Pip was right. Jasmine, too, but she'd picked at him

longer and it was just irritating now. He considered himself easygoing, but since Singapore—he had to think of it as one entity or he'd count off each moment trapped under a house for three days—his tolerance for four walls and a roof was stretching thin. There weren't enough hours in the day for all he wanted to do. Only problem, his plate was full and it wasn't satisfying.

He heard a sharp whistle and searched the restaurant. Jasmine nodded to the front windows and the gold Expedition emptying of his friends. Time to regroup, he thought, tossing off his barkeep's apron as he entered the kitchen and crossed behind fry cooks and servers. It was a pleasant madness, cooks sliding orders on the pickup shelf, servers loading up, and sous chefs prep chopping. He gripped one teenager's shoulders, physically moving him out of the way, then he slipped out the rear and into the hall. He passed the staircase leading to his place above and opened the door to the street.

"Nothing's changed for you, huh?" Max said, cha-chaing his way inside.

"The last hurricane tried." The loud music drummed against the dry wall, the clank of dishes and shouting coming from behind him. "Never a dull moment till closing." He greeted everyone, getting hugs from the women, then he inclined his head. They followed to the second floor. He didn't have a problem abandoning Jasmine. She ran the place when he wasn't around and it was half hers anyway. He'd seen to that while he was still in the hospital in Singapore.

On the second floor, he crossed the apartment to throw open the French doors of the rear balcony. He stopped short when he saw the table heavy with platters of shrimp, crawfish, and half the menu's appetizers.

"My sister's great," he said.

"'Bout time you admitted it, sugar," he heard as Jasmine slipped inside with a tray, giving Max a wink, then crossing to the table. "The butter would have chilled." She set out the steaming crocks, then tucking the tray under her arm, she greeted the team. She got chatty with Viva and Safia for a bit, then headed back. "Have a pitcher of ice-cold Hurricanes downstairs if anyone's interested in something stronger," she said on her way out the door.

"Keep an eye on the college boys," he yelled down, then gestured to the table. "Eat. There's crawfish étouffèe."

Viva sprang to action. "You don't have to tell me twice. Thank you." She slid into a chair, and plucked a bite of peeled shrimp, tasting. "Divine. Almost orgasmic."

He chuckled, Sam hanging back for a second as Riley and Safia joined her. Killian was MIA, using his alter ego Dominic Cane for the DEA, and Alexa, he suspected, was chasing after their daughter. Doctors Without Borders had Logan's time with Tessa . . . hell, he forgot where she was this time. The Congo? He slid into a chair. Drinks poured, and poured again as they dined, dunking shrimp in spicy cocktail sauce. Sebastian preferred hardening his arteries by drenching fresh cracked crab in butter. They didn't come up for air for fifteen minutes, finally settling back to dine slower.

"Got to pace myself around here," Riley said, wiping his mouth with a napkin.

"Oh the hell with that," Safia said, peeling a crawfish, then shoving it into her mouth. She moaned, mouthed, "You're a god," then ate more. He winked and took a sip of his beer.

"We're out of business and it royally sucks," Max said, passing a bowl of Cajun dirty rice.

"No business license, then no insurance, and without a clearance, certainly no work in Europe," Sam said.

"So we vacation." They all looked at Riley. "The D-oh-D, Homeland Security, they won't change their tune. Not anytime soon. There's a lockdown and it's tight."

"McGill said the same thing," Sam added. He glanced up from cracking crab and shrugged. "I thought he could yank some chains, but our last op with him was off the books, and he wouldn't speculate. Hell, after he learned they pulled our chit, he wouldn't consider digging and warned me not to hunt right now and to just wait it out."

Even McGill's doors were slamming, Sebastian thought. The Suit copied everything they'd had in Georgia, and it was a small blessing McGill's Venezuela file wasn't on the jet's computers and stashed in a safe deposit box. But it was damn clear Beckham was on to something highly sensitive or they'd still be in business. He sipped his beer, then said, "What did we stumble into then?"

They stopped eating, except Viva.

"Hell if I know," Max said, grabbing the pitcher and refilling beers. "Mills won't talk to us, so that means Ground Zero came down on him, too."

Safia gestured with her fork. "The Pentagon is sealing any link to Beckham. It was his op the Chechens were gunning for, I'm certain of it. Satellite imagery has a MiG dropping five-hundred-pounders on the return north."

The room went quiet.

"Are you shitting me?"

Viva made a sour face at Max. "I should hope not."

Safia fished in a tote bag, then handed Max satellite photos.

Sebastian peered at the target hit. "We were on the other side of the mountain by then," he said, thinking, *if we know, so does Beckham.* "There's nothing left after a thousand pounds of explosives, but on the Georgia side, it's a military road into Chechnya, a supply route."

"Bombed often, too," Max said, flipping through the photos. "Russia invaded Georgia for that stretch of real estate."

"So the Russians were hiding something and blew it up?" Sam said sourly. "I'll alert the media." Viva nudged him, then offered a peeled shrimp.

"When Lania Price was a field agent," Safia said, "her theater was Moscow. She tracked KGB." Her brows knit. "After Kincade's involvement, maybe Beckham's cleaning out their bad assets, tying off some old ops." The silence stretched and Safia sat back, staring at her lap. Riley slung his arm over the back of her chair, tipping his head to whisper something private.

"Ya know . . . I don't have a problem with believing Kincade worked both sides. I knew that early, but now I'm re-thinking every op with him. Believe me, the Company is too." She frowned harder. "But I can't help wondering if *I* helped him shuffle weapons or something worse."

"He accomplished a lot of good," Max said and Sebastian elbowed him.

"He crossed the line," Safia snapped tightly and the room grew quiet again. "Sorry. Guess I haven't gotten over being betrayed by my boss who set a bomb to kill me and killed thousands instead." Across the table, she met Sebastian's gaze. She'd called in a squad of Marines from the embassy to help dig him out and according to Logan, because of internal bleeding, he'd had about two hours left to live by then. He'd be a corpse if not for her help. Instinctively, he flexed his fingers, rotated his wrist. He had several pins holding it together now. The scars were still a little bright. When he looked up, Safia's gaze was on his hand, her expression growing from guilt to anger.

"It's okay not to forgive," Viva said into the silence, and Safia frowned at her. "My mother was murdered in front of me because of a vendetta against my father. He's slowly rotting in prison for it. Like Kincade—who I didn't like when I met him," she clarified with a glance around the table. "My father had years to end the feud, but did nothing. So imagining him alone with only his mistakes for company . . . that *so* works for me." She broke a bread stick, then offered half to Safia. She smiled, accepted, and they knocked them like swords.

"*Maary* mother," Riley said. "This could be a dangerous friendship."

Laughter erupted around the table and Viva blushed, then tipped her chin up. "Safia trusted me when you guys didn't. And I didn't do so bad my first time, did I?"

"You were fantastic and *I* sent her in," Safia defended, then looked pointedly Sam.

Sam's eyes narrowed. "She isn't trained like you or Alexa."

Viva reared, gunning for a fight. "So . . . all that weapons practice, rappelling, dogfighting in the choppers was what—? Busywork?"

"Careful, buddy," Sebastian warned.

"Field experience overshadows training," Sam argued.

"Killian was stuck in the Ukraine with a commercial flight delay," Safia said. "And the Georgians couldn't offer air support into Chechnya. We were against the wall, no pilot, and you guys either hoofed your own butts out of there or Viva did. What would you have done?" Her expression dared anyone to contradict her decisions as D1 Ops Commander.

"I stand corrected, ma'am," Sam muttered, silencing the debate. Viva and Safia smacked palms, gloating.

But Sebastian didn't need anything more. Viva proved her mettle in spades. "Mills lied." They looked at him, half of them scowling, and he leaned forward. "Or at the very least, he's holding out on what else his captors wanted. Anna Mills was North Atlantic communications, and all classified transmissions are stored. Without access and pass codes, it's impossible to get in and she left the Company years ago." Riley opened his mouth to speak, but he put up a hand. "I'm not dismissing that because Vince was a sonar technician aboard a nuclear sub, all classified, also years prior."

The submarine sonar specialist had turned his Navy service into a money-making career. Unlike government contractors like KBR or DynCorp, Mills was his own company. "We read the schematic proposal. It's calibrated to accommodate the salt diversity in deep arctic water." Sebastian left his chair and crossed to the desk. He grabbed a file, flipped it open, and ran his finger down the page till he found the information. "Sonar doesn't work well in arctic temps. The salt content, the extreme water temperature, and floe shift play havoc and distort signals." He looked up. "He's developed a temperature and salt sensitive calibration that makes them much more accurate to map the ocean floor."

Riley's features tightened. "Bad guys are searching underwater. They'd need the calibration codes definitely, and they beat those out of Mills. You'd have to be familiar with the sonar system, but after that, it's practically robotic and self-contained."

"Double duty," he said. "Take him for the sonar to cover needing something else from Mills. Any ideas?"

"That won't get us tossed in jail? No," Max said. "But this isn't making me warm and fuzzy. Not with Beckham in the middle of it."

"Me either," Sebastian said. "It feels like a shell game." One crime to cover another.

"Then we're asking the wrong questions," Viva said. "Radio, sonar, a listening post. What did both Mills and his wife *hear* that anyone would want?"

"You can't honestly believe all that was over a transmission they pulled out of the air nearly three years ago?" Max looked as skeptical as he sounded. "That's a stretch."

All they had was speculation. "Try this on . . . CIA, NSA, DOD . . . whoever, they let us go in after Mills blind, with no assistance because they didn't want anything on the books. Beckham was already operating covert in Russian occupied territory. If the rescue went belly up and came back to bite them, then Dragon One gets the blame."

The team went silent.

"A scapegoat?" Sam's expression darkened. "I'll buy that. Beckham was a dead man till we got there. He knew it, too. He suffered some heavy-duty torture. I'll bet all the intel we gave Vasili was sanitized of anything pointing to him."

"It had to be to maintain his cover," Safia argued. "Mitch is counterintelligence. Always has been."

"They weren't counting on us to succeed," Sebastian said. "They shut us down so we wouldn't go hunting."

Riley tossed his napkin over his plate. "Beckham didn't accomplish his objective or he wouldn't have been left for dead."

Sebastian cringed, his gut pulling tight. Being left for dead was as hopeless as it got.

"We can't ignore this." Max showed his rare temper. "Our reputation is tied up in it."

"I can make a call," Viva said. "Uncle Vlad was—is Russian mafia. He might not talk to me, but it's worth a try."

When Sebastian nodded, Viva dug in her purse for her cell and left the table. "We can still look for answers," he said. "Just not for a client." Dragon One had the latest computer technology and software thanks to Logan, along with satellite capability, GPS, and the net. It wasn't as fast or as far reaching as what the CIA had but they'd operated just fine for years before being dragged into government work.

"When I saw the satellite photos of the bombing, I prodded some contacts, but didn't have any success like I did before," Safia said. "They're either being paid well to keep quiet or there's nothing substantial to get. Though . . . I can go beat the ugly out of them, maybe learn what else was in that area then?" Viva blinked owlishly, the phone to her ear, and Safia smirked to herself. "I'm not serious about beating them up. Well, half serious."

"McGill says stay out of it," Sam said. "We poke and they'll do more than tie us up in paperwork."

Viva moved away, covering one ear, but Sebastian heard her speaking Russian like a native.

"I resent the hell out of this," Max groused. "Not like we haven't walked into a mess before and bailed them out. They didn't have to yank our card and put us out of business. We still have bills to pay." They looked at him. "Okay, without paying that ridiculous insurance premium, we'll survive. But for how long?"

"You've been whining about diving," Riley said. "Go get wet. Bridget is back in Okinawa. She's said you're welcome to join her." That brightened Max's mood.

Viva returned to the table, frowning softly. "Uncle Vlad hasn't heard anything about that area, but reminded me that he didn't know everyone in the eastern bloc. Which is a lie, he's ex-KGB and ran a tidy weapons market across that military road. He knows I know that, so he's keeping secrets, too."

Safia leaned in. "Vlad . . . as in Vlad Dovyestoff?" she nearly choked. "He's your uncle?"

Viva smiled. "Not blood, my godfather. Palled around with my father when he was exiled till Putin let him back into the country."

"I'd like to get him in this one and have a chat," Safia said, then smiled. "Maybe I shouldn't have quit and just worked your contacts." Viva grinned, wiggling the phone and offering Vlad's number. She and Safia sat close, trading tales from Viva's colorful past, when Sebastian's private line rang.

He urged them to make a dent in all that food, grabbed the mobile, then walked to the living room to answer. He glanced at the caller ID. England. It had to be early there.

"*Fontenòt,*" he heard. "*Edward Granlen here.*"

An odd chill worked over his skin. "And this is a surprise." MI-5 never called to chat, and certainly not a former British Royal Marine he wasn't supposed to acknowledge.

"*I wish it was a pleasant duty, but I have disturbing news.*"

He glanced to the balcony, to his friends he considered family. If he had to get bad news, there was no better place to receive it.

"*This isn't our case, but last evening Noble Sheppard was taken by force from his hotel in Chertsey, Surrey.*"

Sebastian's heart slammed to his gut, and for a moment, he couldn't breathe. Noble was more of a father than a friend. He'd spent half his childhood with the man. "Kidnapped? What would anyone want with a rare bookseller?" That brought the team out of their chairs and closer.

"*I was hoping you could tell us that.*"

"Believe me, Eddie, this man did not have enemies. He's a bookworm. Last I spoke to him a week ago, he was still translating a manuscript for some museum or college in Ireland."

"Maybe that has something to do with this. Less than an hour before his disappearance, he'd won the bidding at the Surrey Auction House for a fifteenth-century Portuguese pilot log, the Aramina. *It's missing as well as his phone."*

"Noble didn't talk about the work he was doing. Was it that valuable?"

"He paid nearly four thousand U.S. for it." Eddie's voice lowered. *"I'm out of my rank here, friend. We've received a fax from your DHS—"*

"Let me guess, no assistance."

"I'm afraid so. But I can fax you copies of the preliminary police reports. It's not our jurisdiction, Chertsey Surrey police found your name in his billfold. When it came over the wire, I remembered you mentioning this bloke. The one with all the stories."

Sebastian lips tugged at a smile, and for a instant, the image of him and Eddie outside a rebel camp in Panama blinked to life. Hot, steaming wet, and so tired they were popping NoDoz like candy. "I'm one of Noble's in-case-of-emergency contacts," he said as the image vanished. Just as Noble was his. Noble was with Jasmine when she learned he was presumed dead in Singapore.

He gave his fax number, then crossed to the machine. "Video surveillance? Witnesses?"

"I'm afraid not. Old hotel and it was late. We're waiting for the auction house cameras. But after he won the piece, he returned to the hotel on foot, spoke to the concierge, ordered dinner sent to his room, then went to his suite. Room service likely interrupted Sheppard's kidnapping. The bellman is dead. The room had been ransacked, the lining of his cases cut, but not a single print. Not even Dr. Sheppard's." Eddie paused, his voice lowering. *"The concierge was the last person to speak with Sheppard directly. We found him beside his car, beaten nearly to death. He's in a coma. Sheppard's rental is missing as well."*

One dead and another critical? "Jesus. Over some antique papers?"

"*Apparently so. Have any idea exactly what he was working on and for whom?*"

"No, sorry. He was pretty mum about it. But I'll find out." The first forty-eight hours were critical. He needed to be there.

"*Don't go nosing in police business, mate. Chertsey police are on it.*" His accent was suddenly heavier, but Sebastian got the message. They were being recorded. "*Go visit your pal, Riley. You can't help us here. We have this contained.*"

Sebastian's gaze swung to Riley standing a few feet away, and he frowned, then felt his features tighten. Eddie was telling him not to go to Surrey, but to Ireland before the police could. "Maybe I will. Keep me posted. Thanks, Ed."

Sebastian wanted to push the friendship and ask for photos, but Granlen was already skirting his boundaries. It didn't matter; he'd be in Ireland as soon as he filed a flight plan. He ended the call after learning that Noble's daughter Moira had been notified by the embassy. His friends surrounded him as he relayed the news, and imagining Noble in the hands of a killer over some goddamn antique papers enraged him. The choking fax machine startled him, and while Max snatched up the first page, Sebastian moved to the window to call Moira.

"*Sebastian. Thank goodness. Hold a sec.*" She spoke to someone nearby. "*It's a close friend. No, it's private. Don't you dare record it.*" Then into the phone she said, "*Sorry. The FBI are staked out here, but they aren't telling me all of it, I know.*"

"They're just doing their job, Moira. But as far as we know, he's alive." He didn't tell her about the damage left behind. No sense in giving her nightmares till they knew something, but the bellman's death magnified the danger to Noble. If they'd kill some kid, they wouldn't hesitate to do the same to his oldest friend.

"*I needed to hear that.*" Moira let out a long sigh, then asked, "*Who'd want to hurt my dad? He never made anyone mad. Well, 'cept my mother.*"

Sebastian couldn't help his smile then. Noble and his ex-wife fought over one issue and she was on the other end of the line. "I don't know, darlin', but I'll find him, I swear it." *"I know you will."* She paused, sniffled. *"He's probably counting on it. I am, too."* Her voice lowered to a whisper. *"I want to hire you. 'Sides me, you're the only person Dad trusts. You still have his power of attorney to act on his behalf?"* He did, then she said, *"Good, I want to hire you."*

"Darlin', we're sacked by the DOD."

She scoffed. *"Like that will stop you?"*

He smiled, agreeing, and after he made certain Moira wasn't alone with a bunch of Feds, he promised to call later. He severed the line, swallowing a few times before he could speak without smashing something. He looked at his friends. "There is no rock on the planet this killer can hide under."

"Buddy, I'm with you. But this wasn't just a robbery and a kidnapping." Max handed over the police report. "The bellman, his throat was cut."

Sebastian scowled, took the report he knew Granlen would catch hell for sending, and read. "That's not all. His kidneys were punctured first."

He didn't have to explain. They knew.

A Black Ops kill. Like a target.

25,000 feet
Somewhere over Italy

Olivia crinkled the police reports as she dug in her tote bag for a tissue. Cruz handed her one. "Thanks."

"Ross can be a jerk sometimes," Cruz said.

"He's more than that. How insensitive do you have to be to notify us that Noble's been kidnapped, and possibly dead, through a *damn* fax?" It didn't get any more sterile than that and she wanted Agent Ross to feel some of this pain. Probably good that he was a few thousand miles away, the weasel.

"Everything just changed, didn't it?" Cruz didn't look up

from his copy of the reports till he neatly laid the last page aside.

"People are dead, Cruz, what do you think?" She met his gaze, wiping her nose. "Sorry."

"It doesn't look good," he said, nodding to the summaries. "You believe he's still alive?"

"Yes." She scowled at him. "We can't even think otherwise."

She glanced down at the preliminary police reports and didn't wonder how Agent Ross got them so quickly. When he wanted something, he had a golden touch. He'd already put it to good use. Noble's cell was missing, and it had their numbers. Ross had already disabled their cell phones, and all calls were rerouted to the new phones left in storage on the jet. Ross was covering his bases effectively, but until they'd found Noble, alive and unharmed, his butt was in a deep sling. Hers. This should never have happened.

She'd barely pulled it together when heard the tone she'd been waiting for, and switched seats in front of a flat screen. An incoming call message trotted across the LCD, then blinked, connecting. Ross's face appeared so close all she could see was his nose. Adjusting his chair, he sat back. On his end, he could see a head shot of her through the webcam in the top of the screen.

"Doctor Corrigan. You got my fax."

She nodded.

"We need to move very cautiously now."

Wrong answer. "It would be so very wise for you to just listen right now."

He eyed her, taking the high road, and simply nodded.

"Leads to the people who have Noble?"

"Surrey Police are on it. I imagine the Yard is sticking their nose in as well. It's not a high-crime area. Auction surveillance shows a lot of people. It will take time to interview them. But with the bellman's death and the concierge, we have a definite time line of his capture."

"Ransom demands?"

"None yet. It hasn't been twelve hours. There's a BOLO for Noble, and police are following all possible leads, but nothing concrete beyond the fax information so far."

A Be On The Lookout. That wasn't enough, and she'd bet the FBI didn't know everything. "There weren't any prints left, were there?"

He looked startled for a second.

"You'd have one or two suspects by now, the cleaning staff at least." She gave him credit for looking directly into the webcam. When she was pissed, even her brothers got scared.

"You're right, not even Noble's prints."

"So we have professionals. Did you know someone else wanted the ship's log?"

"Not with any certainty. The day before the auction, we had a flag on a call Noble received from a number another section was monitoring. The caller wanted to deal. If he won the bidding, the caller would pay him twice the price for the artifact. Noble said no, but they called again the day of the auction, repeating the offer. Obviously this was just for a chance to get close enough to take it."

Son of a bitch. He knew. Yet she kept her features schooled, letting that roll around in her mind. It didn't make her feel any less guilty. She'd sent Noble to Surrey for the Portuguese log. They were supposed to meet in Surrey for dinner tonight before heading back to the site.

"If that caller number was monitored beforehand, then you know who it is, right?" They could back-trace the call.

"It was one of several numbers monitored from a classified source."

"Don't stop now, Agent Ross." *You're digging your own grave.*

"I can't break protocol and even I don't know that intelligence."

She didn't believe that, but after a year of working with him, she was accustomed to his need-to-know mantra. "Then find out."

He scowled. "Don't think that you can dictate—"

She leaned in. "Lives are on the line, Ross. We are now on high alert. I need to know who's got their fingers in this pie enough to kill innocent people." He said nothing. "Fine. But I've warned you before, keep me in the dark about anything and you risk me leaving this project permanently." She reached to cut the line.

"No." He straightened a bit. "You wouldn't. This means everything to you."

"Not when people are dying! Jeez, Ross. Where the *hell* was his protection?" She hated that her voice fractured.

"Right behind him. He was protected from the moment he landed in Doneborg. He didn't want it, if you'll recall. He identified his detail after the auction, but the next pickup was taken out, we assume, by his kidnapper."

Taken out. Killed. How kind of them to whitewash the murder of their own agent.

Olivia sat back. Two dead, one critical, and one missing. For a ship's log? It didn't make any sense unless the log wasn't the true target. The project was deeply masked and she knew Noble didn't give anything up. She'd swear to it. Yet she'd spoken to him hours before he disappeared and he didn't mention anything suspicious. Nor the calls. The auction house and hotel were within walking distance of each other, so whoever killed his protection detail had spotted the agents. That took skill. Her gaze jumped back to Ross. "Did your people recover the translation?"

His features tightened. "I was hoping you had it."

That's what they wanted. "He sent me the most recent portion before he left Ireland, but not all of it." Not the final pieces of this puzzle.

"Can you work with that while I find someone else to finish it?"

"No, you can find Noble!" She couldn't even think of this project without him. "Why are you giving me grief here? It's Noble, for God's sake."

"We have agents searching, Doctor Corrigan. I'm in contact with garda and the FBI is in the loop."

She shook her head. "Use your resources, all of them. Noble Sheppard is an innocent victim of misinformation. *Yours*. We should have been warned about those traces." That a division was tracking a cell number more than once said this was much larger than a kidnapping or the translation. The NSA didn't pay attention to just anyone.

"Yes, I agree, if it were in my power. It's not. Now we have to move on with the project."

It was the wrong thing to say, again, and she could almost feel her expression darken. "Don't you dare dismiss his life so easily." His unemotional response was dancing on her last nerve. "If you'd studied the time line, you'll realize that the killer would have no reason to pulverize Mr. Matterson into a coma if they had the translation."

Ross's features scrunched and he finally nodded agreement. "They'd have just taken it and left."

Finally, some logic. "It's not the original and as far as I know, no one else has any idea of its true value. The only reason to need the translation *and* the log is for the project."

"Not possible," he said. "This has been under wraps since the ice core."

The ice core sample had found an air pocket, which wasn't unusual. Just not one so big or with anything in it. "Keep believing that. And if you're going to assume anything, then it's that this killer is well informed and he knows what the translation means. We must find it. What about Noble's place in Ireland?"

"We've sent people to sanitize the house." God, she hated that word. "But our concern is his work, not his toothbrush."

He'd look really good with a broken nose right now. "Are you *trying* to infuriate me?"

He rubbed his mouth, then pulled his jacket tighter around his throat. "Why don't you just tell me what you want and I'll see what I can do?"

Oh, he really didn't mean that, but she wasn't in the mood to hold back. "We need security where we didn't, and that means on anything that connects to the project. Supply lines, systems. Anything. No one gets near the complex that isn't cleared by our people." She folded her arms and wished she could pace and work off this angry energy. "And with a high enough clearance, too, because they'll have to know everything to protect it."

He frowned. "That's how you get leaks."

"Wake up! You already have one or Noble would be here right now." She waited for that to sink in.

"You're upset, I understand that, but we—"

She delivered her best "don't you dare patronize me" look. "I read the ME's report. I'm not dense about the methods of close-combat kills." She leaned in, thinking of those innocent men taking a knife in the kidneys and never knowing why. "Monitoring those calls says you *knew* there was a threat and did nothing to keep Noble safer. You failed. Protection is *your* job. He should have had an armed bodyguard with him twenty-four seven!"

He stared directly, unaffected. "Not without alerting the perpetrator we were trying to identify."

She featured tightened. "You *bastard*. Noble is the priority."

"It isn't my call."

She was damn tired of that answer. "Think that's a get out of jail free card? Don't. He's in the hands of a trained killer, and you have the nerve to act like it's someone else's problem? It's all yours, Ross. I want that number and a name." Though she didn't know what she'd do with it, she had friends who did.

"I can't reveal what I don't know."

"Then I'll get it." She held up the clean phone. "I want to talk to him. Today."

His eyes rounded. "Out of the question. You know the rules."

Screw the rules. "Perhaps I wasn't clear about the gravity of this." She swallowed, searching for calm and professionalism. "Your lies have put us here, Ross, and now people are *dead*. There are no more rules. The agency has the killer's number and I suggest you share it and start tracking because without Noble's knowledge or that translation, we may never understand this. Millions already spent, innocent people killed, and nothing? The boss will be angry and I want it to be with you." Getting him in the money belt was the quickest route. Her only concern was Noble.

His brows knit, and he took too long to answer.

"Well?"

"I'll arrange it when you get back here."

"Not good enough." She cut the line, and sat back, then took a slow deep breath before she jumped to her feet. "He is *such* an asshole."

"He's a government guy. What do you expect?"

"The truth." She met his gaze. "Maybe to give a damn? Noble is missing, they're all presuming he's dead. Would you want anyone to give up on you?"

"Of course not, but they have the skills and manpower to find him. We don't."

She eyed him. "You underestimate yourself, DeGama."

He frowned, looking a little afraid. "Olivia. No. We have a project that's on a time clock."

"So is Noble's life." She shot him a hard look. "We need leverage to help him. Use your skills. Get the big guy on the line."

For a second, his features pulled so smooth, he looked like a teenager. "No. He scares me."

"Man up and do it." Then she strode to the cockpit and opened the cabin door. "Change of plans, guys." The pilot and navigator twisted to look at her, frowning. "When we get to England, hang a left."

FOUR

Mitch Beckham wondered when his life turned into little more than being a janitor for his country. He couldn't recall the last time he had a day off, or a conversation that didn't involve national security. And forget about sex, he thought, navigating the halls of the Pentagon. Not even some wild, no-commitment fun sex. It left him irritated and a bit resigned as he entered the E ring and walked the long corridor to General Gerardo's offices. The newly promoted three-star wasn't going to be happy. *Guess I should have just died to finish off this FUBAR mission.* His black eye and broken nose said it all. And those were the obvious signs.

Mentally bracing himself for an ass chewing, he pushed through the polished door. The aroma of fresh-brewed coffee greeted him, and when the general's admin chief saw him, she immediately picked up the phone to alert Gerardo.

"He's expecting you, Major, but he has a guest. It will only be a moment, sir."

She left her desk, and Mitch admired one of the hottest bodies in the Corps as she slipped past him to the silver coffee service. He deserved a smack in the head for imagining her in less uniform, he thought as she poured a cup, added a hint of cream, then offered the mug handle out.

"Have I been here that often you know how I take my coffee, Staff Sergeant?" He accepted the mug.

"It's Gunnery Sergeant now," she said, and he noticed the second rocker on her sleeve. "And yes, you have."

He gave her a quick punch on her chevrons, and she arched a brow. "Wuss."

"I figured you might be sore." "Pinning" on a new rank was a painful tradition when the bars and chevrons were secured with metal spikes like on BDU collars. He had vampire bites, double holes in his collarbone from fellow marines smashing his lieutenant's bars at his first wet-down. Then the Gunny lifted her short sleeve. Her upper arm was deep purple. He whistled softly. "You have lots of mean friends."

"Love taps, and I punch back." She smiled like the cover of a *Playboy* and sat behind her desk. "Sir."

He took a seat, laying his briefcase aside to enjoy the coffee. "Thank you, Gunny." He cupped the thick mess hall mug. "Ahh, it's the little things I missed most."

She arched a brow, but knew better than to inquire further. "Low threshold of excitement, I suppose."

Mitch smiled.

"Welcome back, Major."

"Thanks, Gunny. Good to be here." To be anywhere. Let's see . . . slowly rotting to death in a dark room, or quickly incinerated in an explosion? Not a tough choice, but he was glad he didn't have to make it. All hail Dragon One, he saluted with a generous sip. They had great timing. That prison closet was a lousy end to a two-month hunt for Price's and Kincade's assets. Considering Adam Kincade had betrayed his country under the guidance of a truly conniving deputy director, Lania Price, the CIA was trying to plug a lot of holes. Mitch got some of the cleanup duty. Nasty work. He'd rather fight Taliban than deal with the assets of traitors. Taliban, he could predict. Former CIA with too much knowledge were impossible to trace.

Price dropped classified material in dangerous hands to see who'd bite, but Kincade was even dirtier. He used outside assets against their own people, undermined agents by with-holding intel, and even sold confiscated Chinese weapons to an arms dealer. Their past assignments had to be dissected, one by one, and Mitch took it personally that Kincade did his best to kill Safia Troy. No, Donovan now. Mercs had a place, sheltering a load to a military already stretched thin, but Dragon One didn't exactly obey the rules. Safia wouldn't marry just anyone, he admitted. Riley had guts, no doubt about that, and part of him was a little jealous she let anyone that close because she shut him down, A-sap.

The door opened, and his Charlies were nearly a casualty as he stood abruptly. Gunny snickered, and he eyed her, set-ting the mug aside. Gerardo appeared, a civilian in a suit be-side him. They shook hands and the man departed quickly, not sparing a glance. Mitch recognized him. An NSA geek, but couldn't recall his name. Gerardo inclined his head and didn't wait for him as he followed inside and closed the door.

"You screwed the pooch, Major."

"Yes, sir. I did."

"I read the preliminary, give me the details." Gerardo slid behind the desk and leaned back in the chair. Leather creaked. "Now, Major."

The ass chewing cometh, he thought, taking a seat. "I met with the asset in Gorzky and he arranged a meeting with the man named Agar in North Ossetia." He glanced up. "My plan was to buy anything they offered. When I hinted at the schematics, they got jittery."

"You should have closed up shop and left, Major."

"Yes, sir. I'm aware." Painfully.

"We can't confirm Price stole the German schematics her-self," Gerardo said. "But her Cayman accounts say she made a profit. NSA can trace the money trail only so far, then it falls off the earth."

He frowned. NSA couldn't find it? Jesus. "That's some creative financing." The general agreed and motioned him to continue. "I pursued Agar, a former KGB informant, to Sha-toy and met him in a restaurant. I was unaware of the mafia involvement." Only his gaze shifted up. "They owned the place. One man they called Vlad, a supposed ex KGB official, arrived and everything changed. He's angry, they're not even talking to me, and guns come out. I escaped, tried to get to the Georgian border, and was taken prisoner when a villager gave me up. The interrogation was short, creative though. They wanted to know who sent me, what I knew." Same shit, different day, he thought. "When they didn't get anything, they left me there. With Vince Mills strapped to a large IED, apparently." He looked up, closing the file he didn't need to reference. "My guards were mafia hitters. From the tattoos, they'd done time. All executed while still armed."

Gerardo's features pulled tight. "That's a big sweep."

"No witnesses leaves no connections. I never saw Mills until after Max Renfield and Sebastian Fontenòt released me."

"You're lucky they did."

"Yes, sir. Very." He'd take the scolding, he deserved it.

"Dragon One's involvement other than the rescue?" Gerardo flipped through his copy of the reports.

"No, sir. Not that they'll tell me. They're pissed."

"We shut them down, that's expected. I'm not fond of using mercs, ever, but they got the job done." He gave him a stinging look that sent Mitch's shoulders back.

"They would have persued." Mitch was certain of it. He would have. "Do you want to bring them into this?"

"God no, they've cleaned up enough dirty laundry." Gerardo scribbled on a note pad. "They know about the schematics?"

"No sir. I have Dragon One's intel. They feel the kidnapping was for the sonar and a cleanup. You disagree?"

"No, but I don't have the whole story yet."

Neither did he. Lania Price covered her back like the pro she was and chasing down intel this old was nearly impossible. Searching for who had their hands on the classified German technology and what they did with it led him in different directions. The United States needed to be prepared for the possibility that whoever paid for the stolen plans built the horizontal launching system for ICBM missiles. For him, it was a given. The question driving him was, what did they build it *in?*

"Sir. Mills was convinced his kidnapping was a mistake, that they were after his wife for a listening-post transmissions. But anyone hunting intelligence has to know a former employee couldn't access anything. Pass codes are individual and would be outdated. Even the storage system has changed since last year. Sorry, sir, but I don't get the connection."

Gerardo rolled a quarter over his knuckles, watching, then suddenly flicked his wrist and caught it in his palm. "I think Dragon One intervened faster than Mills's kidnappers. We put up the money, but they had his family under protection before the kidnappers could work on his wife. Double threat. One will talk to save the other."

He needed to learn to roll a quarter. "Neither had anything to offer that's a threat, sir. Mills's Navy career is long over. I don't believe it's significant, beyond the loss of the sonar."

Gerardo shook his head, straightening in his chair. "You're not thinking of what Vince or Anna Mills might have heard."

"Begging your pardon, sir, but that's one helluva long shot. Does anyone remember what they heard someone else say over three years ago?" He could barely recall his last conversation with his family.

"I'm aware," Gerardo said, not looking enthusiastic either. "But reviewing every transmission on Anna Mills's watch gives us thousands of possibilities."

And a lot of work, even with the parameters narrowed. "Why didn't we go after this guy, sir?"

"Because you were in the same soup, MIA, and Lania Price isn't cooperating."

Mitch's features tightened. Letting the guy die because he was on another op nearby was not a good strategy. "Intel that Dragon One was launching a rescue should have been passed to me. I could have done something. They had to have put Mills there before my meet with the asset, sir. If I'd known, I might have—"

Gerardo stopped him with a wave. "Don't go there. We had our reasons. The priority was to keep you alive and this quiet."

Considering he was staring death in the chops till D-1 showed up, that plan was a failure, and Mitch shouldered the guilt. He grabbed a file from his briefcase, offering it. "Maybe these will give us something. Pictures."

Gerardo took it, looking surprised. "How the hell did you get these out of the country?"

He smiled. "Google mail. During my escape. That's fifty-eight miles northwest of that meeting. I know they're not great. I was evading. I sent them a second after I took them, then tossed the phone in the river before they captured me." God. Just saying that stuck in his throat. He consoled himself that he was outnumbered and outgunned, but it didn't soothe his pride. "Look carefully, sir." He leaned, pointed to the photo that was a close-up of the rugged terrain, the river. His fingertip followed a hazy gray line. "That's a damn straight line for being underwater."

Gerardo drew his lamp closer, peering. "It angles. Looks thicker and taller nearer the mountain. A retaining wall?"

"I thought that, too. During pursuit, I paralleled the military convoy road toward Georgia. Or what's left of it after two wars." Shelled often like slaps from Mother Russia. "If there was anything to find, it's destroyed now."

Gerardo looked up from scrutinizing the photos. "The MiG. We got it."

"Did Deep Six note the MiG dropped those on the *return* trip to Russian airspace?" Gerardo scowled. "I saw the release before the MiG was nothing but jet wash on the other side of the mountain. Probably killed twenty thousand people and wiped whatever was there off the map. The chopper was out of range when it hit. Dragon One didn't notice."

Gerardo scoffed. "Don't count on it, Major."

"Roger that, sir. Also when I was evading, on the Chechen side, I noticed the unpaved roads to that area weren't rutted by military trucks. Too narrow a wheel span. All farm trucks, oxcarts."

Gerardo lifted his gaze. "You don't think they built it."

Mitch shook his head. "A launching system isn't small. We'd have seen something. The invasion of Georgia, the Chechen war, they could use the chaos to hide a facility in the mountain, but they also risked a bomb hitting. If they built it, then their cover-up is better than we've ever managed. My contacts inside Moscow say no. No troops, nothing."

"And we tell *them* everything? Christ. I feel like I'm sitting here with my thumb up my ass," Gerardo muttered, scrutinizing the photos, and Beckham wondered what he hoped to see. Finally, he gave up. "Send them to David Lorimer. He can go back and compare with sat imagery. Maybe we're just looking in the wrong place."

"Roger that, sir." This whole case felt off track, but he kept that to himself. He didn't have anything to back it up. Just a hunch and a lot of unanswered questions. "Orders, sir?"

Gerardo looked up, scrutinized him. "Stay in Deep Six and heal up, Major. You're scaring the locals."

Mitch smiled, then winced. His lip was split enough to need stitches. He was glad the general didn't force him on leave. It brought too many questions he couldn't answer.

"Immediately," Gerardo said. "Dismissed."

Mitch stood, saluted, and was at the door when the general said, "Glad you made it back alive, Mitch. I didn't want to have to call your parents."

"Thanks for holding off, sir." Now he had some Russians to find.

Rossnowlagh, Ireland

Olivia drove in a wide berth around the little cottage, avoiding the neighbors and notice, but only getting a glimpse at the front before she circled behind the little Tudor house. No sign of anyone near. Nothing had changed since she saw it last.

"The police should have been here by now," she said to Cruz on the other end of the phone. She wasn't that far ahead after landing, renting this car, and finding a hotel to leave Cruz's pansy butt behind. Not that he'd consider joining her. He had the backbone of licorice. She left her car in the glen, staring up at the back of the little house. "No police tape on the back door either," she said, adjusting the wireless earpiece.

"*All the more reason to stay back. God, Olivia, what is it with you and authority figures?*" Cruz said, his voice crisp in her ear.

With four older brothers? "We butt heads," she said. "Agent Ross is very good at what he does, but he's not my authority."

"*Tell him that. He's called no less than four times.*"

"Convince him to turn my old phone back on. If the kidnapper has Noble's phone but no translation, then he'd contact us." She needed to find something to barter with to get Noble back. She hoped for his flash drive copy of the translation so far.

"*He won't go for it and that's if they really want it. You're convinced Noble didn't have the translation.*"

"If he did, then why kill anyone connected to him for it?"

Witnesses dead or comatose were a pretty good testimony to how far these people were willing to go for the translation. Her conviction over that floundered constantly, but she couldn't think of any reason to go after Noble. It's all he'd been doing for the last months. For her. No, the leak was on her side. At least it was small group, but how anyone learned about the Irish translation or where Noble was at that precise time—well, she hadn't figured that out yet. She really needed to talk to her director. He wouldn't like this either, she thought as she neared the cottage, her legs burning from the climb up the hillside. She reached the back door. No footprints and the grass could use a trim, she thought as she flattened against the wall.

She inched toward the window, and felt incredibly vulnerable without a decent weapon, but couldn't get one through West Knock or Enniskillen airport customs. She didn't have time for Ross to make arrangements. Not that he would. This jaunt was unsanctioned, as Cruz called it. That never stopped her before, she thought, withdrawing the knife she bought in Ballyshannon. She rolled her eyes and ripped off the price tag. *Amateur.* An instant later, she heard a loud crash, then another.

Oh crap. "Someone's here." Not smart, not smart, she thought, yet slipped to the nearest window.

"Then get the hell out of there!"

She winced at the burst of sound. "You're not helping." She peered inside.

A man the size of a fridge searched the little house like a wrecking ball, fast, leaving nothing to chance, opening each book and fanning pages before he threw it aside. She ducked when he strode into the kitchen and she felt his violence though the thin walls, each hit making her flinch and rabbit hole herself low to the cottage wall. She needed to leave, now, yet when the noise in the house lessened, she chanced a look. The guy was in the center of the living room, surrounded by his own demolition, and she saw him slip a massive knife into a sheath at his back. He wore latex gloves. He covered the weapon with his shirt, then suddenly turned toward the kitchen. Olivia felt his stare like a slap and ducked, frozen for a heartbeat, then she started running.

"What's happening? Olivia?"

"You're right, it wasn't smart. I'm leaving." His knife, she thought, three inches wide, eight inches long, the same depth of the fatal wound of the bellman. She prayed the cottage covered her escape as she raced down the hill, turning sideways so she wouldn't fall on her face. She slammed against the car door, then flung it open and slid behind the wheel.

"Talk to me!"

"I think I just saw the killer." She didn't feel any safer inside the car as she turned over the engine, suddenly glad the rental was a BMW and hummed quietly.

"*What? Jesus! You need to get out of there.*"

"No? Really?" Putting it in gear, she backed out of the glen, then burned rubber turning onto the highway. Behind her the land rose and fell in gentle slopes and craggy rocks. She checked the rearview mirror. The man stood outside the back door of the cottage. He held a scope to his eye. Trained on her.

Dimitri followed the dark blue car till it reached the highway, then turned back into the house, and dialed Rastoff. "A blue BMW is coming toward you. Do not lose her." He rattled off the license plate. "She is the link to the diary." Dr. Corrigan, he thought. One of the names in the translator's Web phone. "Do not harm her, Rastoff." The man had already forced their hand with the bellman and the man tailing the translator. "Or I will kill you myself."

"*Da, da. And cut my throat, disembowel me alive. You've spoken of that before.*"

He smirked to himself. "Call when she stops."

Dimitri glanced at the interior, frustrated he could not locate the translation. The failure ate at him, brewing an ache behind his eyeballs. Suddenly he drew his S4M, screwed on the suppressor, then emptied it in a sweep, and strode out the door. He retraced his steps, then jogged a little faster to his truck parked a half mile away. He was fortunate to find her. The woman was an avenue he needed to exploit for the cause.

Rossnowlagh, Ireland
One hour later

Sebastian unfolded from the compact car and stared at the cottage that looked like a throwback in history. Noble's rental. A reluctant smile tugged as he looked up the coastline to the ruins of a castle or manor overlooking the water. The south turret was still visible, tall, round gray stone perched on the edge of a cliff. The water crashed and foamed at the rocky base. He looked back to the cottage as Max joined him on the stone walk, hitching a duffel bag.

"The thatched roof made him rent this one." The other homes were shingled, modern, but this looked like something out of a fairy tale. Curved shutters and a wide front door added to the historical feel of the place. Sebastian hoped the four-room rental would give him something to understand his kidnapping and the murders. But the kill method was telling. Noble had secrets.

"Very *Lord of the Rings*," Max said.

Sebastian nodded absently, studying the quaint cottage in a village that appeared untouched by the centuries. He'd sent a FedEx here a couple months ago. Twenty pounds of gulf shrimp on dry ice for Noble's birthday. Damn. *I swear, buddy, I'll find you.* Dragon One was squeezing resources, and doors were locked tight. The law in two countries were investigating, and he didn't know if they'd searched here already. Eddie wasn't talking. We're working with crumbs, he thought, starting up the stone path.

Thirty feet from the door, he stopped, pointing right. "A visitor. No one's walked on that lawn in months." The grass was about ankle high and smashed in intervals toward the forest so dense moss grew on the rocks.

"The footprints edge the rocks," Max said. "He didn't have a choice near the house." It sat alone with more than an acre cleared on either side.

"Could be the police," he said. Nothing else was disturbed and he'd check it out once they searched the cottage. He walked the stone path to the door. The key slid in smoothly, yet the door swung on its hinges. *Rut-roh.* He glanced at Max, and they flanked the door, pushing it wide. The living room looked like it had been shaken, everything toppled on the floor.

"Now I really feel naked without a weapon," he said, moving inside. Max slipped a knife from his boot and handed it over. Sebastian scowled.

He shrugged. "Riley's sister, Kathleen." He palmed another like it.

Sebastian inclined his head and Max spun away to circle the rear as he entered through the front. He cleared each room, empty except for the destruction. Nothing was spared and little survived.

Max came through the back door. "Prints out back. They lead down into the glen. Tire tracks, too. They're fresh."

Sebastian scowled.

"The footprints are two different sizes."

"We just missed them?"

Max shrugged, sheathing his knife. "We missed *someone.*"

A book dropped off the shelf and they turned sharply, then relaxed. The cottage wasn't big, two bedrooms, a bath, eat-in kitchen, and living room. But a spray of bullets cut through the walls. Sebastian turned slowly, fixing the trajectory. "The guy paused here." He gestured to the line to the desk. "But he didn't shoot anything else up." He did it last, he thought as he studied the living room, trying to imagine the "before" picture. Noble was a pack rat, but neat about it, particular, and he could barely make out dust rings where the bric-a-brac had been. He'd been in Surrey for only two days before he was taken, and had a return flight that next afternoon. The "why" of this was in here somewhere.

"I'll call the police," Max said.

"Delay that. We need to search before they bag and tag it."

"A CSI? I don't think there's even a coroner in this town."

Sebastian swung a look at him.

"Fine, but if we get kicked out of Ireland, the Donovans are not going to be happy." Max grabbed the duffel from the stoop, then handed him a pair of latex gloves. "I'll take the bedrooms."

Sebastian pulled them on as Max headed down the short hall. He didn't want to search Noble's things. It put an edge on finding him alive when anyone connected to his disappearance was dead. Some belongings were familiar and he smiled at the houndstooth jacket with leather elbows hanging on a hook. Too hot for New Orleans, but he'd bet the scholar enjoyed looking like one for a change. Though it would take a lot for Noble to give up his usual chinos, polo shirts, and loafers just to blend in.

Sebastian grabbed his camera and photographed the place, pausing to examine the book titles. *History of Ireland's Clans, Spanish Armada, Spice Traders.* Same stuff on his shelves at home, he thought, noticing that every book was on the floor. Frowning, he crossed to the desk. The file drawer was pulled out and spilled on its side, yet the files were intact. He slid a couple from the fanned stack and smiled at the filing system known only to Noble. The Greek letters and symbols were a language he'd created to communicate only with his daughter when she was little, a way to keep their relationship strong and his ex-wife out of it. He'd never shared it. But using it here meant he felt it was necessary. Flipping through files, he wasn't all that surprised they were empty. He was hoping for some college letterhead or a business card. He knelt, his penlight spying in corners. He saw a tiny slice of white, and wedged behind the desk was a single sheet of paper. A credit card statement from two months ago, paid in full. He ran his finger down the charges, committing the businesses to memory, then just pocketed it.

He straightened, his attention sliding to the fat striped club chair and ottoman, both stabbed repeatedly, then to the cabinets and debris spilled on the floor. He let that simmer as he went to the computer, righting the screen and pulling out the tower. Bullet holes cut across the front and side.

"That looks like toast," Max said, coming out of the hall. He pointed back over his shoulder. "Nothing different than in here. His clothes in the armoire are intact. They even found a hidden compartment, but the bed is shredded."

"Why is this even here?" He righted the computer. "The police would have taken it."

"We beat the cops? Damn. Then they're coming."

"Think you can rig this hard drive through our laptop?"

"Possibly, but those bullet holes are close together." Max grabbed a stool and went to work.

Sebastian turned in a circle. "There's a copy somewhere."

"Copy of what?

"Whatever he was working on. Noble was keen on saving his work. Not obsessive, but he's computer savvy." More than me, he thought.

"The police in the UK didn't find his phone," Max reminded.

"If the killer has it, then they know his entire life."

"They have your number, too." Max looked up from unscrewing the computer casing. "Should we warn his daughter?"

"I did. She's taking time off and it's a good bet she won't be social with the Feds there. Killian lives near and promised to check in on her." Despite that the FBI were with her, waiting for a ransom call, the team had updated her alarm system. Aside from putting a bodyguard in her house—which she refused—he prayed whoever took her father wouldn't have reason to get at Moira. But he just didn't know. "Noble said he was translating documents for the University College Dublin for about a year now, but he wasn't chatty about it."

Max opened the laptop and connected it to the hard drive, then rigged the power source. "Doesn't sound like him."

It wasn't. "Clue number one I should have recognized." Noble taught, shared his knowledge of history and culture, often the obscure parts, and was always fascinating. Roped him in when he was eight.

"He *really* didn't want anyone knowing about this work, or he'd have shared," Max said. "At least with you. Especially if it was dangerous."

Sebastian didn't answer.

"Holy crap, we have tone," Max said, and the screen

blinked to life. He tapped keys, then said, "It's workable for now, but no files, just Windows. Wiped clean."

"Erased it and left it behind? This is twisted bullshit. Why show your hand with the bullets and wrecking the place?" They'd covered their trail well, killing witnesses. This was just anger, he thought, then went to the front window, the muddy panes distorting the lawn and forest beyond. The nearest house was a couple acres away down a paved road. Any vehicle would be spotted coming, and his attention slid to the forest. They'd waited there before assaulting the house.

"Whoa. The e-mail is still here." Max looked up. "Why not delete that, too?"

"They already have it. He routes e-mail and voice mail through his Web phone when he's traveling." Max's brow shot up. "I told ya, he's savvy. *I* couldn't figure out how to make that work."

"I'm copying it," Max said.

Sebastian nodded absently and closed his eyes for a moment, clearing away images for a fresh look. He grabbed the mini video camera and filmed slowly around the rooms, crossing to the hall and into the bathroom. The claw-footed tub was filled with jumbled rods and the shower curtain, and he checked under the sink, the drawers, then went to the first bedroom and stopped short. The bed was stripped of sheets and quilt, and the mattress had long slices every eight to ten inches. Stab, slice back, stab and slice back. He returned to the living room and Max looked up.

"They're looking for something that's at least eight inches wide and solid." He gestured to the club chair with a couple dozen short slices, but not torn. Not ripped apart. "Every book is off the shelf and open, yet anything wider than a shoe box is gouged. But with the exception of the computer, the electronics are untouched." He turned in a circle. The mantel and fireplace were untouched as well, yet the stack of firewood in a brass caddy was upended on the floor.

Max stood, looked around, his attention stopping on the

kitchen. "The cereal boxes, too." Anything larger than an egg crate was on the counter or the floor.

Sebastian searched inside the bric-a-brac, the hatboxes, even the Irish porcelain candy jar that was nearly transparent. Max's look questioned. "The backup, a flash drive. Sometimes he even backed up his Web phone."

"Maybe they found it already." Max went back to hijacking e-mail.

"No. The entire house is wrecked. They didn't find what they came for or they would have stopped this sooner." And maybe Noble would be here. He twisted a look at the kitchen, then crossed to the freezer. No. It's too common and Noble is smarter, he thought, opening the freezer anyway. Empty.

"I'll have this in a couple minutes." Max put the screw in his mouth and kept working.

"Excellent, no pressure. The cop shack is in Bundoran, so they're probably on their way."

Max groaned, moved a little faster. "You know evidence tampering is a crime anywhere."

"We're not playing by the rules this time," he said as his phone chimed. He glanced at the caller ID. He hoped Riley had something good. "What'd the dean say?"

"Not a lot. Noble wasn't working for the University College Dublin. There is no record, though they were quick to say they knew him by reputation because he could translate ancient Gaul. But I've called every place I can think of and I can't find any institution in the area that employed him. At least not on this side of the island. He did use the university archives and had inspected clan records. I'm getting a list from the department head, but I don't expect it soon. What's his daughter have to say?"

"Same thing I do. Nothing." Noble was strangely quiet about his work.

"How's the cottage looking?"

Sebastian moved to the window, watching the road. "Like a frat party with knives."

"Mary and Joseph, what's he into?"

"I still don't know," Sebastian said. "But it's obviously not just translating."

"Sebastian, you're closest to him. What would he do in a tight situation?"

"Call for help. He knows his limits. He didn't like traveling and that's why he rented this place." Sebastian pinched the bridge of his nose. "We have to hand this over to local cops. We can't even take prints or we'll catch hell for tampering."

"I'm taking a commuter flight to Enniskillen," Riley said. *"I'll look for his car at the airport. I have an appointment at the National University of Ireland, then Saint Angela's College."*

That was south of the cottage. "Thanks, man." He ended the call.

"I got into his e-mail account." Max looked up from his spot on the floor. "They erased the documents and photos but didn't go into the e-mail." Max typed on the laptop. "Nor did they copy or forward any of it. Not surprised. The program was under a different name. Chaucer's House."

Sebastian swung around and smiled. "That's what I called the bookshop when I was a kid. Can you open it?"

"Yes, but there are only three, all to the same screen name. DOCorri on a Google mail account. No name, no signature. I'm copying it, but there isn't anything attached to the sends, even though the e-mail says there was."

Sebastian frowned, kneeling by a small trash can. "The attachment should be there so they erased all extended files."

Max flicked to the computer. "Not my strong suit, sorry. I'll send it to Logan to see what he can find."

Sebastian poked in the wicker basket. "He's in the Congo, unreachable." He dumped the can, flicking at trash. Noble liked to doodle, and writing out his thoughts helped clarify them. A lot like Max, he thought, but there was nothing except used tissue. "Found a sticky note with a reminder to buy some clothes. The writing is Noble's, but it's faint." As if the

pen was out of ink. He looked between the trash and the up-
heaval that was the living room. No files, no personal papers
from a man who was a neat pack rat? "This place has been
sanitized."

"See now, I thought I was just being paranoid."

"Yeah, but by who, garda?"

"No print dust, so I'm thinking no." Max disconnected
the hard drives and did his best to return it the way it was.
He spared a glance at the sticky note. "I know that brand, it's
exothermal. Extreme cold weather gear."

"Winter isn't for months and he was supposed to be done
with his project before October. Like it was a deadline."

"This DOCorri is part of this, and it's a good bet he's in
danger as well."

"We need to find him, warn him. Send an e-mail, it's the
shortest route." Sebastian pocketed the sticky note. "They
killed for antique paper, they'll go after him next." Why it
was costing lives still baffled him and until he learned what
Noble was translating, they didn't have a direction to hunt. *I
need a target to acquire.*

"We have all we can get here. I'm going to trace those
footprints." He tossed Max a walkie-talkie, then left the cottage, pulling off the gloves and stuffing them in his back
pocket as he crossed the yard. He stopped at the first set of
footprints, then compared it to his own. He toggled the
walkie-talkie. "Our visitor wears a size eleven, maybe."

Max toggled back. "*Shoe size in no way affects height,
weight or the length of . . .*"

"I get it." He chuckled and followed the prints.

He was near the woods when he heard the crunch of
gravel and turned to see a white sedan speeding up the road
to the cottage. "Uh oh, company's here." He waved, retrac-
ing his steps to the front walk.

"*Stall! I still need to stuff the guts back in the HD.*"

"Hurry, I think it's the police."

A stout man struggled out of the car and Sebastian watched
him make his way toward him. Make his way was accurate.

The guy waddled a bit, suffering from short legs and a belly that threatened to topple him forward. In a suit that was years past its prime, the man's jowly face and bright eyes reminded him of Burl Ives . . . and the Pillsbury Doughboy.

"I'm Officer MacAwley." He showed him his Garda Síochána badge and Sebastian introduced himself.

"Noble Sheppard is a close friend," he said.

"I was just notified by Surrey police because he lived here. How did you learn about it?"

They were probably wondering over the kill method more than anything. He showed him his license, though the U.S. government put a lock on them, it would take a while for MacAwley to learn that. "His daughter hired me to find him. I'd appreciate any help."

"Well now, you need to let us do that, lad. Interfering with an ongoing—" MacAwley stopped, frowned a bit. "Fontenòt? He mentioned you. You're the one with the restaurant in New Orleans?"

He hoped that's all Noble said and didn't mention details of Dragon One. "Yes sir. Do you know Noble well?" He helped MacAwley get his kits from the trunk.

"As well as anyone around here, I expect. He kept to himself. I'm the landlord, too." He flicked a chubby hand to the cottage, then grabbed a bag. "It once belonged to my grandmother."

"I'm afraid it's been ransacked."

MacAwley stopped, looked to the open cottage door, then to him. "Well now what on the earth for? Noble was nipped in England."

"Not sure. The door wasn't forced. It's not bad. We just arrived and haven't touched anything." The lie came too easily, but being thrown in jail for tampering wouldn't get Noble back. "You're out a computer and some furniture."

MacAwley huffed. "The computer is his and the furniture is old." The officer whipped out a cell phone and ordered their CSI to the cottage.

"Do you know what he's been working on?"

"A book. He said he was writing a book. He rarely left except for groceries or to visit the pub in the village."

Rarer then, Noble didn't drink. "Did he travel often while he was here?" He hated that he didn't know already and felt the sting of guilt riding him.

"Inside the country, mostly. Donegal, Sligo, Enniskillen. I knew he was in England this time, he called to tell me as a courtesy. My wife cleans the place for him, sometimes cooks meals. She said he spent a lot of time up there." MacAwley pointed up the coastline to the castle ruins, then walked up the path. "Let's have a look at the damage."

Did the ruins have anything to do with this, Sebastian wondered, or was it just Noble's insatiable need to put his mitts on history? "We found footprints." Max needed more time or he'd have shown himself by now.

Thank God the policeman veered with him, kneeling and using a pencil to lay back the dry grass. "He's a heavy man. We haven't had rain in a few days and that's a deep tread." MacAwley straightened, trying to match the footprint stride, and failed. "He was running, too."

Okay, that's a surprise and Sebastian rethought his first impression.

MacAwley followed the prints to the forest, stopping near the rocks. "They go farther." He waved at Sebastian to go look, out of breath.

Smiling, he climbed over the mossy rocks. He didn't have to go far. Beyond the edge of sunlight, it was much darker; elm and hawthorn trees entwined with gorse bushes and yellow flowers. He flicked on a penlight and recognized where the guy sat, the moss crushed and smeared. He shined the light around, walking farther away, yet kept the cottage in sight. When he could see the front and back of the house, he looked around. Clusters of moss and the vines covered everything. He bent closer, and behind a tree too slim to be cover, he found footprints. A lot of them.

Kneeling to see if he could tell the boot type, he spotted bits of curled orange brown paper near the roots of the tree, another bit a couple feet away. He picked up a piece, sniffed, then flattened it. Dirt smeared, and his features pulled tight. Shit. He returned to MacAwley, showing him the shreds.

"There's more to collect. They're skinny cigars and strong enough to make you light-headed."

MacAwley poked at it. "Can't buy them here. We haven't had any talk of anyone new around. The population is small. We notice visitors." The officer retraced the path, placing markers on the prints, then grabbed his bags and went inside. He scowled at the destruction, then focused on the kitchen. Max had his face under the faucet, taking a drink. Sebastian cleared his throat, then introduced him.

"So how long have you known Noble?" MacAwley asked, snapping on latex gloves. He grabbed a camera and worked with the precision of someone who'd done it a thousand times.

He stood near the door, out of the way, yet impatient to move on. "Since I was eight."

The policemen glanced, eyeing him. "Oldest friend you have, I'd say, eh?"

"Yes sir. He is. I was a little troublemaker and broke into his bookshop. He caught me, but didn't call the cops." MacAwley glanced. "He took me right to my mother." Sebastian remembered her disappointment in him more than anything. The look on her face still cut him. "Noble had a vise grip on my arm and dragged me four blocks to Mom. I knew I was about to catch a serious ass whooping and didn't go quietly." His mom had been cooking fish and shrimp, selling it to the locals to keep a roof over their heads. His father had gone off gigging in the bayou the year before and never came back. Deep in his soul, he'd never forgiven him for abandoning them. His mother died still believing he'd return. "Mom was livid, but Noble asked her permission to punish me himself. She was mad enough to let him. I thought I was going to jail, I swear, but he made me come to his shop every day and work off the broken window. Then he forced me to sit and read aloud for hours."

"You poor, poor lad."

He heard the humor in MacAwley's voice and smiled. "Actually, I couldn't read all that well till Noble helped me. The Shakespeare and Chaucer weren't bad, confusing as hell, but then he took pity on me and gave me a Hardy Boys mystery, a first edition. After that, I was hooked." Reading books was the only time he could completely escape anything troubling his life.

He watched MacAwley smooth the plastic, then lift the dusted print off the computer. Good thing it wasn't Max's. As MacAwley crossed to his print book, Sebastian discreetly offered Max the trash from the woods.

Max peered, tipping his head to check the brand, then looked up sharply. "No friggin' way."

His thoughts exactly. Captain Blacks. Made and sold in Russia. In Chechnya, there were smokes around the dead guards. But this brand was only outside Beckham's cell and the tattered one in his palm had been military field stripped.

FIVE

Kilbarron Castle
Ireland

The sun pierced a line of gold across the water of Donegal Bay.

Sebastian felt the twelfth century on the edge of his vision, yet all that remained of the castle beneath his feet was crumbling into the sea. Noble visited here often but didn't come here for the beauty. He wanted to touch history. This area in particular.

"What were you doing here, old man?"

And why didn't he tell him, tell anyone? Noble was his friend, his mentor when he needed it, and sometimes, his father when he wanted one the least. Sebastian understood Noble better than himself, and it wasn't in his personality to be this secretive. He rubbed his face, pushed his fingers through his hair. Frustration rode his spine. He had too little to go on, but after the destruction of the cottage, he couldn't get near the crime scene. Garda were all over the place. D-1 was shut down so tight, they couldn't learn beyond what Eddie gave them. Major Beckham was into something heavy duty in Chechnya for CIA to clamp a lid on the team, and setting them up to be a scapegoat to cover Beckham's tracks was top on his list. He didn't take kindly to that. Calling in the favor Beckham owed the team was a chit Sebastian planned to use prudently. But he would use it.

"Over this way is the Friary." He swung around. Sean MacAwley leaned against his car, nodding behind himself. "It's just as inhospitable."

"I appreciate you giving me a tour of the grounds." He walked to him, pebbles and stones blending into tight mossy ground the closer they came to the copse of trees. Years ago, the ruins had been excavated and while the archaeologists put it back the way they found it, the ground was weaker. Too many had gone too close to the edge and signs warned to approach at your own risk.

"That there was the home of the Maguire, clan chieftain, eleven seventy-three or -four, I think." Sean gestured back to the castle. "There are lots of ruins and for the locals, it's commonplace. You Americans are more fascinated."

"The fascination of youth. America is a toddler by comparison."

"Well, Ireland has her stories. Perhaps he was writing a book about one of them."

"Enough to murder to get it?" He shook his head, and Sean muttered something about never really knowing what motivated someone to kill. All depends on the target and the cause, he thought.

MacAwley brushed back branches bright with pink blossoms and ducked under. Sebastian caught it and followed him into the copse leading up an incline. Thin tall trees made the land feel dense and tight. Sunlight barely penetrated the forest canopy. Ahead was a hollow tree wrapped in vines with tiny white flowers. The breeze tore the blossoms free and Sebastian went still as the flutter of white sailed through the air like butterflies. An elfin tree, Noble called them. When he was much younger, he'd told him stories of legends and myths from every culture and country. Probably why mystery novels were his favorites, he thought, touching the tree as he passed it, smiling. He followed Sean down into a glen.

"Watch your step there, lad, it's muddy."

They crossed a shallow stream and up a short ridge. Sebastian saw the faint lines of a road, overgrown and rutted. "This is an old church road. The Friary wasn't notable, there are hundreds. The Normans built them and brought their priests to change us heathens to Christianity." Sean chuckled to himself.

"The pagans gave some payback," he said and Sean looked at him. "They used the Irish pagans for masons to build castles and cathedrals, and they left their own idols all over in gargoyles."

Sean grinned, corking a little laugh. "Aye, serves the greedy bastards right, eh? The Normans were hording Ireland like a prize, and there was fighting here, but after a fashion, the Maguire, he submitted. The Norman earl gave him back his own land and he ruled till his death." MacAwley moved his bulk around the scrub bushes. "It's a tale that's been changed, romanticized over the years. The way I heard it is there was a bit of clan feuding." Sean grinned, his cheeks bulging. "We do love a good argument. The English baron ordered the Maguire to marry. Fathers sent their daughters. Women were land and dowry, marriage stopped feuds, melded clans." He wore a funny crooked smile. "The story says the brides were murdered by the Maguire. No reason why, but that's the tale. Go south a few miles, it will be a wee different. Go north into Donegal and it's something still further from the truth."

"What is the truth?"

He shook his head. "No one really knows, I guess. Tourists had come up here about three years past, a small family, and the youngest wandered off. The search for the girl found this."

Sebastian approached the ruins of the monastery. Trees grew in the center courtyard, vines draping in a blanket of green, yet he could see stone squares on the ground, and part of a wall beneath vines and scrub bushes. He stopped at the old doorway, a pointed arch above him, and inside the crumbling walls was an open room. Toward the rear, the row of small, narrow rooms was unmistakable. "It looks like a prison."

"Aye, it does, ey? These are the priests' cells. They were Dominicans, I think, a life of poverty and helping the less fortunate. They had minimal to survive and were beholden to the ruling clan for food and such."

"The overgrowth is not as dense here," Sebastian said, marveling that he was walking where ancient priests had a thousand years ago.

"Archaeologists dug everywhere, just months at a time, then buried it all back up like the castle."

"Why isn't this on the local tours?" Max was scouring guides and museums, trying to link the research books in Noble's cottage.

"No money, I suppose, but it's dangerous. There are old coal and copper mines near here. Some so old they're covered up with this." He waved at the vegetation trying to swallow the land. "We don't know all the entrances. This"—he grabbed a piece of vine and moved it aside—"grows wild everywhere. It's the bane of my wife's garden."

Sebastian was beyond the outer wall, trying to imagine the monastery eight hundred years ago. Because right now, it felt like a cave. The sun barely reached back here, and he drew his penlight, following the roofline. "No windows on this side. A chapel maybe?" He worked his way inside, kicking at the ground, and after a few minutes, his boot hit something solid. Pulling at the vines, he uncovered a short broad hunk of rock, unmarred until he felt the flat chiseled side.

"That looks like an altar," Sean said, moving near.

Sebastian yanked at vines. "It's a kneeler. Look at the dents." There were dual curves in the stone block and Sebastian tried it. He only managed one knee. "Man, that's punishment."

"Suffering as the lord did," Sean snickered. "Want a palm to thrash yourself?"

Sebastian smiled, straightened. "Do you remember any more of the story?" They headed back to the car.

"I recall something about the Maguire's woman. That she came from the sea with an elf and a giant."

Sebastian laughed to himself. "That can't be right."

"I don't know them all. Didn't grow up around here."

"Know anyone who would?"

MacAwley eyed him.

"It's a start," he said. "His work has something to do with his kidnapping and if he was researching this . . ." He let that hang, and felt like he was swinging in the wind, helpless. Time was closing in on Noble and still without a ransom demand. He checked the time. Riley's flight should have landed by now. Maybe his sister Bridget could fill in some blanks, although reaching her would be a problem. She was in the Sea of Japan right now and the time difference was hell on communications.

As soon as they cleared the woods, Sean pulled out a cell phone and dialed. "My wife mentioned Mister Sheppard visiting the archives in the National Museum. The former curator is a childhood friend of my son's. She's in charge of the Kilbarron Manor now. Busy woman this time of year, but I'll see what I can do."

Sebastian thanked him and stepped away to give him privacy. Noble wasn't working with anyone he could pinpoint, and he wondered how a vague folktale connected, if at all. This could have just been a place of solitude for Noble and he was chasing his own ass, but doubt drained away with the condition of the cottage, the lack of his financial records, or even a slip of paper inside a book, Noble's preferred bookmark. No, this was nothing as it seemed. Even the scrap he'd found for thermal clothing was odd. Noble hated the cold, and remarked that he didn't want to spend the winter in Ireland. Exothermal was overkill for Ireland's weather, regardless. Max was hunting down the sales on the credit card statement he'd found, but there were few, for gas mostly. Noble's ticket to England wasn't on it. Sebastian learned the hard way not to ignore the obvious, even if it didn't make sense. The field-stripped smokes connected with the method of the kills. A trained hunter.

And while he tried not to think it, that said Noble was already dead.

His cell pinged with a text message and he brought it up. It was Eddie breaking the rules for him again.

2nd blood trail. BIG. 3 blocks from Crown Hotel. No body.

"Well, that was a bust." Olivia collapsed in her hotel room, falling back on the bed. Her stitches burned and she rubbed it, closing her eyes and trying clarify that man's face in her mind so she'd recognize him again. "Don't want to meet his ugly ass in a dark alley," she muttered to the pretty crystal chandelier hanging overhead. The rest of the room was just as opulent, and the deliciously soft mattress begged her to sleep off jet lag. The knock on the door denied it.

She listened to the incessant hammering on the other side of the adjoining room door for another second, then pushed herself off the bed. She crossed to the door and opened it, then flinched when Cruz laid into her.

"Can you be anymore of a doofus?"

She resented that. "Ya know, I'm not a novice at this, *you are.*"

He spun, tense for a second, then deflated. "I was worried."

"I'm touched, really, but I'm fine. See." She turned in a circle.

"But he *saw* you."

"Not my face, I'm sure of it." She was already driving away when he'd spotted her. She hoped. She didn't see a tail on the way here and had made a couple stops, just to be sure. She glanced at the crystal clock, then went to the bathroom to check her appearance. She came out to grab a fresh blouse and found Cruz peering out the window like a pedophile.

He looked back at her. "You aren't seriously considering going to the meeting."

"Liz is fitting me in between appointments, of course I am." Elizabeth MacNamara had e-mailed her, asking for Noble's address. She'd been the museum curator at the National Archives and helped Noble with his research. Yet now her grad school housemate was the curator of a sixteenth-century manor turned museum.

"The killer, here, in Ireland, that doesn't scare you?"

She shrugged. "I just don't think that far ahead." Giving in to fear wouldn't help Noble. He was her priority. She still didn't know if she was dealing with one man or a group. Treasure hunters were notorious for going to extremes, especially the black market sort. She crossed to the phone and ordered room service, tea for Cruz. He needed something. He looked ready to come out of his skin.

"The director?"

He shook his head. "Not available. I left a message to call *you.*"

"Fine, till then, get Ross on the line."

He couldn't move fast enough back to his room, and while he made the connection, she changed quickly, then swept her hair up in a twist. She stared at her reflection. Dumb. *Do you really think a new hairdo will keep big knife guy guessing?* She left the bathroom and checked her phone. She'd put Noble's number in it, and was tempted to try a call, but without the translation, she had nothing for barter. She entered Cruz's room. Ross's image was on the laptop screen. She took a seat. He didn't look happy. Maybe it was just the grainy transmission. The rotation of the earth and satellite links were disastrous in that end of the world.

"Since there's no stopping you now, what have you accomplished?"

She let out a relieved breath. She didn't want to argue. She was right, he was wrong. She relayed the visit to the cottage and the man destroying the place.

"It was sanitized already. They didn't find anything. We didn't either."

She arched a brow. "That was quick."

"The project is exposed and we have to get it back under wraps quickly."

"It's one of our own," she said.

His lips pressed in a tight line. "Or someone further up the chain."

"There's only three and let's face it, they're the ones who scrutinized my staff." She inclined her head to Cruz. Though anyone connected to the project had their backgrounds thoroughly sifted, her team was handpicked for their expertise, not for the ability to play cloak and dagger. "News on Noble?"

He shook his head. "No ransom demands yet." Her heart felt the weight of that. He wasn't a young man and she didn't want to imagine the treatment he was suffering right now. "Police are looking at street traffic videos. So far, the killer didn't leave a trace."

She agreed, then was forced to tell him the guy at the cottage might have seen her. When Ross opened his mouth, she put up a hand. "Don't. Alone without backup wasn't wise, I know that, but it was early. I wasn't expecting anyone to be there except maybe the police." She waited till he settled back and described what she witnessed. "He had a knife that's the length and width of the puncture wounds to our agent. Double edge, nine inches maybe." He worked another computer and the screen split and the photo loaded. "Similar, but I didn't get that close." Her own was in her bag and might as well be a Swiss Army. "The man I saw was wearing latex gloves, but he had a tattoo on his hands. Here." She pointed to the web of skin between the thumb and forefinger on the muscle.

He frowned, scanning papers in front of him. "You're certain?"

He knows something. "Not without seeing them up close,

no, but it was black, and unless he's got a skin disease or broke a pen, my guess is a tat."

"Several gangs have tattoos there."

She tipped her head. "Too organized. If that's the same man, then they got out of England and did it easily. Probably by boat. That means Noble could be here in Ireland."

"I'll alert the garda and the port authorities." He leaned in and she noticed his nose was a little pink. "Now you going to tell me what you found in China?"

The glow was certainly off that, she thought, her smile reluctant. "The origins of the legend."

His eyes rounded and she savored this moment. His stunned expression. Priceless. "Now do you understand exactly how important Noble is to our success?" He was the one who'd found the khan well hidden in history. She'd found the tomb. "It gives us a positive link. Cruz will load up the image and you can see for yourself. Get Dana on it. She has my notes." Ross scribbled on a notepad, nodding. Cruz cleared his throat and tapped his watch. "Gotta fly."

"Consider taking Cruz with you."

"Oh, please." She left the chair and was about to cut the line when Ross said, "You were right."

She sat back down. "Keep going."

"I was insensitive and driven by the job and the time line. We will never find the relic without the translation or Noble."

"I appreciate that." But she wasn't letting him off that easy. "It's a good start. The security I requested?"

"Perimeter sensors have been increased and expanded, and the armed detail is doubled. Though I don't think it's wise to have guns anywhere near a bunch of geeks who can't function without their computers."

He had a point. Living on the edge of the world was a stretch for most of them.

"I'm personally inspecting everything coming into the site, including intelligence. Noble's cell number is being tracked, but it's not turned on. There is a possibility they simply dumped it somewhere."

She had a feeling the director had a hand in that, but she wasn't complaining. At least her staff was safe. "The phone that called Noble, that got the alert from your undisclosed source?"

"They're still tracing it, but it hasn't been used since."

"Who is he, the caller?" She suspected it was the guy at the cottage, but he could just be hired muscle.

"Don't know. It's related to another operation and I don't have clearance to pry." He flushed a little. "I've tried and got smacked down."

Olivia was sort of proud of him, and it made up for his pissy "by the manual" attitude. "There's hope for you, Agent Ross." She smiled. "Now that wasn't so hard, was it?" Although being shut out with one inquiry said the tracked caller was into more than just her project.

His lips quirked. "If I get my clearance handed to me, you're the reason."

"That's because I'm good at guilt trips. Thank you, Andrew."

"Keep a link to Cruz open and anything suspicious, alert us."

"I'll try." The hair on the back of her neck hadn't settled down yet, but wired to Cruz wasn't useful. He couldn't help her if she got in trouble, anyway. A big weapon would make her feel better, but using it on someone breathing—not so much. She ended the transmission and went back to her room for her leather satchel. She was brushing dirt off her shoes when she heard room service delivered in the adjoining room. Cruz's brilliant self wasn't up for this kind of intrigue. He needed sustenance. She left her room through the partition to his, closing the door behind her. She found him near the window, sipping Irish Breakfast tea and spying the parking lot.

"No one is near the car."

"I love your vigilance, Cruz." She bit into a teacake and washed it down with strong coffee. Her stomach screamed for more.

"Someone has to keep tabs."

She wiped her mouth with a linen napkin, then turned to the door. She was glad someone had her back. Cloak and dagger wasn't her specialty. "If you get worried, I don't know . . . go try on my new shoes."

He blinked owlishly, and she closed the door on his laugh.

Olivia wasn't taking chances and drove evasively, managing side streets, and ignoring the GPS bitching about recalculating. She approached the manor and was always blown away that wedged next to a sixteenth-century mansion the size of a football field was a modern bakery and chocolate shop. That chocolate shop and me have a date, she thought as she pulled though the gates of the estate and parked the car in front. Her credentials got her past security quickly, and inside, she followed the docent deeper into the manor. Her shoes clicked on the polished hardwood floors and she couldn't resist stopping to admire the oil painting of the clan chieftain in full regalia before she crossed the dining room. That table would accommodate thirty, she thought, then looked ahead as Liz stepped out of her office, meeting her halfway.

Olivia smiled at the friendly face of her grad school roommate. "You look fabulous!" The tall brunette wore a fitted navy suit, a scarf of her clan tartan across her shoulder. The heirloom brooch securing it was familiar and nearly two hundred years old. "Killer shoes, girl."

Liz grinned and they embraced. "Welcome back, but I didn't mean for you to fly here, Olivia."

"I was in the neighborhood." They turned in to the offices.

"Here to see Noble? He wasn't answering his phone."

"There's a good reason." Olivia closed the door and broke the bad news, revealing the situation with the least amount of information.

With wide eyes Liz said, "You think it was because of the ship's log?"

Olivia skirted mentioning the translation. "It was worth about eight grand, more on the black market. It was especially well preserved." Kiss that good-bye, she thought and tried to redirect. "I'm sorry, I should have called." Her stomach growled noisily and she felt her face go warm, embarrassed.

Liz leaned back against her desk. "Yes, so we could have lunch maybe."

Olivia felt a little sting of jealousy. She could use a not-about-the-job break right about now. Food and several hours sleep wouldn't hurt either.

"This just saves me the post." Liz reached around to her desk to the little wood box near the phone. She opened it, then handed her a bright green flash drive. Olivia felt a flush of relief. "He's never asked me for anything since the archives, so I thought it best to get it to you or send it. I just needed an address. I didn't expect you to show up in person."

"Thank you. May I borrow your computer, see what it is? Or do you know?"

"No, I didn't peek. He's left that here more than once. Absent-minded professor, I suppose."

Far from it, Olivia thought. Noble was sharp.

"I assumed it was simply a copy of clan records he'd made here."

Olivia took a seat at Liz's desk and slipped the drive into the port, then accessed it. She sat back, scowling at the screen.

"Not what you expected?"

"Some. His research." She clicked, opening several, giving each a quick look before closing them one by one. There were copies of all sorts of documents. Huge amounts of old e-mails, more ship logs, trade letters, but no diary. As she opened another, she realized Noble was following a lead she didn't understand yet. This isn't anything to do with Ireland, she thought, then closed the files and removed the flash. She stuffed it between her breasts.

Liz arched a tapered brow. "They'll have to get really close to get at that."

"Like any man has in . . ." She thought a second. "Forget it. If I have to count, it's too embarrassing to mention."

They laughed and Liz sobered first. "If someone would kidnap Noble, for whatever reason, they could come after you as well."

"I know. I'm going back to the hotel after this." She thought of that hulk in the cottage and the damage he'd already done. If he knew of the translation, then he knew far more than anyone should. "Let me know if anyone comes asking about him, okay?" She plucked a business card bearing only her name and new cell number from her leather satchel and laid it on her desk. All calls were rerouted through blind connections.

Liz walked her to the door. "What are you doing, Olivia? Aren't the police looking?"

"They are, yes . . ." Oh hell, she didn't have a lie handy, and hated giving one to a friend. She was saved when Liz's cell phone buzzed, and she turned away to answer. Olivia grabbed her arm, and motioned she was leaving. Liz squeezed her hand, then went back to her crisis. Olivia left the offices.

In the main hall, she skimmed the visitors for anyone without a purpose before she went out a side door, then walked to the outer yard. White catering trucks pulled into the delivery lot and she skirted around them to the front. Deciding to leave her car in the lot, she walked to the street. Traffic moved past, stymied by the crowds of people here for the festival. She smiled at the mix of medieval and Jacobin costumes—a lot of nice kilts, she thought, walking. Getting this flash to Cruz was essential. He had a mind like Noble's and could unwind a puzzle faster than she could. But her stomach rudely demanded attention, and she headed toward the aroma of food. And maybe some chocolate.

Fifteen minutes later, she was dusting off the crumbs from a buttery scone and sipping a decadently rich latte when her cell phone rang. She juggled the Styrofoam cup to grab it, walking. She glanced at the number and stopped short. The cup slipped from her hand.

Noble.

Sebastian waved as Officer MacAwley eased back into traffic, and he sipped coffee, closing his eyes for a moment and wondering when he'd get to sleep. Flying Dragon Six with a red-eye flight plan was catching up to him. He drank more, the hot liquid waking him up enough to notice a car slowing traffic and he followed the black sedan as it slid to a stop at the curb.

Riley hopped out. "It's Noble's. It was in the Enniskillen Airport lot."

"It's a relic from the eighties," Sebastian said. Noble hated spending money on cars and the Allegro was a prime example.

"Runs well, though. Horrific mileage." Riley yanked the passenger door, and popped open the glove box. "I found plane tickets to Greenland in here." He handed them over.

"That's a new one."

"Garda has been all over it, but since it was in the lot when he was kidnapped, they processed it and let it go. Safia says those tickets were not paid for on the credit statement you found at the cottage."

Sebastian frowned, examining them. "He was supposed to board the day after he was taken. The return date is open."

"He's ready to rock, that much I know for certain." Riley walked to the rear of the car and unlocked the trunk, then stepped back.

Inside were two boxes, opened and filled with cold-weather gear, still with the tags. Sebastian poked through it. "He even has snowshoes, for pity's sake. What the hell is in Greenland that has to do with research in Ireland?"

"Maybe Dr. McNamara can tell us." Riley closed the trunk, and tossed him the keys. "We've got just a few minutes of her time. None if Officer MacAwley hadn't called." He gestured to the catering trucks at the side doors a block away. "There's some event tonight, probably why the streets are so crowded."

Sebastian's gaze followed a man dressed like Friar Tuck and thought, tame compared to Mardi Gras. They went inside, the cool air greeting them with fragrant flowers decorating a grand foyer rising nearly two stories. Their path was marked with rich polished woods and amazing detail molding. The massive house beckoned for a slow stroll and study.

"I know a lot of history because of Noble. It's kind of hard not to get excited when he gets into it." Noble was full of oddball facts.

"He's a great storyteller," Riley said with a smile. "He should be writing books instead of selling them."

"Then he'd be talking more about it." He shook his head. "For him to be taken at that time says he was watched. I'm not much help. I can't recall him ever saying exactly what he was working on. Neither can Jasmine." Who wasn't happy about being woken to answer that.

"I didn't get anything from the local colleges, but Noble visited the National Museum briefly, researching a bunch of different subjects," Riley said softly. "Vikings, mostly."

Sebastian's brows shot high. *The giant,* he thought.

"Vikings tore through Ireland, Wales, and Scotland centuries ago," Riley said. "Few Norsemen settled, but they're still finding proof all over Ireland."

"But there isn't a piece of history worth lives, so what's so dangerous about research?" Still no answers, he thought and vented his frustration by squeezing a little rubber ball, forcing the torn muscles in his wrist to obey. It was productive, he told himself, because he couldn't stop envisioning Noble in the hands of someone trained . . . well, like Dragon One. But right now, he'd like to wring the old man's neck for not talking to him.

They walked to the information desk and the cute blonde sitting behind it looked up and smiled. "Well, well. Riley Donovan, this is a surprise."

Sebastian glanced at him, highly amused because he could tell by Riley's expression he didn't have a clue who she was. "Saved by a name tag," he whispered.

"This proves I should not come home," Riley muttered.

"Your misspent youth catching up to you?"

Riley sighed, resigned. "I'm lucky Safia thinks it's hysterical." He plastered on a smile and walked closer. "Rowena. How has life treated you?"

The woman's smile was electric, and it took seconds before she noticed Riley's wedding ring. She busted with laughter. Riley showed off a picture of his bride till Sebastian tapped his watch. He got to the point. Within a minute, a statuesque brunette appeared, a clipboard tucked to her chest.

Introductions made, she stared curiously at him for an unusually long moment before she said, "Forgive me for being so brisk, gentlemen, but I have lots to accomplish and few hours to do it."

"I appreciate you seeing us," Sebastian said. "Would you like us to walk along with you? I just have a couple questions."

"Brilliant." As she walked, she handed him several crisp sheets of paper. "This is the history of the Kilbarron ruins and what we have on the folktale, but as Officer MacAwley mentioned, the story has several versions depending on the area and the clan sects. It's never been a solid fable. So what can I answer for you?"

Sebastian got to the point. "What did archaeologists find in the Friary near Kilbarron castle?"

Her gaze narrowed sharply and he could feel the door closing with her expression. "What makes you ask that?"

Sebastian shrugged. "The search for the missing child uncovered the Friary. It was excavated, then returned to its pre-excavation state. Archaeologists would have kept going and restored it. That makes me think you found something tremendous and didn't want to bring attention to the site."

She glanced between them, silent.

"It must be very controversial to be kept hidden," Riley prodded. "But it's Ireland's heritage."

"I'm not at liberty to discuss this. Forgive me."

"Ma'am, I'm sure the officer mentioned it has to do with an investigation. We only need to know what was found, not the contents. Please. We won't reveal it." He put on his best hound dog face.

For a moment, she looked as if she battled with some mysterious line in the sand, then said in almost a whisper, "A book, a diary, if you will, written by a monk." A young man in a white smock and black slacks pushed through the doors and went right to her side. "I'm so sorry, I must attend my duties. Please keep that to yourself." Before he could thank her, she disappeared though the door with the server.

"That was chilly," Sebastian said, then looked at Riley. "This is shaping into a nice little cover-up."

"I don't see why," Riley said. "And if Noble was really translating a monk's diary from the middle ages, then how did he even know about it, much less get a copy when it's not public knowledge?"

"The same source of the plane tickets and the thermal gear, I bet." It made sense in a crime that had none. They headed toward the exit, passing displays of Roman coins and medieval slings. "We have someone with enough power to get their hands on an Irish relic that's national treasure kind of stuff." He flicked a hand at the Iron Age jewelry and pottery displayed. "A document? No way. Ireland's government didn't give him access."

"Whoever's on the end of that Google mail address did," Riley said. "And they've got some clout."

But DOCorri wasn't answering Max's e-mail, and as they headed for the exit, Sebastian glanced at his cell phone for a signal and nearly ran into an exhibit. He stepped back, then suddenly moved closer to the tall glass case. A massive iron shield hammered in the shape of a bird's wing rested on a stone block. A third was deteriorated, but what struck him wasn't the unusual shape, but the markings. Runes. Viking runes. He read the history printed on an acrylic tile. It was discovered in the same castle ruins he'd stood on only an hour ago. He photographed it with his cell phone, and when they were on the street, Riley called Safia, relating what little they'd learned. He put her on speaker.

"Find out what's in Greenland. Anything. No matter how obscure." He was open to anything right now. "Call Viva, ask her to see what she can find on that fifteenth-century ship's log." Noble bought antique books all the time, but nothing worth four grand or that old.

"*Roger that. But a little FYI . . . just because they shut us down doesn't mean Ground Zero is ignoring us. I've found three traces on my searches already.*"

He arched a brow. "Any idea where from?"

"*No, but they let me find that.*"

"A warning."

"*I'm ignoring it, naturally. But this has very long arms,*" Safia said, her voice tinny on speaker phone. "*Moira called. Someone broke into Noble's bookshop.*"

"Christ, they're thorough." He rubbed his mouth and asked about the damage.

"*Jasmine sent me pictures, I'll forward, but it looks like teenagers trashing. Moira's going there to see if she anything was stolen.*"

Moira wasn't in the shop often enough to know. "The kidnapper really wanted the translation, not the *Aramina* log." *If* that's what he was working on.

"Or both, but it appears they're still searching."

"Jesus, how the hell did *they* know about this when I didn't?"

"Sebastian," Safia said patiently. *"That's when spies do their best work."*

The steam went out of him just then. He couldn't imagine Noble doing anything clandestine, but it was stacking up that way. Riley spoke to Safia for a moment longer. Max was on his way to meet them, yet before he hung up, he asked if she had new satellite from Chechnya.

"We need to know so we can cover ourselves. They're still blocking us." He'd no intention of being swept up in their mess again. His cell rang and he glanced down, then frowned. "Impossible."

Riley hung up, then peered at the screen. "An overnight express pickup? I want to see you make that deadline."

He looked up. "It's Noble's."

"Say again?"

"I'm on his overnight express account because I sign for his book orders when he's not around." The bookshop was four doors up from the Craw Daddy. "He hasn't shipped anything since he left for Ireland." He opened the message and scowled. "Noble sent something to himself."

Sebastian went to the car, grabbed the GPS, and programmed the route to the pickup location. "Finally, a break. It's two blocks east, but it's going to close in fifteen minutes."

He didn't bother with the car and finding another parking slot. He hurried across the street, moving between people and slowing for the crowds. He glanced at the street signs and crossed, slipping left. He spotted the door and slowed to a walk, and drew out the documents he'd need. His passport slipped from his grip and he snatched it off the ground, growing cold when he saw the cigarette near the wall. Like the ones he'd found at the cottage. He glanced up the street and searched the crowds for smokers, but the chime on the door reminded him he was out of time. Ten minutes later, he left with a broad overnight express parcel. He'd taken ten steps when he saw Noble's handwriting. *For Dr. Olivia Corrigan* and a number was written across the seam.

DOCorri, he thought. *No.* He couldn't be *that* closemouthed.

Sebastian hesitated opening it, an understanding he didn't want to make settling. Noble knew he was hunted. He tore the seal strip, peered inside. Books. A second later, he smelled tobacco smoke. He scanned the sidewalk for the thin cigars, spotted one and rushed to it, then searched for another. Don't ignore the obvious, he thought and quickened back toward the manor. Thirty yards from the cars, he stopped. Traffic moved in front of him. The light changed and people paused, then rushed quickly. His gaze ripped over the intersection. A big man worked his way between the idling cars. His attention shot ahead.

A woman looked west up the street, turning in a circle. When she saw the man, the redhead took off.

Sebastian crossed several yards behind, and called out to Max and Riley leaning against Noble's car. As he neared, he tossed the package to Riley. "Lock it up and go north. Max, hoof it east. The man in the black shirt and pants. He smokes Russian cigars."

Max and Riley split off while he kept his focus on the man, nearing. He took his picture with his cell phone just before the guy palmed a knife, smoothly folding the blade against his wrist, hand against his thigh. He quickened. The man neared the redhead, and she darted left and tried to get into a shop. The guy was on her heels before she reached the door, and he grabbed her elbow, pulling her into a center walk between buildings. Shit. Sebastian booked, and as he passed a vendor selling replicas of a castle, he slapped a twenty on the counter and snatched one. He ran, turning into the Walk. The man had his knife against her stomach. Her knee came up and missed. Sebastian drew his arm back and threw.

The weighed souvenir clipped his head, knocking hard

enough that he staggered. The woman twisted her wrist, slapped his elbow the wrong way, and freed herself.

Clutching his head, the man lurched for her, catching her shirt. But she didn't hesitate, bolting.

Her attacker rounded on him, tossing the knife from hand to hand. Sebastian needed to kick someone's ass and launched into him. He struck, once in the throat, the nose, then a hit under his arm. The man folded, dropping the knife, then hit back three times in a beat down that took everything Sebastian had to fight off. Sebastian landed one under his jaw and the man staggered, collapsed. Sebastian lurched back, poised to strike, but the guy leapt to a squat like a Cossack dancer and swept his leg, clipping him behind the knees. Sebastian dropped, his back smacking the cobbled stone. That's going to leave a mark, he thought trying to catching his breath and roll, but the guy dropped his weight on him. He felt his ribs give. Sebastian clapped his ears, stunning him, then rolled hard, gripping the bastard's hair as he went. The man barely made a sound, and Sebastian struck him in his carotid artery, then threw his weight on him. He slammed his arm across his throat, digging in.

"Where's Noble?" The man's eyes widened. "Where is he?"

The guy just smiled and a second later, Sebastian's head exploded with pain. A heartbeat more, and he felt nothing.

Dimitri shoved the man off him, and nodded his thanks to Rastoff. He climbed to his feet, rubbing his throat and looking down at his attacker. His accent was American. Interesting.

"Should we take him? He said the man's name, I heard it." Rastoff's words had a bite, daring him to countermand him again.

Dimitri hurried away, shaking his head. "Nyet. Come." He scooped up his knife, sheathed it as they ran down the busy street to the junk of a car. They needed to get another before this one failed. Rastoff offered the keys, and he shook his head, and swallowed several times. The man's arm felt like a steel pipe against his throat. He dropped into the passenger seat.

"People care about the old man, we need to use that." Dimitri scanned the streets and did not see the woman. At least he knew her name, and now her face.

Then he saw a man running toward their car, and he smacked the dash. "Go, you fool! There's more!" He saw the man draw from behind his back. Dimitri palmed his S4M and aimed out the window. He fired once, aware the bullet would not reach him, but it had the desired effect; he ducked. The small car raced away from the village and toward the sea. They knew his face. This changed things.

She will not be pleased.

Olivia raced to the end of the Walk and as she rounded the edge of the building, a man caught her.

"Whoa, lady."

Instinctively, she kneed him in the junk, then pushed him off and ran.

"American! Jesus. I'm an American!"

She stopped, looking between him and back down the Walk. "They're fighting, two men. One has a knife."

Rushing into the Walk, the guy opened a cell phone and said, "He's down, come west, look for a black shirt."

Black shirt. Were they watching him? Yet when she looked down the alley way, and saw her rescuer on the ground, she rushed back. His friend checked for a pulse as she knelt. "Oh God, he's bleeding." She dug in her satchel for a something and only found airplane tissues.

"Stay with him," his friend said.

She nodded, and blotted the blood at the back of his skull, calling to him. "Sir? Sir?" He moaned, and she brushed back a lock of black hair and froze. An odd familiar feeling poured over her. He tried pushing up, then simply rolled onto his back. She hovered over him.

For a second, she couldn't speak. *"Sebastian?"*

He blinked, his smile slow. "Hi ya, Livi."

"Hi. What the hell are you doing here?"

He sat up, holding his head, then inspected the blood on his fingertips. "I could ask you the same thing."

"I asked first." A thousand emotions crashed over her, but shock ruled them all.

Good God. The very last person she ever expected to see again was her ex-husband.

SIX

Max ran, darting between the shoppers and aiming for the car. He threw himself over the rental's hood, keys ready, and climbed in. A moment later, he pushed into traffic. He spotted Riley running hell-bent for leather down the sidewalk, darting into the street, then back to the Walk. He was flying. Max drove like a Londoner, zipping between compact cars, laying on the horn, and annoying just about everyone. He drove around a bottleneck, taking a right, then squeezing the car down a narrow, very old street. Be just my luck to get stuck, he thought, then breathed easy as the car lurched onto the paved road. He angled toward Riley, coming up behind him. He stopped, Riley grabbed the door, dropped inside. Max accelerated.

"They're heading to the docks. The shore, at least." Riley swiped at his forehead. "I got a look at this guy. He shot at me already."

"Well, shit, that's not fair. He smuggled guns in the country when we can't carry." Carrying a weapon in Ireland was by certificate and only to a shooting range. D-1's license to carry internationally was under Diplomatic Security Service and suspended. That shit pissed Max off. D-1 had earned that in Venezuela and Singapore. But then, operating inside the legal boundaries never stopped them before. He needed to get to the plane and their arsenal. But till then, "Up for breaking a few more rules?" He reached into the console, handed Riley the long slim knife. "Use your skill."

"Where the hell you get that?"

"Your sister has an amazing collection."

"Kathleen. Dougal's going to be really pissed," Riley said, then tested it on his thumb. "Bugger me, it's sharp. She's probably waiting to fight the Brits again," he muttered, then leaned out the window and threw. The tire deflated, but it didn't stop their rush down the coastline. Thirty yards more and the tread peeled off, the hub shooting sparks.

"Where is he going?" Riley said. "There's no docks there, it's just beaches, tourist traps. Witnesses. Oh shit, police!"

Max heard the eee-yaw of sirens. "Busted," he said. "They're heading to the shore." He couldn't miss the trail. The car was spewing black exhaust. Max drove around the curve of the road and braked when he saw the car abandoned. The doors were open, the engine smoking. "You see them?" He stopped and climbed out, then turning in a circle, he sighted through binoculars. The coastline was a stretch of beach with a few sunbathers gathering their belongings. Hello. "They're on the sand, up there." Max ran across the street and down a rocky slope, but he didn't need binoculars to see the speedboat in the water and the two men running toward it.

Riley moved up beside him and he handed him the binocs. On the road behind them, a line of white police cars with the lime yellow stripe sped past.

"He's got an 'in case shit happens' plan." The men were in the water, sloshing, then diving under. Max looked to the sky as the distinct whop-whop of a helicopter punctured the air. "Let's get out of here before they think we're accomplices." They hurried back to the car and were driving back to Kilbarron before the chopper appeared.

"Notice that boat?"

Max smirked. "You mean the sixty-thousand-dollar floating price tag." It was a Scarab, maybe thirty feet long; Dragon One's preferred chaser on the water. Max loved the slick streamlined boats. They could travel over sixty miles per hour and he'd seen one race at one twenty-eight. Those guys could be in international waters in under a minute. There were two more men on the boat, armed.

"Someone has money to burn."

"Bad guys always do." Max didn't see a ship on the horizon, but knew those men weren't leaving by the Scarab. "They murdered to get to Noble. I don't think a few Irish cops will stop them." All this for some ancient book? No, he thought, there was more.

"Well?" Olivia said.

"I'm looking for Noble's kidnapper." Her eyes widened. "Your turn."

When she didn't answer, he climbed to his feet, his hand out for her. She took it, standing. It brought her within inches and her body jumped with memory, damn it. "I'm on a grant. For the American Research Institute."

His brows knit tightly. "I'll bite, what did he want from you?"

"He was trying to rob me."

He scoffed, glancing at the people coming to investigate. "You never could lie convincingly," he said, then grasped her arm, ushering her toward the end of the Walk. But he didn't make it, his legs folding a little, and he put his hand on the wall. "Christ, what'd he hit me with?"

"A Guinness bottle. They're thick." Olivia immediately wrapped his waist and urged him with her. "We need to stop the bleeding, at least." Sebastian regained his footing easily, but she couldn't ignore his shirt collar stained with blood. It had to hurt. When they reached the delivery lots of the manor, she let him go and strode past the workers and inside. She searched the area and waved to Liz. Liz crossed the immense dinning room and Olivia flinched when Sebastian appeared beside her. Liz stopped short, staring at Sebastian as if he'd bite.

"I was accosted on the street and this man helped me. Can we use your office for a few minutes?"

Liz snapped out it. "Of course, do you need an ambulance?"

"No," Sebastian said, his gaze sliding to hers.

Liz led them into her offices, then she crossed to a cabinet and returned with a medical kit. Sebastian lowered to a chair and his WILL WORK FOR SCOOBY SNACKS T-shirt made her smile. Olivia checked the wound, then went to the bathroom, grabbing paper towels and soaking them.

Liz slipped close. "I was just talking with him an hour or so ago." Olivia met her gaze. "He wanted to know what we found in the Kilbarron Friary." She went still inside. "But . . . why does his name sound so familiar?"

She reddened. "That's because he's my Sebastian." Was, she thought. *Was.*

"Your ex?" Liz swung around for a second look, then stared at Olivia. "You're kidding!" she whispered. "Granted you were young and stupid, but how could you ignore *that*?"

"As easily as he did me, Liz." She squeezed out the towels. "We'll be out of here in a few. I'm so sorry to intrude."

"It's fine. Are you okay?"

She nodded, but she wasn't. Not with Sebastian twenty feet away doing something with his phone.

"Just don't repeat bad judgment." Olivia frowned at her, shutting off the water. Liz inclined her head to Sebastian. "This looks like a twist of fate you shouldn't ignore."

She nudged her. "Oh, get out of here."

"Ha. My office, wench. And I'm queen of this castle."

"Show-off." Liz left and Olivia crossed to Sebastian, tossing the bloody tissues and cleaning the wound. It wasn't that bad.

"Olivia."

She winced at the sound of his deep voice. "Yes."

He tipped his head up, grabbed her hand. "I'm waiting."

She didn't speak, couldn't, and he arched a black brow. The move had an effect, like a dart, and she suddenly felt twenty and such a marshmallow near him. "I told you. I'm here on business." She held his wrist, slapped a cloth in his hand and placed both over his wound. She walked away. "It's confidential."

"I know you work with Noble. And considering he's been kidnapped and people are dead, right now you're high on my shit list for not coming forward."

His words stabbed. She had a problem with that, too, but she was bound by her oath. She hoped the director was offering information to the police, but she didn't know. When she didn't respond, he stood, looming over her.

"Don't start this way, Livi. I was at his cottage. I know it was sanitized."

Damn. She popped open the medical kit and found bacitracin. She stood still, waiting for him to sit again, then applied the salve and finished with a butterfly bandage. "You could use a stitch." She thought of the ones in her arm and how she got it. She could handle China; this would be a snap. Right.

"Stop." He forced her to look at him. "I found field-stripped cigarettes in the woods near Noble's cottage and across the street from this place ten minutes ago. He was waiting to kidnap you, or take you out. A knife is a quiet kill."

She crumbled. "I know." She still felt its weight against her stomach, saw those hollow blue eyes. Dead inside. He'd enjoyed her torment. "He threatened to disembowel me or he'd send Noble back in pieces." A chill shot up her spine. If Sebastian hadn't intervened . . . God. She was so out of her element right now. "Early this morning, I saw him trashing the cottage and ran. I was a good hundred yards away before he spotted my car, but I didn't see another tail."

"That's the whole idea." He flipped open a cell phone, dialed, eyeing her darkly. "Max, I'm at the manor. Pick us up." A pause and then, "She's coming with us."

He closed the phone, giving her a look that said don't push him. Something in her struck like a match and she opened her mouth, then clamped it shut. They both had the same goal. Find Noble. The man she'd married had skills, now he had more. "Fine. But we go to my hotel. The Sand House. Because I'm not going anywhere with three men." She cleaned up the trash and resealed the medical kit.

"That hurts, darlin'. And the way you handled that guy, I'm surprised you're worried."

She looked up, then pushed her hair out of her face. That crooked smile made her stomach tumble.

"Who taught you that move? Your brothers?"

She scoffed. "*You* did." His soft chuckle danced down her spine as she turned away to put the medical kit in the cabinet. "We should leave." She flicked a hand at the beautiful blue period gown hanging on the back of the door. She'll look great in that, she thought. "Liz doesn't need us here now." She grabbed her satchel, slinging it across her body, and Sebastian went suddenly very still, staring at it.

His gaze flicked to hers. "Noble has one just like that." He touched the smooth calfskin, her initials burned into the tan leather. But his reverent motion told her so much more, and her heart simply ached for him. Noble was like his dad.

"He gave it to me for my birthday."

Only his gaze shifted.

"Yes, we work together, and we both took an oath of confidentiality." His expression darkened like a cloud passing over it. "I know you understand oaths, and my need to keep it, so save your breath."

He leaned in, crowding her. "Then you're attached to my hip till I find the truth."

She pushed on his chest. "You don't scare me, Sebastian, you never did. You forget I have brothers? Talk all you want, I can't say more than Noble was transla—"

The door flung open and Liz rushed in, glancing between them. "There are two men out there flashing your picture, on a cell phone." She looked at Olivia. "Yours."

Sebastian pushed past them out office door and down the short hallway. The double doors separating the estate house from the newer offices and loading docks were open a few inches and he searched beyond the grand dining room. Visitors crowded the madrigal singers who were the center of attention in the foyer. Behind the group, a man slowly walked, ducking and weaving to look at each woman. He searched for the second man and found him near the front door. The guy put his hand on his ear. Rookie, he thought, but the motion opened his leather jacket. He spotted the pistol stock. He turned back to the offices, thinking the rules just changed.

He motioned to Olivia. "We need to leave now. Thank you," he said to Dr. MacNamara. "Is there an outside exit to this office?"

"No, but at the end of the hall is the fire door."

He shook his head. "Alarms will go off. We don't need a panic."

"I can shut it off for one minute. No more because it sends a signal to the firehouse. You have to go through the old barracks to the fire door leading outside." She went to a panel near the door, running her finger down the switches. "I'll count to ten before I switch it off, then you'll have to run."

"Excellent." He stepped into the hall and nodded to her, mentally counting till he stood outside the door. Olivia slipped off her shoes and stuffed them in her bag. He pushed through. The next door was at the other end of an arched stone corridor and the entire length of the manor. He ran, Olivia right behind him as they splashed through puddles to reach the secondary door. The thing was refitted and looked like a vault. He turned the dial and threw his shoulder into it. His ears popped with the suction and sunlight blinded. He pulled her through and shoved it closed. The manicured grounds were populated with tents and festivalgoers. Few people noticed them.

"How the heck did they get my picture?" she said, putting her shoes back on.

"Cell phone probably, but with two more inside, they're closing ranks and being obvious. You're a target to them now."

Her expression pulled tight, fear flickering in her eyes. She should be scared. These guys meant business in a big way. He walked around the right side. The newer section of the catering kitchen and offices jutted out and blocked the view to the street. Olivia hurried behind him as he rushed to the corner, the smell of exhaust strong as trucks pulled in. He looked at her.

"Stay out of sight. I'll be right back." He walked around the edge, then across the front of the trucks, sidestepping workers unloading trays of food. He met the edge of the stone manor, and scanned the people not in costume.

"What do you see?"

He groaned and glanced over his shoulder. "You need to behave when I tell you. These guys are armed and communicating with each other."

"My car is in the front, on the right near the gate. It's blue, a BMW."

He inched out, looked toward the gates, then lurched back. "Not an option. Two inside, two at your car." They had to hoof it out of here and worst case, get a cab. Hopefully Max would be back with the rental car. He suddenly patted his pockets, then clutched the keys to Noble's heap. "We go out the gate and back down that street." He pointed to where they'd started this. "You ready?"

She met his gaze. "Thank you." His brows knit. "For stopping that guy, for this. I don't know where I'd be now if you hadn't been here."

Not with him now, he thought, and that Olivia was in the middle of this still rocked his world. He grasped her hand. She clutched back. "Let's just get out of target range." He started walking with her beside him and let his eyes do the roaming. "On the left, inside the gate under the tree. Green T-shirt?"

She glanced. "Oh crap. Personal role radios?" He looked at her, a little more than surprised. She just shrugged. "I've been busy."

He walked quickly, the thickening crowd heading to the

estate forcing them apart. She tried to cross the crowd, and he pushed through, grabbing her jacket sleeve. He threw his arm over her shoulder. "Running?"

She laughed without humor, glancing back. "Ha. I'm not stupid or armed and I want to get Noble back as much as you do. Staying alive is, I don't know, a major plus."

He chuckled, the sound rumbling in her ear, and Olivia felt the threat jump a notch with the tightening of her spine. Avoiding Sebastian wasn't an option—not that she could anyway.

He stopped at an old Austin Allego. It was Noble's and a piece of junk. "Does it run?"

"It did an hour ago." He quickly slid behind the wheel.

She strapped in. "This is not how I imagined the day going."

"Your attacker called you, didn't he?" He turned over the engine and pulled into traffic.

She met his gaze. "Yes. My phone's clean. It was a reroute. From Noble's phone."

"We figured they had it. They only left his suitcases and clothes behind." He checked the rearview.

"How do you even know all this?" He flashed a sly glance. "Forget it," she muttered. His military career was getting into places no one else could. She shouldn't be surprised, she thought, and watched her side view. She saw the man in jeans and a green T-shirt rush across the street, another man on his heels. "They're going mobile. White Fiat, blackwalls."

"Oh yeah, this will be fun." Sebastian drove, turning down a street, then maneuvering them back to the main road. "They've got to have more watchers on foot." They knew this car. His speed increased and he took a sharp corner. The Fiat was right behind them and driving so recklessly that pedestrians jumped off the street.

"We've got to get out of the village before they kill someone."

"I'll lose them, but your hotel's not an option anymore."

The Sand House was out in the open, almost standing alone on the Irish coast. He looked at her. "Yes, go."

"I wasn't asking permission, just seeing if you're going to go ape shit on me or something."

"I promise, no ape shitting." He snickered under his breath, then scowled at the mirror and smacked the gas pedal. The car lurched sharply and she slapped the dash, catching a glimpse of the Fiat barely miss hitting them broadside. The other car spun while they fishtailed and he braked, then made a deep right, speeding toward the highway. "Sebastian, he's got a silencer."

"I see that. We need to stay a moving target and out of his range." He sped over eighty. She watched behind. No sign of the Fiat.

Then suddenly it darted out from a side road and headed toward them. "He wants to play chicken?"

He let out a diabolical chuckle as he aimed toward the oncoming car. The other wasn't giving up. "This car will peel him like a grape."

"Oh, let's not do that." She put her hand on the dash, muttering, "OhGodohGodohGod!" as the man lifted a gun and took aim. "Sebastian!" She ducked.

"Hold on!" Sebastian veered left, coming so close they sheared off the side view mirror, then creamed the right rear. The jolt threw her back into the seat, but Sebastian never stopped, struggling to keep the car on the road and moving. The other guy wasn't so lucky and hit the shoulder. The car's rear end slid sideways and flipped on its side. It rolled twice and was still sliding as she sagged into the seat.

She patted his shoulder. "Good driving, oh jeez that was hairy."

He kept speeding. "We're not done."

Another car, this one black and from the direction of the village, jumped on the road behind the wreck. "Man, I wish I had some charges," he murmured as he took a hard curve around a lush hillside, the Allegro swerving. He gunned it and nothing happened. The engine sputtered. He looked down. "Horrible mileage, Donovan? We just ate half a tank."

He glanced in the rearview, then veered off the road and down a slope. The ride felt like an earthquake, rattling her teeth till he drove between rows of narrow trees. The car struggled up the hillside, thirsty for more gas.

He thumb dialed his cell. "Base, open up, we're coming in. Got company." He glanced her way. "Female. Noble's boss. No, I didn't kidnap her. Leave a weapon ready." He closed the phone and looked at her. "All I want is to find Noble and bring him home. It ends there. So if you've got some classified project you need to keep quiet, fine, give me an oath to sign if that makes you happy. But I will learn it all."

"Are you saying you know people?"

His smile was infectious. "You could say that."

"Believe me, the only thing holding me back is my boss. I'd rather not get fired for breaking protocol." Not after she'd worked so hard to get to this point. "But I'm not alone." His brows shot up. "My assistant, Cruz DeGama. He's at the hotel, waiting for me and probably going nuts because I haven't called. If they followed me from there, they'll find him and trust me, he's not capable of defending himself by any means."

"I'll get him safe." He told her to call him, prepare for Max and Riley, and make him ask for IDs.

He was on the phone to his friends while she spoke to Cruz. "Bring your equipment, everything," she told him, ducking as the house came into view. It fit the landscape, the house reminiscent of a castle. It even had a tower, though the three-car garage threw off the aesthetics. The engine suddenly died and momentum slid the car into the garage.

"I don't like this. Neither will Ross. Just who is this guy, Olivia?"

She looked at him. Someone I used to love, she thought. "All you need to know is that I trust him." Sebastian met her gaze, looking like he was going to say something, then left the car. The garage door leveled down as he scraped a gun off a worktable. He peered out the carriage window.

"Have Ross run a deep search and alert the director. I need you here with me." She closed her phone and climbed out, frowning at the pair of motorcycles in the next section, and farther down, a massive SUV you didn't normally see in Europe. He took a duffel out of the backseat, then opened the trunk, stuffing something in before he went to the door leading to the house to reset the alarm system. They went inside.

While the outside looked medieval, the interior said it was a new house. An expensive one, she thought as she walked through a designer kitchen that blended with a massive family room. The rich, jewel tones were gorgeous, and it made her ache for home and weeks of just screwing off. The place was fully furnished, and on the left were tall windows offering a clear view down the twisted hillside to the road. Whatever he does for a living, it sure paid well, she thought. The house sat on a hilltop surrounded by miles of rolling green peppered with clusters of trees. The shoreline was a mile away, but the view was spectacular. The sun was starting to set over the bay.

Her gaze strolled over the computers and flat screens, more electronic equipment on tables drawn together, and a double row of duffel bags on the floor near a hall. Some equipment was running, but still in their big black cases.

"You really need to see this satellite image," a dark-haired woman said, coming toward them.

"Give me a few minutes." Sebastian ushered her into a small office and shut the door. He dropped the duffel on a chair and leaned back against the door. "Talk."

She stared back, mutinous, pulling off the satchel and letting it drop to the floor.

"Fine, then you listen. The American Research Institute is an NSA front, a think tank. There's nothing on you after your doctorate, no job record, not even a bank account. That says government work." She blinked, startled, and he scoffed. "I learned that much in ten minutes, darlin'. The man who attacked you was Spetsnaz trained, Russian black ops."

Olivia eyes widened, but she didn't doubt him. His Marine career was validation enough.

"Damn it Livi, talk to me. Noble understood the danger. He knew he was hunted."

"How can you be so certain?"

Sebastian unzipped the duffel and dug. "Because he mailed this just before he disappeared." He upended a package on the desk.

Olivia approached slowly, and a wash of anguish swept over her as she recognized the leather book. "Oh my God." Her eyes burned. There lay the reason for his kidnapping, for the brutal slaying of two innocent men.

The monk's diary.

She didn't touch it and sat in the chair beside it. Tentatively, she reached, laying her palm on it, then drawing the book to her lap. "Oh Sebastian, I'm so sorry. I sent him to Surrey for the *Aramina*'s log." She choked, and something clutched inside her. "If it wasn't for me, he'd be here with us." She sniffled and searched her pockets for a tissue. "I should have gone myself." One appeared before her face.

"Then you'd likely be dead." She looked up. "These people know everything you do and are willing to kill. That"— he pointed to the diary—"is not worth lives."

"None of this is. I want him back safely, too, and I'll help any way I can, I swear it. But I'm not the enemy."

He sighed hard, then cupped the back of her head and pressed a kiss to her forehead. "I know you're not, *cherie*. Forgive me."

She folded a little more, and smoothed her fingers over her name written on the torn seam. Then she went still. "He sent this the day of the auction."

"I don't know how you'd ever know of it because he sent it to himself. I'm the only one on his express account."

"Maybe he knew you'd come looking for him."

"I need to know what I'm up against, Olivia."

She caught the edge in his voice and sighed. "Yes, we're NSA, but it's not what you think. Let me talk to my superior first." He started to protest, and she cut him off. "Come on, you know the drill better than I do. I need to inform them about the last hours *before* I break protocol for you."

His lips tugged in a half smile. She'd known she would the minute she recognized him, and she accepted she was a little out of her league right now. And scared, if she'd admit it. She clutched the book, then brought it to her nose and inhaled.

"Smells like his aftershave." She palmed the buttery calf-skin, then unwound the grosgrain ribbon securing the leather jacket Noble said he'd carried since college. "Noble loved old things. I think he was just born in the wrong century."

"He'd have disagreed." She looked up. "He loved technology, was very adept at it considering he grew up with a rotary phone. He liked his comforts, especially air-conditioning, and he said he wouldn't want to miss out on the simple pleasures of a hot shower after a long day."

"Me, either, and lugging buckets would have put *such* a damper on that." The pages crackled as she opened the journal. The copy of the original was on the left, Noble's handwriting on the right. She flipped to the last page. "He finished it." She looked up. "It's all translated."

"Other than its historical value, why is the diary so important?"

"We think . . . it's the only documented account of a legend." She turned a page and found an envelope. She flipped it over. It was addressed to her. "It's from Noble."

She tore it open, a little cry escaping and she covered her mouth.

Olivia,
  I am closely watched and I fear for my security detail. If we do not meet soon, follow the traders. If the worst comes, contact Sebastian.
        Noble

She looked up, blinking back the sting of tears, then handed him the paper. As he read, a pained look passed over his face. He met her gaze, handing it back.

"Call whoever you need, now. Noble's clock is ticking." He left the room, taking the book.

Olivia stared at the empty doorway, then followed. "Now who's not trusting who, Fontenòt?"

Before he could answer, a dark-haired woman wearing a headset strode down the hall. Middle Eastern blood, she decided, and smiled when she gave Sebastian a smack on the arm, and said, "Chill out. We have it under control." She looked at Olivia. "Hi, Doctor Corrigan, I'm Safia Donovan. Welcome to Dragon One."

She looked at Sebastian. He stared at her in the strangest way just now and she couldn't decipher it. "And that is what, exactly?"

"Retrieval experts for hire, bodyguards, security." She shrugged muscled shoulders. "Whatever."

"Mercenaries?" She swallowed, annoyed with the screechy pitch of her own voice.

"It sounds so cheesy like that, but accurate."

She cocked her hip, her hand planted there, and looked at Sebastian. "Same game, different club, huh?"

A smile threatened, but his eyes studied her. He had every right to be skeptical, considering their marriage split was over his covert operations and her need to know all about it.

"Don't worry about your assistant, or your things," Safia said. "I know it's hard to trust strangers, but we're very good at what we do."

"Apparently." Her gaze skated over the gear, then to Sebastian. He hadn't moved, clutching the diary. He looked so deadly and sexy and she was ready to give up anything if he'd just come over here and kiss her.

Safia glanced between them. "Want to freshen up? Max and Riley shouldn't be long."

She looked down at her slacks and blouse, just noticing the blood and dirt. Her latte decorated her shoes. Damn.

"That would be great." It was hard to believe she was sneaking into China about this time the day before yesterday. Safia led her down a hall, and she glanced back long enough to catch Sebastian watching her retreat. He wiggled his brows, smiling, and she suddenly didn't feel as bad as she knew she looked and gave him a show, working it. His dark chuckle followed her.

Safia led her into a bedroom. "The bath is there." She pointed behind herself. "I'll just be a sec."

Olivia sat on the edge of the bed, then flopped back, staring at the ceiling, and tried piecing together the last few hours. *Face it, girl.* Dragon One was right behind her and she was alive because of it.

"Doctor Corrigan?"

"Call me Olivia, please." She sat up. Safia handed over a stack of towels. "Thank you." She clutched them, feeling a little rudderless. "What's your part in all this?"

"I'm the Operations Commander." Safia grinned at her surprise. "Yes, I get to boss them around. I'm a bit of a control freak, so it works."

"I can't imagine Sebastian letting anyone tell him what to do."

"I was CIA. I'm skilled at getting my way." She winked. "You knew Sebastian before today?"

"Oh yes. In a wildly impulsive moment, I married him."

Safia gasped. "Sebastian? Really." Her smile turned mischievous. "That little stinker never mentioned it."

Neither did she. Their breakup was by far the most painful time of her life. "It was such a long time ago. Almost Jurassic."

Sebastian's chuckle, deep and rich, gave her goose bumps and she looked up. Safia slipped out of the room, giving him a dig in the side as she went.

"I didn't have a chance to say . . ." His voice dropped an octave, "You look really great, Livi." He was the only person to ever call her that, and while she noticed his Southern accent had faded, the elegant hint of it was still there.

"Thank you." The compliment did wonders for her ego. "You look good, happy. Still in one piece, I'm glad to see." He looked surprised. "Noble didn't tell you?"

"He wouldn't even work with me unless I agreed to never ask about you. He said if I couldn't find out how you were before then, I didn't deserve to know."

"Whoa, that's harsh, especially for him."

"He wouldn't even hint." She shrugged. "He's right though. I couldn't bring myself to search. I was terrified I'd learn you were killed in action."

"It wouldn't have changed things. Your brothers made it clear that you were off limits, permanently."

Her eyes went wide. "They didn't!"

"Oh yeah." He said it with a smile, then sobered. "I backed off. Their threats were meaningless. I just didn't want them to talk trash about us and ruin your memory of the time we did have." He shrugged broad shoulders. "It's in the past. I'm not the same and you're certainly not the wild rebel who ran off to Vegas with a Marine on leave."

She smiled. "Oh, some of her is still here."

His dark eyes pinned her, left her breathless. Then suddenly, he crossed the room and scooped her off the bed, holding her tightly. She stared into his dark eyes, felt the mesh of his body to hers, and the instant electricity that came with it. Then his mouth covered hers. Oh. My. God. It was like coming home. Intense and kinetic, a charge lacing around her like a cocoon, and she drank him in, molding her mouth over his, and urging him to paw her like she wanted. Needed. Then he did, and her body reacted with swift hot memory, pushing into him. She moaned, feeling devoured, and when he lifted her off the floor for a better fit, she fought the need to wrap her legs around his hips. Tumbling to the bed would be so much easier that way. He savaged her mouth for another second, then he drew back, breathing just as hard as she was. He set her down with a thump.

"What was that for?"

He smiled, palming low on her spine. "Just checking."

He let her go, and she stumbled back a step as he walked out the door. She chucked the pillow at his bandaged head. His laugh echoed in the hall. She smiled to herself and dropped to the bed, then flopped back. Well damn, Sebastian. She licked her lips. They were a little numb, and somewhere in her mind, a little voice whispered it wasn't bad to know some things hadn't changed . . . then dared her to name the last man to kiss her like *that*. She failed miserably.

You are in such *trouble*. But then, she already knew that. When it came to Sebastian, resistance was futile.

With a long-suffering sigh, she reached for her phone.

FSB headquarters
Lubyanka Square, Moscow

Leonid Sidorov strode down the corridor, his thick heels clicking time with his urgency. He did not want to make this visit. Conferring with the directorate of counterintelligence was rarely pleasant. The tall wood door loomed ahead, and reaching it, he did not knock, pushing into the director's offices. The secretary hopped to his feet, then recognized him and immediately sat. He ignored the people waiting to see the director.

Out of respect, he rapped once, then entered the office. The director glanced up, scowling, then signed a paper before handing it off to the man nearest him. Assistants and officers surrounded him, hovering like handmaidens.

"We are done," the director said. He waved at the door, but it wasn't necessary. The officers were in a hurry to leave. It was wise not to know all the secrets. His superior was a ruthless man, devoted to the party, to Putin, as he was, though Leonid felt the ruling elite had taken their power too far. He kept his thoughts to himself. Many of the opposition had died. This could begin a bloodbath, he thought, looking down at the red leather case, waiting until the last man was gone. Leonid didn't particularly care for the director. In fact, the man repulsed him, not for his slovenly manners—atrocious—but that he thought there was no consequence to death warrants issued for anyone who stood in Putin's way. The PM might have another office, but his presence was still here.

"It is urgent."

Golubev waved him closer and Leonid dropped the leather envelope on his desk.

The director gave it a passing glance. "Tell me why."

"Andre Molenko is dead. His neck was broken." The director showed no emotion beyond the lift of a brow, and sat back to hear more. "His personal safe was opened."

Now the director leaned forward, bracing his arms on the desk. "Do we even know what he had? What was taken?"

"Nyet, we do not, but he was, as you know, privileged to several cases of special importance."

The highest level of classification made the director pale. He opened the leather case. "He had American contacts. You are certain they did not silence him?"

"Nyet, I am not certain. But he was not in active reserve." Neither was Molenko fit for duty, Leonid thought, having seen the photos. The former KGB operative was found wearing only a robe, spread open to show more than his increased waistline. "His guard was killed as well. There are traces of activity."

The director eyed him. "A woman, perhaps?"

Leonid didn't know. "There were no prints, nor even a drinking glass."

"A professional, then."

He knew that, of course, and despised that this man treated him with such condescension. "They left everything as it was. Only his safe and the files were disturbed. Those"—Leonid nodded to the untouched stack on the desk—"were in his personal possession." It was a violation. State secrets, copies no less, were never to leave the headquarters. He did not need to know how Molenko acquired them. He was high ranking within the party. Smuggling them out would have been simple. But from the lifestyle Leonid had examined in the last twenty-four hours, he was living well only by the benefit of blackmail. A cloak of a different color, he thought. More secrets to hide.

"You were aware of these files?"

The director shook his head as he stood slowly, a delicate teacup dwarfed by his palm. He brought it to the window and he stared onto an empty street. Cars were routed away from the square, never close enough to inflict damage.

"You must search then. Begin with his American contacts."

He already had. "Only he knew their identities, comrade."

The director scoffed, returning to his desk and drawing the files close. He opened one and read the first page, then went onto another. He stopped at the fifth and looked up. "You have read these?"

"I have."

The director's face flamed with anger. He was mentioned several times.

"I should not be kept out of these matters," Leonid said, condemnation in his tone as he flicked his hand at the folders. The director started to chide him, but he would have none of it. "You did not notice they were still in chronological order? They were found in this same manner and brought to me." No one would dare touch anything without an FSB officer near. The police did not even enter the apartment after the cleaning woman had found him. "Molenko's killer was after one file, at least three years old."

The director looked up sharply, his eyes narrowing. I have struck the nerve, he thought.

The director closed the file. "Do not delve, Leonid."

This was an outrage, he thought, and stared at his superior, waiting for him to rescind. It did not come. "As you wish."

Yet he could not ignore this. Not after reading the files that contained such detrimental secrets. He started to turn and the director put out his hand, stopping him. Leonid frowned when he opened his desk drawer and pressed a button, shutting off the recording. Keeping secrets from the gatekeepers, he thought as the director took a breath, stretching his white shirt tight across his torso. A moment later, he motioned him to the window near the heavy velvet drapes in Kremlin red.

"You must find this person."

"Person or file?"

"It does not matter, both must be destroyed and all suppressed. All of it. It is of special importance, Leonid. The tragedy in the north seas."

Leonid stepped back, his eyes flaring. Near Brønlundfjord. Three years ago. A special mission so covert even he was not privy to details. "It was not as we were told."

The director scoffed rudely. "Is anything?"

SEVEN

An hour later, Sebastian was still feeling the effects of Olivia in his arms. Christ, that was a stupid move. She had the *it* factor, the ability to turn him on like a switch. Slumped in the couch, he knew he had to get some perspective before he grilled her. The question was, could he keep his hands off her?

Someone nudged him. "Snap out of it." Safia rolled her chair closer. "I don't think the assistant knows, by the way."

He glanced at the young Latino man talking with Max and hooking up the rest of the equipment. They didn't have time for much when they'd arrived, but once again Max found outstanding digs for a secure location. Olivia was in one of the bedrooms, talking through the computer to God knows who. Sebastian just wanted his suspicions confirmed.

Safia eyed him, looking infuriatingly amused. "There's something to be said about second chances."

Sebastian scoffed. "I'm not looking for one."

She'd left *him*. Though, he really didn't blame her. He wasn't around much and he'd brainwashed himself into thinking he could keep her waiting till he was ready to come home. After a while, he was just a paycheck, she'd said before disappearing from his life. The next time he heard from her it was divorce papers. But seeing her again didn't bring back the pain and heartache, but the good. The fun they'd had and memories of her rushing to greet him as he stepped off a C-130. It's just how he wanted it, and he mentally ushered the past where it belonged because on the other side of the house was the only woman he'd ever loved. Ever. A dangerous fact he wouldn't reveal, or she'd have him under her thumb so tight he'd squeak.

It didn't matter that he'd loved her over a dozen years ago and was already making the Marine Corps his career then. He'd enlisted at seventeen and when they'd met, he was twenty-three and so freaking gung-ho he scared himself. He'd been in Serbia and Panama by then, and couldn't talk about the rest. She didn't like any of it. The Corps, his deployments, the secrets, nada. But he'd admitted a long time ago that she really didn't know what she was getting into when she'd eloped with him. The blame for that rested on him.

The irony that she was hiding her job from him wasn't lost on him either.

He pushed off the sofa and crossed to the kitchen, pulling out pans and mentally fusing the past with today. Hands down, she was still the most beautiful woman he'd ever met. She didn't think so, he knew, always a little tomboyish. It wasn't just the dark red hair and Irish green eyes that set her apart, but her deep passion for life and a nearly uncontrollable curiosity.

He opened the fridge, fully stocked as of an hour ago. At least he remembered her favorite foods, he thought, and started creating. Halfway through chopping, Max said the police were directing traffic around the accident. He could care less about the men trying to kill them, but no civilian casualties was always good. He shifted pans and sprinkled in a last kick of spice, listening to Max read aloud a part of the Maguire legend of a child stolen from the shores of Ireland by Vikings and made a slave. Some years later, she returned with her Viking stepfather and Mongol soldiers. Elf and the giant, he thought. The rest went as MacAwley has said, yet Dr. MacNamara had given him several accountings. One version told of wild animal attacks, rival clans, and the princess's skill at reuniting the people. Another had the killer dogs and a myth about a glass globe that changed the appearance of things. Like a witch's glamour, he thought, tossing a pat of butter in a pan and shaking the skillet. He wondered what version was in the diary and why Noble hadn't backed it up.

Thirty minutes later, he heard, "Oh my God, that smells heavenly," then saw Olivia enter from the hall. She'd changed into a jeans and a white T-shirt, and her hair was wet. Then he frowned at the laptop under her arm. When her gaze fell on him, she reared back a fraction, then crossed into the kitchen and slid onto the stool on the other side of a granite counter. God, she looked terrific.

"Hungry?"

"When am I not? I can't believe what I'm seeing. You cook?" She lowered her voice, leaned over the counter. "I recall you doing some cooking before, but it was, ya know . . . guy food."

He chuckled, and turned to the cabinet for plates, then laid out silverware.

"Sebastian is a *god* in a kitchen," Safia said from her spot at the screens. "He owns a restaurant in New Orleans, the Craw Daddy." From across the room, she winked at him.

He just smiled. "You're telling all my secrets, woman."

"I thought Dragon One was what you did for a living," Olivia said.

"It's not steady, and I can do it only so long." He served up the honey-glazed chicken, then from another pan smothered it in caramelized onions.

She hovered over it and inhaled deeply. "They say you smell your favorite food before you die. This is mine."

Sebastian grinned, adding dishes of wild rice with slivered almonds, baby green beans, and a rich curry cream sauce. She didn't waste time and started eating. Max and Cruz crossed to them, and Sebastian plated more, then stepped back, sipping a cup of fresh coffee. Olivia chewed, and he waited till she swallowed before he said, "What's going on in Greenland?"

Cruz froze midbite, but Olivia lowered her fork, tipped her head. "Now I see why the director wants to speak to you guys." She inched up to check the clock on the stove. "Ten minutes." She pushed the laptop to Cruz. "Set it up, please." Cruz looked forlornly at his plate, then took the laptop and went to rig it through the big screen.

"Director of what, Olivia?" She met his gaze, and he realized she seemed more relaxed than before. But Cruz went still, staring holes in her back. Safia stopped doing whatever and crossed to them.

"The Second Sight Unit." She blew out a breath, some tension leaving her face. "Sorry. That's the first time I've said that aloud outside my team." She met his gaze. "And yes, you were right, we're a unit of NSA. At the *far* end of the spectrum. Like the crazy uncle no one acknowledges." Her lips quirked. "Acronym, SSU. We're not discussed in senate committees, no oversight. We're scientific research into the unusual, the bizarre. If it's weird, unsolved, a phenomenon, a legend, we're all over it."

Sebastian leaned back against the counter. He'd never heard of it and it explained why Noble was so secretive. He'd sworn his duty to the SSU.

Olivia glanced around at the team. "It's a bit to digest, I know. Take your time."

Even stranger was that she was a part of it. Not a career choice he imagined archaeology taking her to, yet he was not all that surprised she'd gone this route. She liked the challenge. Probably pissed off her anti-establishment brothers, too. "How the hell does something like that get started? How long has it been in operation?" Sebastian thought he knew it all. Hell. This put a whole new spin on things.

"Only about ten years at the capacity we are now, but it started, actually, in 1908 when a mysterious explosion occurred in Siberia."

"I thought the Tunguska explosion was a meteor impact."

She practically beamed. "Yes!" she said, doing an arm pump. "Thank you, Sebastian." She twisted to look at Cruz. "See, it's not as uncommon as you believed."

"I said one in one million, Olivia. There he is." Cruz waved at him. "Now give it up."

Sebastian chuckled, took a sip of coffee before setting it aside. "Are you saying the Tunguska crater wasn't a meteor?"

"No. It was. We learned about it and actually had the opportunity to investigate and take samples."

"Without a passport, I 'spect."

Her shoulders went back. "We research for the good of the whole, not just the United States."

"And if you don't like what you find?" He topped off her coffee.

"It's not a matter of like or dislike. It's the effect and any danger it poses. I know, somewhere someone is passing judgment, yet most searches have disproved a hoax, or are explained with science. But some are not." She wiggled in her chair. "Those are the fun ones."

"Was translating the monk's diary Noble's only part?"

"Ha, not by a long shot. He was documenting the Irish legend of the Maguire's princess. The diary was written by a monk who lived at Kilbarron in the eleven hundreds when the legend was first formed."

"How'd you get the diary," Riley asked. "Even know about it?"

"Liz McNamara told me about it." Her shoulders moved restlessly. "It's a copy, of course. The original is in the National Archives. I didn't have anything to do with getting it, a government-to-government thing with the express condition it was kept *secret*." She sent him a sassy look that made him smile. "Noble was researching the legend for his own pleasure and we ran into each other while I was doing it for SSU. Even without the diary, he'd gathered more information than I had." She speared a bite of chicken and onions. "He's got a remarkable way of finding the weird stuff."

DAMAGE CONTROL / 135

That was Noble, Sebastian thought. "I don't get why it isn't public knowledge."

"See, that's the rub." She gestured with her fork. "It's what the monk wrote that kept it under wraps. It's his own observations of everything from the church's views to his daily life, a very candid conversation with his God. Some parts are a little whacked for the church to let it loose, I suppose, but that's where it gets interesting. The friar writes of witnessing supernatural events and attributes most of it to the princess, a very pagan woman, by his own observation. This coming from a devout man of the cloth?" She shook her head, taking a last bite, then nudged the plate back. She picked up her coffee. "It was never meant to be read, and I think the guy was just having some fun talking to God. SSU set out to prove it was a true account."

"Of an eight-hundred-year-old legend?" Max said. "That's got to be all uphill."

"Not as much as you'd think," she said cryptically, then Cruz called out to her.

"We're up and they're buzzing us."

Without thinking too hard, he reached behind himself for the diary, handing it to her. She blinked owlishly, then held it to her chest for a second, smoothing her fingers over the edge, and met his gaze.

"Thank you."

"Don't go far. It's a book I want to read." Her lips curved in a beautiful smile, making him feel almost rewarded, and Sebastian reminded himself that he was an old man. She shouldn't affect him like this still. It wasn't working. He inclined his head, and they walked into the living area as the screens blinked to life. The face on the other end of the satellite transmission appeared. Sebastian let out a short laugh and crossed to the chair, taking a seat. "Hello, General. I see you haven't really retired after all." Though he wore a polo shirt instead of his uniform, he'd bet he'd earned another star since Venezuela.

"Never said I was. Rumor. And neither have you, so shut your yap."

Off to his left, Olivia said, "Is there anything you guys don't know already?"

Sebastian chuckled, shot her a wink. "SSU? Noble Sheppard was working for you."

"For Doctor Corrigan. I'm just the figurehead."

"More like the cracking whip, I'm thinking. The second blood trail in England. One of yours?" McGill arched a gray brow, then nodded. Olivia folded a little. "A shame. Did anyone have a clue someone else was in your business?"

"No, and we still don't know how. A possible leak, but it's hard to determine. SSU is isolated and small, mostly scientists and historians."

And harder to keep leaks plugged, he thought. A little persuasion went a long way with the untrained, and he frowned to himself, praying Noble wasn't suffering. "They've covered their tracks well so far. We know their target, and that diary is the only thing keeping Noble alive right now. They can't know we have it." Noble had to stay valuable to them.

"Agreed," McGill said and Sebastian glanced at Olivia. She clutched the diary with a white-knuckled grip. "We're tracking Noble's phone. It's not on. But since they have it, any calls are rerouted through ghost towers."

Then no trail on this end, he thought. One advantage, at least. "If these people are as smart as they're behaving, they won't keep Noble anywhere close. I think they're going to run. I want in, sir."

McGill leaned forward, folding his hands on the desk. Sebastian recognized the offices in his house. He'd cracked open a few beers a couple times in there. "I figured that much."

"Though you might have a problem with DOD." It frosted him to even say that. They'd played by the rules and their own tried to screw them.

McGill scoffed. "Not a concern." Sebastian scowled. "We're . . . Venezuela." The general fought a smile and Sebastian thought, holy shit, that's deep. "Doctor Corrigan can answer any questions. But the attempt on her life is desperation."

"They're beyond that, sir. I bet there's ten men here all searching for that diary and now, Doctor Corrigan. Max and Riley followed them to the water—"

McGill put up a hand. "They're in international waters. Interpol already has aerial surveillance on the boat."

Spying from the skies wasn't working for him. "Noble could be on that boat, sir. We have no problem going illegal and cleaning a few clocks to find out."

"Christ. Do not, Fontenòt." Sebastian conceded with a nod. "We don't have provocation that we can give the garda. Revealing the monk's diary is for Ireland to decide. Without evidence to pursue, it's up to us."

"I hear you, Mac, but understand from the get-go, Noble Sheppard's safe return is my *only* objective. And sir, we're not working for you." McGill's lips pulled into a thin line. "We're retained by his daughter, Moira." A technicality. Even without Moira, he'd be right here. McGill stared for a long moment and Sebastian could almost see the gears working as he weighed his options. Bring them on or lock them up, because he wasn't sitting idle if there was even a slim chance Noble was on that boat.

"Roger that," McGill said. "Now you're mine, Fontenòt. Be discreet and try not to use deadly force." He tapped a key and the screen went black.

Sebastian swung the chair around to look at his buddies. "Let's get wet."

Max let out a sinister laugh. "We're just breaking all the rules this week. I'll get the gear. And just so you know, that includes lots of weapons." He grabbed the truck keys, Riley following.

Olivia was unusually quiet, just staring at him. He knew she didn't know what to make of this, but that McGill wasn't concerned about the DOD said the SSU was *way* out of the normal intelligence channels. Fine with him. He was tired of getting crapped on by people like Beckham. He turned to Safia. "Want to show me those satellite photos now?"

Safia spun in the chair and tapped keys. "I was searching Greenland and went back a couple months, and didn't see more than increased activity. It wasn't until I went farther north that I found this." He was expecting Chechnya photos when the screen blinked with an aerial photo that was mostly white. "This"—she swept her finger over the middle right— "wasn't here a year ago."

He scowled, leaning in. "You were expecting something besides snow on the seventy-fifth parallel?"

She intensified the focus. "I know, it's like a piece of rice on snow except for this." She traced shadows and darker shapes. Sebastian could make out the silhouette of buildings. "There's definitely something happening at the top of the world."

"It's my project." They turned to stare at Olivia, but she spoke directly to him. "That's what this is all about, Sebastian. Ice Harvest." She walked near.

Sebastian frowned harder, glancing at the screen and thinking, she's an archaeologist. She excavated. "You're digging in Greenland, on the Arctic Circle?"

"A kick, ain't it?" Her smile hit him like a punch. "And yes, for several months now. The diary is vital because the monk tells us where the legend begins. And that"—she pointed to the screen—"is where it ends."

Deep Six
Satellite Intelligence

Mitch was comforted by Deep Six. Two days had turned his face from black and blue to a hideous shade of greenish yellow. He looked like a troll, wanted the reminders gone, and working several floors belowground had two advantages. No mirrors and silence. Well. Beyond the analysts tapping on keyboards.

In his favorite chair, he tipped back, lifted his feet to the corner, and closed his eyes. His fingers rolled the black ball, the sound through his headphones like sliding the dial of an FM radio. He reviewed calls made at the time of his capture. A couple yards downwind, David Lorimer still studied the photos from Chechnya. Mitch had looked at them so long he was going blind.

David swung in his chair, inclined his head. Mitch stood, grabbed his coffee, and limped down the amphitheater landing. "Tell me it's not just wasted megabytes."

"Then I'd be lying, sorry. Most of them will take time to redigitize, sir. Except this one." He brought up a photo. "That line you photographed is visible by satellite." David tapped keys, then pointed to the screen. "Fortunately for you, we've been watching since Russia invaded Georgia in 08. No, we weren't looking for this. Just troop movement."

David narrowed the field of vision, showing rooftops and roads. Then it went deeper, images focusing on the prison where he spent his last days till Dragon One liberated him.

"There's nothing there," Mitch said. "No movement, nada."

"Sir. Look closer. Here."

David focused the overhead view of Chechnya. On either side of the river near the incline of the mountains were two straight gray lines broken up by shrubs. Man made. A launch canal.

"Send that to Gerardo. Mark and highlight the area. Print a copy, too."

David nodded, turning back to the screen. "If you tell me what you're looking for sir, it would help."

"No, it wouldn't. That area's destroyed so we're just confirming."

David scoffed, sliding him a dry look. "Gerardo made that a priority, sir."

Mitch arched a brow. Gerardo was pissed enough to give David the authority to dig deep and anywhere he wanted. If there was a chance of salvaging anything from this embarrassment, he was all for it.

"This is Price's mess, David." His eyes flared and he looked suddenly very angry. It was because of David that the former director was found out and the young man managed to get to McGill in time to stop a hit on an agent. "We need to know what those lines mean, because it could be the launch of a Russian weapon she failed to tell us they had."

David's features tightened and he turned back to his bank of computers. The photos popped up, filling the screen. "This is four years ago, sir."

Mitch scowled.

"I figured the lines were cement or stone." He shrugged. "They had to construct it and couldn't do that easily. About four or five years earlier, there's a hell of a lot of movement, mostly farmers. The daylight shots show nothing. It's practically deserted. We can see a hell of a lot during the night, but nothing is clear enough to show us exactly what. They were clever with hiding it. But one twilight image *three* years ago shows this." He increased the focus on the base of the mountain on the Chechnya side, about a hundred yards from where he was captured.

"Enlarge there." He pointed. David obeyed. It was winter, the snow deep, and while the white stuff didn't contrast with the straight lines he thought was a retaining wall, the river did. Mitch saw a distinct rounded shape through the shroud of trees and bushes. Too broad to be a missile, he thought, and got closer. Jesus. The nose of a sub. He was wrong. They did build it.

"I've got more." David scooted his chair to the left and at another console, he typed. A moment later, he leaned back in his chair. "This is before Russia invaded Georgia. Notice there's no armament, no troops or trucks. They're all a couple hundred miles west, South Osseita. Everyone's attention was on the force coming in the east, not farther south, along the mountains. Your accommodations were—"

Mitch's eyes narrowed.

"Reviewing satellite before and after showed me what happened," David said. "Eight against one, you put up a good fight."

"I should have plied them with liquor and rubles, and let them do the talking." But he'd pushed and blew it. He started to return to his desk, then looked at the screen, moving in. "Can you get imagery just after Dragon One assaulted?"

David nodded, fingers flying over the keys. He searched though feeds by coordinates and date. The screens rolled with data, one, then two highlighted and blinked. David pulled up the first. "There's Dragon One crossing to the prison." The men were no more than dots on the screen. David fast-forwarded the feed. "Now coming back out with you, but look north." With a tap of his finger and dragging, he moved the focus south. "Two large trucks." David used a stylus to circle it. "There are the men unloading, then advancing to the prison, then just before the explosions." He froze the picture. "These two stand back from it all and watch." He brought up the images, then narrowed it.

Aerial shots. Mitch could see the top of his head. "He's making a call." His arm was bent, hand near his ear. "Oohrah. Back it up a little." David did. "He's the only one within fifty yards on a phone."

"If it's satellite, I bet I can get the call."

David turned to another console, rising slowly to his feet, and nimbly typed like a rock star playing a keyboard. "Transferring to your console, sir."

Mitch retuned to his desk, sliding on the headphones.

"It's Russian," David said.

Mitch waved, translating in his head.

They have taken him, commander, and the krasnaya prisoner.

That would be me, he thought.

A curse and then, *We have made our point. Moscow will respond with force. Now there must be no trail to follow. Leave the area. Now. Or you die with them.*

The man responded with only "Da," and the call cut off immediately. While the voices weren't clear, the commander was definitely a woman and remarking on the MiG about to drop bombs.

"Work your magic. Get me that number," Mitch said, tossing down the headphones. "Run it against the database and listening posts." If he could lock on it, then they might be able to trace the call if the phone was used again. The search would take days. There were a thousand surveillance posts, and they were looking for key words that made it a little easier for the computers to search. It would help if he had a name.

David glanced back, looking doubtful. "The frequency matches a million disposable phones."

"Just need one, Davey-boy." At least he could give Gerardo something to chew on besides his ass. He closed his console and headed for the steel elevators. "And now you have a time frame. Check North Atlantic, Eastern Europe first. Listen for Russian in Chechen dialects."

As the elevator doors swept closed, Mitch realized that Anna Mills had been assigned to a Eastern Europe listening post. He looked down at the printout of the photograph, enlarged and detailed. "Oh shit." Right around the time the sub would have been launched.

Off the coast of Ireland

Thirty-five feet beneath the water covered their approach. Night diving wasn't the norm in Ireland, too damn cold, and Sebastian felt every inch of the icy water flowing through his neoprene suit as the diver propulsion device dragged him along. Max had amped them up, and their increased speed brought them to the Scarab in under an hour. His buddies kept in tight formation with him, visibility a decent fifty feet if it were daylight. In the dark, twenty feet, tops. His mask gave him an advantage with night vision as Riley cut away from them to spot any approach. He and Max circled the thirty-foot Scarab to the stern. From underwater, the hull of the boat looked like a dull brown whale, and he tagged the Sea Scooter with a chemlight and secured it to the anchor line. Max's equipment joined it, Riley staying back and armed with a harpoon. Making a racket with guns wasn't going to keep them under the wire.

Sebastian inflated his buoyancy converter and rose slowly to the surface. He shallowed his breathing, then climbed onto the vessel. He stepped out of his fins.

This was a long shot, but he had to be sure.

He drew his Glock, advancing to the pilothouse. The keys were in the ignition, swinging with the chop. Not good, he thought, and felt the boat list as Max boarded. The deck was wet and he moved between the pair of captain's chairs and below to the Scarab's version of a stateroom, a miniaturized kitchen, a lavatory, and bunks. He didn't have to go far to find evidence. Two bodies were sprawled across the larger bed, stacked like flour sacks. Missing fingertips looked as if dipped in acid, and inspecting closer, he realized molars were gone as well. The head injuries were a nasty mess. Killed playing chicken, he thought when he recognized the face of one corpse. It was bloated, the clothing wet, but the bulging tattoo on the neck gave him chills. They did this to their own.

"Bad guys are sweepers. There's got to be a reason for that shit," Max said, then opened a drawer, a cabinet. Then he froze, scowling. "Smell that?"

Sebastian sniffed. Over the scent of the sea, he caught the intense odor of ammonia. "They just left." Max backed out, and topside, Sebastian fitted his mask, the night vision lens showing the chop of sea.

Then Riley appeared, hanging on the massive outboard. "Something out there, I can hear it."

It was an anxious moment before he spotted the white churn in the water. "Fifty yards out. I want prisoners." He shoved on his fins.

"Oh shit, more company."

Sebastian twisted, saw the lights of a vessel in the distance. Police? He tapped Max and went over the side. Ahead, jumpy light speared the black water. He unhooked the Sea Scooter and hit it, finning hard, lights off. Black on black shapes moved in the water, and he spotted two separate beams of light. Flotsam floated in the current as he finned toward them, drawing his knife. They were heading out to sea, and he counted three men, the scooter pulling them along a helluva lot faster than theirs. Max shot up alongside, lights off.

Sebastian was less than five feet from the last man when he twisted, immediately reaching for his regulator. He blocked, and the diver slashed up with a knife. Sebastian cut his air hose line. The man struggled to reach the surface as Sebastian switched on his light and went for the others. The second aimed a gun and fired. The bullets left a current, missing, and he slammed the scooter into his side, then gripped his face mask, tearing it off with the regulator. The gun sank.

He filled the other's buoyancy converter, driving him up to the surface.

The man choked and coughed, spitting water. Sebastian dunked him again, disarming him, then let him surface. He gripped the BC, the knife to his throat. He spit out his reg. "Give me Noble and I won't kill you."

"Kill me and you never see him."

Russian. The guy worked his neck against the blade, as if he wanted him to cut his throat. He adjusted the blade so it wouldn't.

"I got plans for you." It involved pounding the stupid out of him for Noble's location. But the guy's underwater escape said there was another ship farther out, waiting for him. He heard the chirp of Riley's signal and knew police sailed closer. Then he heard a motor, and saw the swell of a small boat sidewinding toward him. He almost didn't see the man aiming an AK-47. Machine gun fire ripped across the surface toward him and he ducked under, taking his target with him. More gunfire followed him as the guy pounded his arm, tried for

his regulator, then kicked him in the stomach. He jerked
back, but managed to keep his grip, looping his hose with the
knife. The man went still. Fight or lose air, he thought.

Then he heard five short chinks of metal to metal. D-1's
SOS.

He spun them both. Bullets rained down on them as he realized Max wasn't around. Then he saw him floating, barely
a trail of bubbles. Immediately he cut the bastard's hose and
punctured his BC, then finned toward Max. Riley was closing in. He speared himself deeper, finning hard. Max was suspended like a ghost, blood coloring the water. His reg floated
useless. Jesus. He grabbed his weight belt, gave him air, then
pumped up his BC, and rose to the surface.

He came to halfway up and Sebastian held his regulator
until they broke the surface.

Max coughed and spat, fresh blood blooming on his temple. "Jesus, where are these guys coming from?" He coughed
more.

Sebastian added air to his BC. "They have a RIB. They
must be idling somewhere," he said, looking around for the
rigid inflatable boat. Not a wave in the water.

"Sorry, man, he's getting away." A pause, and Max said,
"While we go to jail."

Sebastian spun. "Well, shit." The spotlight hit him a few
seconds before he heard the loud speaker declaring Interpol.
No amount of shouting for them to go west got them to
move. From the deck, the agents made them targets.

Riley scootered near. "McGill's not going to be happy."

"Tell me about it." With mangled bodies aboard the
Scarab, this was going to take some fast talking.

EIGHT

Dimitri felt himself sinking underwater, the rush of bubbles around his head. He experienced a strange softness in his limbs, water quickly replacing his last breath. He sank deeper, his heart slowed. The jolt to his body barely registered and as he felt a pull, he sought the tranquility trying to take him. His head broke the surface, hands dragging him aboard. The sudden thumping pressure on his chest was excruciating and in an instant, the reality of pain crushed his lungs struggling to find air. At once, he shoved Rastoff back and rolled to his side to vomit up water. He gasped for air.

"You were ordered to leave!" he blasted and his body racked with violent coughing again. Someone pushed a regulator into his mouth.

"We did not all have to die today," Rastoff said, tucked low in the boat and breathing hard. He pulled off his mask, then shouldered off his tanks. Blood streamed from his nose, from the corner of his mouth, and he turned his head to spit.

Dimitri yanked out the regulator for a fit of coughing, his chest wheezing as he drew in clean dry air. He sank to the floor of the rubber craft, swiped water off his face, then worked off his buoyancy converter and weight belt. Cold air whipped off the water and spun around them. Someone tossed a thermal blanket over him. He started to give it back, then wrapped it tightly. Failing to obtain the diary and now this? His adversary was far more skilled than he anticipated, and he accepted his mistake. He had further duties to complete and keeping them invisible till she was ready to reveal herself was essential. Traveling underwater was a flawless plan till the Americans interfered.

He smothered a cough and peered over the rim of the rubber boat. The docks were lit with lights of the police cars and he smiled to himself, sinking back down. The trail had to die in Ireland. There was nothing left except the bodies of two men who had accepted the challenge and their fate in it willingly. It would be difficult to identify them, regardless. He'd seen to that himself. He sank into the hull.

Dimitri didn't realize he'd dozed until he felt the lulling vibration lessen. He sat up, and saw the vague outline of the ship, the small yellow lights along the bow glowing brighter as they neared. He climbed to his feet, and as the small boat swept alongside, he reached for the ladder and climbed. He felt incredibly weak when he dropped onto the deck, then stepped back as men hoisted gear with nylon lines, then the outboard engine. The boat followed, plopping noisily on the deck. He moved to the rail and faced the distant shore, then jerked to attention, lifted his chin, and saluted his dead comrades. The others joined him. After a moment, he stepped back, struggling against the roll of nausea and dizziness to stay upright.

He walked toward the bridge. The engines rumbled to life, vibrating under his boots as he stepped inside. He strode to the communications console tucked in the far left. A radioman sat beside it. Dimitri waved him away. He did not want to speak with her, not now, but she was waiting. Impatiently, he knew. The satellite link connected and she responded in seconds.

He gave his report, sparing her the details. "Elan and Mika are dead." He hesitated, then said, "They have seen my face, commander."

From a thousand miles away, he heard the little burst of

anger, quickly smothered as she'd done for three long years. *"Da. Evidence?"*

"Nyet. They search for the old man." How they knew he had him still confused him. He had erased any trail, but knew the American would not relent, and that they were in the water with them warned Dimitri. His foe was not simply law enforcement. He'd fought men like this before.

"Then we will see them again, da?" she said. *"If they are willing to die to find him, let us give them the chance."*

The line went dead, and Dimitri returned the microphone to its cradle. He stared at the radar winding continuously in glowing green. She had a bloodthirst even he could not match. "Stop all electronics." They could be tracked by them. "We travel silent." The captain looked at him, scowling, and started to speak, but Dimitri's expression silenced him. "Show us your skill, Captain. Navigate by a compass and the stars."

He turned away and walked the empty passageway to his cabin. Remaining covert was essential, and while his new adversary would continue his hunt for the old man, he would find nothing. Veta had seen to every detail and contingency, leaving enough trails to confuse. He admired her precision, for the historian, he thought with a glance at his watch, was already a thousand miles away.

Svalbard, Norway
Twenty-four hours earlier

Veta Nevolin stood on the forward deck of her ship, her legs braced against the wind as she watched the plain white truck roll to a stop on the dock. Two uniformed men jumped out, looking toward the ship, searching the decks, and she flicked her hand for notice. Androv nodded, waved back, then, with Geld, he went to the rear of the truck and began unloading. She looked away, to the sea, snuggling into her jacket. The temperatures still held the warmth of summer, the breeze laced with a fresh, earthy scent rolling off the land. It tasted crisp. It told her the snow was coming, the first signs of summer's death. It would grow darker soon and her purpose had to be done before the freeze of winter could bite them.

She glanced at the truck, then turned fully when she saw Androv on the gangway. He held one end of a platform housing a large container, Geld at the other end as they smoothly transferred it to the deck. She'd inspect the equipment later, but was satisfied her backer was good to his word. He'd provided all she'd requested, including the massive vessel capable of extraordinary scientific research.

But more was necessary and she was impatient for Dimitri to join them. His failures had far greater ramifications than she'd expected. He must not bring more notice, she thought, walking to the rail, her palm barely covering the wide surface designed to repel the adhesion of ice. The gathering of forces under her command were prepared for every contingency. She would take the blame for not snatching the diary sooner, but she would not be swayed. She'd worked too long for her mission to fail on poor timing. Now she would make up for it.

Her men returned to the truck, and after letting a laundry vehicle pass, they helped the old man down from the bed. He did not look well, she thought, and they'd at least clothed him for the climate. He was not difficult to transport, sedated and packaged as cargo for most of the journey and only woken to respond to his body and eat. His confusion would only help her cause. She didn't want to come to this, involving anyone outside her most trusted, but he had cleverly disposed of the translation and without it, she fed her impatience with how she would use this man. Revealing her possession with a ransom request wasn't a consideration until she knew what he could offer. It would take a little time to understand the perfect way to treat this man and get him to divulge the information she needed. Men were easy to manipulate, she thought, and she'd done it a thousand times in the last three years. There was no risk when you had nothing left to lose. Until now. The efforts of her sacrifices were so close she could taste victory on her tongue as she watched the scholarly historian walk up the gangway. She crossed to the ramp. He stopped, stared, and in his eyes, she saw bright intelligence and outrage. His temperament wasn't a concern. His mind held the key. If he did not give her what she needed, she would destroy his body.

"Who are you people?" he asked, then cleared his throat.

"I am Lizveta Nevolin, commander of this expedition."

His brows rose with surprise. "Expedition for what?"

She did not answer. He had no reason to know the truth.

"You've put yourself as far away from the diary as possible."

She smiled, slow and thin. She enjoyed his reaction; his skin pricked with cold paling further, the slackness of his features. "I do not think so."

A fire truck, ambulance, and about two dozen police officers filled the end of the pier. Headlights and flashing cruiser lights lit the area. Traffic on the road a couple hundred yards back was already bottlenecking. Just wasn't his week, he thought. Riley paced in front of him, his dive boots squishing with each step.

Sebastian turned down his wet suit to his waist, the evening air prickling a chill across his skin. He grabbed a blanket from the ambulance and sat on the bumper, watching their equipment being confiscated and grouped. All Max did was bitch about how they were treating his new ultra light tanks. His forehead was bandaged neatly, the blood trail down his throat drying. There was plenty of evidence they'd met trouble on the water, including cuts in his wet suit. Two officers stood guard a few feet away. Neither looked older than high school. Lots of fidgeting. Sebastian was tempted to bark to see if they'd jump. Interpol had scanned their prints and were checking them out, but he couldn't convince them the bad guys were escaping. Radar would tell them that much. McGill's touch hadn't reached them yet and the wheels of bureaucracy weren't turning fast enough.

Sebastian's gaze followed three officers as they boarded the boat towed from a half mile out. A photographer and a stretcher followed a minute later.

"See, told you so," Max said as if the cops could hear him.

Sebastian slid him a glance, arched a brow. "Want to call your mama and whine a little more?"

Max chuckled. "It's just so obvious now. If we could spot them fifty yards out, so could Interpol. They suck at surveillance."

Or were bribed to delay, Sebastian thought. Then Riley leaned in to say, "We'll be charged for boarding it, and probably evidence tampering, or being vigilantes. Just pick one."

He was right and Sebastian didn't think it would all come out in the wash, though they offered plenty of motivation for the attacks. Not that the average criminal needed one, but D-1's background gave them enough suspicions to warrant a deeper look. The police had the truth, that they were following the man who attacked Olivia and a possible lead to Noble's location. But with the looks the police tossed their way, they were going to lose valuable trails by sitting in a holding cell somewhere.

Sebastian's gaze followed the bodies being passed from the Scarab to shore. The EMTs laid the bodies on the ground and the coroner examined them again, holding up a mangled hand. A detective motioned to a uniformed officer, and the guys slipped out his handcuffs and started toward them. Shit.

"Guess we should have waited for those credentials," Sebastian said.

"Jesus. Someone's in a hurry." Max nudged him, and Sebastian saw a dark SUV barreling down the docks. A red light pulsed from the dash and the truck maneuvered around the fish shacks and deserted vendor shops. He could feel the vibration from here and stood, pushing his arms into the sleeves of his dive suit.

The truck stopped, the light still flashing, and from the passenger side, a woman slipped out. The driver stood by the front of the vehicle, dressed in a dark suit and staring straight ahead. His gaze shot to the woman striding toward the police, carrying a briefcase. "It's Olivia."

Max frowned, taking hit of oxygen. "Doesn't look like her."

Yeah, but he'd know that tight behind anywhere, he thought as she walked briskly past, not sparing them a glance. Her deep red hair was swept back in a barrette and she wore a simple gray jacket and skirt, but her legs in heels twisted with muscle and every man here turned to watch her approach. She was wearing a weapon, he realized. She spoke to one man, walked to another, then flashed an ID. The man reared back a bit, then took it, looking closely. When he returned it, she set the briefcase on the hood of a garda car and opened it, handing over a couple sheets of paper.

She talked with them for a few more minutes and Sebastian simply enjoyed Olivia on a power trip. She had an air of absolute authority that was scaring the officers. *Go get 'em, baby.* She strode to the two bodies laid out and frowned, pointing to the one man he'd recognized from the chase across Ireland. Then with the garda officer, she crossed to them, her NSA ID leading the way.

"Not another word, gentleman. Collect your equipment and board the vehicle please."

"I think I'd rather duke it out with the garda, ma'am."

She stiffened, and he was impressed with her stern expression. "You don't have a choice. *Now*, please."

"Yes, ma'am," he said respectfully, then looked at the officer. "Keep the Glock for ballistics. You'll learn I never fired it."

The officer flushed and reluctantly conceded with a nod. With Max and Riley, he gathered the tanks, regulators, and DPDs, then took them to the truck. Cruz was at the rear by the door. All he needed was some aviator shades, a PRR rigged up the back of his neck, and he'd pass for Secret Service. Though they rarely wore Hugo Boss.

Sebastian came around to the side and over the open door, met her gaze. "Nice job, Olivia," he said under his breath.

"We aim to please, and get your ass out of trouble," she whispered, pinkening a little as she slid into the passenger seat. The doors slammed shut, Cruz behind the wheel. He started backing off the docks.

"McGill know about this?" Sebastian asked.

She scoffed, flipping down the visor to talk to him in the mirror. "Are you kidding? McGill knows everything even when I think he doesn't. We haven't needed this kind of clout in a while. A project barely draws attention normally." She watched to see if the garda followed, then looked at Max. "You okay? That looks painful."

He touched the bandage on his temple. "Fine, just pissed he could hit that hard underwater."

"Safia tracked you and I heard it on that police band. They were sending a wagon for you guys." She switched on the heat, and Sebastian got a whiff of the sea and wet neoprene before he felt the warmth. When they were on the highway, heading back to the house, she turned in the seat. "One of those bodies was the guy from the estate."

He'd recognized the Fiat driver, too. "Forensics will tell them he didn't die on the boat." The missing fingertips and teeth would make the identification tough, if not impossible. "Notice the tattoos on his hand?" He could feel Max staring a hole in his head.

"There wasn't much left of them." She made grossed-out face.

"Between thumb and forefinger. A symbol like a fork."

"Yeah," she said with wonder. "I think it's a trident or maybe a rune. The guy who tried to fillet me, he had one, too. Well, more than one, but I saw the fork when he grabbed my arm. He was wearing gloves in the cottage. His tattoo is bigger and more detailed than the guy with no fingers."

He slid a glance at Max. "He had them on his knuckles, too. Hard not to miss when they're trying to rearrange your face." Like the dead Chechnya soldiers, he thought, and should have anticipated the guy had more backup. "I'm hoping your admirer is swimming with the fishes, but I doubt it." Not with the RIB so close.

"Knife guy?" She shivered. "Pretty blue eyes, but there's nothing there. It's scary."

He agreed. Eyes like glass, he thought, square jaw, flat forehead, and several deep scars on his face and throat. He was Noble's kidnapper. He felt it in his gut. If he'd known they were on the water, then Blue Eyes cleverly set them up, but he doubted it. The propulsion device carried the team from shore without detection by Interpol till they started up the RIB's motor. "There's got to be a ship waiting for them. That RIB doesn't take on enough fuel to get very far. Not in those waters. We need active satellite." He turned over ways to track the bastards. "About three miles out."

Olivia nodded. "Safia has it. She's watching *sixteen* ships off the coast of Ireland right now. When the RIB meets with it, we'll know."

Riley asked for a phone and she handed over hers. He dialed. "Leaving Ireland now is just wise," he said, putting the cell to his ear. "I'd like to come home for a visit someday."

"Noble's nowhere near here," Sebastian said and they looked at him. "The Russian was just too confident and well prepared. Leaving those bodies is a distraction." He looked at Olivia. "They want everything you do. The threat isn't here, now it's your dig. So I'd say, the ball's in your court, ma'am."

"McGill's ordered us to Ice Harvest. Our jet's waiting."

"We brought our own," Sebastian said and his ego swelled at the little flare of disappointment in her face. "I'm flying it."

She arched a brow, looking him over in a way he remembered. Intimately. "Fine. I didn't want to share my G-five with you anyway."

He grinned.

"A G-five?" Max said. "Shit. I want a ride in *that*."

Spring, 1175

Having lived with the Irish for some time now, I hazard that my experiences could fulfill some adherent questions for my brothers. As no one shall read this afore my demise, I will do my utmost to speak without hindrance. God is, after all, my supreme confidant. In these pages, I shall question what I cannot speak to even my brethren of Saint Angela's. I wait and hope for that day.

My faith in the church's true message is tested daily. A fact, I'm certain, the Irish pagans would relish. I have known in my heart since I was a small boy that understanding leads to acceptance and compromise. The church is unbending so it is God's message I bring. I often stroll through the countryside, offering counsel to our newly converted disciples of Irish blood. Yet far more pray to pagan gods. I have seen their ritual offerings on the road and near homes. They are mere requests in food and fruit, ribbons, and stones. A gathering of wishes, I feel, to the power stronger than themselves. Is that not where all faith begins? Do I not make an offering of bread and wine for blessings on my flock? I seek a common path, my lord. The church brims with ritual and ceremony and to deny thus to others is a duplicity I cannot abide. I pray I am not forced to choose.

Whilst trying to understand the pagans is indeed fascinating, many compromises have been forced on the Irish. I do not wish this monastery to be one of combat, but one of sanctuary. For any faith. The bloodshed of this crusade was as horrific as I have seen. This hamlet of Ireland is wounded, and I shall continue to extend a hand in friendship in the hope of bridging the divide England has wrought on these good people.

Svalbard, Norway

Sebastian hurried away from the nearly empty parking lot and ran down the pier. He paralleled the trucks from the airport and spotted them between warehouses. Riley waved to him and split off, heading northeast. He ran harder, darting left and slipping between buildings to the waterside.

"Well, aren't we all full of money," he muttered. "Finn, you see that?" A massive ship berthed at the end of the pier. Workers marched like ants from trucks to the gangway but no farther. The trucks' license plates matched from the airport.

"*Roger that,*" Riley said. "*They aren't letting anyone aboard. I'm getting eight by tens of the crews. They either need a diet plan or they're carrying.*"

"Roger that. Looks like your sister's expedition ship, ey?"

It was rigged for a purpose, but Sebastian couldn't pinpoint it. A research ship, maybe. His dark self wasn't getting closer, not in a sea of pale-skinned blonds. The trucks blocked the cargo being unloaded. Sitting in the water would give a better view, he thought, holding at the warehouse wall. Across the road were the dock and about four big fishing trawlers that looked abandoned and barely seaworthy. He didn't want to sail it, just get on it, and waited for some cover, then ran across the road and down the dock. He jumped into the middle trawler, and worked his way to the mast rigged to swing giant nets over the sea. He climbed, and used the nest of ropes and pulleys for cover. He sighed through a single scope binoculars. One of Olivia's gadgets she had handy. It had thermal, night vision, and a camera.

"*Northern Lion.* Nuke powered and loaded for something," he said in the PRR. Cranes poked like broken arms on the deck. The equipment was completely shielded with tarps, but whatever it was, pushed the ship's waterline.

"*The stern is an electronic hoist system like we use in*

hangers," Riley said. *"They're putting something big in the water, but I can tell what it is. I'm thinking a bathyscaphe."*

Safia was so tight on satellite she'd caught the RIB hooking up with the mother ship, a freighter. That couldn't have been easy. The inflatable boat's wake was no more than a white dot, but when the world turned, and she was in perfect range, she got one telling bit. Tattoo guy on the deck, saluting his dead. For him, it just confirmed the guy was Spetsnaz and without a thought, he rubbed the cut behind his ear. The freighter ported in Iceland. Flying from Ireland, they'd arrived hours ahead of it and saw it unloaded. Crates, numbered, no names. He photographed everyone and recognized the bastard who'd gone after Olivia.

On target, he thought. He'd followed those crates to the airport and bribed his way to learning it was headed to Svalbard. Cold-as-ice Svalbard, he thought, zipping his jacket and watching the traffic on the end of the pier. For a minute, it looked like a fight starting and he saw a man rush to adjust the swing of a crate to the deck. Accident avoided, though he'd like to know what was under that tarp.

"Coonass, deck of the ship, near the blind passageway. The woman. She's the only female so far."

She stood in the corridor in the shadows, but yeah, definitely female. As the trucks unloaded, the workers were paid and the population thinned. He watched the woman speak into a radio. A moment later, a man waved to her, grabbed a big case, then headed down the gangway to the pier. He shouted at the workers, then opened the briefcase.

"The case is full of Norwegian kroner and they're overpaying," Riley said.

The last two trucks pulled away as the dockworkers rushed off to spend their ging-wah. The crew was still moving the crates belowdecks and Sebastian thought, there's got to be four floors to it before the cargo level. Mean-looking ship with barely room to move on the forward deck. It was another half hour before the docks were barren except for the ship and a couple men at the stern, smoking.

158 / Amy J. Fetzer

A short white truck rolled up the street. Sebastian climbed down, and from inside the abandoned fishing trawler's wheelhouse, his gaze followed it till it passed. He left the boat and ran down the dock. He couldn't cross to the warehouse without risking being spotted, and he crouched on the short pier, using the stern of the boats for cover. The smell was enough to gag a maggot. He couldn't see Riley, yet knew he was somewhere across from the *Northern Lion* in a warehouse. The truck stopped. From the cab, two men climbed out.

"We win the Kewpie doll." The Spetsnaz from Ireland. Sebastian wished he had a sniper rifle. "Opportunity to get aboard and look around?"

"Negative, they're locked and loaded for war. Topside and bow."

He swung left and had to search for them, then spotted a shooter behind a crate, another in sniper position on the roof of the wheelhouse. "Shit. We need more guns." One man looked his way and Sebastian ducked, waited, then on his stomach, jungle crawled till he could see. The dock rocked on the water. All the cargo they'd seen unloaded was marked with diplomatic seals he knew were fake, but that got them anywhere without an inspection. He hated to think it, but Noble could be inside one of those wooden crates.

"Safia had a frequency track on the ship. It's been right here for four days. The plan filed with the harbormaster doesn't give a destination port. Only Greenland Sea. They accept this shit?"

"Money talks, buddy, and they're swimming in it."

"The Northern Lion *has been this route before. This is the third time it's berthed here. I mean right here, this slip."*

Sebastian frowned to himself. "A dry run?" He narrowed the lens on the man's face as the blond woman stepped into the sunlight and addressed Spetsnaz. She was pretty in a severe sort of way and as she spoke, he saw the man soften and smile. With the docks empty now, the men didn't try to hide the weapons.

"If they have Noble aboard, they need him, Coonass. They'll treat him well."

He hoped so, and he prayed Noble obeyed and survived till he could figure out how to get him back. "We hang till night, maybe opportunity to—"

"Coonass, back of the truck, back of the truck!"

Sebastian leaned out and risked exposure, clicking off photos as the stocky man walked a dolly down the truck ramp. "Well, color me surprised. That sure looks like a sonar case."

The broad white case bore a few scrape marks but it was identical to the one in which Vince Mills stored his deep-water sonar. He'd never actually seen the case, only photos, but it was the right size. Then Spetsnaz tipped it on its side. "Check bottom left."

"Roger that, Mills's logo," Riley said. *"See, I knew they were hunting underwater. But Jesus, someone with mafia ties has Noble?"*

"Sure explains the abundance of cannon fodder." Risk the hired mafia and keep his own men safe and undercover. "Drivers, start your engines." He could feel the vibration of the massive icebreaker powering up. "Back off, we track from the sky, but we bring our chopper onto the ice."

And armed, he thought as he watched the bastard push the dolly up the gangway.

Aboard the Northern Lion
Svalbard

Veta stood at the bridge of the icebreaker, and through the windshield, watched her men load the last piece of equipment. The crane swung the cabled platform onto the forward deck, and she stepped closer to the windows as the men secured it. She let out a breath she wasn't aware she held, then lifted the radio to her lips. "Be very certain she is secured as instructed, Androv, da."

From the deck, he turned to wave. *"Da, Commander, as you ordered."*

She would like to be down there with them, supervising, but she trusted her men. They joined her eagerly and looked to her as more than a commander and maintaining discipline, but to keep them focused. This would not be a pleasant journey, yet within each of them was a sacred vow to fulfill it to its end. They understood that all would not come back alive. So many had already perished.

She moved to the right, and peered down toward the street, keeping her features schooled when she saw the truck. Excellent. Her gaze shifted back to the cargo and along the lash lines. Well done, she thought, her anxiousness untempered since she started down this path three years ago. A crewman bumped her and she moved back against the only vacant wall to give them a clear path to their duties. At the bridge, the captain called down to the cargo hull, giving specifics to lashing the valuable equipment. Piloting such a vessel required great skill and an experienced crew, and her confidence in them magnified after the voyage across the Barents Sea.

Then the captain looked back over his shoulder, nodding. "Ready for your orders, Commander."

"We need only wait for Comrade Kolbash, Captain. Then we will be under way." She lifted her radio. "Androv, pay the workers and get them off the dock." He responded, then walked to the briefcase near a spool of rope and went to do just that.

Signaling the captain, she left the bridge, taking the passageway, then the short stairs to the deck. The cold air stung her eyes and she zipped her jacket. She waited for the docks to clear a bit, then walked toward the ramp. Her gaze followed the short fat truck rolling down the pier, but her focus was on the driver. Her palms dampened.

She shoved them into her pockets, feeling somehow incomplete till this moment.

He was here.

* * *

Dimitri Kolbash parked the truck and tossed the keys on the floorboard before he left the vehicle. He stopped short, darting back for his duffel, then strode to the rear, hopping the bumper to throw open the retractable door. In the back, he unstrapped the dolly, positioned the hard-sided case, then unloaded it from the truck. He walked briskly to the ramp, ignoring the workers hurrying off the docks and shouting happily over their quick pay. She was too generous. Less money and they'd work harder for it, but she was in command and he respected her choices, yet not always her reasons behind them. She thought money bought silence. He did not.

Dimitri pushed up the ramp, giving a hard look at a man rushing to help. He would deliver this to her and no other. They'd already risked much for the mission. He didn't anticipate her disappointment and shouldered the blame. The bookseller had outsmarted them, and the translation was gone. She had the most important pieces, he reasoned, and should stop this quest for the relic, but he knew in his soul, she would rather die than let her father's work perish.

She met him on the deck, smiling. She was such a beauty when she did that, he thought. She spun on her heel, and he followed her, turning onto the passageway barely wide enough to accommodate the dolly, then into the conference room. The case was awkwardly large, yet not heavy. He lifted it to the long table, then stepped back.

Her gaze slid to the bruises on his jaw and cheek, and she frowned. "It is good to see you well, comrade."

His gaze lingered over her before he spoke. "And you."

Her beauty still affected him, and seeing her dressed so severely did little to change that. The dark gray uniform designed for a man fit her well enough to silhouette her voluptuous figure, yet it was buttoned to her throat, and she appeared unapproachable. As she wanted. She closed the door, her gaze skidding once to the case.

"I knew you would succeed."

"Ahh, my Liziveta, you honor me with that smile."

She rushed into his arms, kissed him deeply. "You have made this all possible now."

He released her and stepped back.

"What is wrong?"

"I did not recover the translation." She strode away, cursing foully, and he long accepted that he'd failed her. "Forgive me, Veta."

She spun, her angry expression dissolving into a gentle smile. "The blame is not yours, Dimitri. We still possess the means to get it."

He folded his arms, his feet spread wide. "It's foolish." The old man's silence was enough to know he would be difficult to persuade.

"So you have said." She stared, her oddly dark eyes unblinking. He recognized this side of her, the methodical woman who thought nothing was out of her reach, and none were beyond the scope of her venom. She'd proven that by killing the mafia lieutenants and a least one member of FSB already. "The rescuers?"

He did not break eye contact, his shoulders moving back. "Our path is cleaned, and none left to speak of it. Be satisfied." Mills or the American spy were of little consequence now. Moscow sent MiGs to destroy the factory, the evidence of their crime against NATO. Attention would stay there.

"The krasnaya served us well enough."

No one had any inclination to the outcome. Every step behind him had been erased or lead astray. Confusion was their best asset. She'd anticipated their every move so far.

She nodded, moved closer. "Show me this wonder."

He turned to the casing, flipping the eight latches and lifting off the top.

"So small, da?"

Dimitri shrugged. "I know nothing of such things."

She understood the electronics and could have built it herself, he thought as she leaned over the sonar device. She opened a small hatch, closed it, then ran her hand over the slick surface. "Did he confirm the transmission?"

When he didn't answer, she looked back over her shoulder. "Dimitri?"

"Da. It was as you predicted. In the same area."

Her shoulders sank. She wanted to be mistaken, that it was as they'd been told. This only confirmed the lie.

"The wife?"

He shook his head. "We could not get close." He waited for the explosion of her temper, and when it did not come, he frowned. "Veta?"

She looked up and the gleam of violence in her eyes didn't surprise him. "We do not need her. Our wrath will find its target. Now give me the log." He swept up the satchel and tossed it. She dumped it on the table, and grasped the linen-wrapped book. She carefully removed the linen, then took a seat and opened it.

"Amazing this still exists," she murmured peering closer, turning a page in a plastic sleeve.

He scoffed, caring little for the antique. "I could have just taken it from the auction house."

Her gaze shifted to him. "Nyet. That would bring Interpol. As is, it stays with the local police." From her leg pocket, she pulled a pad and pen, jotted down a note, then closed and rewrapped the log.

"Not after Rastoff killed in England. The men in Ireland were not police and will follow," he warned again.

"Only if you have left a trail to follow."

His lips tightened. "Do not misjudge our adversaries, Lizeveta." Her gaze snapped to his. "They were skilled enough to find us on the water and now the garda have bodies." He tried for calm. "Moscow will keep disguising their crime for they cannot allow you to expose it. Killing Molenko was a mistake."

Her eyes gleamed with barely suppressed rage. "Nyet! Molenko gave the order!"

"You speak as if I know nothing! Molenko kept state secrets and FSB is hunting us now. Do not doubt that. They sent MiGs to destroy the factory so the Americans wouldn't learn of it."

She drew a deep breath, suddenly calmer. "That was their own mistake. Now the Americans are watching."

"They are always watching." She was not in intelligence long enough to understand how skilled the Americans were at spying. His body bore the scars to prove it. He rubbed his neck, a headache brewing. He did not want to see her harmed, but felt she was opening her trap too wide. She should have taken all the files from Molenko's house. Leaving the others behind offered too much to men who saw crimes against the state around every corner, and never their own duplicity.

"You will keep us safe, Dimitri. That is what I do not doubt."

Her confidence was misplaced. He'd failed to gain the translation and now she would force the old man to re-create it. Dimitri pitied him. Lizveta was a woman unrestrained with her vengeance.

A knock jolted the door, and he found a crewman standing in the corridor. "We are ready to be under way, Commander."

She nodded once. "Weigh anchor." The man disappeared down the passageway and she looked at Dimitri and said, "It is time."

He remained by the door till she left the room, then followed her till she was outside her cabin. She entered first and he hesitated, waiting for a crewman to pass. Though he'd spent many nights in her arms, he would not shame her in front of her men. He slipped inside, sealing them in, then immediately grabbed her, pushed her up against the door, and kissed her ravenously. For it would be their last. Their lives had taken separate routes to end here, on this day, and to launch the expedition she'd sacrificed everything to make happen.

"Dimitri, I am nothing without you."

"Nyet, you are the strongest." He palmed her body one last time. "It must be this way."

"Da, but it does not mean I like it."

His mouth moved over hers with maddening desire, and he knew well this vow they'd make was for him. She would never stop. He could not allow his heart to rule when following her orders would put her in grave danger. He'd give his life to protect her, but she made him swear to complete the mission, even if she was no longer alive. He swore to himself, even as he kissed her once more and drew back, that if she died, he would leave no one breathing to exact his own revenge.

"*Do svidaniya*, Veta." Then he snapped to attention, staring above her head. "My loyalty is yours. I swear it." He saluted her, and she returned it, sealing their vow. She was his commander now and he would not touch her, would not taste her mouth again till the mission was over. Emotions must be left behind. As if marking the moment, the ship rumbled with the pull of the anchor, rocking a bit.

She tipped her chin up. "Stage two begins." She straightened her clothing, smoothed her hand over her blond hair twisted tight and high on her head, then stepped out of the cabin. Dimitri followed, remaining a respectful step back as she strode down the passageway. Her boot heels were soundless on the rubber flooring. The vessel had been retrofitted with the latest equipment, solar and petrol powered. But that was her business and she'd bargained with the devil to get it. He was here to see that no one interfered with her quests, regardless of how futile he thought them to be.

Deep Six
Satellite Intelligence

Mitch paced the floor in front of his console, ignoring the looks Lorimier was handing him. The kid was tracking that Chechen phone number and he mulled that it was a long shot, and with all this technology, they still didn't have enough to hunt. He wanted to chat with Price and Kincade. Gerardo was stalling. The photo didn't confirm the sub—not to the brass's satisfaction—and without proof, they couldn't confront Moscow with it. Mitch was itching for that. He didn't need more evidence and knowing they built a submarine, possibly with the stolen German technology for a vertical ICBM missile launcher, gave him that "shit's about to hit the fan" feeling he'd lived with for most of his career.

Worse, that it was most definitely roaming out there, loaded for war.

The phone number might give him a link to the money, the operators that were all over the place then. His mind tumbled back to his captivity, the wounds on his chest and legs far from healed, but it least his skin wasn't screaming with pain. His ankle had a hairline fracture, a fact he didn't learn till three days ago. It pissed him off. He wanted back in the field, to find the bastard who did this to him. He ignored the cane propped against the desk, and finally took a seat, bracing his leg on the desktop. What he'd really like was about twenty minutes in a room with Price, no cameras.

"David, talk to me."

"You're not long on patience lately, anyone tell you that?"

"Bite me. I'm in pain, look like a zombie, and I need some payback."

David chuckled and kept working. It annoyed him that the kid was so focused. Suddenly, David swung his chair around, looking a little wide eyed. "There's a flag on it. We're already tracking it."

Mitch squinted at the screens, scowling. There were hundreds of feeds and satellite technicians from sections even he couldn't name. "The reason?"

"Person of interest. Tracking for a while, too. Printing the call list."

Mitch didn't ask how he managed that and stood near the printer, wiggling his fingers as if it would spit it out faster. He snatched it, and ran his finger down the list, scowling. The calls were spaced months apart. That said, the caller knew he'd be tracked and used different phones. His gaze slid to the last on the list. Same time frame as Chechnya.

"Last call from that phone was in England, Surrey, four days ago. I need to know who received it."

"That recipient number belonged to Noble Sheppard. I checked the registration. He's an American."

Mitch crossed to him, hovering over his shoulder. "I want Sheppard's call list, everything you can get on this guy."

David tapped a few keys, then slid back from the counter. The information spilled down the bigger screen. "Noble Sheppard, bookseller from New Orleans and at his address for over thirty years. Sixty-three, divorced, one child." David swung the chair around. "He's under police investigation in Surrey. He was kidnapped from his hotel."

His brows shot up. "Get me the police reports and contact Surrey police. Did Sheppard make any calls to the tagged number?"

"No sir. Only incoming. Sheppard's phone isn't on, and it was last used yesterday. In Ireland. Man, he gets around."

"Not if he was kidnapped, Davey-boy. The kidnapper has it. Start a trace."

"You might want to look at the last four numbers on Sheppard's call list then."

Mitch scanned the list and went still.

"I thought that would get your attention."

Mitch looked at him. "Fontenòt? Christ. Research Sheppard, this Corrigan, and Fontenòt. I need to know where they are and what they're doing, A-sap."

"Why not just *ask* Dragon One?"

"And eat crow after we shut them down? Not till Gerardo lifts the restriction. Find another way."

David scowled at him. "You're trusting the wrong people.

Just my opinion, sir. If Fontenòt is associated with this Sheppard, and he's missing, don't expect D-1 to be sitting on their thumbs."

"They're restricted."

David scoffed and looked back over his shoulder. "It just warms my heart that national security is in your hands, Major."

His expression said otherwise and Mitch's face pulled tight. "Is that doubt I'm hearing, Lorimier?" And why wouldn't he? It's not like he didn't just get his ass handed to him by a bunch of mercs.

"All I'm saying is . . ." David didn't look at him and typed, humming a funeral dirge. "What goes around, comes around, sir."

NINE

Olivia cranked up the music, wiggling in the seat to "Ain't too Proud to Beg." The song made her happy and it was one of Noble's favorites. She was trying to be positive. Sebastian hadn't seen him in Norway, but the blue-eyed guy was there. Yet while she didn't have details, Safia was tracking everything from the dig and around it. The *Northern Lion* was sailing slowly south. Dragon One came prepared with cases of gear, half of it she didn't recognize. The weapons she did, and she glanced down at her SIG Sauer on the seat, loaded. She'd locked it up on the NSA jet before China and hadn't had it on the dig till now. She felt better armed, but wouldn't wear it inside the habitat. Too distracting. Besides, that's what Sebastian and the detail were for, thank you director, but after having that big knife shoved in her face, she wasn't going to be defenseless like that again.

She turned down the volume as her MP3 player slipped to the next song, enjoying the only privacy she'd had since leaving Ireland. She'd caught up on sleep, and indulged with a soak in a tub, her last for a while, then videoconferenced with her team to prepare them. Sebastian had done the same with Ross and McGill. Her team was a little nervous and anxious for her return, but Agent Ross didn't seem the least bit insulted that someone else was taking over security. Then again, she thought bitterly, he'd failed to protect Noble in the first place. Blaming him didn't ease her own guilt and she was feeling a lot of it with Sebastian in her life again.

He was a few minutes behind her and on reflex, Olivia glanced in the side-view mirrors of the Snow-Cat, big hawking things fitted with two-inch steel pipes. Another reason she wasn't comfortable riding in this kind of tonnage on the ice. It was a tank, and the rolling trends pulled its massive shell across the endless blanket of white that looked pink through her lens. Her goggles were less the cyborg style and more like some pricey wraparound Guccis. The best part was the switch that would turn them to night vision. Ideal for being on the ice in the dark, though right now, it was daylight about twenty hours a day.

From the treads, shaved ice and snow fanned out like white wings and it was another ten minutes before she spied the habitat, downshifting. Beside and behind her were supplies, mostly food, and she was dying to try the Polish sausage she'd seen loaded earlier. Her hips wouldn't like it, but she had the winter to worry about that. Time was literally growing shorter by the day up here and hitting hard ice wasn't helping the project she'd ignored since Noble was taken. Her heart sank a little more, and she slowed the Sno-Cat to a crawl, then stopped several yards outside the habitat and behind the marker. She shut down the engine, then pressed her forehead to the steering wheel, flinching when the horn chirped. She fell back into the cushioned seat, aching down to her soul.

I wish you were here, Noble. Safe and doing what you love.

He had to survive. It would kill Sebastian if he didn't.

She heard the distant thump of the chopper and blotted her eyes, mentally preparing herself for weeks of practically living with Sebastian. She admitted that given the turn of events in the last three days, she was glad there was one person she could trust to keep them safe. Archaeology didn't usually bring bad guys. Her own training was minimal, and Ross's skills weren't even close to what she knew of Sebastian fourteen years ago. Clearly, he'd added a few, though he'd never talked about it when they were married. She was much more informed now and understood the drive that kept him in the field. Like climbing the cliff and sneaking into the khan's crypt. She *had* to see it, screw the risks.

Anxious to get back to her job, she pushed the safety on her weapons, and zipped it into her pack, then exited the Sno-Cat with quick moves. It was going to take a few days to get used to the cold again. Yanking the wrap over her mouth, she strode to the domed habitat, her boot spikes digging into the ice. She dropped her bag there, then attached the Sno-Cat battery to the heater to keep it warm and ready. She faced the horizon to watch Sebastian fly in. Another skill, she thought, and her eyes widened as the helicopter approached. *That's some chopper.* It reminded her of a fat arrow with a hook tail. Painted matte black, the metal nose was layered like scales of a dragon. Wicked cool and big. The skids retracted inside its smooth fuselage, she supposed. Neon green lights outlined the undercarriage and blinked.

Seeing Sebastian at the controls was sexy and she admitted a freakin' turn-on. Gawd. Knowing what he looked like naked wasn't helping either. He hadn't lost that self-assured edge that made her feel incredibly safe and protected—and yeah, loved. It was his trust and confidence she'd wanted then. What do you want now, a voice asked, sounding too much like her mother. The impossible, she thought.

The aircraft neared. Very James Bond, honey, she thought, smiling, and a little excited to show him her world.

Sebastian had plenty of cold-weather training in the Marines. Six months of living in Norway with little more than standard-issue gear; he'd spent most of it repairing and maintaining choppers. He hadn't learned to fly the things till a couple years later. It had taken him ten miles to get used to the arctic temperatures and wind currents. A wild view, he thought flying over gray jagged rock and patches of lush green. He passed over a massive lake so still it reflected a perfect mirror of the snow-capped mountains surrounding it.

Beside him, Max studied the screen showing the terrain. He pointed out Olivia's Sno-Cat ahead. "You should have forced an escort on her."

Sebastian snickered to himself. "While she was armed, are you crazy? She's an expert shot and doesn't take orders well." He was behind her by minutes and could see anything coming. Then the radio crackled with his call sign and he tapped Sam through.

"Just checking freques."

"Loud and clear. Y'all almost set up?"

Sam was as close as he could get to the dig and not be on the ice, positioned a few miles west of the Nord Ice Station, a weather tracking facility manned by the Danish Navy. The Sirius Patrol was out there somewhere, he thought, noticing snowmobile tracks. The *Siriuspatruljen* executed long-range recon patrols solely to maintain Danish sovereignty. Sort of a roving ice police. Sam was south of them, a Huey on standby in case they needed to airlift the scientists. Olivia had a bush plane at her disposal, but Sam considered them no better than balsa wood and a rubber band. Choppers could go places a plane couldn't.

"Roger that. Just trying to stay warm. Got you on satellite, but if anything goes ass up, you're on your own. It'll be a few minutes reaching you."

Trying to anticipate the unknown was never easy. On the ice, even harder. With so many on this ice dig, he went for overkill. "Stay locked and loaded. The security detail are all young pups fulfilling their cold-weather duty." He signed off and lowered his altitude a hundred feet. Flying low was better than high. The glaciers were hell on wind currents and it was a bumpy ride, more dangerous with fuel barrels right behind his head. He could have done without that, but there were no free rides. Supplies had to be transported, and today he was a flying gas can.

He glanced at the GPS, a little bit of anticipation making him strain to see ahead. After another minute, the habitat bloomed on the horizon. "Well, ain't that a sight." The wide sloping, dome-shaped structure had to be the length of a football field at least. Wider, he thought as he flew closer.

"Looks like a golf ball cut in half," Max said.

The rising sun blinded, and he pulled down his goggles, then positioned for landing. He peered left, aiming for the circle of blue strobe lights. He lowered the craft.

"The welcome mat is out," Max said. "Lowering skids." He flipped a switch.

Sebastian felt the hum as the skids unfolded and he lowered till metal touched smooth ice. Wind and fresh powder buffeted the doors, blinding till the rotors slowed. He shut down the aircraft, and radioed Sam.

"I'll get the cables," Max said, pushing open the door. The gust of wind made him fight for it.

The landing zone lights flickered neon blue and as he shut down, his gaze followed the cable lines running to a building far from the habitat. It was white and large enough for an eighteen-wheeler. A power station, wind, solar and combustion fuel, he realized, impressed. He looked back at the facility built over an archaeology dig, his mood lightening.

He pulled on the gray ski cap, thinking it was completely dorky, but it kept his ears warmer than a hood. He opened the door, hopping down, turned back for his pack and duffel, then locked it up. He went to the rear cargo for the stakes. He wasn't taking a chance on the winds kicking up, and with a sledgehammer drove the two-foot iron divot into the ice. Max cabled the chopper to the divot. At the fourth one, he was overheated and stripped off this parka, then tapped the stake and stepped back to slam it home.

"Put your jacket back on," he heard and looked at Olivia running across the ice.

"Even I know not to run up here, woman."

She stopped short, smiling. "Put your parka back on." She grabbed it off the ice. "It's not wise to chill and warm over and over up here. At least till you're used to it."

He lifted his goggles to his forehead. "Hang on to it. I'll be a second." Sebastian turned to the stakes, sent the last into the ice, then with Max, roped the chopper, testing the slip line so one yank would release it, then secured the knot with a carabiner clip. He grabbed his gear and crossed to her. She offered the jacket with a "you're a stubborn ass" look and he slid it on.

"Hey Max, how's your head?" The wind pushed at her fur headband.

"Frozen." He pulled up his hood, gestured between him and Sebastian. "We were going for a matching set."

She tipped to look at his two-day-old wound. It was no more than a scratch now.

Sebastian hitched his duffel. "Let the crews know, four barrels are yours, the others, for the chopper."

"I bought more food." She wiggled her brows. "Any chance of you cooking? We have a full kitchen."

He looked at the habitat. "You're kidding. No MREs?"

"Not on my dig. We even have a cappuccino maker."

"Your tax dollars at work," Max muttered as they walked to the figure standing near a door facing away from the wind gusts.

"Hello Ross, nice to meet you," Sebastian said, biting off his glove to shake his hand. He offered his ID and Sebastian introduced Max.

"It's a pleasure. Your team comes highly recommended by the director." The agent seemed a little too relieved to meet him. Maybe twenty-eight, Ross looked completely out of sorts in about thirty pounds of down. His cheeks and nose were chapped and red.

"Appreciate that." Sebastian's gaze rose up the curved wall at least forty feet tall. "Amazing. How long did it take to build this out here?"

"A few weeks," Olivia said. "It breaks down into sections for transport. The weather cooperated, but it won't for long. The temps hover around forty now, but in a couple weeks, they'll plummet and we have to be gone."

"With all this equipment and people on the ice, doesn't it melt faster?" Max asked and they started walking.

"It's a couple hundred feet thick," Olivia said. "And yes, it melts, but not enough to be significant to the dig yet. However, we're close to the water, and glaciers break off in massive chunks there. I wanted a helicopter, just in case."

"Your way or the highway?" he said, then regretted it when she went still and met his gaze. Ultimatums broke them apart.

"I've learned to compromise," she said with a sassy look. "But I can still throw a mean tantrum when the situation calls for it. You'd be proud." Her grin was toothy, totally fake, and he chuckled. "Let's get out of the wind." She headed to the entrance. "Watch the electrical cords."

Sebastian followed her into the crooked wind tunnel and felt the breeze vanish at the last turn. He came to a dead stop inside. There weren't many things that impressed him, but this certainly topped the list. It was a high-tech lab on the ice and surprisingly quiet with the hum of computers and equipment, sections with tables, a centrifuge, microscopes, and large hi-def screens. About thirty technicians manned them, voices low, and it was cold enough inside that your breath frosted a bit, but he already felt overdressed in his cold-weather thermal gear. One-half of the dome was shielded by a white tarp, but he could see a wood boardwalk and metal framework under the silky canvas. The dig. Tubing and hoses ran in tied bundles across the ice that was covered in rubber mats to the wall and somewhere beyond. Noble planned to be here, and he felt compelled to take it all in at once. Just how the legend of the Maguire's princess ended in the arctic, he was anxious to know. The diary gave him a hint, but he'd only glanced at it. Olivia promised a dive into the dig.

Then very softly he heard, "Welcome to Ice Harvest, Sebastian."

He looked at her, smiling. "Thanks. I'm still getting used to the idea that you're up here digging and then this . . ."

"It does have that wow factor."

The dome was an engineering marvel. He'd half expect it to be jiggling, yet wide sloping walls allowed the wind to slide unimpeded over the shell. Like a missile, he thought as he lifted his gaze to the ceiling, and instantly saw a disadvantage in the venting above. A drop right through it would put an assault team in prime position to take out everyone. About thirty yards away, he counted two squads outfitted in white and gray cold weather gear. Hell, we could stage a coup with that many.

He looked at Ross. "Those troops should be on the outside to cover territory this size."

"Really." She swiveled to stare at Ross, then arched a brow.

"The teams make regular rounds and a night watch," Ross explained. "It's never completely dark here."

The viperous look she leveled at Ross didn't escape him. "I said we needed to be better prepared," came through gritted teeth.

"You still aren't." He didn't wait for a response, dropped his duffel, and with Max, strode across the rubber flooring toward the men. Agent Ross wasn't telling the troops the whole story or they'd be patrolling instead of sitting on their asses.

Olivia remained a few yards behind Sebastian as he addressed the troops, thinking she liked that dust of whiskers. When they were married, he was always clean shaven. Right now, he was a specter in gray and white, like the troops, but it was the way he handled himself around the equipment and tubing, with an easy grace, that fascinated her. Her brothers were that tall and not nearly as agile as Sebastian.

Agent Ross moved up beside her. "He's not what I expected."

She turned her head to look at him. "You will give him the reports on the other section tracking that call to Noble's phone." She hadn't forgiven him for that. She'd swear he was raised in the NSA, he was so miserly with information. Especially when he was supposed to report everything to her. "Your neglect was instrumental in Noble's kidnapping."

He flushed even redder. "McGill has said as much. He's looking into that personally." Ross sighed hard. "Look, Olivia, I know we haven't always seen eye to eye lately."

She scoffed, watching Sebastian. The squad was standing at attention in a line in front of him. Ross couldn't get them off the chairs. "You don't believe, that's your problem. It makes you a bad choice because a love of history, most especially the obscure, has to be a requirement. They have it, you don't." She waved at her team working over delicate equipment with the expertise they were hired for. Them, she trusted. Ross, about as far as she could throw his skinny butt.

She looked at the papers, the official seals, and thought, Sebastian's been damn busy and she needed that expertise now. "He's got an Alpha One clearance, and has more than enough skills." She met his gaze. "If he says we need more protection—"

"I'll get it, I swear."

"I know you will." She smiled brightly. "Or you could end up right back here." He'd stick around for a couple days till Sebastian understood the ropes.

Ross rolled his eyes. "God forbid. How can you stand the cold?"

"I grew up in Minnesota, Ross. Don't you read the dossiers?"

"I read his, or rather the parts that weren't blacked out."

Her gaze snapped to him. "Excuse me?" She glanced briefly at Sebastian as he gestured to the vent in the roof that was about twenty feet wide. Max was inspecting equipment, ordering the table and chairs collapsed and stored. Two pairs split off, jogging east and west, while another climbed the scaffolding to the roof.

"Blacked out as in Black Ops. Don't get too comfortable around him, Olivia. That"—he nodded to Sebastian—"is a very dangerous man."

To her heart, yeah, she thought and almost laughed. Almost. Ross didn't need to know their past, and since joining NSA, she had a fair idea just how hazardous some of Sebastian's tours of duties were and why they were covert. Noble captive, people dead, and yet no one else thought there was a darker threat except Sebastian? Dangerous was good.

"I feel safer already," she said when he was within earshot.

He smiled gently, hitching the pack and scooping up his duffel. "Outstanding." He winked. "We aim to please." His gaze slid to Ross. "They're used to taking orders, not suggestions."

Ross reddened, and Olivia hid her smile, moving between them toward the living quarters. "Let me assign you two a cube." She inclined her head. Sebastian spoke to Max over the PRR. Ross rushed ahead to find warmth somewhere.

"Excellent, gonna give me a look at your hole in the ice?"

She met his gaze for a long moment, then said, "It'll blow your mind."

"Baby, you've already done that."

She blinked, then smiled, her laugh infectious as they walked to a walled section, then down a corridor fashioned from tarps. Sebastian pulled off his glove and touched the flexible wall. Lightweight, sturdy, and taut. It was easily collapsible, he realized, in sections about fifteen feet long and just as tall. The corridor was wide enough for them to walk abreast.

"We get to be test cases for a lot from R&D," she said, noticing. "That's a metal alloy fabric, like Kevlar. It's heavy enough not to snap with the wind, which can get irritating."

And the reason it shielded from satellite, he thought, glancing as Agent Ross dropped off. He followed Olivia around a corner and his brows shot up at the accommodations. A good thirty white boxes probably ten by ten lined a portion of the habitat walls. They were the type the military used for satellite surveillance and air traffic control on deployments. Push it out of a C-30 with a parachute and it could be up and running in minutes.

"Home sweet home, for a while," she said, stopping at the last three. She punched a key pad and the door sprang. She leaned against the frame, and inclined her head. "Yours."

He looked inside. It was a friggin' bedroom, with storage, climate controls, and thermal bedding. Even a microwave. "That's some pricey equipment. Who pays for all this?"

She gave him a cheesy grin. "Think of us as the pork in bills."

He laughed shortly, tossed in his duffel, and she gave him the code, another for Max, labeled the units with their names, then led him back to the center of the dig. She pulled off the fur headband, and fluffed hair the color of toasted nutmeg. For a second, he saw her naked, that hair hiding some of her best parts.

She smacked his arm, blushing. "Stop that."

He chuckled under his breath, and said, "How does the U.S. fund a dig on Danish territory?"

"They can't afford to excavate and don't want to. This kind of digging is expensive, more than a land excavation. We want to do it, and most of the team are Danish nationals."

"How'd you get a gig like this, Livi?"

"I was on my first dig after earning my doctorate. In Iraq of all places, before the last invasion. I'd uncovered a relic thought to be the Spear of Longinus."

"The Roman staff that pieced Christ's side. It wasn't?"

"No. Right time period, but not Roman. It was stolen from the dig and well . . . I recovered it. It turned out to be a ritual sword of the Hashashin so it wasn't a total loss. NSA paid me a visit and brought me in." She stepped over massive tubing piped to the center of the habitat. "What'd you think I'd be doing?"

He shrugged. "Digging, just not at this magnitude, but I shouldn't be surprised." She looked at him. "Your curiosity is a dangerous thing." She'd needed to know his secrets, his missions, and at the time, she couldn't understand then that knowledge would make her a target. He'd bet she did now.

"Ready to see where it took me this time?" She flicked a hand toward the giant hole in the ice. "We're all about the theatrics here." She crossed to a metal shelf filled with equipment and gathered gloves, boot spikes, harness, and a keel of rope. She tossed half at Sebastian and started rigging up. He buckled the harness and tied the belay line as she walked to the boardwalk, hooking herself to the anchor.

He peered over the edge. Strings of lights glowed deep inside the pit. "That's got to be a hundred feet."

"One thirty-three, so far. The platforms will be used for bring up the artifacts. We avoid using them to get them frozen in place. Stay close to the south wall." She went over the edge. "But this will be fun, for me at least. Even though the legend is there for anyone to find, I haven't been able to show this part of it to anyone except SSU."

"Well, rappelling into an ice cave is a first for me." He swung around and pushed off, taking short hops. A curl of icy air swept up from the spiral of ice. Sebastian zipped his parka. "Like crawling inside an ice cube."

"When we get down there, if you feel light-headed, there are those." She pointed to the row of small oxygen tanks no larger than an aerosol can anchored to the ice wall about ten feet down. "Take a hit, it will clear the fog. With the ancient ice melting, the sulfur dioxide is dangerous at this level." She adjusted her footing. "That"—she pointed to a focus heater—"melts the ice and the tubes draw out the water. Another for exchanging the air. While we try to filter, it's not possible to purify it with each level. The techs take a sample reading every foot. That's what the climatologists are playing with up there." She poked the air above her head.

"You'd rather be sitting down there with an ice pick."

"Oh, yeah, and I will be soon."

Sebastian checked his watch. "Tango three, report," he said, adjusting the PRR for second.

"*All clear, sir. No movement for two miles.*"

"Roger that. Drac?"

"*Got them in four-hour shifts right now. A second squad was at the power station. That cush gig is o-vah!*"

"Roger that, buddy, make 'em wish for boot camp." He signed off, smiling. Max was a drill instructor and could kick troop ass in gear, A-sap. Olivia stared, not frowning, just sort of studying. "You're never that quiet."

She blinked, then smiled. "It's interesting to see you this way." She waved at the PRR. "In case you haven't guessed, I've had an awakening in the last decade or so."

He winked. "I gathered that."

"I'm glad you're here and in control of security."

"I don't want to be anyplace else, and bossing you around, well, that's just an added benefit." Noble's kidnapping was over far more than a diary and something stuck in the ice, but he kept that to himself. The Russian tattoos and smokes were just a little too close to Mills's rescue to ignore. The sonar case was the kicker. "Show me your playground."

"Just keep an open mind, okay?" Olivia inched lower, and he noticed the air change a little. "The legend says that a thousand years ago a child was stolen from the shores of Ireland by Vikings. She was taken as payment for the loss of the Viking's son, who'd died in battle. She lived in his household as a slave, yet the Viking grew to love her and adopted her into his family. In Iceland, I believe. We've found Celtic markings there, but can't confirm the origins."

She shifted a step carefully, and he was aware of the depth below them. He didn't trust the strength of the wood platforms or the ice.

"Now, as the child grew, the Viking understood he'd taken something precious from Ireland, a princess."

He smiled slowly, working the rope. "How romantic. But then, women ruled in Ireland a thousand years ago."

"I don't think the title was warranted by that, but because she had some unusual skills. She was a shaman, a sorceress, for lack of a better word. His village grew afraid of her and she asked to return home. He took the long way. I guess he didn't want to let her go." She shrugged, and lowered a few more inches. "With two ships he sailed, but not to Ireland. He took his trade route to China."

"Vikings in China, what's your proof?"

"Oh there's plenty." Her smile was full of anticipation. "In Tarim Basin in Xingjiang, they discovered mummies dating 1800 BC, blond and blue eyed."

Sebastian frowned, moving farther into the dark ice. "Those could be Germanic tribes."

"DNA sequencing says Teutonic and Celtic. The garments found with a family of ice mummies was woven from wool from Ireland." She stopped, looked at him, securing the rope. "It was the first find of Celts in China. On the Chengdu Plain, they found Scandinavian artifacts of the Bronze and Iron Age as well as in Siberia. Vikings were a busy bunch. You have to give them credit, raiding marauders till about 900 AD, then they used the fear factor to become traders. Real capitalist." She turned and walked backward on the platform. "It gets a bit steep here. Careful."

"You found this legend in China."

"A reference. Viking symbols, runes, on a stone sarcophagus in Jimaisu. Manchuria province," she said when he frowned. "The Viking traders went farther than we suspected. The ships were wide with a shallow hull and they could traverse rivers."

"But the Viking symbols don't prove an Irish legend in China."

"True, but it was the origins of it. This woman made

enough of an impression for the Khan to include her and the Viking in his tomb decor which was only unearthed two years ago. There was a Celtic endless knot carved. I'll show you the rubbing, so yes, it's not just a folktale, the legend is true." She pushed off and let a few inches of rope slide through her gloved fingers. "The markings on the sarcophagus tell of a long battle for some sacred relic. The emperor's people had been slaughtered for it and he wanted it gone."

"Why not just destroy it?"

"Apparently it couldn't be destroyed." At his doubtful look, she just shrugged. "I don't make the story up, just fill in the blanks." She shined her light on the walls, frowning.

"So what was the relic everyone's so hot to get?"

"That was the big mystery. The monk's diary says it's a sphere, but there wasn't any other mention of it anywhere that we could find." She studied the walls, the pumping equipment, her spikes in the ice keeping her from twisting. "We didn't know it even existed till the diary, and there wasn't any solid reference of it till I found markings in China on the emperor's tomb. The khan called it *di nény ér*. A changeling. In Chinese that could just mean people who were different from them or just growing old, but in most cultures, it means a spirit inhabiting a child's body. The legend stretches too far for it not to have more substance." She lowered a few more feet. "The Chinese emperor insisted she take the gift with her, far away from his land enough to send along a ship, Manchurian soldiers, and an assortment of bling for their trouble."

The elf and the giant, Sebastian thought, a strange prickle working over his skin. It was *real*.

"They sailed to Ireland with it, but something happened, the murder of the Maguire's potential brides, I'd say, and she sent the gift away with her adopted father."

"No more story?"

"Not exactly. We're here."

Sebastian looked down. "Holy shit." It was a cavern of ice so thick it looked blue, the walls sweeping elegantly back and like an offering on a plate of ice was a massive wooden ship. He looked at her, then back to the dig. "It's the Vikings."

"I hope it is, or I'm gonna get a really big bill for all this." He glanced, smiled. "We've retrieved enough to know the period coincides with the legend. The mast was removed first. Even the sail fabric was still attached."

Sebastian slid closer, and could smell the decay, the chemicals in the melting ice. "How much longer till you reach the deck?"

"About six hours," she said, studying the walls, the water collected and forced out the tubing.

"Are you going to excavate the whole ship?"

"No, too dangerous. There are cracks all through that ice." She pointed out a deep one. "Chunks can fall without any stress. As long as the weather holds, we can study it. We're not excavating any farther than the deck. But do you see that?" She focused her penlight on the bow and Sebastian could see the outline of a body trapped in the ice, perfectly preserved, yet lying as if sleeping. "I'm hoping that's the Viking chieftain."

Even from twenty feet above, the deck of the ship showed oars, kettles, and more ice mummies. He looked up; the surface was a good eighty feet away and the walls were slick. He could feel cold air swirling inside the cavern, keeping the wall frozen, he supposed, but was just damn awed by the ship below. "Jesus, look at the size of that broadsword." It was thrust into the deck at an angle and he imagined the Viking using it to keep himself standing. "What's your theory on how this got here?"

She tipped her head, thinking. "Blown off course, maybe. Paleoclimatologists say it was a season of big storms then. They were coming home. Maybe to Iceland, Svalbard Norway, or Greenland."

"And the *Aramina* log Noble bought?"

"It records the last sighting of this ship above the ice floe. The *Aramina* sailed near these shores and her Portuguese captain saw the vessel trapped in the ice. He made a note of it in his ship's log with the coordinates by the stars."

Sebastian's featured tightened. "The Russian has it, Olivia. They know this exists."

"Another reason I'm glad you brought more guns and the chopper. The *Aramina* log was the third reference in a pilot's log of the sighting." She shrugged, then heard her name. She craned her neck to look past him to the surface. "Yes, Cruz?"

"The air needs to be replaced and I detect shifting."

"Which side?" she called up.

"Your left," he said after a moment.

She twisted, her feet braced on the wood platform, her body nearly parallel with the Viking ship as she spied her light over the walls. "We need to get out," she said. "No one has been in here for a couple days. You first."

"You're the boss." Her soft snicker followed him as he worked his way back up, securing himself though it wasn't necessary. The scaffolding and platform were strong, not even shifting with their weight. But then, it was in ice that was melting. He thrust himself onto the landing, then reached for her as she stepped onto the wood platform.

Her boot spikes caught and she flung forward. Sebastian grabbed her and swung her away from the opening. She was sandwiched against him and his body practically moaned.

"I planned that," she said.

He smiled back. "Ross doesn't know about us, does he?"

"No, no one does. I'd like to keep it that way." She stepped back, unlocking the boot spikes and stripping off the harness. "I'm not embarrassed, but it's a small group, young, they like to tease." She returned the gear to the racks, then faced him "Ross thinks you're too much of a badass to be around." Her expression said that amused the hell out of her.

"Good. That little puke needs his clock cleaned for being a slacker."

She smothered a laugh. "Don't hold back now, tell me how you really feel."

His gaze slid over her incredible body in thermal slacks

and a turtleneck that fit so well, he could tell she was cold. "Really want to know?" He rolled in the ropes.

"I think I have a good idea." She moved in closer, keeping her voice low. "Wild monkey sex in a Vegas penthouse for starters." That memory slammed through him, stirring him in all the wrong places, and he groaned. "Ooo, that's a familiar sound," she added even softer and he wanted to take her somewhere dark and attempt to re-create it.

"Behave," he warned when Cruz approached.

"I'm glad you're here, Sebastian. Some people take too many risks." He looked pointedly at Olivia, and she made a girly eye-rolling face at him. "Speaking of which, I need to take your stitches out of your bullet wound."

Sebastian swung a look at Olivia, brows high. What the hell was she doing lately?

"Mention that again and I'll revoke your security clearance," she said through gritted teeth, and Sebastian smothered a bark of laughter he knew she wouldn't like. "Just what do you *want*, Cruz?"

The kid flushed, leveling a pleading look to him. "Hey, your stew, man."

"I thought you had that whole protect the civilians vibe going," Cruz shot back, "Because she needs it."

He moved alongside Olivia. "You need to get to the point, DeGama."

Cruz sobered instantly and looked at her. "I loaded the flash drive and scanned the monk's diary into your PC."

"Thank you. I need you to go through it, and look for commonality." Cruz hurried away. Olivia spoke softly, and explained that she was in the manor to pick up a flash drive Noble had left behind. "It's copies of his research. His note with the diary said to follow the traders. I'm praying whatever he wants me to find is in those files. If these people are doing all this to find the relic, then we need to find it first so we can bargain with it to get Noble back."

Sebastian doubted that's all the Russians were up to, but that she'd give up what would probably be the find of the century settled a warm comfort somewhere in his chest. But then, he knew she would.

"From what Noble told me, its significance wasn't in the artifact, but the danger it presents. Think about it. Wars fought over it, then paid to take it away, and it couldn't be destroyed? I think the Chinese emperor called it a changeling for a good reason." He met her gaze. "They were terrified of it."

TEN

May 5, 1175

I met a most curious woman this day. Whilst taking my morning walk and as well, my daily conversation with you, my lord, I was drawn to the cliffs. I find where water meets land with such anger oddly stirring and this occasion was not without its merit. I watched for a measure of time, then made to return to the monastery when I spotted a small group camped beneath the trees on the old ruins of a manor house. I cannot recall the name of the family landowners, but its defense is left to the chieftain, the Maguire. It was the reunite's peculiar ensemble that brought fear and reservations. Aye, my lord, I did not offer my presence. Cowardly, mayhaps, but how can I serve here if I'm dead and at your side?

I happened on the smoke from the fire first, and found a man standing far from it. The fellow was astonishingly tall and wrapped in leather and furs. He carried a shield on his back and didn't take a single step without his sword. I have never seen such a weapon. It equaled my own height and was most certainly difficult to wield. Yet 'twas his stature that startled, more so that it forced him to bend to speak with a much darker, fierce looking man from the East. If you'll recall, my lord, I had met several such people near Prussia when I was much younger. Few understood their manners or the curiously long queue of hair that fell from the top of his *head to nearly his middle like a horsetail. Yet his garments were regal, the fabrics rich, and even from the distance I could see the sparkle of golden embroidery.*

I shall admit to only you, my lord, that when they noticed me, I was afraid. We stared for a moment so long I felt my heartbeat against my bones. As is my vow, I sought out a possible disciple to bring into your flock. When I walked toward them I heard soft murmuring atween the odd pair, but could not understand the language. I was nearly abreast of them when the tallest with light hair shouted at something over his shoulder. From the forest stepped a woman. A beauty. You did well, my lord. She is lithe and graceful, almost floating over the land. Her escorts parted and she beckoned me closer.

I will confess, as you already know what occurred, my lord, I feared her as well.

Olivia tried to imagine this fabled woman with hair that swept the ground. She read on, the monk's observations wonderfully descriptive and even kind to the woman and her entourage. The monk had visited her twice more before he saw her in the mountains and followed her, the sneaky man. She tried to imagine his life then, his daily toil. He wrote of the mundane duties, the final rites he'd given, and his duties of preparing the dead for burial. Pretty glum, she thought. Bet that princess was as exciting as it got.

She flipped past the list of duties, the blessing of a child to one of his flock, and searched for a mention of the murders. The date was a month later.

Whilst the unusual reunite has made no trouble, nor asked aught of the villagers, they live still in the ruins, as if waiting for something. The rash of crimes against many has brought the Maguire and this woman to a heated battle of words. He lays the blame with her. She is bold, her captivity with the Norsemen obviously having an ill effect. She spares no words. Most especially for the Maguire.

Ahh, there was a romance waiting to happen, she thought.

My sin is that in indulging my curiosity to visit with this pagan female, I have witnessed the most unusual and quite extraordinary events. I am still feeling the tremors in my hands as I pen this. I cannot understand my own reasons for following the woman again, but I feel commanded to learn what she and her odd family are about. Why have they come?

I observed the woman they call simply Cat kneel on the ground, I thought in prayer, but then she began digging in the dirt. For a time she used the blade she always carried, but she was patient, at one point, she removed her cloak and turned back her sleeves. She would allow none to assist her. The ground had been churned. By animals, I suspect. Several paces behind her, the Viking stood, his sword piercing the ground. It was coated with blood. He did not watch her dig but studied the forest surrounding us all.

Then from the earth, she pulled a knot of fabrics, and with her reunite of protection she returned to the campsite. Most especially, her adopted father. I cannot fathom any man, English or Irish, besting the Norseman, Jal, in battle. I have yet to see a soul confront him and I admit, my lord, I feared they knew I observed them and kept further back than I was wont. I do remember feeling suddenly refreshed and stronger for I returned near the campsite afore they arrived. This day was full of moments I do not understand. She crossed to the fire that never seemed to die and unwrapped the cloth, layer by layer. Her lips moved in a silent prayer to her deity. She lifted out a round green object large enough that she gripped it with both hands.

I neared for a better look, aye, when I chose to disobey the laws of God, I am wont to excel. It was fortunate then, for she held the object higher, nearer the fire's light. I confess my breath escaped when I understood 'twas in the shape of a human head, yet green. 'Tis cut from a stone, I have decided, for I have seen gems in the Holy City with that soft, milky hue. The lady placed it carefully on the remains of the old well. Then I heard her speak.

For the protection of these people or the man who leads them, grant me the power. She raised her arms and spoke to the heavens in a language I'd heard a village elder once use. Imagine my surprise when the lady's delicate hands glowed with long tips of blue fire. Aye, my lord, fire. Thrice, she circled the stone, repeating those words, then stopped and threw her hands toward it. The light grew suddenly blinding and not even my fears, they were surmountable I assure you, nay, not even that could make me look away. She had cut it in half. I do not question what I have seen with my own eyes this day. Without sword or mace, the woman severed the stone cleanly. I know, for I saw the two halves fall to the ground. My legs could no longer hold me and I fell like those stone halves and remained so until I no longer felt I might expire. I swear to you my lord God in Heaven, I speak only the truths I have seen. It was incredible to witness and I will keep my own counsel. To speak of this to anyone is heresy, aye, but to know such power exists has certainly altered my perception of all things. Aye, my lord, including you. I understand You gave such a wondrous talent to this woman for her life has not been joyous since she was stolen as a slave. All she loved has forsaken her again.

She wrapped each piece of stone in the fabrics whilst chanting to her Goddess and bound it with chains. Then she handed one to her adopted father, Jal, the other to the small man from the East. Both men secured them into their baggage, then turned back to the woman. From her satchels, she drew a long strip of dark blue cloth. The dye alone was costly, yet I recognized this piece. She had worked her needle on it and the silver thread shone. She placed it around the neck of Zhu, the leader of the eastern men. He did not kiss her, nor embrace her, but dropped to his knee and bowed. She touched his dark head, and he rose and turned away. The woman sobbed quietly as the others bid her farewell, then walked the path to the sea and their ships. Only the Viking remained. His immense stature was now hunched with the burden of his loss of the woman he loved as his daughter. She touched his face, kissed his cheek, and then from her girdle, offered him a scrap of a tartan no larger than her hand. He took it, kissed it once before tucking it beneath his garment and breastplate. Then he wrapped her in his arms. His furs obscured her face, yet the pain was clear on his own. My heart ached for them.

Olivia sniffled and searched her pockets for a tissue, and was about to use her damn sleeve before she found one. She blotted her eyes and wiped her nose, feeling sad for Cat. To be so alone.

The lady stepped back and I heard Jal asked her, Where shall I hide them, my sweet? To which she responded, You must choose for I am well tired of this rock and would leave it on the ocean floor. Travel south as far as you dare. Find a land with no people and place it back into the earth. Keep your vow, speak of it to no one. He nodded his accord, his eyes cool as he looked her over from head to the tip of her boot, then turned away. She remained there, watching the Viking leap into the boat and shout orders to the scurry of Zhu's men. She did not leave until they were a smear on the horizon, then turned back to her fire, sitting on the rock and warming her hands. She was alone now. Without friends or loved ones. Why did she not leave with them?

Come, Monk, she said to me rather loudly. You linger like a thief and I know you are not. I was shamed for intruding on her privacy and she beckoned me again, more gently. I stepped from behind the tree and walked to her. She gestured to the fallen log and I perched opposite from her. What was that? I asked.

Know that the stone is the reason the wolves have changed. I shoulder the blame, for I am the one who brought it to Ireland, and with my own hands, I buried it in the mountain. I have taken it back. She stared at me over long. Aye. Curious, eh? It has a humming that calls to the living.

But not to you? I asked. She shook her head and the chime of trinkets and bells laced in her hair made me smile. I saw you. Did I not? When she nodded I asked the single question that plagues me still, How did you cut the stone? You know well, Friar. You have watched me from your little haven. She pointed to the path from the monastery. I felt the flush of my own shame and spoke what I dared not repeat to a soul for it would mean this woman's life. You are a sorceress.

Nay. I am me. I know only this woman. She swept her hand down her length. Do not judge what even I do not understand. She stood and walked away, but I felt her frustration as it were a cloak in the summer. I can do no more than wield the elements, Friar. I cannot change a mind, stop a rock from falling. That treasure, I cannot destroy it and naught can harm it. Thousands have sought it and died for their greed of it. She kept her gaze on the sea. I will never see him again, will I?

Mayhaps. The world, I have learned this day, is never as it really seems.

She made a disappointed sound. Of all things, dear Friar, I know my fortune was never to find peace.

She did not appear sad about it. I offered the only counsel I could and told her my thoughts. Peace often comes to us when we understand what we need to have it. Mayhap happiness has not graced you for you seek thus in the wrong places? She smiled then, laughed bit at herself and me. We enjoyed each other's company and I am most heartened by her candor. I have never met a female with this woman's intelligence and free will. She is ruled by no man, no faith, or society. She is Eve in the purest form.

We sat long into the night, and I listened to the tales of lands she had visited with her father. Those places have shaped her. Then she entrusted me with the story behind the glass orb she has named Siofra. Show-fra she teaches me and she says 'tis the Irish word for changeling.

Olivia felt a chill slid over her skin that had nothing to do with the arctic temperatures. The changeling.

She read further, little checks going off in her head when she recognized parts of the legend she'd already learned. Emperor Jin, the princess told the monk, was a very old man, with many concubines and offspring full grown. Yet to her estimation, he appeared but two or three years senior to the princess. *She saw this most precious stone in a guarded room of its own. No men stood near, their duty given to mongrel dogs as big as a man. She admitted to me she feared those animals and insisted they were not of this earth any longer.*

Like the wolves, Olivia thought and read the paragraph again. She looked up from the diary on her lap to the flat screen as if the digital version would give her a clue as to where the Viking went with the relic. Follow the traders, she thought again. Norsemen were traders as well as the Spanish, Portuguese, and English. Heck. Traders were all over Ireland then. She looked down at the diary copy. The princess sent it away with the Viking and his trade route would have been all over the map. She glanced at the clock, anxious to get back inside the site, and hoped the excavated remains would tell her where they'd been.

She opened Noble's flash drive, then split the screen with the images. One by one, she opened a file and searched its documents for the fifth time. She frowned until her face hurt and after an hour, she'd closed two. Her eyes burned and she rubbed them, mumbling to herself. "I'm trying, Noble. Hold on." She looked up, flinched at the reflection in the screen, and twisted in the chair. "Make some noise next time. Jeez." She covered her heart.

"Sorry. It's the rubber floor," Sebastian said. "Shouldn't you be digging?"

"Dana and Kit are lifting out what we've excavated so far. We need the preservation tanks set up first." She wished they'd done that while she was gone, but waved him closer, opening Noble's leather book. "I think I figured out why this sphere was so coveted. We know it's made of jade or alexandrite by the color and it heals enough that it reverses aging. I think it's the equivalent to the fountain of youth."

"Then why send it away?"

"Apparently its effect isn't the same effect on everyone or everything." She lifted the translation, her finger keeping her place. "Especially animals. The monk describes the stone as a skull with eye sockets and a mandible." He scowled. "I know what you're thinking . . . crystal skulls, aliens, and special knowledge stuff, but most of those were fakes, the bane of archaeology, but the monk says it wasn't smooth. Now I'm trying to understand where Jal and Zhu might have gone with it."

"You know their names?"

She lifted the translated diary. "Cool, huh? The Friar never mentions his own name, but he liked to talk. Great detail. It's a bestseller."

"It's mine next," he said, then eyed the screen. "What's all this? That's Noble's handwriting." He pointed to one document.

"It's his backup. No diary though, but lots of copies of antique trade papers." She opened a scan and narrowed the focus. "He said follow the traders and I'm not getting very far."

He studied the screen. "Yeah, you are," he said, then searched for the mouse.

"It's a touch screen." She left the chair and waved him on. "Go ahead."

"Man, all the bells and whistles in this joint." He sat, tapped, enlarging two documents. "It's not ships' logs, they're trade invoices." He glanced. "A list of what people bought or traded from the traders." He pointed one out, enlarging a digital replica of a fragment from a merchant's pay book. "It's Spanish. Four sheep, three female, one male, traded for pelts of white fox fur. Norwegian blue fox, maybe?"

She hung over his shoulder and smelled his aftershave, distracted for a second. His face was next to hers. "*Roos*, the name for Vikings in the Middle East and Spain. It's dated five months after the monk wrote about it. It's possible it was Jal's."

"Where were these found?"

She thought for a second. "That one, in Cadiz."

"Wait a second." He studied the files. "Chaucer's House. That's where he listed his e-mail on his computer in his house."

She frowned at him curiously. "You misbehaved, didn't you?"

"All the time, baby." Sebastian opened the file and spread the e-mails, then sorted by date. "These are old, four years old. Why would he keep them?" He opened the last one, read, then studied the most recent. "Rut roh." She nudged him, smiling. "I think the leak is Noble."

"No way, I'd swear to it."

"Not intentionally or recent." He leaned to read for a second. "He's corresponding to a running conversation about the Maguire's princess. Before you recruited him."

"I knew about that. He was up-front. He was on a discussion board, a couple blogs. Like I said, the legend is there for anyone to find. We just happened to find the Viking's ship and the diary."

"This e-mail address originates in Russia."

"Yes, I know that." Her brows knit. "What are you getting at?"

"The guy with the tattoos, he's Spetsnaz, darlin', and if you think the NSA snoops, try the FSB on for size. Someone has seen these on the other end."

"But there isn't any conversation in three years. It's a dead issue." She inhaled, her eyes going wide. "Before Noble was kidnapped, someone called him offering to buy the *Aramina* log. The call was from a number U.S. intelligence was monitoring already." When he scowled blackly, she cursed. "I'll kill him. I told Ross to tell you this morning. He said he couldn't find out who or why the call was on a watch list."

"Then it's beyond his clearance," he said. "But I'll find out. Did you learn who this sender is?"

"Gregor something, a Russian national. They didn't exchange personal information, only a lively discussion." She touched the screen, right clicked, and matched the e-mail with Noble's address book.

Sebastian opened his phone and spoke to Safia. "I need anything you can find on a Russian, Gregor Nevolin."

It was a moment before she said, "*I can tell you he's dead.*"

His brows shot up and he put her on speakerphone. "Dead. How so?"

"*The name's familiar because he was the captain of a Russian nuclear powered fast attack submarine, Akula class, that went down in the Bering Sea. Russian authorities pretty much blamed him, though I don't recall more than that. So what's up?*"

Sebastian recalled the news reports of an explosion aboard, all hands lost. That was the FSB version. "Noble knew him by Internet contact." He gave the details, and mentioned the monitored phone number. "They were discussing the legend. When did the sub go down?"

"*About three years ago.*"

Sebastian's spine stiffened. "Mills and his wife were listening to the airwaves then and Vince was aboard a submarine somewhere in the North Atlantic."

"*It's what they heard, too,*" she said, catching on. "*Then maybe you need to look at those Sat photos I sent you.*"

"Will do. Call ya back." Sebastian unzipped his Gore-Tex jacket and walked to the other end of the communications room. Like everything else, it was state of the art, big screens and superpowered. Most of the computers were for scientific use, the three in here were NSA linked. He sat at Ross's computer, glad the guy made himself scarce. He was nice enough, but pretty much out of his element. A slacker, he thought, and earlier, he'd spent a half hour deleting games the agent had loaded on a classified computer. What an ass, he thought, and brought up the photos. Safia sent several and he was about to call her back when he noticed the time and date stamps. Each group was a year apart and he pulled them all up, moved them side by side, then called Safia. He put her on speaker. "What am I looking at? It's all trees and mountains." He spotted the river, but not much else with all the snow.

Olivia inched around the edge of the partition, and he beckoned her closer. She pulled up a chair beside him and studied the screen.

"Look at the base of the mountain where the bombs dropped after we escaped with Mills. Near the river."

Safia gave the exact coordinates and he typed. The focus narrowed. Olivia pointed, and he felt his skin tighten along his arms when he recognized a nose cone. The next photo, taken seconds later—from a surveillance drone maybe—showed the outline of that nose cone along the riverbank before it went under.

"Jesus. It's a submarine."

"Oh yeah. I think it's where they built *and launched it. I've gone back over sats and all the work had to have been done at night. I've got spots of lights, headlights maybe, but those are the only twilight shots that show something. It's not at a known military facility, possibly a Stalin-era bunker, but you don't have to be smart to get that they did all this against the NATO arms treaties and right under our nose. That's why they destroyed it. I'd bet good money Beckham was in Chechnya looking for that subfactory or the sub and got too close. Moscow cleaned the trail."*

"I don't doubt your theory. Those MiGs showed up too damn fast. Someone was watching that area before we showed." With the exception of the few men they encountered on the way to the prison, everyone was dead before they arrived. Erase the trail, leave no proof, he thought. He rubbed his neck, a headache brewing. "So the Akula class that went down in the Barents Sea is the sub that launched from Chechnya."

"Timing is too good," Safia said. *"Nevolin was stationed at Ana Bay, but wasn't officially assigned an Akula boat. In-*

cluding the one that went down. That's an alarm, Russia doesn't have that many skilled captains just hanging around. Whatever sent it down didn't matter, blaming Nevolin was FSB being expedient."

He remembered the story from the Russian's failed attempt to rescue the crew. He looked at the images. "That nose cone is smaller than the Akula class. It would have better maneuverability. But if that sub went down, why is Beckham investigating it now?"

"Secret factory and secret sub, breaking about ten UN statutes, not to mention NATO treaties, what do you think?"

He smirked to himself. "With all this maneuvering, it was loaded for war, but I give the Russians credit. Good snow job."

"The E Ring knows about this, Sebastian. The question is, when? Price was a big mover in Moscow then. She had Kremlin contacts, KGB hard-liners, corrupt as hell. My bones say she covered this up or we'd have known about it before Chechnya."

"Oh hell yeah."

"We need to send this to Deep Six."

"We work for McGill, and to them we're shut down. Send your intel to McGill, give him your theory, too, but he'll handle the Pentagon. He knows how to use those stars." In Venezuela, McGill practically wore the shine off them for Logan's wife, Tessa, when she was infected with a virus.

"Roger that. I owe him." When Safia was active, she had constant intel feed in the field, all from McGill sitting in the CIA director's chair for a few months. Safia said something, but her voice faded out with a hiss of static.

"We're going out of satellite range," Olivia said. "You can use the net for about ten more minutes, but we're blacked out for the next twelve hours."

He closed his phone. "That would have been helpful to know." Then the dome lights suddenly lowered.

"Quitting time, too," she said. "If we didn't keep a day-night schedule, we'd all go slowly nuts." She smiled, then looked at the screen, the images of the blue-gray nose cone. "What's going on, Sebastian?"

He stared into those wicked green eyes and knew he wasn't going to hide anything from her and not because of her security clearance. He told her about rescuing Mills and being shut down, and finished with his feelings that Dragon One was set up to take the fall for Beckham's screwup.

Typical Olivia, all she had to say was, "You can disarm a *bomb*?"

Deep Six
Satellite Intelligence

Mitch rubbed the bridge of his nose with thumb and forefinger. His eyes burned from reading page after page of intercepted transmissions. It was a waste of time and while David was running it through the computer, Mitch searched through intelligence on Russia's arsenal and came up empty. It was constructed in the mountain and when he got too close, they bombed away the evidence. Though at the time, he didn't know they'd actually built it. He needed a chat with Lania Price, he thought when he heard his name. He looked at David. The kid was a little pale.

"Transmissions from Vince and Anna Mills are a match."

He stood, grabbed the cane, and walked to the main console. "It doesn't surprise me."

"Mills was aboard the USS *Bowman*, and at the time, traveling under the polar ice cap when they intercepted a distress hail."

"Under the ice?" So they really wanted Mills for what he'd heard. Then he remembered Mills's sonar was designed for arctic temperatures. Now we're getting somewhere, he thought. They wanted both.

"It's Russian, and I should mention that all this"—David waved at the screen flowing with listening-post data, satellite images, and dossiers—"was around the same time that Russian submarine had a reactor mishap and went down in Barents Sea off the Russian coast." Mitch scowled. "The transmission interception was *after* the *Bowman* broke through the ice in Greenland, sir."

A hard chill worked up from his bones. Fontenòt was in Greenland. He'd flown Dragon One's behemoth of a cargo jet there. After that, nothing. Not even a car rental. He tapped a key and held the headset to his ear, translating in his head.

The distress hail was standard for Russian. System failure and he thought they said gyroscope, and if that was screwed up, it would be hell to navigate. Reactor problems, possibly, the captain said, unable to move, but the transmission stopped abruptly after a minute. "That's it?"

"The commander of the *Bowman* tried to hail them again and offer assistance, but the Russian naval command claimed it was in Russian territory and they were handling it. Three ships went to the location, but I'm having trouble swallowing that story."

Mitch made a rolling motion.

"It's not possible for the transmissions to be that clear under the ice unless the Russians were there at the same time as the *Bowman*."

"A Russian sub went down, the Akula class." He glanced at his notes. "The *Trident*. Seventy-three men died."

David was already shaking his head. "I'm sure that's true, but that transmission interception wasn't even close to where the *Bowman* broke the ice to pick up that signal."

"Your theory? I know you have one."

"Our subs don't go under the ice cap from anywhere near Russian territory. They skate by the Bering Straits on the way *out*. But it's slow going because there's some big curve of underwater ice to navigate. Russian subs are out there since they always try claiming the north pole as federation land." He snickered to himself as he brought up a map of the arctic. "U.S. subs, say out of Newport, drive up Denmark straits, then go deep north of Iceland near Svalbard." David traced a line from the U.S. East Coast, along Greenland to the white ice just south of Norwegian territory, Svalbard.

It was another fifteen hundred miles to come out on the other side in the Bering Straits, taking over a month, but that's not where the intel insisted the transmission originated. He'd been on subs numerous times as a Special Ops detachment. He never got used to the feeling of being in a tin can and on a sub, the teams left the boat out a torpedo tube like Jonas spit from the mouth of a whale. He honestly admired submariners. It took guts to live underwater for months at a time, especially going under the ice cap.

"The exercise is completed maybe once every couple years and it's more to test the crew than whether it can be done. It can be, just takes a great sub captain and crew and we have them in spades." David's smile fell a little. "But navigation is the real problem. Arctic water distorts radar and communications. Especially at that depth. At certain points in the crossing, they are running without any outside link." David shivered. "A floating coffin. The *Bowman* didn't get a clear transmission." He nodded to the printout that was at best a third of the transmission. "But arctic listening posts got it. The problem is, if the *Trident* was sending a signal the *Bowman* could pick up when they broke the ice, it wasn't in the Bering Sea. It was on the other side of the world, somewhere on Greenland's coast."

In launch range, he thought. Big-time. Mitch threw down the headset, then reached for the phone, dialing Gerardo. While he waited for the pickup, he walked closer to the screen, tapping it to focus the satellite imagery. Arctic water distorts sonar and transmission signals, repeated in his mind, and he thought of the sonar Dragon One was certain the Chechens were after. Mitch admitted they were right. But even as he heard the Gunny say she'd put him through, he realized it was entirely possible that Mills's kidnappers were trying to pinpoint where that sub was last. Moscow really didn't want this getting out—enough to drop a bomb and kill about ten thousand Chechens.

"Sir," he said to the general. "I think its time we paid a visit to Leavenworth."

"*Perhaps you should come to my office, Major. There's been a development.*"

"On my way, sir." He hung up and headed for the elevator, then darted back for the cane and his cell phone. "David, if that sub was nuke powered, then there'd be radiation, heat, something."

The kid frowned at him. "But the report said reactor trouble. I doubt it would be giving off anything to register thermal in that water."

"Try. News reports came from FSB, a twisted truth is a given, buddy. If it wasn't the reactor, then it would still be running and show a hot spot." A minor one if it was deep under the ice cap. He stepped into the elevator.

David turned back to the screen and before the doors closed, Mitch caught, "If it is, there's your reason for global warming."

ELEVEN

Aboard the Icebreaker Northern Lion

Noble lay still on the bed, fighting the groggy edge lingering from the drugs. Days were lost to him. He'd seen no
faces till he woke inside a crate, for God's sake. Buried alive,
he thought at first, and was thankful the bunk above him was
folded back into the wall and lashed. He glanced around,
lying still. He'd slept with no idea of how long. There were
no clocks in the cabin. The engines still rumbled and he felt
the speed of the giant ship pushing through the water.

Destiny unknown, he thought, throwing the covers back.
He sat up and swung his legs over the side of the bunk. The
air was frigid and he rubbed his arms, pulling the blanket
from the bed and wrapping himself in it. The room wasn't
large, but without windows and one way out, adequate for a
prisoner. He tried the door first, then walked to the small
lavatory, grateful for the single comfort. He splashed water
on his face, rubbing his chin and wishing for a blade, but
knew there would be none. He investigated just the same and
found cold-weather clothing in the drawers. *For you, Dr.
Sheppard* was written on a slip of paper. He considered refusing anything from these people, but his own ripeness had
other ideas. He showered in lukewarm water and was shaking violently by the time he pulled on the heavy cable knit
sweater and a second layer of socks. He rubbed his hands,

thinking of his family and friends and what they must be feeling now. Olivia must be going mad, he thought, then warned himself not to dwell on what he could not change. He was still alive and surviving was his only goal. He searched the cabin again, finding more toiletries, but little else.

Wrapped in the blanket, he sat in the only chair before a small collapsible desk. The man with the blue eyes wanted the diary translation enough to kill that poor young bellman. The moment was forever etched in his mind: the two men dragging the boy in the hotel room and killing him so quickly he didn't scream. He'd obeyed from then on, not that they gave him an opportunity with all the drugs since. The hour or so before coming aboard was only the second time he wasn't in a pickled stupor. He wasn't educated on ships, yet thought it was an icebreaker, and considering he'd heard a little Norwegian, maybe ported out of Iceland or Norway? It didn't matter. Trapped at sea was the invisible fence. The water temperature alone would kill before you could fight it.

The door lock rattled. A young man entered with a tray, setting it on the desk without sparing a glance. "The commander wishes you to eat and wants to know if you need a doctor."

He didn't speak and only shook his head. The crewman left, but not before Noble noticed the embroidery on his dark gray shirt. A silver trident. Beneath it was Russian, and translated, he thought it meant People's Justice. His hand bore the same mark though much smaller. Neptune's trident was not an uncommon symbol for the sea. He looked at the tray, drawing back the linen. To say he was surprised was mild. Steam rose from the lobster tail, beside it a steak as thick as his thumb. Ply me with pleasures, he thought, so he'd recreate the diary. He'd understood that from the moment the blue-eyed man realized it was gone. He had to be useful or he'd be dead.

He cut the steak and ate, confident that Sebastian would not fail him. Nor would Olivia and General McGill. NSA did not go to such great lengths to hide the diary and dig to have some renegade Russian female infiltrate. He'd only glimpsed the decks to know he was aboard an icebreaker stacked with gear and all covered with tarps. An expedition, she'd said. But to where? For what? Logic said they were searching for Ice Harvest, and his uncertainty gave him little hope. The ship's log, if they understood it, would point them right to the dig.

He felt measurably restored as he pushed the plate back, wishing for something to read, and considered napping again when the door abruptly opened. He tensed when he saw the woman. Lizveta Nevolin. Gregor's daughter. There was nothing gentle about this beauty, he thought, noticing the bundle under her arm. She looked decidedly different than when he was first brought onboard. Her blond hair was loose and falling over one shoulder. Her dark blue slacks and turtleneck belonged at a ski lodge in the Alps. But Noble understood instantly. Soften her appearance to soften him.

He'd known the girl's father a few years ago and only through Internet conversation. Gregor was passionate about the legend and they'd shared theories before the NSA had recruited him, but when his correspondence stopped, he'd searched, and only then, learned he captained submarines for Russia's Nordic fleet. His death was a tragedy, and Moscow had blamed Gregor for the explosion that destroyed the submarine and all seventy-three lives. Or so he'd read in *Pravda*. A scapegoat, perhaps? His daughter didn't grieve quietly, vigorously defending her father and his crew in the press. She gained a gathering of outraged Russians. Then abruptly Lizveta Nevolin disappeared from the news and went into seclusion. Some speculated she'd been permanently silenced. The party deemed her harmless and grief stricken.

Not a wise choice obviously, he thought, and his gaze followed her as she inspected the cabin. He considered himself an observer by nature. Living in New Orleans near Bourbon was always a treat for people watching, especially from his balcony above his shop. The reason behind a person's behavior didn't often present itself, and he watched her inspect the room. She tried for grace and failed, her moves too rigid, methodical. Yet he had the feeling this was the Dr. Jekyll to the Ms. Hyde he'd met above deck. He'd accept her threats as truth, and let himself be lulled to learn what the blazes she was going to do that was worse than murder.

She finally looked at him, clutching a small computer notebook and a familiar linen bundle. "How are you feeling, Doctor Sheppard?"

"Captive."

She gave him a polite smile. "I have brought this for you." She laid her stack on the bed, then unwrapped the *Aramina* log.

"A thief returning the booty. How generous." Being lulled had its limits, he thought, then noticed the long knife sheathed at her hip.

"Doctor, I'd hoped we could work together and share our knowledge. I think you'll be interested in the pieces my father had found."

"What do you want from me, Lizveta?"

Her gaze sharpened on him. She didn't like him using her given name. "To repeat the translation, of course."

"If you know of the monk's journal, then you certainly understand that's impossible." A lie. He'd read it so many times he knew it in reverse. "It's hundreds of pages and not a single word in it is worth taking lives."

"I have lost people as well."

He made a sound that was just not rude enough. "Your *people* killed a nineteen-year-old bellman, for God's sake. Please don't imagine I give a damn."

She pawed the rope of hair spread down her chest. "But you did care about my father. He liked you, Noble. I read your correspondence. I have followed you and your work since his death."

He frowned, and assumed she'd gone through her father's estate, yet following him? He'd have spotted it, and he wondered where she was going with this.

"After he died, I found his papers on the Irish legend. He

had told me the story a few times, but I had already chosen to carry on his research." Her heavy accented English was textbook precise and monotone. "I went to Ireland and visited the castle ruins." She met his gaze. "The excavation was under way and I saw the archaeologist unearth the diary from the altar stone."

He would have liked to have seen that and tried not to let it show.

"When the discovery did not appear in the news, I understood it had value for its contents." She shrugged lightly, then sat primly on the foot of the bed, her hands folded on her lap. "A few inquiries, and I knew the eras coincided. I envy that you have read it." She paused, staring as if he were transparent. "My father's notes are here," she finally said, touching the notebook computer beside her. "As well as scans of his personal collection. I think you'll be interested in a letter found in a family Bible that not only mentions the legend, but its origins in Manchuria."

He tried to school his features. Other than the monk's story, the tomb was the only reference to the changeling relic. He knew he didn't hide his surprise when she said, "A Russian in China is not a problem nor was learning of the excavation there," she smiled thinly, "perhaps eighteen months ago."

That will irritate Olivia, he thought, trying to keep her involved. "What did you learn?"

"That Emperor Jin was desperate to free himself of its yoke and gave his most hunted prize to the Irish woman with the Viking father."

Noble wouldn't confirm or deny. Olivia was in China last he knew, proving just that, but the monk's words agreed with Nevolin's. "Interesting that you followed that path."

She eyed him. "You study the legend same as I do and my father did."

"I do, but the diary is only one man's reflection of a story." You are simply racking up the lies, he thought. In his own archaic way, the monk had been decidedly accurate in his interpretation.

"My father had spent many summers searching for it. I never understood his passion for the legend. He was murdered before he could share it." She stared, unblinking. "I seek the gift the emperor gave her."

Something inside him went still as glass, and he frowned.

"The jade stone."

Good God, he thought. She or her father deciphered the legend enough to know the relic was jade. However, only the diary mentions it being cut in half.

"The meaning behind this?" She gestured to the log lying on the mattress. "The captain of the *Aramina* guided by the stars. How strange that I found an entry that points, I believe, to Brønlundfjord." She opened the log and lifted a ribbon where she'd marked her place, bent over and pointed. "Come, read this, Doctor."

He didn't. He knew what it said or he wouldn't have bought it.

She glanced at him, arching a thin brow. "I know who cares about you. My men have been to your bookshop and your daughter's house."

Noble felt his gut wrench at the threat and he clenched his fist. "I'm a kidnapped American, the FBI is with her, looking for you and waiting for a ransom demand."

"One that will not come. How long will they remain with her?"

"Point made." She stepped near and his skin crawled. He wasn't in a position to antagonize her, but did not doubt the capability of NSA or the FBI. Or, thank God, Sebastian and his friends.

"I know of your partner, Doctor Corrigan. We believe she has the diary now."

"It doesn't matter, it's gone. Move on, Lizveta." Giving her even a shred of information was dangerous. The diary would not lead her to the jade stone. Only Ice Harvest could.

She stood and walked the small circumference, then stopped with her back to the lavatory door. She folded her arms, her feet spread, and he thought, there is the viper he met above decks. She shrugged, but it was not a casual move. "No matter. I do not need it, Doctor. I have you now."

"That's not your good fortune, Lizveta."

Her name made her tense, and she grew more agitated, almost hyper as she pushed away from the bulkhead and paced for short steps. "There is only one remarkable entry, Doctor. The *Aramina*'s captain says he has seen a ship trapped in the ice. Is this true?"

"Your man stole it before I could read it." Though he was surprised she'd translated the Portuguese, he wasn't going to lead her to Ice Harvest. Yet as she stepped near enough that he smelled her flowery perfume, he knew she would not suffer his stalling.

"Know that if you do not cooperate in every way, I will simply find those you love and kill them."

"This is how you honor your father's memory, Lizveta? With threats?"

She slapped him viciously. The sting exploded through his cheek and made his eyes water. He turned his head and met her gaze. He'd sworn his duty, but that didn't mean he couldn't re-create a lie. He'd given her enough of them to start. "I will do whatever you want."

She let out a breath that didn't seem to calm the rage in her eyes. She stared, her fists white knuckled, then suddenly she was inches from him. Noble leaned away, but she grabbed his hand and with surprising force, flattened it on the desk. Before he realized what was happening, she drew a knife and brought it down on his hand. Pain rocketed up his arm as a segment of his little finger rolled off the desk to the floor. He screamed unrestrained, and clutched his hand to his chest, trying to stop the bleeding. The woman crossed to the lavatory and tossed him a white towel.

"Are you mad? I can't use my hand now, woman!"

"Do not deny me again, Doctor Sheppard. Complete the

diary or you will lose more." Nevolin walked to the door and paused only to collect his fingertip in a handkerchief. She met his gaze. "It is your only purpose here. You have eight hours."

The door closed and Noble slumped in the chair, applying pressure. He swore foully. The woman was savage in her grief, he thought, and three years had stripped compassion from her. He read it in those black eyes. She would kill before admitting defeat. He adjusted the towel, his arm throbbing. He had to keep her from learning of Ice Harvest and he was only guessing that she hadn't searched the *Aramina*'s star coordinates on a current map. He recognized the uneasy feeling slipping up his spine. Lizveta Nevolin possessed the exact location of Ice Harvest and didn't realize it yet. God forbid when she did, he thought, looking down at the bloody bundle in his lap.

After a few minutes, the bleeding stopped, but the pain was excruciating, and when he thought he'd pass out, a young man entered the cabin. Without speaking, he dressed the wound, injected a drug to numb it, then collected his first-aid bag and left Noble alone. But the depraved smile on the young man's face was enough to make him turn to the laptop and start it up.

Find me, Sebastian. Whatever her purpose, it's twisted.

Ice Harvest
2400 hours

Sebastian couldn't sleep, and the endless daylight had little to do with it. The longer Noble was with Nevolin, the more the scales tipped against him. Safia had a lock on the *Northern Lion* since Svalbard, and he kept wondering about the sonar and why Nevolin needed it desperately enough to kidnap Mills. But his biggest concern was that the *Lion* was heading south, toward them.

He tipped the cutting board and slid the diced onions into

the pan, then shook it gently. It took him about two minutes in the mess hall to realize that sound traveled inside the dome. Other than the sizzle in the pan, the only sound was the chug of the equipment sucking melting ice through a tube. Everyone was sleeping except for him and the duty watch.

He cracked a couple eggs into a bowl, whisked, then added it to batter. A moment later, the griddle puffed with pancakes. He glanced up at a noise and saw a figure moving in the dark. A second later, Olivia was showered in light. A surprise, since she'd worked like a madwoman today to keep up with the approaching winter deadline.

"Evenin'. I thought you'd be comatose." She was inside the dig for twelve hours with few breaks.

"I'm just a little sore." She waved it off, tightened the belt of a really thick robe, and shuffled closer. "Nothing some good drugs can't handle." She moved nearer, a little sluggish, her boots unlaced and the rest of her wrapped in layers of fleece and flannel.

"You look cold."

"I am. I only get this way at night and that's because sleeping in my thermal suit isn't recommended."

The thick shirt and slacks she wore under her clothes, he realized.

She took a seat on the steel counter a few feet away and looked from the pans to him. "I'm still shocked you like to cook that much." She studied him for a moment. "Your mother taught you, didn't she?" He nodded. "She was a great cook."

He stacked pancakes on a plate, then slipped it into a warming oven. "A couple of her specialties are on the Craw Daddy menu."

"Let me guess, Gracie's Damn Hot Shrimp, conch fritters, and . . . cinnamon glazed beignets."

He grinned, oddly pleased she remembered. "On the money, honey. I like to think she'd be happy it was open again."

"She would. Gracie loved feeding people."

"Good food, and some zydeco music, make people happy. Cooking is relaxing for me. Not much different from mixing explosives." He poured more pancakes.

She scoffed. "Somehow I doubt that."

He met her gaze, smiled. "Yeah, but it's still cookin'." He flipped a pancake, then from another pan, lifted the bacon onto a paper towel. "When Mom died, Jasmine was alone, barely legal age, and too wild to be unsupervised. God, she was a handful." He shook his head. "She was angry with everyone, including me." He started another stack. "The house was falling apart around her, and Mom's restaurant wouldn't pass a health inspection without being gutted." He shrugged. "Noble kept her in line, but she wasn't a juvenile. When I got out, I renovated everything. I have the mortgage to prove it . . . then gave her a job and home."

Her brows shot up. "You left the Marines then?"

"I was on hardship leave, then—yes, I did."

An uncomfortable silence pushed between them. His constant absence was the biggest hurdle between them then. Like a peace offering, he held up a strip of bacon.

She ate it quickly. "You planning on eating all that yourself?"

He flipped pancakes, shook the pan of sautéing veggies. "No, for the troops." He pointed to the ceiling and she looked at the scaffolding, but couldn't see more than the Marines' boots from here. "How about one of Gracie's omelets?"

"With onions and cheese?"

He laughed to himself and pointed to the large fridge. "Work for it." She hopped down and a second later, brought him a massive bag of cheddar.

"I love to eat, just wasn't excited about cooking."

He glanced at her as he whisked a half dozen eggs. "You were better at other things." The instant it was out he knew it was a mistake.

But she just smiled brightly. "I'll take that as a compliment, since my ego could use one." She pushed her hair back, and glanced at the the chaos of knives and bowls and the simmering pans. "Clearly there's more to you than I got to know."

"Not really." She watched him make the omelet, encouraging more cheese and leaning over the pan to catch the aroma.

"Bullshit. Bombs, a pilot, a chef, you've been busy."

To keep from missing you, he thought, then jumped to flip the omelet. She gathered plates and silverware, and he plated up the omelet with a side of pancakes and bacon. He set it on the counter, then kicked the stool closer. "Chow down, rebel." She met his gaze, her lips curving and a playful glint in her eyes reminding him of the last time he saw it. It involved sweaty skin and about every surface in their little apartment. "God, Livi, don't look at me like that."

"I have a certain look?"

"Yes, and you damn well know it." He pulled her off the stool and that was another mistake. Despite the layers of flannel, she was like a heat-seeking missile; everything in him was attracted to her in a big way. The layers of flannel and fleece didn't make a damn bit of difference. He knew that body too well to forget. "So behave." He pushed her into a chair when he wanted to kiss her senseless.

"Only because we have an audience," she said, then took a bite. She moaned. "Your mother would be *so* proud."

Smiling, he touched the pad on his throat. PRRs were rigged for voice activated. "Tango One, Chow is on."

She barely glanced up as the Marines worked their way down the framing. "Fabulous, Sebastian." She tasted pancakes, bit into the bacon. He took a seat beside her. "You're not having any?"

"Had four pancakes while I was cooking them."

"When this is over, I'm coming to New Orleans to see your place."

"You're always welcome."

She went still, the fork halfway to her mouth. "I never thought I was."

A crook of her finger, and he'd have come running, willing to risk the heartache all over again. The noise of the Marines put the kibosh on anything further.

"Save us anything, Doc?" Recker said.

Sebastian hopped up to grab the food out of the warming drawers.

"Hey, I have four older brothers. I know it's get in here first or you guys leave nothing behind." She shifted on the stool, snuggling into her robe, sampling the pancakes. He heard her mutter, "They're light and fluffy carriers for butter and syrup." She dunked a piece and he noticed she'd scratched her arm while she ate.

"Your stitches itch?"

"Yeah, they're only three days old, no, four, but I'm mad at Cruz, so they're still in."

"I can take them out for you." Her gaze swung up. "Or Max, he has the training."

"He's sleeping," she said, then looked at the Marines hovering over plates. The serving platter was nearly empty.

"We won't be missed," he said lowly and she left the chair, heading to her cube. He grabbed the small medical kit from the comm room and joined her. She hit the keypad and the door popped. He followed her in, glancing around at the simple décor. Everything had a place, neatly tucked in a wall of cubicles, but he could tell a scientist occupied the room. There were bone samples in bags tacked to the wall.

She took off her robe and sat on the bed while he searched the medical kit for scissors and forceps. She tried rolling up her flannel pajama sleeve but the wound was too high. "Oh, hell," she muttered and unbuttoned the top. He arched a brow. "Not like it's all unfamiliar." She pulled her arm free as he sat on the bed beside her.

He glimpsed the rounded curve of her breast. "My memory is excellent." He started cutting the stitches.

"So's mine." He met her gaze and she wiggled her brows. "We had some fun, didn't we?"

"God, Livi, don't go there."

Her expression fell, and she stared at her hands. "I'm sorry. It must be hard to be around me, let alone work with me."

He caught her chin, tipping until she met his gaze. "No, it's not. Being with you is as comfortable as it ever was. It's keeping my hands off you that's tough."

Her lips curved in a slow smile and she looked relieved. "Who says you have to?"

"God, do you have to be so honest?" He didn't expect an answer and pulled the last stitch free, cleaned the tiny dot of blood, then applied a bandage.

"Then you'd know I'd be lying." She slid her arm back into the pajama top, then pulled a down blanket over her shoulders. "Thank you."

He replaced the tools and snapped the kit closed, then started to stand, but she grabbed his arm, pulling him down.

"If you don't kiss me right now I'm going to attack you."

"No."

She arched a brow.

"A kiss isn't enough. It never was."

She gripped his jacket, pulling him nearer, and he saw the mischievous glint in her eyes. "But it's a good start." Her face neared, her gaze lowering to his mouth, then meeting his gaze. "Or are you afraid of me now?"

He scoffed. "Afraid I'll drown myself in you."

Her mouth brushed his and she whispered, "Man overboard."

He sank into her, into her mouth, and like a thousand times before, the sensuality between them didn't have levels; it rocketed straight to lush excess. He took her mouth like a man dying of thirst, his arms slipping around her and under her top. She moaned, a dark sultry sound that ignited him in several places, and when she pulled him with her as she fell back onto the bed, he went eagerly. His mouth trailed her throat, then lower. Olivia wasn't shy, and flipped a button, then another. His hands slid beneath and closed over her bare breasts.

"Sebastian," she said, her warm little hands finding his bare skin beneath his clothes. He nudged the flannel aside, exposing her lush full breasts, and Olivia encouraged, "Taste me."

He did, his lips closing over her nipple. She gasped, arched, offering more and he indulged in the taste of her, the smooth feel of her skin. The little sounds she made were just more fuel for the fire, and he covered her mouth, silencing them. She responded wildly, her kiss mauling, drawing him tight as a bow. Then she tore at his Gore-Tex jacket, the layers of sweaters and shirt.

"God, you taste good."

"And you do that so well," she said as he laved at her nipple, tugging, and slid his hand down her hip and between her thighs. She spread wider, and he was about to touch her more deeply when a knock echoed in the cube. They went still, and he met her gaze.

"I'm gonna beat whoever's on the other side of that door."

He was, too, and it made him realize the dig was not the place to start this. Not with the close confines and everyone knowing each other's business. He pushed off her, then went to the door, glancing at her before he opened it. Her disheveled hair and the hint of bosom was enough to give him a dangerous hard-on. He gestured and she buttoned up, but not before she flashed him. He chuckled, shaking his head, then opened the door.

Max stood on the other side. "Second watch, I'm on it." His gaze slipped past to Olivia sitting on the bed, his grin telltale with amusement. "Carry on." He chuckled as he walked away. "Cuz I know you will."

Sebastian shut the door.

"Okay, that was a little embarrassing."

"This isn't happening, not here." He flicked at their surroundings. "Not now."

She looked crestfallen, and fell back into the pillows. "I have no dignity around you."

And he had no restraint. But Sebastian wasn't certain he

wanted anything temporary with her, then knew he didn't.
Old heartache kept him cautious. When it came to Olivia, he
had only so much willpower in his arsenal. "Try to behave,
Doctor Corrigan. You *are* the boss."

She tipped her chin up, her green eyes daring him. "But
being bad is much more fun."

Smiling, he shook his head, opening the door. "G'night,
Olivia."

Just before he closed it, he heard, "Sweet dreams."

Sweet? Not a chance.

Ice Harvest
0900 hours

Photographs, grids, and readings were done and Olivia savored the single moment as she stepped on the freshly constructed wood platform one hundred thirty feet below the
ice. It stretched over the deck of the Viking's ship and she
didn't fight the tears blurring her vision. Finally. She hadn't
slept much, the anticipation waking her. That and the sub
thing Sebastian was checking out. She didn't really understand how something in Chechnya three weeks ago mattered
to Ice Harvest, but he'd find out. Noble was hostage for
whatever she'd find in here.

The ice cutting was slow when the average temperatures
were below zero inside the cave. She didn't feel it, her thermal suit keeping her toasty. Fine tubes of some liquid she
couldn't name ran through the suit fabric and worked with
her own body heat. A little warmth went a long way in that
liquid conductor, and she loved that she got to test it. She
could see the use of it in lots of cold-weather gear. Inside the
ice cavern, it was quiet, the occasional slurp of water being
sucked through the tubing, but other than that, she could
hear herself breathe. Heat was direct and water immediately
drawn out. The air was circulated every hour without anyone
inside because it created a pudding-thick fog. She shined her

light into the far recesses and she imagined the Viking's crew struggling against an ice storm, unable to maneuver away from shore as most mariners did then.

She looked up, the roping to her harness flopping loosely as Dana and Kit prepared to come down. All three of them would catalog samples for testing. The technicians above were champing to get more than bits of dirty ice under their microscopes. She was happy to oblige, and knelt, turned up the lights, then set the timer. The equipment produced heat and they would excavate in two-hour intervals, allowing the temperatures to remain frigid. The entire surface of the deck had an electronic grid set with lasers. Not a single stream hit the ice and it had taken her half her dig time to get it right. The laser levels were feeding data to Cruz above, including the seismic sensors, and he'd re-create it in CGI. The guy was a genius, but he didn't know what he was missing, she thought, glancing at the supports and platforms before she pulled long tweezers from her tool vest. She got close to the deck and the light on her helmet showed the grain of the aspen and spruce. She used her rope system so she could lean out and not fall into the Viking's face.

"Hello, Jal," she whispered and simply held there, staring at the long hair that still held its yellow shade. Gently, she pried his cloak apart, the rankness of decayed wet fur making her slide up her mask. She'd passed two layers of animal skins before she found fabric. She slid a frayed thread free and bagged it. Then she found a leather string around his neck and worked it free. A small purse hung from the end. It had weight and she tipped it. Moldy coins slipped into her palm. Coins and pebbles, she thought, bagging it as well.

She moved to his feet and took a scraping from his boots. Cruz could analyze it and tell her where Jal had been. It took her over an hour to tag the surface artifacts, and she moved to the Chinese warrior nearly flattened around the broken mast pole. He was face out, his body bent from the pressure of ice. It was sorta gross seeing a human body that way, but she was interested in his queue, the long braid of hair. She worked it free, feeling perspiration on her upper lip, and stopped.

"You must be Zhu," she said when she recognized the emperor's symbol on the clasp anchoring the braid. It was still dark despite the burn of freezing temperatures. The mummy was dressed in layers of clothes and she gently peeled back a level and almost screamed when she saw the stole embroidered with the never-ending Celtic rope. Her heart pounded. "Yes, yes, freakin' yes!" She wiggled a happy dance.

"*Doctor Corrigan*," came through her personal role radio. "*Come to the surface, now, the ice cave is shifting.*"

She looked up. Dana and Kit were on their way back up already. "I don't feel anything." Just the same, she pocketed her tools, worked the ratchet to bring herself upright, and stood on the new platform. "Which side?"

"*East, the water side. Don't risk it.*"

She started climbing back up. "I'm coming up, I swear. How big a shift?"

"*Forty percent!*"

Oh God, she thought, moving faster. "Are you sure? Check it again. It's stable down here." She shined her light over the interior that was more than forty feet wide. It looked more like a cavern now with arches cut into the ice to support the tremendous weight. She could see the sensors implanted every five feet to detect any fracturing. Olivia hoped it held off and strained to hoist her weight, the walls too hard to gain any traction even with her spikes. She aimed for the next platform. Then she heard a soft crack, and spied her light around. Above her was the slanted end of the three-foot-wide platform fastened into the ice. The anchor bolt had worked itself out. I can fix that, she thought and worked the ropes. She reached for it, but could barely get her gloved fist around the bolt. She climbed higher and with her feet together, aimed for the bolt to push it back in till the engineer could repair it. She pushed off and hit it, feeling the smack up her legs. The anchor didn't move. She pulled on the rope, swinging free in the center. Her arms trembled. The air smelled fetid and she reached for the oxygen canister. She couldn't and grabbed the rope, pulling.

"Cruz. Get some muscle and pull me up, will you?"

She'd barely taken a breath when the platform broke free.

Sebastian shifted his position on the dome roof, and sighted on the blinding white horizon stretching to blue water. The *Northern Lion* was somewhere in the Greenland Sea with Noble aboard. With a killer. Safia was tracking, and all photos were running through their database. He was impatient for a hit. He was interested in the woman running the show because the Spetsnaz was bowing and scraping to her and that just didn't sit right with him.

The wind barely cut across the dome and he felt the warmth of the sun. Not even forty, though he'd bet Max was feeling every degree on that snowmobile. He'd sent Max out with two Marines for a spin around the neighborhood and see what was near. Satellite images didn't mean much when everything was covered in snow and ice. Behind him was land so green it looked like velvet, and he turned in a slow circle back to the horizon.

The Marine beside him checked his watch. "Two hours to de-Rossing time."

Sebastian smiled. He'd fly Ross out of here in an hour or so, McGill's orders, and none too soon. The man had a way of pissing everyone off, the troops especially. The young devil dogs considered him no more than a pencil pusher and not physically fit enough to be out on the Arctic Circle. Sebastian thought the guys were just glad to be busy instead of loitering.

He felt a shudder in the soles of his boots and looked down the scaffolding. Like something hit it, he thought. "You feel that?" He glanced at Collins.

"Tremors, happens a lot, sir. We're on an ice island."

"I guess I need to learn more about archaeology, huh?"

"We got a lesson from Doctor Corrigan, sir." He smiled

tightly. "We're at the mouth of a fjord. It's big, lava, and a mile or so long. The Doc said that's why they have only a short time. In the winter, the upper ice floe shifts, and puts pressure on it, then." He shrugged, "It just folds into the sea. Like with the Viking ship, I guess."

Sebastian went back to inspecting the horizon, thinking that digging in the ice was just nuts, but admired her for it.

"Tango One, be advised, there's trouble in the pit."

Sebastian looked down through the scaffolding to the giant cave in the ice, then started to work his way down. "What's the problem?"

"There's been a shift. Doctor Corrigan's in trouble. She's not answering her PRR."

Sebastian kicked into high gear, swinging out to the scaffolding poles and sliding down like a fireman. He rushed to the dig. "Back off, everyone who does not need to be here, go. Esposito, Collins, my six, A-sap." He looked around at the equipment, grabbed a keel of rope, then stepped into a harness and linked himself up. He shined his light down.

Oh Jesus. Olivia dangled on the rope line like a dead fish on a hook, slumped and not moving. Below her was the jagged point of the broken mast.

Three Marines showed.

"We need to secure that platform first. Belay me and I'll rig it so it won't go anywhere before we get her out."

Cruz appeared, Ross beside him. "She's not responding."

"That's cuz she's knocked unconscious." He kicked his boots into ice spikes and latched the straps.

"Be careful," Cruz said. "The sensors say stable, but I don't know for how long."

He nodded, waiting till the Marines had the rope behind their backs and feet firmly in the ice. Two others stood by to pull Olivia's line and prepared with another rope. He tested comms, then went over the side. Sebastian descended the first twenty feet rapidly and the Marines slung a rope down. He grabbed the end, securing the platform and sliding the rope between the slats. He looped a knot, then radioed to pull up the slack and secure from above. He let a few feet of rope slide through his fingers and called to her. She didn't move, spinning in the air over the Viking's ship, the mast pole a few feet below her. He suppressed his impatience and lowered methodically, stopping at eye level. He secured himself, then reached for Olivia and tipped her head up. Her pulse was strong, but her helmet was badly dented. He pushed it back and touched the bit of blood on her widow's peak and trickling down her forehead. He steered it away from her eye.

"Olivia, talk to me." He patted her cheek. "Come on, *cherie*, wake up." She blinked and flinched, her feet working wildly, and he grabbed her, locking her legs with his. "It's okay. You're okay. Be still."

She met his gaze, tears working to the surface. "This time I *asked* for help, damn it." He smiled and hummed the Indiana Jones theme. "Oh, please." She laughed shortly, though her death grip on his arm was cutting off circulation. Then he heard a sharp crack.

She looked somewhere past him, then scrambled to pull herself up the rope. "It's going to fracture," she said. "We have to be careful. It could crack more."

"Why you want to work like this is beyond me," he muttered to himself, rigging a secondary safety line.

"Oh, this from a bomb disposer guy?"

He chuckled, and secured her with back clip, then looked up. He gave the loose line a tug. "Look alive."

"*Ready to hoist, sir?*" came through his PRR.

"Heave away." He needed to keep her still as the Marines hoisted them up the tunnel of ice. Yet Olivia wasn't buying that, inspecting the walls as they went.

"There's a lot of cracks that weren't here yesterday."

He frowned. Her speech was a little slurred, and he grabbed the mini oxygen tank and made her breathe through it. It was a minute of short pulls till they reached the top platform and her foot touched. She grabbed the scaffolding anchors. Sebastian was behind her and she kept slipping, then cursed like a sailor, jammed her spike in the ice, and flung herself over the rim. A Marine dragged her from it, then offered a hand to Sebastian. Topside, he straightened, then winced when he heard noise in the dig. On her stomach, Olivia looked over the edge. Triangle-shaped chunks of ice fell, fracturing the platform over the ship.

"Shit!" She smacked the ground, dropping her head forward for a second, then scooted back to unclip from the rope. She looked ready to explode, he thought, removing his harness.

He patted a Marine on the shoulder. "Thanks, guys. Appreciate it."

"About as exciting as it gets out here, sir."

Esposito handed him a bottle of water and he drank, watching Olivia angrily strip off her equipment, then her helmet. She inspected the dent as she stood, then touched her forehead. She stared at the blood on her fingertips and Sebastian heard her mutter, "Oh for pity's sake," before she used her thermal suit for a rag.

He was just glad she was okay. She didn't seem to care she was almost impaled on a stick and he definitely didn't want to feel that fear again. Digging in the ice was more dangerous than he first imagined.

"Everyone back off," she said. "No one goes down." Her team didn't look happy about that. "Shut down the melting, Cruz. Bring the temperatures back up and recycle the air. We're either going too fast or we're in for a jumpy day or two." She called over two women and an Indian man about thirty and discussed diagnostics. She gave orders like a sergeant major, he thought, and when she was alone, he crossed to her.

"My hero," she said a little breathy. "Thank you."

"Shucks, ma'am." He smiled, inspected her cut. It was minor, from the inside of her helmet. Suddenly, she gripped his jacket, pressing her head to his chest. He frowned, ran his hand down her back. "Olivia?"

"I'll just be a sec."

He smiled with tender humor, feeling her sway. After a

moment, she tipped her head back. Her eyes looked a little dreamy still.

"I was sweating down there, and I shouldn't be. Those bolts were eighteen inches long. No way they could work out of the ice. It took a shotgun to get them in." She stepped back, then sank to her rear, and grabbing the mini oxygen tank, she inhaled.

He sat beside her, checked her eyes. "You're the expert, darlin'. Hypothesize away."

"The walls aren't slick, it's not melting. It's blue ice." When he frowned, she said, "It stays below forty degrees. Cracks, chunks falling, happens often enough, and this isn't my first dig in the ice. No one does it because it's dangerous."

"Then you've got to look for what's changed. Something's heating that ice."

"Not from in there." She flicked at the hole. "We have alarms that tell us of any change in temperatures, shift in the ice. They extend around here for about two thousand yards as a warning system for seismic activity." She pulled her gloves back on and stood. "We're at the start of the Gakkel Ridge— it's under the ice—a mountain ridge stretching twelve thousand miles to Siberia," she explained. "Granted, it's a deviating tectonic plate, but shifts only about a centimeter a year." She shook her head as if to check it off the list, then suddenly turned and met his gaze. "Could be a hydrothermal vent."

Geothermally heated water bubbling through a crack in the earth's crust. "Not unless there were a few dozen vents, I can't see that doing damage to a glacier. Not at these depths."

"You're right, it shouldn't. I'm going with seismic activity." She called to Cruz. "Water output levels?"

"Same as always, decreased in fact. It's not melting."

"Then it's structural. No. It can't be. To push the bolts out? The arch supports distribute weight and the blue ice shouldn't fracture—" She sighed and pushed her fingers through her hair. "I really don't have a clue."

She walked across the lab to a Poindexter-looking kid and talked with him. The glaciologist, or volcanologist, he couldn't recall. But as he neared she called for results from three scientists, then suddenly put up her hand. The talk died as she scribbled on a pad. He saw math and thought, she's way smarter than me.

Then she met his gaze, looking horrified. "It's not melting, it's vibration."

Fort Leavenworth, Kansas

Mitch sipped bad coffee and waited beside Gerardo in the secure conference room. He'd run a check-through to make certain they weren't heard. This was not going to be pleasant for anyone. Least of all Lania Price. The door opened, the sound echoing in the nearly empty room. There were two plastic chairs and a solid steel table. Not even a trash can.

Gerardo stood, smoothed his uniform, and stepped back beside him. "Your ball game, Beckham."

He glanced. "Sir?"

"Damn near dying over this puts you with the most to gain. I'm just here to observe."

Mitch had interrogated terrorists. He considered Price a step below.

"Solitary confinement hasn't softened her. I've been trying for over a year now. Have at it."

Price walked in a hunched shuffle, her wrists manacled. The guard followed closely and told her to sit. Every day of her incarceration showed on her face. Her hair was stone gray, made even more hideous with skin that looked like paper. Rough, he thought.

"Take these off." She lifted her wrists.

"You're fortunate not to be chained, Lania," the General said.

She eyed them both. "So whose ass are you after now?"

Mitch gave her a smile he didn't feel. "Today, it appears to be yours."

She stared at him, then tipped her head as if to say, bring it on.

"Sir," he said to Gerardo. "A moment alone, please."

Gerardo didn't react and strode out the door.

"That's not necessary, you know."

Mitch looked at Price. "Yes, it is." He smiled thinly, thinking of the bastards that locked him in that closet to die and how this all came back to her and what she *didn't* tell the CIA. How could they fight their enemies if their own betrayed them?

"How much did they pay you to keep quiet about the sub built in the Chechen mountains?"

Her expression didn't change, but her skin went paler. "A lot."

He sat on the edge of the table. She didn't like anyone being that close to her so he leaned in farther. "Your reason for smothering the transmission's location of where the sub went down?"

She looked away. He turned her face back and she jerked from his touch. Mitch stood and walked around behind her. He knew how to make her talk. He didn't have to prepare. She'd sent hitters after their own, killing Americans to further her stronghold in the spy game.

Within ten minutes, she was gasping for air and begging him to stop. Mitch had barely touched her; descriptive threats were more useful. He swept his index finger behind her ear and she flinched, ducked.

"Okay o-kay! It doesn't make a difference now."

"You could have saved yourself all that, Lania, but then, I think you like pain."

"Yeah well, your face looks like you do, too, Major."

He smiled and said nothing though he really wanted to smack the shit out of her. Every wound radiating under his clothes was from hunting down her lies.

She stared through a curtain of gray hair. "What do I get out of it?"

He looked her over. "A decent bath? My fist not in your face?"

"The guards do worse than that." She turned her head, her hair rasping against her jumpsuit. "Call in the general. I don't want to repeat myself."

He did and Gerardo zeroed in on Mitch. He stepped back. "Continue," Mitch said.

"Yes. Russia built a fast attack submarine. I didn't learn of it till it launched."

"The German schematics?"

"I didn't steal them," she said, defensive. "Ex KGB Vlad Dovyestoff did, with help, I'm sure. That cow can't walk a straight line. He sold them to Moscow. He's probably set for life after that. Moscow kept it quiet with threats, and did all the transporting and construction at night. It took them only seven months to build it inside a Stalin-era bunker in the mountains. It launched three years ago from Chechnya."

Seven months? That had to be the maiden voyage. "Why did you not inform E ring or the director?"

She made a rude sound. "Because it was more useful to hold it over their heads. How do you think Putin signed the SORT treaty? Or left Georgia after a month? I used it to push them out. This stuff doesn't get done with talks, you know. With the Russians, you have to be ready to take down the government to get them to agree to a treaty."

Blackmailing a government wasn't how democracy worked, he thought, but, he admitted, it was useful. "Tell us about the boat."

"It's much smaller than a Borei class, seventy-three-man complement, and it had stealth cavitations, seven pin. It's barely detectable even at full speed, and has deep submersion launch capabilities. That's the German technology. It can launch vertically without surfacing. So maybe you should ask Moscow why a submarine like that was heading toward the U.S. coastline?"

Jesus. The sub could fire and be gone before we realized the missile was in the air. And she kept this quiet? Beside him, Gerardo stiffened and she swung her gaze to him. "Reports say the submarine sank in the Bering Sea."

"We both know that's a lie." She scoffed rudely, and Mitch thought, what a vile woman. The polished CIA officer he'd met once before was thoroughly erased. She looked like she belonged at a truck stop waiting tables on the night shift. "If it did, you'd have more information. Come on, you know or do I have to say it?" She answered herself a second later. "Fine. I'm not leaving here, but this should get me a bottle of scotch, at least. Russia launched that thing with every intention of hitting the U.S. When it sank, the threat to the U.S. was gone, but Moscow didn't want us or anyone else to confirm that they broke several arms treaties by coming that close with loaded ICBMs."

That wasn't as unfamiliar as most people thought. Russian subs were off Florida's coast often. The United States stayed alert and watched. But Moscow sent three ships to the Barents Sea to investigate. It was all for show. "You're saying they falsified where it sank." That matched David's findings.

"Yes, I am. Golubev orchestrated it. Molenko executed it. Down to killing a couple of my contacts who knew the truth."

Golubev was the current head of the FSB. He shouldn't be surprised her skirt lifted that high in Moscow. "Molenko is dead." That development the CIA learned yesterday, and he suspected FSB was cleaning house, but Price's reaction was a self-satisfied smirk.

"Justice is slow this week in the Kremlin. Golubev should be next. That disgusting slob knew they could have rescued that boat." Mitch's brows shot up. "The *Bowman* was in the water then. Neither boat was down deep. The *Bowman* had just started its arctic crossing in the Greenland Sea. A rescue of the entire crew was feasible, but Moscow cut us off from helping with territorial rhetoric and threats."

"Russia attempted rescue."

"No, Major. They didn't even *try*." She sat back and crossed her legs like she was in a boardroom meeting. "Russia had knowingly broken treaties. They had to smother it, completely."

She glanced between him and the General before she delivered her bomb.

"Moscow cut off all communications *from* the sub. They intentionally silenced the *Trident*'s distress hail and let seventy-three of their own countrymen die an ugly death to keep it quiet."

TWELVE

Ice Harvest
One day later

Sebastian walked into the crooked hallway and the bite of the wind instantly lessened. Maneuvering around the tubing and cables, he pulled off his ski cap and scraped his hand through his hair. He needed to check the weather. It wasn't looking peaceful out there anymore. He strode into the dig and instinctively searched for Olivia, smiling when he spotted her near a large tank. Inside it was a frozen mummy, a short one, and he could feel her excitement from across the dig.

She looked up, smiled, and pointed to the tank. "Chinese warrior, his name is Zhu."

"How the heck do you know that?" He crossed to her.

"The diary mentions his name but a big clue is the stole," she said when he was close, drawing an imaginary line curving the mummy's shoulder.

"Well damn." Around the decayed throat was a piece of fabric and even though ice surrounded it, he could see the twist of Celtic knots.

"The monk tells of the princess giving this to Zhu before she sent them away. She made it herself."

"Looks like you have all the pieces."

"Quite a few. We brought up the cargo from on deck." Sebastian went wide-eyed and she said, "Yes, there's a crate of fabric and barrels of pepper and ginger. That says a southern route. The pressure of the ice crushed it, but some were in the ice beside it so I think maybe the ice storm was sinking the ship, or they were taking on too much water and were trying to lighten the load. There was water in their mouths. They all drowned before they froze."

"Doctor Corrigan?" She turned sharply to the excavation. "I think you need to see this."

She crossed to another archaeologist, Dana, and Sebastian's curiosity made him follow. A Plexiglas plate suspended with rope and wires rose out of the dig as a technician worked the pulleys. She'd been taking artifacts out of there for a steady eight hours. The tech swung the plate over to the metal table, and Olivia switched on the under-cabinet light, then put on a high-powered scope and bent over it. She prodded a small section that wasn't encased in ice, then went suddenly perfectly still.

She looked up, pulling off the bug-eyed scope, and smiled brightly. "It's a piece of a tartan. A small scrap, very faded when it got into the ice, and it's embroidered."

He glanced at the ice cube on the clear plate. "A Maguire tartan?"

"No. Mine." He blinked, peering closer and she said, "According to the monk, she gave it to the Viking before he sailed. She was wrapped in the tartan when she was captured. I guess that was all that was left."

Sebastian laughed to himself. "The princess was a Corrigan."

"It is a sect of the Maguires," she said primly.

"So . . . your relatives are responsible for this."

She grinned. "It appears so."

"Then I guess you *should* get the bill."

She went breathless for a second, grabbing his arm, then her laugh melted with, "Not with my bank account, for sure. But being indirectly connected is kind of cool, huh?"

"Proves you have troublemaking in your blood." He motioned her away from the finds already tagged and laid out on tables that were quickly running out of surface. "Any more shakes?" He looked at the forty-foot-wide hole in the ice.

"No, and I still don't understand it. I've been down twice and haven't seen a single sensor blink. Outside the dig we have a couple going off, but thermal say it's wolves."

"I'll check it out." He needed a visual, but before he could radio Max, Ross's voice came over his PRR.

"We have activity off the coastline. Agent Troy says the Northern Lion *is just sitting there."*

He gestured to the PRR and turned away. "Don't count on it. McGill's in Deep Six by now," he said, walking to communications hut. "Connect with him." A hand on his arm, and he turned. Olivia looked worried and he told her about the icebreaker.

"The one with Noble is here? Right here?"

He glanced. Scientists moved closer. "Let's not cause a panic." He swept his arm around her, guiding her with him. In the comm center, it was even colder and he ached for coffee and instead stood to the right of Ross. "Bring up the dossiers, will you?"

Ross typed wildly. He was good at searching data, and finally, useful. The guy had come off a year tour at a listening post in East Asia. Sort of explained his lack of social skills. With the *Northern Lion* off the coast, Sebastian canceled his leave. His butt remained parked right here, watching any and all movement. Sebastian stared at the pictures on the screen, the personal stats beside it.

"Knife guy," she said, then leaned in to read. "Dimitri Kolbash and Lizveta Nevolin." Olivia inhaled, looked at him. "As in *Gregor* Nevolin?"

He nodded. "His daughter, and McGill already confirmed the lady has a money trail in the millions and no means to earn it." He'd let the CIA learn who was backing the woman,

234 / Amy J. Fetzer

but her shopping list said she was prepared for any contingency.

"She's taking up her father's search for the relic," Olivia said with certainty. "She has the *Aramina* log. She knows something is here, or that we are."

"I think that's secondary to looking for her father's sub." He told her the latest scenario of Moscow cutting off communications from the downed submarine and letting them rot under the ice.

Olivia looked stricken, her hand on her throat. "Those commie *bastards,*" she said, looking at the screen. Radar fanned out, illuminating the dig, but nothing near it. "Nevolin's opening a wound. Wide. I can't say as I blame her."

Nor could he. But that didn't have a damn thing to do with killing innocents and kidnapping his friend and for that, he'd show no mercy. "We're looking for a hot spot under the ice."

"Hot as in heat?"

He shook his head and knew she was thinking of the bolts loosening in the ice. "Radiating. The sub was nuclear powered. I doubt the *Trident* would be in operation, but that depends on what really sent her down. The last transmissions put the sub in this area and Mills's sonar could map exactly where it was located."

"You still think this was all a shell game?"

"It's playing out that way. In Chechnya, they killed witnesses before we arrived, but the explosion would have been seen for miles. Not to erase the trail, but to bring attention. She's uses Russian mafia to do the work, then wipes the trail. She's equipped to the nines, with enough to have a rigid inflatable boat aboard." He remembered the hoist and pulley system at the stern. "I bet she has a sub under those tarps and she's going under the ice."

Olivia eyes went wide. "That's insane." She looked at the picture of the thin blonde. "The depths at those temperatures would require a specific oxygen mix and you risk dementia."

"She'd have to use a dry suit," Sebastian said. "And even if there wasn't any water inside the sub, the air would be toxic with nearly a hundred bodies aboard."

"The bitch is off her rocker," Olivia said. "She'll do anything to win."

He knew she meant kill Noble if he didn't do what she wanted.

Ross said, "In the last eighteen months, there's been a lot of ships passing by. None of them stopped except one. The *Northern Lion* sailed as far as Danmarkshavn, then turned back. That was three months ago. Can't tell more than that. Everything goes out of range up here."

It was continuously daylight through the summer months, dusk coming yet never quite reaching darkness. He was glad he lived by military time or he'd never know when to sleep.

"Separate Mills from it and it's all about exposing this sub." Price was in this to her eyeballs, and he knew she'd used it against Moscow. He glanced at the pictures still wet from printing. Price having dinner with Viva's unofficial godfather Vlad. She looked like she was holding back a barf jag, but she'd done a bang-up job of muddying the waters for the United States. "The *Northern Lion* isn't going anywhere. It's sitting exactly within the legal limit of international waters."

He met her gaze. "You need to do whatever it is you do to start getting your artifacts off the ice. Any unnecessary personnel, I want them to leave with it."

She agreed. "All but Zhu is almost prepped to go. The Viking's ready to lift. We'll keep everything we can encased in ice for transport to the university." She looked thoughtful, then said, "Transport by sleds and Sno-Cats over the ridge; after that, it has to be flown. It's not a smooth ride."

"You pick a place big enough to land, Sam and Viva will be there." He glanced at his watch. They should be at the house with Safia. Riley was on the top of the dome with a Marine. He radioed Max and warned him of Kolbash and Nevolin.

Deep Six
Satellite Intelligence

"*Vibration occurred at 1445 hours. Must surface.*"

Under orders not break cover, Mitch realized, rewinding the *Trident*'s hail recording and playing it again. He watched the counter. Two hours later, there was another hail this time, Mayday. Static then, *ice crev—prope—crush—*. Obvious, he thought and it was the fifth hail, weaker each time. The *Bowman* responded to the third one in four hours. They hadn't had much time then, and it would have been a miracle if the *Bowman* could have reached the *Trident* in time. Sinking on her maiden voyage had to be a massive blow to Moscow, and stupid for not testing its crush depth in open water. Machines had their limits. David Lorimer was jumping military satellites to use their thermal imaging for a hot spot. Not easy in the North Atlantic ice cap.

Mitch flicked on the recording of Lania Price's confession. He debated the truth of most of it, yet understood the bombs dropped in Chechnya were because he asked the right questions and got too close to the factory. The *People's Trident* sailed capable for World War Three, and when it failed, they let the military rot and branded the captain for it. Bastards. The inhuman right of Molenko and Golubev to make that decision to save themselves was an abomination. But deep in his frustration of fighting terrorists, Mitch understood whoever was opening this wound had a right to do it.

Where's that leave us now, he thought, rubbing his forehead. His brain was smoking, and he wondered what the kidnapping of Noble Sheppard had to do with all this. Snatching a scholar just didn't figure in and Sheppard's phone hadn't been used again. But if Fontenòt was on Greenland, near where the sub was supposed to have gone down, then he needed to know all about Sheppard. Gerardo was searching because he kept getting slapped down. It made little sense with his clearance, but he figured there was some politics making them wait. He looked up when the elevator opened. His brows shot high as General McGill stepped out.

He jumped to attention. "Sir. This is a surprise."

"At ease, Major."

Mitch met his gaze. He didn't look happy, nor did Gerardo as he followed him. McGill wore more stars than the last time he saw him, and Mitch figured he'd be commandant of the Marine Corps soon. He called to David and the satellite expert spun in his chair, then leapt to his feet.

"General." He threw him a huge grin. "Long time, sir. I thought you retired?"

"Christ, why is everyone ready to shuffle me off to the old vets' home?"

"If they did, you'd stage a coup." They laughed and shook hands. McGill's stern expression softened for a second. Until it landed on him. Okay, his ass was in the sling again.

"You owe my men a big favor, Major, and I've come to collect."

"Sir?"

"Dragon One. They're working for me." He offered his NSA deputy director credentials.

Shit. Oh, shit. Did he slam down NSA?

Mitch looked at Gerardo, but the man didn't offer a thing.

"So why don't we see what you've turned up since you shut my boys down?" McGill spared a dry glance at Gerardo. "You're tracking a phone number used during Mills's *and* the major's rescue in Chechnya."

Mitch felt that dig like a knife. Dragon One was McGill's sacred six and offering that he was under orders to close them down wouldn't make his case. From the looks of the brass, McGill had exercised rank. "Yes sir. It hasn't been used."

"I have pictures to go with it."

"Sir?" McGill handed David a flash drive and the tech went to his console and brought it up. Four photos popped on the screen, then four more.

"That's your caller." He pointed upper left. "Dimitri Kolbash, former Spetsnaz. We believe he kidnapped Noble Sheppard in Surrey. Chertsey police say that phone was used outside Sheppard's hotel. He is partnered, we believe, with the woman, Lizeveta Nevolin, daughter of the Red Navy submarine commander Gregor Nevolin."

McGill went on to fill in some empty spaces and add a few. A dig on the Arctic Circle, a legend, a diary, and an ancient relic this secret unit considered a threat. Oh for crissake. Like a philosopher's stone. He felt a smirk coming and kept his face bland. Not hard, his bruises had turned an interesting shade of canary yellow—but if this relic hunt gave him intel on Chechnya and the bastards who'd left him to die, he'd believe in aliens.

"Nevolin is educated in everything she needs right now," McGill said. "Submarines, arctic navigation, the legend. I think she's hunting for the trapped sub to expose it, and from the money trail behind her, she's been planning this a long time." He dropped a folder on his console and flipped it open. "D-1 encountered them in Ireland and they have backup and men to expend. Fontenòt has tracked them to Svalbard, and saw Mills's sonar moved aboard by Kolbash."

He gave Mitch pictures to prove it and he thought, *Fontenòt was right, all for the sonar.*

"The *Northern Lion* left Svalbard ten hours ago. We believe Doctor Sheppard is aboard." He looked directly at Mitch. "I don't give a damn about Price or Moscow covering it up, but my people are on the Arctic Circle, and now so is this bitch. Where's the goddamn sub?"

"Greenland," David said. "I'm trisecting the coordinates of the *Bowman*, Atlantic listening post, and the *Trident's* hail."

"Get specific, go thermal. Find a hot spot, because if this thing is underwater and its reactor wasn't the reason, it's possible the boat is operational. Nevolin is extremely well funded and you can bet she's going to bring this crime to light, and do it with those missiles. She's a woman on a rampage. It's going to get ugly."

Brønlundfjord, Greenland

On the eightieth parallel with binoculars, Max thought. Madness.

The fjord was a massive inlet, a tongue on the edge of the world and frozen solid. Ice blocked the water flow from the Greenland Sea, but farther inland, it was jagged mountains dusted in green. Fifty miles south people were in shirtsleeves. Max wasn't having any of that shit and decided he was not made of the sterner stuff. The two Marines, Recker and Lewis, were from Wisconsin and just brimming with it. Max didn't mind being the weenie of the bunch. His Florida blood was in shock over the temperatures.

"Lewis, take point, let's move out a bit."

He adjusted the lens on the dig site across the frozen water, barely discernible. Snow drifted smoothly onto the dome, sweeping it into the glacier. Lewis kicked in the snowmobile and shot across the ice. "No hot wheeling. Soft ice."

"*Roger that, sir.*" Lewis was beyond the ridge, nearer to shore.

You got to be nuts to be chopping into the ice, he thought, but for morale's sake, kept that to himself. The vibrations Olivia couldn't pinpoint were trouble waiting to happen. You don't mess with the powers of the earth when there's nowhere to run like hell, he thought, then wondered if Sebastian was ready to bail. After Sebastian saved his life in Kuwait, and they were sharing a beer and first aid, he'd told him about Olivia and their marriage—once—then never mentioned her again. Max understood Olivia was the man's Achilles' heel. Living with her now had to be torture because even Max could see that after all this time they still loved each other.

He felt more than heard a rumbling and he pulled his hood back from his ear, listening. "Motor, two of them," he said and scanned the horizon. It was another minute before the Sirius patrol showed up on a pair of souped-up Ski-Doos, moving wicked fast. The drivers looked almost space age with streamlined helmets that reached past their necks, and not an inch of skin exposed. He radioed Sebastian. "Denmark army is paying us a visit. I'll make nice." He waved.

The soldiers were aware of the excavation and its detail, and they'd radioed them before leaving the dig. When it came down to it, Danish authority ruled. They had to have permits to be this far north on Peary Land, the world's largest national park. Nothing about it said camping and hot dogs, and only the skilled and experienced could survive up here. Some dangerous land, he thought as the snowmobile veered and slowed to a stop. One man remained behind as the other approached.

The Dane pushed his windshield up, but kept the helmet on. "You are Renfield? With the American archaeologists?"

Max reared a bit. "Yes, I am," he said in Danish.

He felt Recker staring at him and glanced. "Speak up, Marine."

"I know him." Recker smiled at the Danish soldier and stuck out his hand. "You almost arrested me two months ago out here. I was on patrol."

The Dane shook hands, smiling. "I am Gunderson. We've come to warn you, no farther. Summer is over, but ice still soft."

"We know, but thanks for the warning," he said. The ice was deceptive and while it would freeze back up quickly at night, the dig was on the tip of the inlet, what Greenlanders called a Ghost Island. Geology said there was land beneath the ice, but out on the edge, the ice ruled. Several islands were discovered in the seventies, never to be seen again. About a half a mile away, the water was chunked with ice and so cold life expectancy in it was under a minute.

"This is good," the soldier said, pointing to the ropes securing them to their snowmobiles. If the ice cracked, it was their only anchor. They weren't on anything you'd call a road, only the last path taken on the glacier. Supplies were routed through this area, kept surprisingly busy with geologists and climatologists collecting data. North was snow and ice dotted with bits of bedrock. South, the land rose in dimples and mossy green mounds, the wind sweeping snow into peaks. Fifty miles away was a village.

And hot coffee, he thought.

"If you travel on the ice, radio us, yah." He gave their frequency. "Stay two by two."

In pairs, he guessed, then shook hands with the soldier, and waved to his buddy who was watching the terrain as if terrorists would parachute down. Very Sirius soldiers. Max walked back to his snowmobile, then climbed on. Recker mimicked him. He rolled in the rope, stuffing it under a Velcro strap, but didn't unclip. He turned over the engine, then headed onto the ice. The soldiers were flying east across the snow, deeper into Perry Land.

After a couple hundred feet, Max stopped and swung the binoculars into position. He narrowed the focus. It was shades of white till he moved left.

"Fox leader, I've got people on the ice," came over the radio.

"I see them, Fox one." White camouflage wasn't easy to spot, but the machinery, he couldn't miss. It was huge risk to be on the edge of the ice and he counted ten people with Ski-Doos. He zeroed in on the weaponry. "Back off and return to base immediately. Stay covert."

"Roger that. They're awful busy out there, sir," Lewis said over the PRR. *"Negative ID on anyone."*

Not bundled in cold-weather gear, he thought, then said, "I better see your ugly mug in two minutes, Lewis." He changed the frequency and radioed Sebastian. "Coonass, we got company on the ice, and they're packing. Looks like they're digging, too."

"Copy that. We need to get personnel off the dig."

Civilians and weapons didn't mix and even from here, he saw handguns and counted four assault rifles. What the hell were they expecting, a polar bear stampede? "No chance of a rescue assault on the *Northern Lion?*" Recker brightened at the prospect.

"Negative, too dangerous on the ice or that water. We have a storm front coming."

He looked to the sky, then behind himself. The cold front was a gray blanket heading this way. "Roger that." It was killing Sebastian to know that Noble was this close and he couldn't reach him, but a struggle in arctic waters was just unwise unless they had the supreme advantage. And they didn't.

He turned the snowmobile back toward the dig, keeping the motor low. Recker was behind him and they paused for Lewis to catch up. Max radioed the Sirius soldiers, warning them.

He'd bet one of Olivia's cappuccinos that was the little Russian psychopath, Nevolin.

Veta eyed the giant boring machine and the hole it cut into the ice with a thousand blades spinning at once. She was concerned about its weight on the ice, but the cut was clean, shooting a soft spray of shaved ice in four directions and creating a rainbow. She felt a little childlike for a moment, watching it turn crystal pink. The grinding noise drew her back and she found Dimitri staring at her. She smiled. He did not return it and she crossed to him.

"Share your opinion, comrade."

He stared ahead. "The decision is yours, commander."

She eyed him, not liking what she was seeing in him. Why was he doubting her now? "Continue."

"Wounding the old man?" He shook his head.

So there it lies, she thought. "He was uncooperative. He would have lied, and written lies. He's obeying now." She waved, cutting off the discussion. Sheppard made her uncomfortable and she knew the lilt in his voice reminded her too much of her father. "The star coordinates are near here. The captain wrote of seeing a ship trapped somewhere." Like her father's boat, she thought, looking inland. A crest in the drift prevented seeing a portion of land, but the rocky mountains rising behind were bright in the sun. Few lived this far north and certainly not on the ice fjord. A phantom island, she'd read somewhere, and she thought it oddly appropriate. For this small piece, there were many spirits under the ice.

"If it does not lead to this rock you believe changes . . . things?" He waved uselessly at the machinery.

She tried to keep emotion from her face. He did not believe in the legend and wanted her to let it go. She could not. He didn't understand the love of a parent, the trust you gave them and the inconsolable loss. Dimitri was raised in an orphanage and grew to a man in the military. His life was violent and his view tainted by his own "most expedient route" practicality. She was in her father's footsteps now, and the stone was Papa's desire. He was obsessed with it, she admitted. Because Moscow ignored their calls for help, he never had the chance to find the truth. She would accomplish two goals for him. Avenge his death and find the relic. But her need to fulfill it wasn't driving her as much as to know the truth of the stone's power. The Chinese fables her father had uncovered spoke as if it offered youth and health, and those who warred over it, sought immortality. A wild tale, yes, but as she looked at Dimitri, she hoped it was true.

"I will not stop till I find it. I cannot."

"I know why you hunt the stone." His expression hardened. "And you waste precious time and money, Liz—commander. You cannot change that—"

"No!" She couldn't meet his gaze and stared at the grinding. "For my father and his crew first, comrade, then for myself."

He scoffed, the sound disgusted. "You only want to rub Moscow's face in it."

She tipped her chin up. "I will rub the *world's* nose in this. Moscow has already brought attention by those MiG bombs."

She'd predicted that with a small sign of trouble, they would rush to smother the evidence. It had taken her four months of tolerating the company of her enemies and using the mafia troops to secure Mills and his sonar. Killing Molenko was a euphoria she relished still, but she'd known from the beginning it would come to this. When there was no ceremonial launch, nor family allowed to see the sub, she knew her father had been on a secret mission for the state. Yet after the catastrophe, the more she fought to recover the submarine, the harder FSB pushed back, and threatened. Blamed her father. The betrayal and the accusations in the news had killed her mother with a shame she did not deserve. Veta had gone into seclusion after her death, to learn and prepare to battle the lies. Moscow saved face with the Americans at the expense of seventy-three of their countrymen. It was an abomination.

Father would never have risked his crew. He would have surfaced at the first sign of trouble as a precaution. Arrogant, poor navigation, the news had said, all provided by FSB. Her father was the most skilled of all boat commanders, awarded several times for his bravery. He was a national hero, and to defame him was unacceptable. But even the pleas of the families of the dead had not been enough to extract the truth. Until a man visited her, warning her that screaming her claims only made her an annoyance to Moscow. She had to become a viable threat and willing to execute those in her path to prove it. He'd provided the money to do that, and there was much blood on her hands now. Unearthing the conspirators was only the beginning, and she knew killing Molenko put FSB on her trail. *Let them come.* She was where she wanted to be, ready to strike back.

"The responsibility is mine, comrade." She eyed Dimitri. He was staring at the hole, looking as he often did. With regret. He was to have been aboard the *Trident*, but a chest cold kept him from joining his Special Operations unit. He was the only one of his unit alive. But she was alone as well, and didn't care for his morose mood. Not now. They were just starting this phase and she needed him focused. "You will have your revenge," she said softly, aware more than anyone that it was their single purpose.

"Da. At what cost to you?"

"Only justice matters." She dismissed his concern with a wave.

He grabbed her arm, drawing her from earshot. "Those men are coming for the old man and do not make light of their skills. The woman landed in Greenland for a reason. Hunting *us* now, perhaps?"

She pulled free, frowning at him. "Then when the time comes we will use the old man to get what we want. This woman, Corrigan, goes for the *Aramina* star coordinates and it must concern the diary." The star navigation was during winter then, perpetually dark. What could they have seen from the water? "Sheppard wouldn't speak of them." But the old man was a history scholar, and would not have bid on the ship's log without knowing exactly what was inside it. She'd mapped and readjusted those findings for that particular century and year, but found little that could be seen from the sea. She glanced at the horizon, wondering how far away the star navigation was from her father's grave, then swallowed bitter tears and straightened her posture. She would prove that they'd died needlessly. The Americans could have saved them, but at the first slap, Moscow politics sent them away. The champions of democracy were weak. She was not.

She returned her gaze to the bore and when she saw the bubble of water ordered all stop. She waved them back. "Quickly, before the edge breaks."

The men rushed to pull the boring machine from the hole. She rolled the sonar forward and looked at Dimitri. He nodded, and she pitched the hand cart. The sonar slipped into the water and bobbed. She walked to Dimitri and he gave her the handheld controls. With a touch to the screen, she shifted the ballast and marveled at its maneuverability as it sank slowly. The ground-penetrating radar readings said the ice here wasn't as thick and they'd dragged the sonar behind the *Northern Lion* to map this area, making several turns to get this close. She had considerable assets behind her to do more than hunt for the *People's Trident*. It was part of the bargain, a trade for the ballistic missiles she would retrieve. Remote robotic cameras, the minisubmarine, and dry suits designed to withstand frigid temperatures were prepared. The coordinates from Molenko's files were as accurate as the KGB official wanted and those, she thought, could be another lie.

Her search for the *Trident* would end here, she thought as the sonar submerged further, then vanished from sight. On the screen, she watched the beacon descend. They were several yards from the shore, a line of frozen seawater that threatened to widen. She watched the beacon find current and slow to a stop, then into the fjord. She smiled and maneuvered it nearly three hundred meters beneath the glacier. Then she switched on the active ping, and on the screen, she watched the sound waves map where the glacier met the water.

Her eyes widened when she realized it wasn't deep ice at all. This was their third cut in the ice, and the coordinates were on target, but she could not take the minisubmarine down without an exact location. The sound waves painted a slow picture on the screen and she frowned. Nothing. No shape that should not be there. With the handheld, she swept it slowly back and forth, then lowered the motorized sonar and let it spun slowly in a circle. She stopped it in a hover, letting it do its work. On the screen, the shape grew more distinguishable, and she knew she wasn't seeing a glacier. The curves appeared first. Deep blue and smooth. She covered her mouth, trying not to choke on her own cries. *Oh Papa.*

She felt Dimitri move up behind her, his hand discreetly touching her back. She lifted her gaze to her men surrounding her. "We have found the *People's Trident*." They moved in closely. "She is on an ice shelf." She looked at Dimitri. "Bring the remote camera. We will begin filming this as well."

He walked to his snowmobile and unstrapped the underwater camera. It reminded her of a toy, a tubular camera flanked by lights with small propellers that would tilt and shift to sweep through the seawater. She switched on the camera and Dimitri lowered it into the choppy water that was already freezing over the hole with a layer of fresh ice.

Once they had the exact location, the *Northern Lion* would break the ice to reach it.

THIRTEEN

In the comm room, Sebastian leaned against a steel table, sipping damn good coffee while he waited for the hookup to McGill. The kick of caffeine fine-tuned the edge of his impatience, and for Ross's sake, he stopped pacing. He was trying to figure out a way to lure the *Northern Lion* close enough to board her. McGill wouldn't go for it, but he knew a dozen Marines who would. His gaze flicked to the split screen and the satellite view of the shore. The *Northern Lion* was inside Denmark waters and moving fast. Deep Six searched for the downed submarine. How it evaded the SOSUS sound surveillance bouys, still eluded them.

He looked up as Max entered, throwing back his hood and plucking off the ski cap. "Ten on the ice, I figure no less than thirty to operate that ship. All armed. They were cutting a hole in the ice. Sonar dipping."

Sebastian agreed, gesturing to the right screen. "It's not far from breaking the shore ice. Ross?"

"Got Deep Six coming in five seconds. We'll only have it for about another hour, maybe eighty minutes," he said with a quick glance at the time.

"I only need five," he muttered. Deep Six could jump any satellite, and he watched the stream arrive. McGill's face appeared first. He noticed Beckham and Gerardo standing back to his right.

"Fontenòt. We have the hot spot for the submarine."

He reared back a bit. "In this ice?"

"It's giving off low-density waves. Unstable core possibly."

He frowned, thinking of the vibration Olivia insisted was damaging the ice.

"We believe . . ." the pause held a wealth of doubt, "it's about thirty yards northwest of the Viking ship. Above crush depth. Sending you some coordinates."

If the *Trident* was shallow and disabled, he thought, what the hell was keeping a three-hundred-foot sub buoyant? He tipped his head to Max. "Check the load of the Sno-Cats, buddy. One man to drive them, three on protection. We get them off the ice before anyone starts this party."

"Uninvited guests are so crass," Max said, then brought the radio to his mouth as he turned away.

Sebastian looked back at the screen and McGill. "Noble is aboard, sir. It's not getting out of here with him."

"Agreed. After Molenko's death, Moscow's on it, even though they won't admit." McGill smirked a bit. "They can send MiGs that far, though none are in the area. Danish authorities are aware of the *Northern Lion,* and they're not happy about it. We're under diplomatic service here, we're guests. They make the call."

Sebastian's lips tightened. He'd deal with diplomatic sovereignty when Noble was safe and McGill knew it. "They can blow them out of the water, but not till I get Noble off."

"Gotta plan for that?"

"Opportunity will knock. Already off-loading artifacts and nonessential personnel."

"Get them all off, Sebastian. Ice Harvest can endure an earthquake. SSU can return, but Kolbash and Nevolin will use deadly force and just take what they want."

Sebastian felt a little relief. He wanted the dig cleared and filled the general in on the recent details, arms, men, and cutting into the ice. "They're going under the ice."

McGill looked grim. "Nevolin's money bought her a four-man sub designed for emergency docking with just about any boat. Evidence suggests she's been educating herself on it for a year. She's crazy enough to try to board it."

Her voice echoed inside the small submarine and Veta adjusted her volume.

Through the thick glass, she looked at Dimitri standing on the deck, smiling in the face of his concerned expression. He wanted to be with her, but she needed his expertise on the deck as a precaution. The cables lowered the vessel. The weather wasn't cooperating and she felt the sway of the submarine as it dangled from the clamps. She looked at the dual readouts counting down till satellite blackout, then the other readout beside it showing how long they had until their air ran out. The counter blinked zeros till she hit the reset.

"*Ready to release,*" Dimitri said and she ordered the clamps opened.

The free fall tumbled her stomach, and her body rocked with the sub's impact with the water. It was another moment before it stabilized. She glanced at Stefan beside her and he nodded. "Rastoff?" He sat behind her inside his dry suit.

"I am fine, Commander. Good landing."

She maneuvered the sub away from the icebreaker. The shore of ice lay ahead, their progress mapped on a screen. Dimitri confirmed release of the sonar from its holster. She dragged it for a few yards, and tested the readout. She switched on the cameras mounted over her head. "Camera is on. *Northern Lion,* do you receive?"

Dimitri responded. "*Copy, Hammer. Looks very cold.*"

She smiled to herself, glancing at Stefan. "Prepare to dive." She adjusted the ballast. "Dive."

The icy water swallowed them. The temperature changed within seconds. She watched the sonar screen strapped to the dash, and while the confines were cramped, the four-man sub she'd christened the *People's Hammer* fit like a comfortable old sweater. Its sea crab shape with four outboard propellers gave it amazing maneuverability, and the mechanical titanium arms were extensions of her hands. A year of preparation had been worth it.

She maneuvered the minisub toward its destination deeper under the glacier, and the thousand yards at a slow speed turned the temperatures down another few degrees. She didn't feel it through her heavy clothing, but it wouldn't last. Her training in icy temperatures could not prepare her for the hazards of arctic waters. She searched ahead, glancing briefly to her controls, the oxygen and petrol levels. Impatience rode her as she neared the location pinpointed earlier. The sonar pinged slowly at first, each tone coming faster as the *Hammer*'s lights brightened the cloudy seawater. Then the beam caught the curve of the hull, and like an old movie fading in, the three-hundred-foot submarine came into clear view.

She inhaled, feeling her heart race. The dolphin shape sloped to the tail section, its propeller crushed under black rock and ice. There were no breaks in the hull that she could see, but the far side of the submarine was against the ice shelf that curved deeply over its bridge. *"Northern Lion,* do you see this position?"

"Copy that, Hammer."

On contingency, she'd been prepared to ballast and tow the *Trident* should she be unharmed, but with her tilt and the rock and ice, it was impossible to free it without losing it to the bottom of the sea. Damage was expected, but she was disappointed she couldn't parade the sub into Ana Bay and focused on what she could do. "We proceed to dock." She brought her submarine alongside toward the nose. A fish on a ledge, she thought, and drove the boat left, checking water currents that were surprisingly strong. "Prepare for locking, Rastoff."

She let the craft hover in the water, the temperatures inside making her breath frost. Slowly Veta navigated over the top hatch, the *Trident*'s position forcing her to tip slightly and play with ballast. Her gaze flicked between the *Trident* hatch and her controls as she drew incrementally closer. She lowered slowly, like a bug settling on the back of a rhino. The jolt of metal to metal echoed as she went all stop over the escape hatch. Rastoff lowered the clamp, and the minisub rocked slightly as the mechanism pressurized the suction lock. The air pushed past the front glass in a trail of bubbles.

She turned over the controls to Stefan, then unclipped from the molded chair, rolling out to crawl to the rear. She worked on the dry suit, its thick skin heavy. Her upper lip perspired and chilled until she pushed her feet into the heavy boots and snapped the clamps tight. She fastened her weight belt and sat to secure her tanks. She'd opted for two much smaller ones, and yet knew that even with her size, it would be cramped inside the *Trident*. Rastoff fitted her helmet down over her head and turned on her air. As he fastened it, she tested the communications, then called above to Dimitri. He sounded relieved, and she was simply glad to hear his distorted voice. He'd stopped trying to convince her that finding the *Trident* was enough. She had to see for herself or she'd never put this to rest. She knew Dimitri expected her to die today.

Rastoff locked his helmet in place, then she turned on his air. They switched on the digital cameras built into the helmets. The tiny headlamps were blinding bright as Rastoff knelt, then pulled levers to release the hatch. It opened, the wet hull of the *Trident* below her. For a moment, Veta closed her eyes. The truth, finally.

Rastoff turned the crank, twisted the wheel, and opened it. "Christ on a cross," Stefan said, his expression sour.

She glanced at the gauges. "Air levels are toxic. When we close the hatch, transfer air."

"Do not doubt that, Commander. Good luck."

She lowered into the hatch, the fit tight because of her tanks. The toxic levels forced her to descend quickly into her father's grave. At the base of the ladder, she stepped aside. Rastoff dropped his equipment bag. Veta pulled it out of his way, and he descended, then immediately resealed the hatch. He knocked on it twice. The minisub would remain there until they returned and she would drive it to assist Rastoff at the torpedo tubes. Once they had the missiles released, Dimitri would launch boats to assist with transport. Capture was up to Dimitri, and the *Northern Lion* would tow them. Rastoff would set the ballast that would take the missiles to the surface. She had under twenty minutes to investigate and record this mass murder.

Rastoff looked down at her. "Ready?"

It had all come to this moment, she thought, unable to look at anything until Rastoff took the lead. "Da." The helmet obstructed head movement and the face shield offered only a look at his eyes. But she saw the sympathy there. She touched his arm. "Let us find the truth."

Rastoff walked ahead, his weighted boots clunking on the steel grate floor. She frowned tightly, staring down and feeling a rumbling under her feet. She tapped Rastoff, but he didn't respond. She looked past him to the horror spread through the submarine. Four men were slumped over their stations, their uniforms pristine, yet their bodies shriveled up inside them. She moved forward, the controls dead, the air still. She checked her radiation reading. "Radiation and toxicity are high. We must work quickly." The fumes from the bodies encapsulated in their coffin, she thought, and the radiation from the core.

"Da, but no electricity. There is no breach in the hull. It should start up." He waved to the waterless interior. She'd expected it to be filled as well, and wondered how a submarine of this magnitude would simply stop working. "We need to have electricity to open the tubes."

"The core is leaking." She showed him the gauge. "We have twenty minutes, no more." Rastoff knew his duty and went to complete it, pushing through the next hatch with his equipment bag and moving around the dead to do it.

Veta turned to the bridge, the spot where her father would have stood, and found his second in command. With the lack of reconstituted air, their skin looked pasty brown and drawn around their skeletons like mummies. All the crew were at their stations, neatly dressed. She turned away from it, searching the bodies for her father. She was headed to the cabins when she found him, and with a cry, she sank to her knees. In the communications corner, he was slumped over the radio controls. He still gripped the handset in dry fingers. She choked, tears burning her throat as she struggled with her rage, her grief again, and touched his uniform. Her metal and fiber gloves broke his remains into a power. Dimitri called to her over the radio, and she frantically cut off her communications and video, then let herself cry. She cried for his last moments still believing his pleas did not fall on deaf ears. For the picture of their family curled and gray beside his wrist. She pushed to her feet, sniffled inside the helmet. She switched on communication to hear Dimitri scolding her for shutting it off.

"I am fine," she snapped. "He never gave up. Do you see this? This is not a man who was arrogant nor unskilled. Moscow failed him. Putin failed. Golubev, Molenko ran scared from the Americans!" She walked from man to man, stating the obvious with cold facts. At each body, she called out the name embroidered on his uniform. She wanted the families to know how their loved ones died at the hands of FSB.

She checked her air readings, then walked off the bridge to her father's side. None appeared harmed, she thought and saw papers under his arm where his head rested. It took her a moment to grip the paper and draw it out. She read aloud that when Moscow refused their Mayday, and after their supplies were depleted, they went peacefully. She found the empty pill bottle behind her father's shoe. They'd averted a reactor explosion by shutting down everything, her father wrote. To attempt to restart would ignite.

Suddenly the lights flickered on. "Rastoff! Do not turn anything on!"

The sub went into black again. *"Da. Now why?"*

"It is inoperable by choice. My father wrote that it will explode if we restart."

"I was not turning the key, Commander, only electrical to open the bay locks. The core is hot. I feel vibration down here."

She frowned, standing still and agreed when she felt a humming rising from her boots. Like a slow moving motor.

"We can separate the missiles, but it must be done quickly. The change in weight will surely tip the boat."

"Can we flood the tubes and soft launch?" Commandos often left a sub through the torpedo tubes.

"Da. But it cannot close and will flood the boat. I will go out the tubes with them."

She stopped short. "Nyet! The water is too cold and we are too deep." The only way they were surviving now was the oxygen mix in their air tanks. She glanced at the gauge. They had only twelve minutes left. "Rastoff, that is an order. Send them out and return to the hatch. Let the boat flood. We can retrieve them with the *Hammer* as planned."

"As you order, Commander."

From Molenko's files, she'd memorized the layout of the submarine, the bridge, the cabins, and squad bays. She turned toward the front and the captain's cabin. Her tanks barely fit through the door. The bed was still made. Despite the dire situation, her father held discipline. She searched for the captain's safe. Eyes Only orders would be locked in there, but she was more interested in her father's legend notes. He'd carried them everywhere and liked to read them before sleep. She opened his closet door. In the base was the captain's safe, and she removed her waist pack to open the sealed bag. She held up the glass syringe and applied the acid, stopping before it dropped the lock. She pried it open and removed the contents, and found her father's accordion folder with the worn ribbon. It felt heavy in her hands, and she wanted to read through it to understand his obsession, but there was no time. From her utility belt, she unfolded a waterproof bag and sealed it inside, then anchored it to her weight belt.

"Hammer to *Northern Lion,"* she radioed Dimitri. "Break the ice."

When the ballast took the missiles to the surface, they couldn't retrieve them unless the ice was broken or they'd be forced to tow them from under the ice. According to the design, they weren't more than fifteen feet long but it would take too long and satellite would spot them. Breaking it was expedient.

She headed back to the hatch, moving quickly. Men were strewn like rags. For some, their faces etched with burns. She stopped, looking down through the network of catwalks and corridors to the engine below. A fire? It was suddenly hard to breathe and she checked her air, then immediately hurried to the hatch. She climbed the last level and felt perspiration at the small of her back by the time she reached the hatch. She smacked the hilt of her knife against the hull. A dull clunk was answered and she climbed the ladder and turned the wheel, her arms straining. It opened. She pushed her bag in first.

Stefan pulled her in, saying, "We have some boats on the water and seas are rough. Dimitri says now or give up. We'll die. We could lose the missiles." He closed the hatch.

"Nyet! We will not!" She tore at her helmet, motioning for Stefan to hurry. "I have no air!" The lever clamp gave and she breathed deeply, then worked out of the heavy suit. "Where is Rastoff?" Stephan radioed him as she knelt at the hatch, adjusting her radio. "Rastoff, respond!" He didn't and she tried to unlock the hatch.

"Nyet, the radiation!" She shrugged Stefan off and opened it. The spinning rush of water rose in seconds, and she slammed it shut and locked it. She wiggled into her chair, calling Rastoff as she released the lock. Then the sub shook and she saw bubbles rise from the nose.

"*Lift off. I am in the tubes.*" She cursed him and released the seal. They floated away. She forced the engines and the submarine dived down toward the tubes. Damn him. She would have guided them herself! She saw the nose cone of the missile. The ballast would inflate and force it the rest of the way. She waited, poised near. But the ballast balloons didn't inflate, and when the missile started to tumble, she drove forward, extending the mechanical arms to the binding. She could only flick at it before she saw Rastoff, his weight belt caught in the strap. The missile dragged him down and she aimed for him, lengthening the arms. He struggled to cut the lines and suddenly, they slid free. Rastoff grabbed the mechanical arm. The missile sank into the darkness. She drew the arm inward, and shouted for him to go to the hatch. Then a mass of bubbles blocked his face mask and she realized water filled his suit. She used the secondary to push him closer, swearing they could bring him in. Then he let go.

"No! Oh God, he's rising too fast!" She turned the sub in a swirl and headed toward him, extending the arms to grip anything to make him stop. She reached, and closed the clamp on his leg. His face inside the helmet no longer gasped for air, but was red, swelling, and a moment later, his body ruptured inside the suit. Blood darkened the water where the pressure pushed it out the cut sleeve of his suit.

"Rest your soul, Rastoff." She released him and went for the second missile.

It was sinking and when she thought it was gone, the ballast released. The missile rose rapidly, spinning and she tried to maneuver out of its path. Then, under the water, she heard a tremendous thunder she couldn't define. She spun the vessel. The black hull of the *Northern Lion* was rushing toward them, breaking the ice. Excellent.

Then the rising missile cleaved the air tanks from the *Hammer*.

Olivia hefted the Plexiglas box housing artifacts trapped in ice and walked it to the rear of the Sno-Cat. Dana took it, setting it somewhere inside and leaving the last spot for Jal. She'd thawed the Viking mummy to free it from the furs and cargo trapped beneath him, not really surprised he wasn't crushed flat from the ice. Water encased him. The Viking was six four at least, decomposed, rare even for that century. Intimidation probably worked for him, though he was definitely a trader. The deck was filled with cargo, crates broken open that would later join the artifacts they'd already uncovered and transported. The most amazing pieces were a jar of honey, intact and still sealed, and a plant wrapped in coarse burlap. She couldn't wait for their botanist's findings. Poor guy was bored to tears till now, and she hoped the plant could tell them where the ship had been after leaving Ireland.

She lifted the end of what looked like an Egyptian divan made of ice, straps, and wood, then nodding to Kit, marched it across the ice and slid the container into the vehicle. A hundred yards south, another Sno-Cat was spitting snow as it rode toward the ridge and the plane waiting to take it to the University of Greenland. She'd have to brush up on her Danish, she thought as her hair swept over her face. She let go of the rails, then searched her pockets for her fur headband and slid it on. Her ears stung they were so cold.

"Go get your bags, everyone," she said and they scattered. They couldn't ignore the dangers. Especially with two Marines facing the coast and armed to the teeth. Ice Harvest had gone from an archaeology dig to a strategic defense location. A couple of the team returned through the open end of the dome and climbed into the Sno-Cats. Olivia double-checked the bindings, then closed the doors.

"You're ready to roll."

Kit scooped her bag off the ice. "I'm not happy about leaving, but that scary guy doesn't let you argue."

Scary guy? "Sebastian is protecting us and if he says, go, we go." Though Ross said the same thing, probably why he obeyed Sebastian like a soldier and was still staring at a computer screen like a plant. But scary wasn't what she saw in her ex. She admitted that remembering getting naked with him was way too easy and it brought some especially erotic memories to the surface. The brief moments in her cube were just not enough and she could almost feel his mouth on her skin. She felt a blush stealing into her face and said, "We're lucky to get Jal out now, so let's not piss him off."

Kit laughed, slinging her duffel across her body. "Cruz will. He's refusing to budge till he's uploaded the data to the NSA mainframes. He's as paranoid as Doctor Sheppard about backup."

She'd done the same, and where Noble had left his still puzzled her. Suddenly the tremor alarms sounded and Kit grabbed her arm for balance.

"That's not an earthquake," she said and rushed to the Marines. They were on the radio, running toward the shore. She searched inside her neckline for her PRR, then slid it into her ear. She heard Sebastian issuing orders to take up positions. She came around the edge of the sloping dome and her eyes went wide. The giant ship was moving inland, shattering the ice.

"Oh this is not good, not, not." She heard voices and turned. Kit and a couple scientists were behind her. "Get in the Sno-cat! Go, go, everyone get off the dig!"

The crew disappeared and she saw a Marine follow before she ran down the length of the dome. Sebastian appeared, hauling butt to the chopper, and she rushed to help him pop the cable lines. Max joined them, sliding on the trembling ice. He released the battery from the heater.

"We have to stop them! If they get any closer it could crevasse and the ice will fold."

"Well, that's not happening, I have plans for Christmas," Max said, slinging his assault rifle forward, then climbed in. Four Marines joined them, sliding the doors shut.

Sebastian dropped behind the stick, and flipped switches. The engine kicked over and the rotors started turning. Before he pulled on his helmet, he grabbed the neck of her parka and pulled her close. "Get off the dig."

"No way."

"Thought so." He kissed her, deep and quick.

She pulled the balaclava up over his mouth. "I can see weapons, be careful."

"Just going to shoot something till it stops, darlin'. Get inside the dig. The exterior will protect you from any gunfire." He pulled on his helmet.

Max sighted through binoculars, pointing ahead. "Noble's topside."

She whipped around. Noble's thick crop of silver hair was a bright dot from here. "Trade for him." She shouted above the engine. "Trade the translation for him!"

Sebastian shook his head, pointing to his helmet, and the beat of the rotors sent her running for the wind tunnel. He lifted off. But the ship kept coming, and Olivia saw the widening cracks move toward her.

Three smaller boats swarmed in the choppy water. Chalk-white ice shattered like glass, climbing up the hull and falling away as the icebreaker moved ahead. Dimitri stood at the prow, sighting through binoculars. He caught movement and narrowed the focus. A band of red hair flashed against white and he reached for his rifle and sighted through the high-powered scope.

The woman from Ireland, he realized, then turned to the nearest man. "Bring me the historian. Dress him well," he said, then looked back. He spotted the shape in the glacier, and as they neared, saw white buildings, but little else. He didn't wonder over the structure, nor care. *The diary is with her.* He was sure of it, and realized the star coordinates had led to something on the ice. Nothing would please Veta more than to have the diary and her vengeance.

He ordered the ship forward, and the first fuselage of the missile broke the ice; the red ballast canisters marked its position. He smiled and waited for the *Hammer* to surface. It didn't, and he smothered his worry and ordered all stop. The ice floated on an uneven current.

Then he heard the radio distress calls and Veta's scream that she had no air. He ran to the hoist. The nose of the *Hammer* suddenly appeared, rocking wildly in the turbulent seas.

He shouted to snag it. He had to get the hatch open. She was dying inside, like her father. Nose up, he could see her pounding on the hatch. He ordered the boats to surround the sub and push it to the hoist. It wasn't fast enough and through the windows, he saw her struggling to breathe. Immediately, he slid down the hoist, his boots in the water. The freezing temperature sent needles of pain up his legs but he forced them to move and climbed over the top of the unbalanced sub.

He heard a slow dull pounding from the inside as he tried opening the hatch. The edge was bent, and he stood on it, yanking. The seal broke, and Veta lurched out, gasping and breathing hard. She coughed, then turned back and helped Stefan. Dimitri simply gripped her under the arms and pulled her out of the *Hammer.* He clutched her to him, uncaring of anything except that she was alive. Then he set her back abruptly, glaring at her. "Stupid fool!" he growled for her ears alone.

"Rastoff is dead," she gasped. "He stayed behind to push them out."

Dimitri's face showed his grief, and he turned away from her, ordering the *Hammer* lashed, and found the sonar had torn free. One air tank was gone as well. He accepted this fate, but knew she would not. He looked up when he heard shouting and rushed around equipment to the rail. A second, then a third missile floated between the boats, the red buoys inflated. As the motorboats corralled and nudged them toward the *Northern Lion,* Dimitri turned to Veta. She sat on the deck, shivering, her head in her hands. Her skin was a ghastly shade. He turned away and ordered them to hoist the missiles and leave the *Hammer.*

"Nyet, my bag and the camera!" she said.

"We have a recording and you have your precious trade."

When she started to get it herself, he gripped her arms, dragged her to his face. "You are a fool to do this, Veta, and now Rastoff is gone."

"He gave his life for our cause."

He shook her hard. "For you, they die! Enough!" His fingers worked and he released her slowly when he wanted to throw her. She would end her life for her damn vengeance. He wanted to see her discard these fucking quests and just live a happy life but feared she was too deep in her own misery to envision beyond it.

"I will say when it is enough!" She stood erect, her eyes damning him, then went to the *Hammer*. She nearly fell in the water trying to get into the sub, and he tossed her a rope. She crawled into the hatch, then reappeared with the waterproof bag and her helmet camera. When she was back on deck, she straightened, swaying a little.

"Take your toys to your master, woman. The ships approach." He crossed to the old man standing on the deck. "Put him on the bow." *Let them see him.*

"What?" Veta demanded. "Why?"

"I warned you." He pointed to land, and the helicopter coming toward them. "We are not alone."

FSB headquarters

There are some secrets that must be kept, Leonid thought. Yet in his soul, he wanted this exposed. Perhaps corruption would reduce, but he knew by association, he'd be pulled into the mire as well. Today he felt he stepped closer to crossing that line he'd sworn never to touch. He understood Nevolin's motivation, yet while his superiors insisted on silencing her before she could divulge the truth, the missiles aboard the *Trident* were Leonid's first concern.

In front of him, four screens were broken into segments, different views of Greenland's coast. He was certain Nevolin had found the *Trident*. Molenko's notes had given her the last transmission location. The screen showed her ship, the *Northern Lion*, and it looked as if it had docked. Yet there was no pier. The topographical map beside the view showed the frozen fjord that never thawed. They had no success in defining the smooth lump in the snow near land, but saw buildings. Scientists were always there taking endless readings in the arctic, but at the moment, it had no bearing. If Nevolin succeeded in raising the missiles, she had to be stopped. At least one contained a nerve agent.

He looked down at the thick stack of papers on the table. Her activities of the past two years shifted between dealings with mafia, men holding national secrets, and a historical search of some kind. Her father's hobby of legends and fables, he thought, mostly Irish and none of them Russian. He dismissed it.

Leonid stepped forward and said softly, "Get me the commander in Ana Bay." He'd send MiGs. It would take time to travel there, but he'd sent ships to that quadrant. A deterrent, he hoped, but Nevolin had conducted herself under their nose. She was better prepared than anyone anticipated. Beside him, the head of military intelligence looked on in silence. He was unaware of the powder keg beneath Russia right now. Leonid thought it foolish not to include him in the details but understood he would not be sympathetic.

When he had the commander of the Russian naval command on the line, he gave orders.

"Do not allow the *Northern Lion* to escape the area, but remain *outside* Danish waters." It would be hours before a ship would reach the area, and if they could not take control of this situation, then he'd order MiGs to sink the ship.

The ice was smooth and flat as a lake beneath the chopper. "Dragon Six to base, Keep them armed and ready."

"*Roger that,*" Riley said. "*Don't shoot anything unless you have to. Sirius is riding to the rescue.*"

The Denmark soldiers had full authority to enforce Danish law, but Nevolin wouldn't obey. He approached cautiously, and lowered the chopper to a hover. Noble was at the bow, alone, but a few feet back a man pointed an assault rifle at his head. He could see the stain of red on his hand wrapped in bandages.

He opened the speaker. *"Northern Lion. Stop all engines. Do not come farther."*

The ship kept moving and Sebastian lifted higher when the dots of red punctured through the broken ice.

"Looks like they went shopping," Max said.

The missiles. "Christ, she did it," Sebastian said. "Tell them stop or I'll shoot the ballast."

Max grabbed the speaker mike and spoke in Russian. Their posture immediately changed and he saw Nevolin at the rail, looking deathly pale. "They got the message."

"Warn them again to give us Sheppard or I'll sink the missiles." It was their only bargaining power right now.

Max repeated his words. The look of shock on their faces was priceless, but then Kolbash put a gun to Noble's head. Noble shouted something.

"Let's show some teeth." Sebastian reached above his head and flipped the gun switch. The chopper trembled for a second as the steel shields rolled back, exposing the machine guns.

Max repeated the warning. Kolbash nearly pushed Noble over the edge.

Sebastian fired, blowing the ballast of a missile. It sank, turned nose up, and disappeared. "Three more to go," he said. Noble doesn't look good, he thought, then heard Riley.

"Be advised, Corrigan is on a warpath."

Sebastian twisted and saw the Ski-Doo zip under the chopper and stop at the edge of the ice. "Christ I thought she was smarter than that!" Dumb move, Livi, heroic, but dumb.

"She's shouting to trade," Max said. "Riley says he can hear her through the PRR."

Sebastian opened his own mike. *"—us Noble. I'll give you the diary!"*

He flipped a switch, talking to her. "Olivia, what the hell are you doing?"

"They want the diary. We want Noble. He's injured, look at him. We have to get him off."

"Woman! They'll take you, too!"

"Kolbash called my cell! He demanded the translation or he'd kill Noble! Look at that bastard!" He was taking pleasure in sticking the gun barrel in Noble's mouth.

"They won't negotiate."

Olivia looked back over her shoulder. *"We have to try."*

Even through the dry transmission, he heard the heartache in her voice. She harbored a deep guilt for his kidnapping, blaming herself for sending Noble to England alone. They couldn't have known, but she was too stubborn to see it. "But this isn't the safest way to do it."

"I know, I'm winging it. They've stopped breaking the ice at least."

She climbed off the Ski-Doo, her security rope trailing her as she walked a few steps. She held up the translation, the plastic covering snapping in the hard wind tearing at her hair. Sebastian maintained a hover. With the cracking ice, landing wasn't smart. Then Noble disappeared from the bow. For several minutes, they were helpless as three RIBs grabbed the remaining missiles. Shooting them risked Noble and Olivia. Nothing happened, no one moved, and then the loading ramp unfolded from the side of the ship. The steel hit the ice, breaking it more.

"Jesus!" Max said. "Is everyone playing the odds today? They're at the waterline around broken ice."

"Marines, prepare to rappel." The troops threw open the doors, and positioned themselves on the ledge. Wind currents made the chopper unstable, and he swept around the edges, looking for a bloodless solution. "If we shoot, Olivia's going to buy it." Kolbash looked ready for murder and he was good at it.

"We can take out every man there, but not all at the same time."

The massive ship rocked on the waves, the warm front

smashing with the cold and nearly on them. Water sloshed over the ramp. Then Riley came over the airwaves.

"Sirius soldiers to your three o'clock and Danish Air Force is taking off and packing."

"They're booking and these guys can fire and ride at the same time," Max said.

Sebastian stared ahead at the open jaw of the icebreaker. "What are they planning with a truck in that thing?" Then Noble appeared from behind it, his wrists unbound. Someone shoved him forward and he stumbled, flinched when water splashed him. Giant ice chunks wobbled. "Oh crap, he's not on solid ground."

Olivia walked forward, holding out the translation. Kolbash pushed Noble onto the ice. *"Noble, go to the Ski-Doo!"* she shouted.

Sebastian wished he could hear Kolbash answer, then he motioned for her to bring him the diary first, and Olivia, God love her, refused. Nevolin stood at the mouth of the ramp, wrapped in blankets.

Noble tried to take a step and Kolbash raised his weapon to his head. Olivia rushed to the water's edge and held the diary over the thousand-foot depths. Just when he thought, *plastic will float*, she ripped the seal, ensuring it would sink.

"I will let it go. Don't think I won't." Olivia was damn defiant, poised on the edge of the arctic sea.

Nevolin shouted something, immobile. Danish soldiers shot across the ice. Noble dashed across the ice toward the machine and Sebastian didn't breathe till Olivia backed away from the water's edge. The icy wind whipped inside the helicopter. The seas churned, waves enough to rock the icebreaker

"I believe we have yet another Mexican standoff," Max said.

"More like Russian roulette," Sebastian said. If he fired, too many would die.

Then Olivia made the mistake of letting Kolbash near her secure line.

FOURTEEN

Kolbash grabbed her security rope, pulling it taut, his eyes taking on a gleam she could feel from across the ice. The same look when he'd held a knife on her. This was not looking good for the home team, and her heart beat against her breastbone so hard she could feel it. She held the diary translation over the water, her gaze shooting between Noble and Kolbash. He pointed a weapon at Noble, but a quick glance at the bow, she knew it didn't matter. There were a half dozen men aiming semiautomatics at them.

The whop-whop of the helicopter suddenly felt like Sebastian bitch slapping her on the back of head. She was trapped and knew the outcome, even before the bastard fired a shot at Noble.

"Don't fuck with me, Kolbash!" She let the diary go and heard a scream before it hit the water. Nevolin rushed down the ramp, her boots sloshing in the water as she threw herself onto the ice to grab the plastic before it sank.

"Shit!" Olivia ran toward the chopper, and gunfire chased her. She stopped, her hands up. "Noble, go! It's Sebastian." She could hear the ice cracking, the sound almost painful as Noble ran toward the aircraft. She kept her attention on Kolbash.

He held her rope and his smile was downright evil as he yanked. Her feet went out from under her, the impact to her back rattling her fillings. Pain didn't have time to register before the ice chunk rolled wildly.

"Not in the water! Oh jeez, not in the water!" Water splashed her legs and the sharp stings nearly immobilized her. She prayed it didn't tip or she'd go into the sea like a fish off a plate. Then Kolbash reeled in her security line. She slid across the ice like a hockey puck and scrambled to release the carabiner. Then a rip of bullets cut the line. She tried to stand, to run, but her wet legs refused to move fast enough and Kolbash was there, grabbing her hair and flinging her back. Her scalp screamed and she thought, please don't shoot anyone. Three successive shots were deafening. She heard Noble's screaming plea and opened her eyes to see the black hole of a pistol barrel. It was still smoking.

"*Don't fight,*" she heard Sebastian say faintly and realized her earpiece had slipped out. She didn't dare touch it and hoped her hair covered it. Kolbash barked for her to stand and Olivia obeyed, pushing at her hair and disguising adjusting the PRR. Her Ski-Doo was riddled with bullets, she realized as her boot heels hit the loading ramp. Icy water washed over her legs. She flinched at the pain and backed out of it.

"Oh Jesus, that hurts." Tears burned her eyes and she smothered the pain inside her rage as she unclipped the carabiner and threw it back at Kolbash. "Don't be stupid," she said. "Denmark Air Force is coming. And you don't really think the United States will allow you to get away with missiles, do you?"

"Shut up!" He didn't know whether to help Nevolin or shoot them all. Then he fired at her Ski-Doo again, demolishing the engine.

"You have the diary." The wash of the ship engines churned the water, the ice breaking further.

Nevolin had already crawled off the ice and onto the ramp, tearing into the diary. Olivia knew she was convinced it was the real McCoy when Nevolin stood and walked uneasily into the belly of the ship. She grabbed a radio from the first man she crossed. Dimitri argued with her in Russian.

Olivia didn't understand, but knew she wasn't letting Noble go. Then the ramp started to rise and she looked beyond to the black chopper hovering in the cloud-filled sky and saw a zip line drop and a harnessed Marine fall out of the chopper, aiming for Noble. At least five Sirius soldiers raced toward them. When the Marine grabbed Noble, she bolted, but Kolbash latched on to her jacket hood, twisted, yanking her back. She lashed out, her elbow impacting his throat. He barely flinched, the gun in her face.

"I can kill you now and sleep well, woman." He dragged her onto the ship, her boots scraping against the ramp as she tried to stop herself. He shouted in Russian. The buzz of a snowmobile neared, and he swung his arm and fired. The Danish soldier flew backward off the machine. Blood stained the ice. Oh God. The machine stopped, tipping. As the soldiers ran to their comrade, Kolbash swung his aim to Noble, uncaring of the gunfire around him. Relief swept her when she saw Marines pull him inside the helicopter. Kolbash immediately made her his new target, and pressed the pistol to her forehead. *OhGod-ohshit.* His blue eyes said he needed to pull the trigger and she prayed she didn't pee her pants.

"You need me," she said suddenly and hoped Sebastian understood. It would be a bloodbath if they opened fire. No one would win. "You need me to find the relic."

"Livi, don't."

She ignored his voice. She had to. A soldier lay dying on the ice. She put her hands up. "I give up!"

Kolbash pointed the gun to the sky, smirking to himself, and Olivia looked at the ramp rising like a drawbridge, darkening her surroundings. She tried to make a dash for the edge, aware she'd land in the water. Her ice-bitten legs were leaden and bullets sparked off the iron at her feet, ricocheted. She froze, hands up, and the moment for escape was lost as the chopper swept left.

A Marine was poised on the skids with a rifle. He fired, and she actually heard it speed past her and hit Kolbash in the shoulder with a squishy sound. The impact threw him back off his feet. He landed hard and someone screamed. Olivia ran up the ramp, grappling to keep from sliding. But it was too steep. She caught a glimpse of the fiery tail of a rocket spiraling toward the helicopter.

It was on target.

The loading ramp lifted and the icebreaker was already angling away as Noble fell to the deck, and shouted something. A corporal shoved on a headset and plugged him in. "That woman has no self-control!"

That's what Sebastian loved about her. Just not right now. "You okay, cousin?"

"Yes, yes, fine." He grabbed his shoulder, shaking him. "Now get her away from those people."

"Oh, shit. Ramp's closing." Sebastian turned the chopper, spotting three more ships on the horizon, but was only interested in the one below them. And Olivia. He couldn't see her anymore. The ramp was too high.

Esposito was poised on the edge. "Eleven o'clock!"

"Take it!" He fired twice, knocking the man back, but another took his position. Esposito fired again, pinning the man behind the rail.

Sebastian spotted the rocket tip a second before it launched. "Incoming! Hold on!" He pulled back on the stick and the aircraft rose high and hard, banking left over clear ice. The RPG shot under them. Sebastian swore, and a moment later, Ice Harvest exploded.

The air blistered with curses and he circled back to the ship, but knew he'd lost his chance. The ramp was up, the ship in open water, and he took his anguish out on the Russians. "Going postal!" He opened fire, leveling the fucking playing field as he dove over the massive ship, fifty-caliber machine guns ripping a double stream. Bodies dropped, equipment shattered, bullets sparked off a missile half lowered into the bay. It gave him no satisfaction and the misery of acceptance started to sink in. He couldn't land or assault to get her back, not now, but needed to track the *Northern Lion* and the ships closing in on her position.

"God, sir," Esposito said. "I'm sorry. The doc—"

His throat tightened hard and he swallowed before he spoke. "We'll get her back. We're low on fuel. Max, tell me you tagged her clothes."

"All but her lingerie."

He wouldn't sleep till she was safe, and his mind turned over immediate possibilities. He glanced at Max wildly tuning the radio controls, changing frequencies.

Then he looked up, stricken. "No communication with Ice Harvest. None. It's just dead air."

Veta ran as Dimitri fell to the iron deck. She knelt beside him. Covering the wound in his shoulder, she demanded the doctor, a stretcher, then she pulled off her blanket and stuffed it against his wound. She spoke to him, blinking back tears. He wasn't responding and she patted his face. He opened his eyes.

"I have failed you." She shook her head and screamed for help again. Then she swept her fingers over the contours of his face. She heard footsteps and the doctor knelt, throwing aside her blanket, then pushing Dimitri on his side to check the exit wound. It was hideously torn and she grabbed cloth and stuffed it in the hole. Four men came forward with a stretcher and quickly transported Dimitri onto it, then started for the upper deck ladders.

"Lock her up!" she ordered, and Stefan grabbed the woman's arm. Veta hurried after Dimitri. "The infirmary, quickly!" She squeezed ahead, clearing a path, and the men laid the stretcher on the exam table. She stepped back, and the doctor ordered his clothing cut away as he washed and pulled on latex gloves.

Dimitri hadn't opened his eyes yet, and Veta took a step closer, only to be asked by the doctor to leave, that she was not sanitary. She turned away, clutching the translation, its plastic casing bloodied and wet. She rushed to her cabin, entering and slamming the door. She could not bear it if he died, and paced the stateroom, searching for calm. She laid the package aside, then used the intercom to be certain the woman was secured before she washed away the blood and changed into dry clothes. It did nothing to stall her impatience, and she checked the time. She was surprised at how much had passed and grabbed her waterproof bag, then left the room, her steps brisk, for the infirmary. She entered and stopped short. Dimitri lay still on the table, his body wrapped in blankets. A metal bowl of bloodstained cloths was on a tall tray beside him. The doctor washed his hands, then stripped off his bloody lab coat. He pulled on his parka.

She held the bag to her chest. "How is he?"

"He will live. The bullet went clean through, but he's lost considerable blood and must remain still and warm." The doctor crossed, checked the IV and blood plasma. A monitor registered Dimitri's heartbeat. "He cannot be left alone and I must see to the wounded and the dead." His look was accusatory.

"I will have that duty first," she said, ignoring his insubordination. Today had not gone as planned, and she was well aware of the price paid. Her heart felt heavy, but they all knew the risks and had agreed to them. The missiles were already belowdecks and she was pleased with their performance. The Americans were unexpected and while she wasn't certain where they'd come from so quickly, she would learn it. She owed it to her men.

The doctor left her alone in the chilled sterile room. She sat on the edge of the bed, her gaze was on Dimitri. He was breathing in oxygen, his pale skin brightening ever so slightly. Seeing that tubing under his nose reminded her his health was fragile, and she leaned to press a kiss to his forehead. His skin was cold and she left the bed to grab another blanket. She covered him, then found a padded chair and pulled it beneath her as she sat. She looked down at the heavy bundle on her lap, then to Dimitri.

She'd had forsaken God for taking her father and then her mother. For allowing so many to die. Yet now she begged Him. Dimitri must live. She needed him.

There was much still to do.

A blond man with a scarred face pulled her along carelessly, shoving her every step upward into the ship. She overtook a ladder and walked a passageway, counting doors, men, anything to help. Her PRR wasn't giving her anything and she didn't dare utter a syllable, but she refused to imagine Sebastian burning to death in a fireball on the ice. She wasn't winning that argument.

Outside a cabin door, Blondie stopped. He searched her, opening her parka, taking her cell, then running his hands over her breasts, her waist and hips. She kneed him in the nuts. He buckled. She glared down on him like the bug he was.

He straightened, spoke in Russian, insults or threats, but after today, insults were child's games. Blondie stared at her for a second, then backhanded her across the face. She hit the wall and fell, her face exploding with burning pain.

"Asshole," she muttered, rubbing her jaw. Her eyes watered. His smile gave her immediate chills as he grabbed her parka and pulled her off the floor.

"He dies, you die." He opened the door and threw her inside. The door slammed shut. She sank to the floor as the lock clicked. Okay, she asked for that. She breathed deeply, fighting the chills rippling up her body from her icy toes soaked in arctic seawater. She put her ear against the door, and heard the thump of his retreating footsteps. Moving away, she hunted for something to dry her feet besides the pillowcases and found a drawer of towels. She sat on the bunk, removed her boots and socks, then spent a few minutes chasing away frostbite. She found men's clothes in the next drawer and went still, glancing around the cabin. The bed was unmade, the leavings of a sandwich on a plate. Beside it was a laptop. It was running.

She turned in a circle. "It's Noble's room."

Then she heard the sweetest sounds.

"Corrigan, I'm going to tan your hide."

Relief swept through her so hard she dropped to the bed. Tears flooded, sudden and hot. *He was alive.* "Oh honey, I didn't know you were into the kinky stuff. That much has changed in fourteen years?"

"Don't anger them and you'll find out."

Too late, she thought, and worked her tongue over her lip. She tasted blood, and looked at the ceiling as if she could see through the decks. The PRR had a five-hundred-meter range. "That Danish soldier?"

"He's alive, but Ice Harvest has been hit." She inhaled, her heart feeling the wound. *"Sit tight. I'm going out of range, but I won't lose you."*

"I'm counting on it." Her throat suddenly hurt and knew she didn't have long before the Russians learned she had communications. "Either way, this isn't looking good and if we don't see each other—"

"Don't. I'm coming for you. Trust me." Then nothing.

She sank into the desk chair, her head in her hands. She knew her odds. Nevolin was too dangerous. She'd reached the sub and now possessed nuke-tipped ICBMs. Whatever the hell she was going to do with them was all in her mind, but Moscow had to stop her. MiGs could drop a bomb on this ship and be home for lunch.

What have I done?

Sebastian bailed from the helicopter before the blades stopped.

Marines were already running in three directions, hoping to find the few who were still on the dig. He helped Noble down out of the chopper and smiled when he batted him away.

"Don't start that. I'm fine. Except for these wet boots."

"I'll find you something better." Despite everything, Sebastian smiled. "It's good to see you well, cousin."

Noble's eyes glossed a bit and he gripped his arm. "I knew you'd come."

Sebastian suddenly grabbed him in a bear hug, thankful for the chance to do it, then let the old man go. He eyed him. "I have the clearance, you know. You could have told me, in case bad—"

"—bad shit happens. I know." Noble looked chagrined. "I wanted a taste of the mystery. Some intrigue."

"Had enough yet?" The black Danish jet flying over head sobered them quickly and he walked around the tail of the chopper.

Noble stopped short. "Oh my."

Max was there, tying down the aircraft. "It's not pretty."

Sebastian secured the chopper with the cables, then looked at the giant section of Ice Harvest that was just gone. He glanced at Noble. "I need to see if it's safe to go in. Max, my six." Palming his weapon, he hurried toward the dome. The RPG hit the twisted tunnel, taking it out nearly to the dome and leaving it blackened and melted. The impact smoldered, yet didn't burn. "Smells like burnt plastic," he said, working his way past the damage. Icy sleet poured, slapping the dome walls like nails on tile. It froze before it slid to the ground. Going to be a cold night. He holstered his weapon and waved to Noble. He slid in his PRR, tried hailing Riley, and got a Marine who said he wasn't miked up. "Get him one, A-sap!"

Max walked farther into the impact area, nudging debris with his toe. "I think it took out the dish. It was on the rise behind the tunnel."

The scaffolding was twisted and collapsing in on itself. The lights were out, but the endless sunrise gave them enough daylight through the yawning hole in the dome's skin. The dig was deserted, the screens for the lab equipment strangely dark. They got some gear off the ice, he thought, noticing that the black storage cases for the hard drives were gone along with a few pieces of the more valuable lab equipment. He hated to think Olivia would get the blame for this. He inspected the damage. "The electrical lines were here, too. Without that and communications, we're isolated."

"I can fix that," Max said, staring at the framing. "Enough to keep it from collapsing, at least, but it won't be an entrance anymore."

Sebastian nodded and Noble moved up beside him, wrapped in thermal blankets. He needed better clothing for the arctic, despite that it was usually only about forty-five degrees around here. The storm was dropping the temperatures.

"I'd only been here once for about two weeks," Noble said. "Amazing achievement, isn't it?"

"Oh yeah. So is the dig." Deeper inside, the darkness shadowed the dig, and Sebastian flipped out a penlight, spying inside the ice cave.

Noble peered cautiously. "Magnificent. Olivia still insist on rappelling down?" Noble glanced, and he nodded. "She's rather skilled and daring from what Cruz tells me."

"He hovers like a mother hen."

"Don't underestimate the boy. He's like Olivia's caution, since the woman doesn't possess a shred of it."

In spades, he thought, righting a table. Her heart was in the right place and he knew she blamed herself for Noble's kidnapping. He didn't care if she wanted to shoulder the guilt, he just wanted her safe, here, with him. Right now, damn it and he needed the communications running to do it.

Then Riley hailed him. *"We're all right,"* he said, and Sebastian felt one burden lift. *"The dig area was empty when it hit. I'm trying to jerry-rig the power station and get us some electricity. Tell Max I could use his help."*

He relayed and Max trotted off as Sebastian turned in to the communications room. The area was lit with a million candle watts of light, but the screens were black, the area deserted. "Ross!"

From under the desk, a hand waved. Wires and cables

crossed on the rubber floor, and Ross leaned out to unhook one line and reconnect another. "I'm trying to get back with Deep Six."

"Who else was in here?"

"Aside from the marines and Riley, Cruz is the only one and I don't know where he is. Dana was about fifteen minutes from the landing strip before all went . . ." He waved helplessly.

At least they were safe. "First chance, contact Wyatt. Why didn't you stop her?"

"She was already outside. I didn't know she was gone till it hit and—" Ross scrambled out from under the desk. "Noble!" He greeted him, and then looked past him. "Where is Doctor Corrigan?"

Sebastian's lips pulled in a tight line. He should have risked it and killed them all, he thought bitterly. "Nevolin has her." Ross paled. "We have to pinpoint that ship *right now*. There's three more closing in, all nearly the same size. Either decoys or prepared to receive those missiles. If Moscow is on the ball, they'll bomb that ship as soon as it reaches international waters." He couldn't even hope Russia would use restraint. They'd already gone too far before this started.

Ross's features pulled tight enough to show his youth and he turned back to his workstation. He made Noble comfortable, then went to find Cruz, overtaking the corridor and down the hall of white cubes. He knocked on each cube as he passed, then stopped short when a door opened. Cruz stuck his dark head out.

"It's all clear."

Cruz crumpled a little. "I was standing right here. The blast shut the door. What was it?"

"A rocket-propelled grenade. Noble is in the communications room." The kid's smile was brilliant, but it didn't last long. "Olivia traded places with him. Dress warmer, we won't have electricity or communication."

"I do. I was already packed." He went back into the cube and returned with a big backpack. "The data is already on the mainframe and my computer's charged."

He was thankful for small favors. "No dish."

"Then we'll have to hit a direct signal." He flipped out his phone, checking the time. "Two hours and we're out of range. I'll see what I can do." Cruz rushed toward comms as Riley responded, and came around the corner.

"All accounted for. We were at the other end when it hit, but we saw it coming." He grabbed his shoulder, smiling. Three Marines trotted past with materials to stabilize the torn dome.

"Sirius soldiers have wounded and are coming here. I need to refuel and get back out till we have the ship tracked." The *Northern Lion* was likely at full speed and without a drone, they were blind. They returned to the communications room. Cables and wires crisscrossed the rubber floor. Ross was on his knees, soldering something.

Cruz was at his computer. "It's my personal computer. They might not answer the knock."

Ross joined him to input the classified codes for Deep Six. "They will now."

Sebastian strode to the locker and opened it. Pistols and hand radios were racked in a line, and he handed them out.

Cruz waved off the pistol. "I was hired for this." He pointed to his laptop. "I'd shoot my foot off."

Sebastian scoffed. "I wasn't giving you one." He reached past him to Noble. His friend loaded it, kept the safety on, and shoved it in his pocket.

Then over his PRR he heard, "*Tango One to Tango Leader, Danes with wounded,*" from Esposito.

"*I'm waiting to play doctor,*" Max said. "*Direct them to the infirmary.*"

Sebastian left the room, and stopped at his cube to add a layer of clothing before he went to the power station. It took an hour to move barrels and refuel the chopper, but he had to put his impatience on hold. They needed to secure everything, then free up the cubes for quarters. Survival first, he thought, listening to the Marine chatter. At the top of the dome, Lewis, his point man, had the *Northern Lion* in his sights. He trekked across the ice to the chopper and knew he wouldn't get off the ground.

The freezing sleet on the blades would drop the chopper out of the sky, and the battery heater was vapor. If he could push the damn thing inside the dome, he would. The Marines collapsed some of the frame, and with a lot of duct tape and a few tools, they managed to seal the hole enough to stop most of the wind from pulling it apart. He hunted down a compressor used to operate the melting system and, with a Marine, rigged it to keep the chopper battery warm, but unless the weather changed, he wasn't going anywhere. Sleet was coming down harder.

He returned to the communications room. Riley was moving cables with Ross. Noble sat in an isolated corner, but it was his hand that got his attention. Crudely wrapped, the bandages were bloodstained. He grabbed a small medical kit from a steel cabinet and crossed to him. "Kolbash do that?" He laid out supplies.

Noble shook his head. "Nevolin, and that's after I agreed to help her. Bluffing, of course. But she kept the digit. Disgusting woman."

He went still, another bolt of fear lacing through him. What was Olivia suffering? Then his oldest friend reached out, gripped his arm.

"She's strong. She'll survive."

Kolbash had already killed for Nevolin. If the witch wants it, Olivia would be tossed overboard. The thought crippled him, and he was desperate for all his training to kick in and stay focused. He cut the old bandages free and cleaned the wound, bringing Noble up to speed as quickly as he could on how Dragon One's last operation in Chechnya was Nevolin's handiwork.

He was nearly finished dressing it when Noble said quietly, "Olivia knew you were hurt in Singapore." His gaze flicked up. "I could tell it was killing her not to ask, but I'd made such a righteous stink about protecting your privacy, I couldn't go back on our agreement."

Sebastian cut tape and applied it. Noble had flown to Singapore and sat by his bedside with Jasmine for a month. "You've never forgiven her for leaving me, have you?"

Noble sat back. "I thought I had. When we met again, she wasn't the same spoiled girl. I knew that." He waved dismissively. "But I understood why she never contacted you." Noble eyed him in a way he remembered from his childhood. "As NSA, she was in the same position you were when the two of you were married. To contact you would mean starting right back where you left off with all that distrust and government need-to-know business."

Oh yeah, he got that back in Ireland. "Lovely irony, isn't it?"

"Especially when you called out her name in the hospital."

His gaze snapped to him. Noble simply arched a brow and gave him that "isn't that interesting" look, but Sebastian understood his feelings for Olivia. They were intensely familiar. Just not with all this helplessness. He was impatient to get satellite eyes on the *Northern Lion*. One thing he could count on was Nevolin had backup plans, and she wasn't done. "That why you didn't tell me you worked for NSA? Or even Moira?" Informing his daughter, Granlen, and the Surrey police that Noble was free was on his to-do list. That and getting Noble some antibiotics.

"Moira didn't need to know, and frankly it just wasn't dangerous, only classified, and that's until we find a conclusion."

Noble wouldn't participate in anything covert that involved defense, but he'd have to get used to the lines crossing. They always did, and he'd admired Olivia for not cutting him any slack. "You need to find those conclusions. Because Nevolin won't stop with the missiles." He thought about the millions funneled into her accounts and how low they were right now. He hoped Beckham was following the money trail because Nevolin was delivering those missiles to someone. Soon.

"She gave me her father's notes to work with, but it felt incomplete. I know what she has and doesn't, but Gregor followed a path that's nearly impossible to corroborate, the Viking's signature, his mark as it were then, on trade documents." Noble's brows furrowed. "Gregor seem to already know that the relic had been severed in half by the Maguire's princess. But the only way he could know that is through the monk's diary or actually finding it."

Sebastian's eyes flared. "Is that even possible?"

"Anything is possible. I would never have thought the Viking's ship still existed." He waved toward the dig. "But the Odd Squad has uncovered things that would just blow your mind."

Sebastian smiled. "Odd Squad?"

"The nickname awarded by non–Second Sight NSA. The few who know about us, that is. Joseph likes to keep a very low profile."

It amused Sebastian that Noble and the four-star general were on a first-name basis, and if anyone could keep this mess quiet, it was Mac. He pitched the medical trash and returned the kit to the cabinet, a penlight in his mouth. He suddenly turned to Noble.

"Where's your backup files for the diary?"

Noble tipped his head. "I back up online at a secure site."

Shoulda known, wouldn't have mattered, he thought, then looked at the flickering lights. He heard Riley bark something at Ross. The agent typed on the keyboard. A minute later, the lights came on, and it was a few more before they could send a signal to the satellite sliding quickly out of range.

The images were static, then twisted before it clarified. McGill was on the wire. Sebastian stepped near the mounted camera.

"We saw it. We have tight eyes on the ship. Danes are out

of Thule air base. Moscow has MiGs in the air, but the ship is moving quickly into international waters. If they can, they'll strike."

"Doctor Corrigan is hostage on the *Northern Lion.*"

McGill looked grim. "We don't have any vessels in the area and it will take hours to get anything closer. I'm ordering an LPH to fast track ahead of the fleet."

A Landing Platform Helo was smaller and could make better time.

"Then I'm calling in every marker, sir, including Beckham's." The man stood just inside camera range and visibly tensed. "I don't care how you threaten or blackmail. Stop those MiGs, cuz if Olivia dies, I'm holding y'all"—he motioned to Beckham and Gerardo—"personally responsible."

Beckham looked like he'd issue a counterthreat, but McGill put his hand up.

"Be ready to fly."

FIFTEEN

Olivia didn't know how long she dozed on the bunk, but was grateful to be warm and dry. She tried to move and her stomach rolled with the bank of the ship. She curled tighter. Clearly we're not in icebreaker mode, she thought and could feel the ship charging through the ocean. From across the room, she watched the water in the glass rock and shimmer, and her gaze fell on the papers and laptop on the desk beside it. She'd tried the Internet connection to reach Sebastian, but it was useless at sea and she could only imagine the tailspin she'd sent Ice Harvest into. Sebastian must be going nuts. And mad. That was a given.

Her heart ached with a dull thud, and she nurtured the comfort that Noble was safe with Sebastian and hoped her last glimpse of him wasn't her last forever. They could have assaulted and taken back those missiles if not for her. WMDs on the loose would have every government fighting for the chance to blow the *Northern Lion* out of the water. Nevolin had to know that. God knows she'd planned everything else well.

The ship shuddered from the hull up, threatening to spill her out of the bunk, and she knew if she didn't get her sea legs, she'd be making an offering to the porcelain god. Counting off like a dare, she sat up, then swung her legs over the side. Her mouth watered a little and she swallowed, then forced herself to stand, then walk. It was the only solution.

She paced, her body warming, and it took another half hour or so before her stomach stopped fighting her. Her boots were still drying in front of the small wall heater and she crossed to them, testing the dampness against her cheek, then sat to pull them on. She was jerking the laces tight when the door opened. Nevolin stood in the doorway, then stepped inside. Olivia quickly tied her laces and stood.

Nevolin inspected her, and while Olivia wanted to belt her, she wasn't in a position to agitate her captors. The woman was younger, her brows dark against her pale skin, contrasting with blond hair yanked so tight her eyes looked feline. Dark soulless eyes. She wore the same uniform as the others, dark gray with an embroidered Trident insignia. Under the heavy jacket, Olivia saw striped epaulets on her shoulder. Playing military commander, she thought, because according to intelligence, she'd never served a day. Kolbash had enough for both of them, granted, but the whole idea of it made her lips quiver. That a Spetsnaz would put up with it said a lot more.

"Are you done or you want to see my teeth, too?"

Nevolin smiled slightly. "You came from the same area of the *Aramina*'s star coordinates. What did you find?"

Olivia said nothing. Revealing even a shred of information on Ice Harvest was just not happening.

Nevolin took a step closer, looked her over like she was spooge on her boot. "You will learn not to fight me, Doctor Corrigan. As Sheppard did." She grabbed Olivia's parka and shoved it at her, then left the cabin and waited for her to follow.

Olivia pulled on her jacket and obeyed, glancing back to see the guy who'd belted her in the mouth walking behind her. He wore the same hateful expression, and as she followed Nevolin down the passageway to the floor below, she knew her life was running to its end. Nevolin wouldn't share anything unless she knew she'd never leave here alive. The thought was sobering. She really didn't want to die today,

God. Really. She tried not to think of all the lost opportuni-
ties with Sebastian as she followed Nevolin through the ship
to a deck below.

"You're an American agent, da?" Nevolin said.

"I'm an archaeologist." There were no links to her background. NSA made sure of it. All they had was her name on
a phone and her association with Noble and his kidnapping.

"Then why send so many after the historian?"

"He's a U.S. citizen. England's hunting you for the murders in Chertsey and Denmark and the U.S. are watching you
right now."

"We're out of satellite range."

She scoffed. "Keep thinking that. You'll sleep better."

Nevolin eyed her for a moment, then walked though the
ship, turning corners. Olivia almost lost her bearings before
she went down a ladder. She negotiated it behind Nevolin. At
the bottom, she stepped back and knew she was inside a lab.
She counted four men in lab coats hovering over specimens,
including the diary translation, and she recognized a few
pieces of equipment. U.S. intelligence suspected the Russian
missiles contained nerve agents. Did she get it out? Was she
planning to release it?

Each man looked up from his task, and Olivia felt hatred
rolling off them in waves. Up yours, she thought, sending it
back. Her skin creeped when she glimpsed a reclining chair
behind a curtain, complete with IVs. One wall was storage
and from Sebastian's pictures, she recognized the case for the
underwater sonar. The woman had big plans, she thought,
realizing everyone was uniformed and armed.

"What is the point of all this, Nevolin?"

That Olivia knew her name didn't seem to faze her.

"Doctor Sheppard and my father conversed on the Irish
legend before he was murdered. That is how I knew of him.
But Sheppard did not learn nearly as much as my father. The
translation filled in some pieces, but Father was far more
skilled at finding the answers."

She doubted it. Noble was the best. "I know you want to gloat, so get on with it."

Nevolin crossed behind the technicians. "We are testing inks here," she said, flicking a hand at the lighted tables like at Ice Harvest.

"For what reason?"

"My father located a letter on a vellum parchment in a family Bible." Her gaze swept to hers. "A Corrigan Bible, the clan of the princess."

Olivia felt suddenly possessive over the letter. "What did you find?"

"The paper is of the period and the ink is from a squid. Rare for Ireland. My scientists believe the ink came from China."

"Entirely possible." The Chinese were the first printers and squid ink was common, but its resilience over the years depended on preservation. The original monk's diary was in iron gall ink, yet the last hundred pages or so were written with squid ink. A gift from the princess, she thought. Whether Nevolin's letter and the diary's ink were the same was just a theory without tests.

"I was in Ireland the day the diggers found the diary, Doctor Corrigan. I know the relic exists."

"Is that right? Have any proof?"

Nevolin walked to a man in a corner sitting at a small table. He was in his seventies at least, hunched and wearing magnification goggles. He probed at a mass resting on a lighted counter, and as she walked near, Nevolin called his name. She spoke in Russian, gesturing between her and the mass of what looked like fabric. The scientist removed his goggles and handed them to her. He stood, backing away, and Olivia slid them on, adjusted the scope, and leaned over the specimen. Her heart slammed to her throat when she recognized the twist of Celtic symbols. She intensified the view and the weave of the fabric was like a calling card from the Viking ship. The needlework on the stole and tartan fragment had the same slant and knotting, and she suspected this piece was embroidered by the same person. But that meant it was the princess. "Where did you find this?"

"My father did. In Benzù."

Olivia looked up, pulling off the goggles. "Where exactly, in what? Its deterioration isn't from a dry climate."

Nevolin spoke to the old man, then looked at Olivia. "It's wool."

"I'm aware of that, but it wasn't kept in a dry climate recently. The fibers are matted and there's mildew growing. Take a sample, see for yourself." She handed the goggles back.

The older scientist murmured in her ear and Nevolin cut him off with a wave. "It was in my father's safe. On the *Trident*."

Olivia could only imagine what she saw or how she got inside, but it couldn't have been pretty. She tried not to feel sympathy and remember Noble's injured hand. "When did he find this?"

"Father took several trips to Morocco before his death. He told me that when he returned from his last voyage, I would understand his obsession. Father never wanted to be a submariner, but he was groomed for it."

Olivia could care less about Gregor Nevolin's career choice, but how did he know where to look for this? Norse runic writing had been found in Jerusalem, Libya, and Egypt and as far as Turkey and Russia, but Morocco was where Olivia was looking because the coins found on the Viking mummy were dirham and one gold dinar. She looked back at the fabric on the lighted table, the illumination showing a pattern. She slid the goggles on, taking up the needle-tipped tweezers and tracing the path.

"What did you see?" Nevolin said from close by.

Olivia spoke without thinking. "The fabric is in long strips. I'd say about eight inches wide, and they pass over each other three times, in three places." Olivia spotted a string of tiny links, and pried a piece loose, then laid it to the right. The distinct *chink* said it was metal. She removed the goggles, handing them over.

Nevolin looked and her indrawn breath said she understood. "A chain, silver perhaps?"

"There's more, and it's on the same lines of the fabric. Three times."

Nevolin straightened. "Three times three. Like the occult? Are you saying there was a spell on this?"

She kept her mouth shut. She'd already given her too much already, but the monk had claimed the princess was a sorceress, and if she truly cut the stone in half, then the Maguire's lady had abilities that couldn't be explained. Even today.

Nevolin conferred with her men, and Olivia let her gaze stroll over the lab. Maps, ancient and new, hung on the wall, scraps of paper and notes were thumbtacked near, along with several symbols. She recognized the runes and the Arabic, then took a step closer to the board of line drawings.

There was a sudden commotion on the other side of the room near the door, and Nevolin dismissed the men and walked around the corner of the tables. She stopped short and a second later, the woman's smile transformed her face. A few feet behind her, Olivia stared at the knot of fabrics, not for its rare qualities, but for its shape. It's a wrapping, she thought as Stefan nudged her away from it.

Near the entrance was a big man, and when he stepped farther into the florescent light, she realized it was Kolbash. He looked amazing, really good. Healthy, not like he'd been shot in the chest a few hours ago. Even his skin tone had lost that pastiness. It was nothing short of miraculous and a glance at the scientists said they agreed. Nevolin ran to him, throwing her arms around his neck. Whatever he said to her sent a hush around the room and he kissed her, then stepped back and crossed to an exam table. He placed an oblong object on the glass. Its soft sea green shade was completely opaque and blocked light from the illumination table. Olivia took a cautious step, then another. She tipped her head and swore she heard angels singing.

On the milky white table was the jade stone.

The *Siofra.*

FSB Headquarters
Satellite Surveillance

The darkness of the room suited Leonid. The screens spanning the wall erased any further emotional attachment. He kept perfectly still as he watched the colored dots representing ships and aircraft near the *Northern Lion.* The ice-breaker had encountered Danish soldiers on Greenland's shores. He didn't know the outcome. Satellite showed a helicopter near the ship, but more than that wasn't possible. Satellite capability was difficult with the storms moving through the arctic. The door opened and he glanced, then scowled when Golubev entered.

He stopped near. "What are you doing, Leonid?"

"Cleaning up your mess," he said, and stared ahead. "The Americans are in the Greenland sea with the *Northern Lion.*"

Golubev lifted a bushy gray brow.

"An entire amphibious battle group is being redirected. They know. Nevolin had the equipment to reach the submarine and retrieve the ICBMs. From Molenko, she had plenty of proof of the *Trident* . . . mishap." The lie stuck in his throat. "I imagine she found the rest quite easily. These three vessels"—he gestured to the lower portion of the screen—"have surrounded the *Northern Lion* since the Greenland coast." He pointed right. "That is a MiG. Make your choice now."

When Golubev didn't answer, he looked at his superior. He didn't hide his distaste for the man and he would not shoulder the blame for this crime. But Nevolin held volatile information that could destroy the FSB, the president, and the entire country. Whatever they did would have to be decisive and final.

"Do it."

Leonid refused to give the order and kept his expression impassive as he'd done for the last fifteen years. Offering judgment of his superior's choices would find him in a gulag in Siberia listening to whales.

"Eliminate the *Northern Lion*."

Leonid looked at the technician. The young man wore the same bland expression. "You heard the director, da?" The man nodded and turned back. "Nevolin has several ships approaching." He waved at the screen. "We know nothing of her plans, but clearly the Americans do. I'm assuming. We have no inside source to question. Anyone associated with her and the *Trident* is with her now. Brothers, cousins, fathers, and sons of the *Trident* crew, director. It is clear how she gained so much information. She had a hundred spies."

"Use whatever means you have. She must not reach any shore with the weapons. Their existence is an act of war with the United States."

He made a rude sound. "I'm well aware of the treaties broken, but I remind the director, the Americans are very close to capturing Nevolin."

Golubev huffed, his jowls quivering. "Then our only choice is to destroy evidence." He walked to the door. "Now, Leonid."

Olivia's gaze snapped to Kolbash. The changeling stone. She went out on a limb and thought, that's how it changes things. It heals, quickly. Not only was the pasty color of his skin rosier, he looked about five years younger. *A fountain of youth.*

Nevolin smiled, then with a smugness that made her want to slap her, she waved toward the jade. "You see, I don't need you to find the relic."

Olivia pulled the magnifier over the stone. Her heart pounded as she realized that it truly existed. A chill gripped her as the monk's words came back to her. *Two halves fell to the ground.* That she was staring at the truth of the legend made her breathless. She studied the fabric and realized it had wrapped the stone. She turned the relic clockwise. Light blinked off the jagged edges. She squinted and saw the original shape. A skull. *The size of a man's head,* the Friar had said. With the tweezers, she traced the lines, seeing an eye socket, the empty nasal cavity, and the mandible. Only the cut side was smooth, and was nothing like the Mitchel-Hodges or the dozen other crystal skulls in museums and private collections. The surface of the forehead, cheek, and jaw were cut like facets on a diamond. Light flickered with every touch. She felt suddenly aware of it, like a tug down to her bones.

She looked up and delivered the bad news. "It's only half."

Nevolin came forward, scowling. Olivia marked the outline of the eye and nasal cavity to prove her point. Nevolin couldn't look more confused and spoke to her scientists.

"You have the diary, didn't you read it?"

A couple yards away, a technician scanned the pages and started to speak when Nevolin said, "My English is not good, what does it say?"

Olivia didn't utter a word, arching a brow.

"Answer!" Nevolin slapped her.

Her cheek exploded with pain, her eyes watering, and without thought, her right arm shot out. Her fist connected with Nevolin's nose. She went down in one punch. "Smacking me like a teenager won't get you any help, *bitch.*" Olivia rubbed her knuckles, then her jaw.

Nevolin was on her feet, coming at her, but Kolbash grabbed her back. She yanked free and paced a few steps, gathering her dignity. Olivia didn't care about her own. Nevolin shouted orders that didn't make Kolbash happy, but the gleam in his eyes said Olivia was going to pay dearly for that catfight.

Nevolin grabbed the relic and the diary, wrapping them

both, then left. The man she'd called Stefan grabbed Olivia's arms and forced her after them. They climbed the next level and it grew steadily colder. Another level, and she felt the rock of the ship, heard the boiling roar of the waves. She zipped up, stuffing her hair inside her thermal suit before she pulled on gloves and wrapped her scarf. She pulled on her fur headband and goggles, grateful the ugly guy didn't take them. Nevolin didn't seem to notice the slap of wind and shouldered the hatch open. Wind whistled through the corridor as she stepped over the threshold. Stefan pushed her through.

He didn't let go, ushering her painfully toward the center of the ship. She passed a small submarine near a lift and hooked up with cables. It looked ready to launch, she thought, and noticed fresh soldering on a tank. Two men working over it glanced up, throwing the same ugly snarls as their comrades. Did they think murder and kidnapping didn't have a price? She looked ahead toward the bow and her eyes grew wide at the ships floating in the distance. *They're handing over the missiles.* She turned full circle and saw the smaller boats launch and guide the larger vessels closer.

Olivia dragged her gaze to Nevolin. She stood near five men in a neat row. A few more men held planks propped on the rail, a sheet-wrapped body on each one. Bloodstains marred the white fabric snapping in the wind. Someone shouted above the weather, almost singsong, and she flinched as the troops tipped the boards up. The bodies slid into the sea. There was no saluting, no ceremony, but Olivia back-stepped when the men walked toward her. Was she going to hand them over to them?

Nevolin blocked them and said, "My men are dead because of you and those soldiers."

She couldn't argue that. "Probably shouldn't have broken the ice, then."

"My father, our families are dead because of Moscow. But they could have been saved by the U.S."

Olivia kept her expression blank as Nevolin told her what Olivia already knew; the secret sub was trapped under the ice and the *Trident*'s plea for help was ignored by Russia, not the United States. Nevolin revealed details she didn't want to know about how they'd died, and Olivia really didn't blame her for her bitterness, just the way she was going about it. Blaming everyone except her father for taking that assignment.

"My condolences to you, all of you and your families. That was horrible and criminal. The Russians responsible should be punished. But I didn't have anything to do with that, nor did my country." Nevolin was all over the map with blame, but reminding her Russia was positioned to attack the United States then didn't seem wise right now. "I'm not your target."

Nevolin smiled thinly. "You are now."

"You think keeping me hostage will stop the U.S.? I'm one person, some collateral damage." She didn't want to believe that, but one life versus nuclear warhead ICBM missiles? She came up short.

Nevolin sent her a bitter look. "America went after one man. They will not fire with you aboard."

"But Russia will." Nevolin had left a body trail with FSB, ex KGB. They were on her ass.

Nevolin scoffed. "They will not have time."

Olivia looked toward the sea at the three large ships; it wasn't their close proximity that scared her, but the deck cranes ready to lift the missiles. She stepped back against the bridge house when the deck yawned open, fascinated and helpless. The ships neared, and the bony elbows of the cranes jerked to life. Transferring missiles at sea. Ballsy. If McGill thought this woman planned, he was wrong. She'd choreographed this like a Bolshoi ballet—in a sea of decoys and confusion.

Sebastian walked around the massive helicopter. Off the port and starboard, the amphibious battle group closed in. Aboard an LPH, Landing Platform Helo, he was suited for an assault. The massive helicopter with double rotors had the fuel and the payload to get to the *Northern Lion*. Everyone wanted the missiles. He wanted only Olivia, and his chest tightened every time he thought of her with Kolbash and Nevolin. Noble's missing digit said she'd suffer. Riley and Safia were on Ice Harvest with Sam. Recker, Collins Lewis, and Esposito insisted on joining him and Max.

The LPH commander gave the order and McGill watched them from Deep Six, but cloud cover lessened visibility. Jets would be pushing the risk factor.

The horn sounded three short blasts, and he stepped onto the platform. The hydraulics lifted the Huey into the sunlight and the flight deck. The crew released the tie downs, and rolled the craft forward. Bright-colored sweatshirts marked the flight crews, and his gaze slipped to the Air Boss. He signaled the pilot, and he boarded the helo with the Marines and a corpsman. The plan was to assault and take the ship, but this far north the seas were rough. It wasn't going to be an easy target, and the reason he wasn't flying this pit bull of a chopper. It had the fuel and power to do the job, but he had a couple rounds just for Kolbash.

They got the wave from the Air Boss and within moments, the helicopter lifted off. Sebastian sat back against the bulkhead. Across from him, Max watched a TDS Recon computer and was thankful Max had been his usual overprotective self. He'd inserted a GPS in Olivia's boots and the TDS screen blinked the green tracking dot. She was still aboard the *Northern Lion*.

The tension in Deep Six was so thick he could taste it.

Mitch sat to the right of David, watching the smaller screen and feeling helpless. McGill was at his desk. Well, not *his*, but he'd grown possessive in the past week since he'd been practically living down here. He rubbed his face, thinking he needed to get a better life, then watched the diplomatic nightmare happening in neon markers.

He glanced at David. "Go ahead, say it."

The kid smiled. "I told you so. All you had to do was ask."

"You following orders now?"

David frowned. "Yes, of course."

"So was I." There were times he questioned orders, but his oath made him obey.

Mitch kept his attention on the screen; the assortment of fishing and cargo ships converged. A MiG approached. He heard the Danish pilot warn the Russian fighter jet in two languages. The satellite coverage was debatable with the cloud cover, but the video from the aircraft made him dizzy, and he looked away. The pilots were flying so fast he heard the punch through the atmosphere on the speakers.

McGill sat perfectly still in his chair, his gaze shooting around the screen and ending on the jets approaching. "How long before our boys get there?"

"Seven minutes."

McGill grabbed the desk phone and demanded General Sarkov. It was a minute to connect, then McGill unleashed. "Ivan, what the hell is going on?"

Mitch heard the one-sided conversation.

"I have orders, too, from my president, not the CIA." A pause and then, "My ass, and you really don't want that kind of firepower involved. Call off the hounds! There are fishing and cargo ships in that lane!"

From his expression, Sarkov refused.

"Think about *your* traitors when the people learn their government willingly killed seventy-three Russian sailors!" His look turned murderous. "I'll be sure to pass that along." He hung up, drawing his hand back slowly. "The Danes out of Thule are incoming. Relay to Fontenòt."

The teams had lifted off thirty minutes ago in full attack to capture the *Northern Lion* in international waters. Sending teams in with a MiG on the loose was suicide, he thought, but kept his yap shut. David tapped him, pointing just as the computer sounded off a warning ping.

"Something's in the proximity of the *Northern Lion*." David opened a panel to try to identify it. "A second MiG, possibly. Lot of jets in the sky right now."

Mitch left his chair, stepping back from the larger screen. "It's another bogey." He pointed, then brought up a satellite visual of the narrow, nearly thirty-foot-long aircraft. "Christ, it's an armed drone." He looked at McGill. "It's nearly on top of the *Northern Lion.*"

David was already sending out a warning of the drone to allied aircraft and the Huey. Then they all heard the jet pilot's transmission. The MiG fired on NATO forces. Fighter jets were engaged.

"The MiG is a distraction. They're covering for the drone." Loaded with cruise missiles and painted gray, they'd never see it coming. He watched the unmanned aircraft close in on the *Northern Lion.*

The Danish jets weren't going to make it.

Inside the Huey, Sebastian twisted sharply when fighter jets shot overhead. MiGs were headed his way and the United States didn't want to get into an aerial battle, but it was looking inevitable. Danish Air Force fighter jets out of Thule raced toward them. NATO forces and UN peacekeepers were scrambling. Moscow refused to confirm or deny a thing and kept their heads in the sand.

Inside his helmet he heard, *"MiGs have crossed into international airspace. Danish will not fire till they cross theirs, but will defend. Orders are to take the ship."*

The pilot started the wide turn to bring the helicopter back to base and Sebastian saw the MiG chase toward the *Northern Lion,* the Danish jet in its jet wash. The MiG climbed in a spiral and Sebastian's heart skipped a beat as a missile released. Guided, it headed right for the *Lion.* He didn't wait for a jet to take it out and threw back the door. Icy air whipped through the chopper as he manned the fifty-caliber machine gun and opened fire. Countermeasures flew through the air, attracting the cruise, and the gun jerked in his hands as he followed the cruise, knocking it off course. It exploded into a countermeasure. His relief was short.

"UAV! Nine o'clock, nine o'clock!" the copilot said.

"Taking evasive maneuvers." The pilot angled the helo and Sebastian saw the Russian version of the Reaper, a thirty-two-foot armed military drone. A hundred yards out, it sped over the *Northern Lion* and let loose two cruise missiles. "Releasing countermeasures." The tubes spun in the sky and one missile shot toward it. But the second shot past. "Incoming!"

The Huey picked up speed, evading, and with the machine gun, Sebastian chased the slim missile as it headed closer to the *Northern Lion.* But he knew. The missile was on target. It plowed into the side of the *Northern Lion,* the explosion shooting high into the sky. Smoke boiled in a black cloud, orange flames chasing it from the gash at the waterline. The Nordic Sea rushed inside, and the weight of it fractured and tipped the giant icebreaker. Men jumped overboard only to be trapped with the undertow.

Sebastian sank into the bulkhead. No one spoke.

Olivia, oh honey.

His eyes burned and he stared at his boots. A horrible sensation poured over him like hot wax and his throat grew tighter and tighter. He pulled off his helmet, rubbing his face.

Max was staring at the TDS Recon.

He shook his head. "It says she's underwater."

Oh God. He tipped his head back and tried not to think of her sinking to the bottom of the arctic ocean.

SIXTEEN

Inside the People's Hammer

Olivia was fifty feet beneath the ocean before she accepted that Nevolin was a genius. After the first missile was moved to a cargo ship, she'd forced her inside the minisubmarine that was so banged up it looked spit from a whale. Her ribs still throbbed from refusing their offer, and she kept herself tucked in the curve of the bulkhead. Small tanks and gear left little elbow room. Stefan the ugly was beside her, and in the cramped space, all she could smell was his rank breath. Was Nevolin planning to ride this thing all the way back to Russia? Because she knew it didn't have enough fuel. Surely they were beyond the ship by now. The temperatures made her feel like she was in a fridge. The ocean currents added to the uneven ride, and Olivia swore she'd never set foot in the water again if she didn't vomit in the sub.

Nevolin was in control, naturally. She was kind of freaky about that, and Olivia wondered how she kept all these men jumping. Nevolin maneuvered the watercraft with skill. Beside her, Kolbash was heavily dressed and grinning like a loon. Even Stefan softened, joining in the completely Russian conversation. They were smug and laughing at her, but she didn't care and settled in for a long ride. She debated closing her eyes when she heard a thunderous sound, the scrape of metal. An explosion? The four-man sub rocked brutally, thrown forward, and Nevolin lost control. Alarms sounded and Olivia braced herself as the force of the water turned the sub nearly upside down. All she saw out the windshield were bubbles and thought, *we're sinking.*

The sub's speed increased and Nevolin dove it deeper. Olivia felt the pressure in her ears and spotted something dark under the water. She was afraid they were under a glacier. After several minutes too many, the rocking lessened, the surf calmer. Their depth decreased and she yawned widely, her ears popping. They broke the surface and when she leaned to look, Stefan pushed her back and stood, hunching. Her heart leapt when he opened the top hatch. A little water splashed down. A loud, hollow rumble surrounded the sub as he climbed out. He anchored them somehow, and she felt the sudden pull in the sub. Kolbash and Nevolin climbed from their seats and out the hatch. Stefan snapped his fingers, his hand out for her. She slapped it aside and climbed out.

The submarine tipped with their weight and she widened her stance on the white deck. She was tempted to kick all the electronics on the top, but not till she was out of here. "Here" was under some giant structure. It stretched a football field wide. The sub was anchored to a leg and the whole thing reminded her of the Eiffel Tower for a second. She nearly fell off when Kolbash launched up a metal ladder in a crossbeam of steel girders. The little sub rocked as Nevolin stepped off it.

Olivia climbed two rails and froze. "Oh my God."

Nevolin's scream scratched hackles down the back of her neck. The *Northern Lion* was a cloud of smoke and fire. Bodies floated on the waves, a few struggling helplessly on the icy surface. Smoke curled up from the leeward side, flames rushing along the deck as the giant ship tipped. The propellers broke the surface, and Olivia started moving faster up the ladder. But nearer, a wave curled higher and higher, and she climbed, desperate to escape the power rushing toward them. She concentrated on reaching the next rung and getting deeper into the protection of the structure.

The wave came like a tsunami, twenty feet high and slapping the rig. Water showered through the girders, the impact vibrating steel. Olivia held on, turning her face away as water splashed like hailing rocks. She couldn't move, freezing water cascading over her, and she shook her head like a dog, then followed Nevolin. Kolbash was already on the next level. Her shoulders ached, but her muscles were warming with the climb. She glanced down, and a sadistic part of her wanted to knock Stefan into the submarine anchored below.

Above her, there were no obstructions, nothing stopping the wind as she struggled through the narrow opening, then threw herself on the deck. Kolbash yanked her to her feet. It was an old oil rig. Really old. Rust dripped off everything and she could see corroded girders ready to break. Nevolin stared at the remains of her ship, then had the audacity to cross herself. When she turned, Nevolin glared at her. Oh yeah, she thought, blame me for that, too, why don't you?

Stefan ushered her across the open platform stripped of equipment and piping. The only building was at the rear, rising three floors above to a steeple point. She couldn't see much beyond the haze, but the jets were fast and loud. She wished she had binoculars and had to keep her goggles on clear lens. The cloud cover ruined the light, but she counted two more ships out there than before. Stefan shoved her forward and she followed Kolbash into the darkened building. The walls rattled, but she was glad to be out of the wind. The dark interior offered nothing, stripped of the equipment necessary to run an oil rig this size. Kolbash pointed to a spot and she backed against a wall.

Computer controls used to operate the drilling were before the bank of windows. From her pack, Nevolin withdrew a heavy-duty notebook computer, and laying it on the console, she opened it and connected it to the terminal. She seemed to know the right switches to flip and nodded to Kolbash on the other side of the room. His hand was on a large electrical breaker. It would take two hands to lift it and then he did, pumping it a couple times. The interior lights came on first, and the energy sparked once, then started one small dash. Nothing else came on except the green light of a switch. Kolbash crossed to her and Nevolin exchanged a triumphant look with the two men.

Then, like a schoolgirl, she kissed Kolbash's cheek, and typed on the notebook keyboard. Olivia heard a humming and didn't understand what she was doing, but Nevolin looked awfully pleased. Then her gaze fell on the laptop, the picture on the screen. She heard the voice-over in Russian, saw the English subtitles. It was video taken from inside the submarine, and she heard a name with each dead body slumped over workstations in a pile of brittle bones. It showed the registry of toxic levels. She heard the turmoil in the woman's voice when she found Gregor. How could she even go in there, see her father like that?

Nevolin looked back over her shoulder, her expression vicious. "Today, we have justice. The world will see what they have done."

Olivia blinked, looked at the small laptop screen, and realized Nevolin must be using the satellite tower to broadcast. "Who's everyone?"

"BBC, Associated Press, Al Jazeera, CNN." Her smile grew. "But it starts with *Pravda*." She tapped the keys.

Olivia saw the video upload pages for networks, video-sharing sites, and Google in a half dozen languages. The woman had her revenge. It would go viral within hours. Talk about a weapon of mass destruction.

Mitch glanced back at McGill and saw the gloss in his eyes.

Doctor Olivia Corrigan was on the *Northern Lion* and while Mitch didn't know her, Sebastian Fontenòt did. Very well. He couldn't imagine what the man was feeling. Ex-wife or not. The general looked stricken, staring at his fists, then slammed one down on the desk. SSU wasn't supposed to be dangerous, and while he didn't get all the intricacies of this Irish legend and the Viking ship they'd found in the ice—that still blew him away—Nevolin wasn't above killing anyone to have it all.

His console buzzed and he turned back. Satellite showed the *Northern Lion* before it was swallowed by the sea. The storm covered a better look and only neon markers on the screen told him where anything was located. He couldn't take his gaze off the Huey circling the water.

David said, "The drone is down and sinking. MiGs are turning back."

The Russians win this one, he thought, but he had to admire Nevolin for her guts. She'd hidden her plan so well Moscow didn't know till she chose to reveal it. Exposing the sub's launch bays in Chechnya was the first tip. Moscow was behind her, covering it up. He watched the glowing markers, the ships clustered. Thanks to Fontenòt they were only chasing three missiles, and the ships carrying them would be surrounded with a battle group before they could get out of the Greenland Sea. F18s were chasing the skies above them. They had no choice but to relent or die. Bad guys were staring down too much firepower.

Mitch rubbed his bruised chin, wishing he was on the assault team. The Huey's mission was a search for survivors now, and Mitch thought it ironic that Nevolin did all this to defend the death of seventy-three men because of the FSB when about a hundred of her own just died because of her.

The speakers burst with transmissions, yet for nearly two hours, the conversation inside the room was hushed or nonexistent. McGill went from pacing to sitting still and staring at nothing, understandably angry that with all this technology and weaponry, the weather was ruling their visual. David hopped satellite feeds to keep the bird's-eye view. He heard a sharp ping and glanced at David.

"It's an alert from another unit." David worked the keyboard. "Command says there's something on the airwaves." Mitch read the flash message and jumped to his feet to switch on the TV. "Which network?" David looked at him. "All of them. In Russia, Polish, and Ukrainian mostly, and the networks are getting slaughtered with a video stream. Ours are trying to confirm the authenticity and background before they broadcast. But they're talking about it." David pushed off the counter, sliding his chair across to another computer. "The Internet is wild with it."

Mitch surfed TV channels, and stopped on a Breaking News report from the UK. He recognized the interior of the submarine. Borei class, but smaller. The voice-over was female and he heard the recount of the cover-up. The voice gave each body a name and rank. He watched for a moment, then swung a look at McGill.

"Oh Christ. So much for keeping this under wraps." McGill looked between the men surrounding him. "Suggestions, gentlemen, because the shit just hit the fan."

FSB Headquarters

Leonid ordered the broadcast blocked. All airways. Dear God, he thought. She destroyed them. She destroyed Russia. Even the technicians sitting at the computers before the line of screens couldn't move as the video played, as Nevolin stopped near her father and shut off the video to mourn. That will have everyone demanding justice. Wasn't that enough? His sympathy was for the families who were seeing this, for the president who was talking to Golubev right now. Any other moment, and he'd take pleasure in that. But this, it would touch them all. He imagined the UN Security Council, the treaties under question. Russia's word would never again be trusted, especially by her people.

He wanted Nevolin to die for her cruelty to her own

country and all who helped her to perish with her. His personal phone rang, and he frowned, glancing at the number.

It starts here, he thought.

"We have the transmission offering to help the Trident. *We will come out of this smelling like a rose, Leonid. Our president is not happy."*

Leonid closed his eyes. "Neither is mine."

"He signed the order. Golubev, he signed it, didn't he?"

Leonid knew his calls were tapped. "Never."

"Then it was you."

He inhaled.

"I thought that would get your attention."

They spoke further, accomplishing nothing more than a dance of words and threats. Leonid ended the call, pocketed the phone, then declared that all FSB agents in the area were to hunt Nevolin and Kolbash and kill them.

Noble stared at the dissolving marker on the screen, then looked at Safia and Riley. "No. It can't be." He stood. "Dear God, please tell me that's wrong."

Safia rapidly typed. Riley was on a phone, looking grim. "No, it's not. *Northern Lion* was hit, it's sinking."

Noble felt numb. *For me. She traded herself for me.* He sank into a chair, his face in his hands. Sebastian will be devastated. Silence reigned with the numbness of loss and he didn't know how long he sat there, staring at the floor. A thermal mug of coffee appeared in front of his face and he looked up.

Safia handed it over. "I'm so sorry. I liked her."

She hugged him and he patted her shoulder. "You would have been friends, I think." He sipped as she turned back to the computer, and kept vigilant over the air and ship traffic. At least the missiles won't get away. He stared into his mug, his heart aching for Sebastian, for the love he knew he'd lost all over again. He'd never wanted Olivia to know how crushed he was when she left him. He thrown himself into Special Operations, volunteering for the most dangerous assignments like he was asking to be put out of his own misery.

It had changed him, made him reserve himself from others. Noble prayed this was a dream and was on his second cup when he heard his name, then rapid footsteps. He turned as Cruz flew around the corner, grabbing the edge to keep from falling.

"TV. Nevolin," he gasped. "She just loaded a video onto YouTube."

He stood, shrugging off the blankets. "What is it?" He went to a computer.

"Looks like a documentary. Intel says the signal came from where the *Northern Lion* went down."

"That's not possible." Safia worked her keyboard and Noble saw the imagery change, narrow enough to show the cloud cover. "There's nothing out there but an abandoned rig that was being dismantled."

Ross waved. "I have the feed." He sent it to a bigger screen and looked up. "Good God. She got inside the sub."

Noble turned to a TV tucked on the edge of a desk and turned it on. He searched for a European channel. It was on a French channel and the BBC.

"Russia has blocked it from their networks," Ross said. "But it's on *Pravda* online, and an RSS feed to about three hundred websites."

"Wait, wait, wait." Noble stepped into the middle of the discussion. "If Nevolin is alive to do that, maybe Olivia is, too." He looked at Safia. "Is there any way to contact Sebastian?"

She shook her head. "He's on a Huey. He saw that missile hit."

"Olivia?" Cruz said. "What's wrong with Olivia?" No one paid him any attention.

"Nevolin believes she needs her. She could be alive!" He looked at Riley, waiting for him to believe the possibility.

"If there's a chance, we take it," Riley said. "If Nevolin is on that rig, she has plans to get off it, too." He looked at Safia. "Send McGill an alert. We need to drop some buoys and submarines need to track. The minisub I saw in Svalbard could easily take deep depths, but she's gone unnoticed so far. I'm betting it's got jamming devices onboard." Safia nodded, already typing as Riley turned to Noble. "You're right. Nevolin's not done. Get on Olivia's computer, see what she's found in the dig. We need to know where the relic is before Nevolin. Olivia felt they wanted it for something very specific. Help me, Noble. I know she uncovered coins and a plant."

His eyes widened as he stood, wrapped in thermal blankets. "Seriously? That will certainly close some gaps."

"Talk to the rest of the staff, " Riley said, beckoning Cruz closer. "If Nevolin survives, she's going after it. She's killed too many to stop now and the way her bank account is looking, the missiles are payment so she can keep hunting."

"I think Kolbash is dying."

Everyone stopped and Riley frowned. "He's as big as a house and sure didn't look it."

"I saw him one time with marks under his nose, like he used oxygen recently. His skin was red, but looked pasty. He'd used a powder to cover it. It was the pinkish shade that looked so odd." Noble rubbed his temple as if it would pull thoughts to the surface. "The diary implies it had healing qualities, perhaps that's her reason for hunting. Nevolin is in charge, but I had the feeling she and Kolbash are lovers."

He didn't feel a shred of sympathy for either of them, but understood her need for the mysterious head of jade. He'd do anything to have saved Olivia the fate laid out for her right now. He hoped Nevolin took her as a hostage.

"I'm betting it's lung cancer," Riley said and Noble frowned. "The one thing that led us to connect your disappearance and the rescue op in Chechnya was Russian cigarettes and tattoos."

"I'll find the stone, you reach Sebastian. He doesn't know about the video broadcast. He's out there thinking there's no hope."

Time seemed to slow down as Nevolin launched it again and again. Kolbash stared at his watch, and Olivia realized he was calculating the time inside satellite range. The cloud cover wasn't interfering, apparently, as the launch icon finished and blinked. Nevolin confirmed each send, then disconnected the laptop. Her smile was extra bright, a little crazed. She stored the notebook inside a waterproof sack, zipped her parka, and stopped a few feet from Olivia. Nevolin gave her a long self-important look, then opened the door. The wet wind snapped hard through the building, slamming the door against the wall. Stefan exited and Olivia started to follow. Kolbash wouldn't let her and put a gun in her face.

"Stay."

Her eyes flew wide. "Oh God. Please don't do this."

He just smiled. "You should not have hit her." He turned away.

Olivia rushed after them. "Are you serious? You can't leave me on this thing." To punctuate her words, ship debris hit and the steel platform shifted. The three of them rushed toward the corner of the rig and the sub anchored below. Every time she started after them, Kolbash fired at her.

I'm going to die out here. Their intention, of course. Icy sleet battered her face, her forehead stinging. Kolbash was the last to disappear down the rabbit hole to the ladder and she ran to it, looking down. The gunshot was loud and she threw herself back. Okay, that's not an option, and her gaze shot around the rig. On the horizon, she saw helicopters. She needed some way to signal them. She ran back to the building and to the electrical pump switch. She forced it up four times as Kolbash had done. Then at the computers, she searched for the switch, for anything to give off a signal. Nothing worked, and she ducked under and realized all but that one portion had been removed. She typed, then yanked off her frozen gloves and tried to send an SOS. She didn't know where those ships originated, but someone was bound to get it. The satellite signal was strong, and she tried everything, but without the notebook laptop, this computer wasn't capable of more than a DOS message. Then the floor beneath her feet shifted steeply, throwing her against the bulkhead.

"You've been out here for decades and *now* you want to give up?" She yanked on her gloves, then covered as much of her skin as she could. She adjusted the seal of her goggles, then opened the door. Moving was a struggle on the uneven platform. The storm raged around her, water and hail splattering the deck. She was a single speck on a massive structure the size of a skyscraper. The low groan of bending steel terrified her and she ran around the building, searching for a ladder, a way to get off the deck and be seen. She found it, climbed, telling herself it was like rock climbing. She had to jump to reach the rung. She felt like the Road Runner trying to get traction on the wet wall as she pulled her weight higher.

She searched the horizon. The *Northern Lion* was gone. God, all those people. The ships containing the missiles were speeding away, but in the distance she could see vessels approaching them. She hoped they weren't Russian. Above her, a gray misty haze enveloped the rig, and she climbed to the only spot she could. A five-rung ladder for maintenance on the satellite tower. It was already crooked, and she tested, then climbed another rung.

The beat of a helicopter grew louder and she saw two divide off, the doors thrown back. They were searching the water and she adjusted her goggles. Freezing rain saturated her head, and she could feel the stiffness of hypothermia setting in. She moved down the ladder to keep the blood flowing. The helicopter swooped past the rig, circling the south side. They'll never see her, she thought and needed something to get their attention. Stefan had taken everything except her clothing, and her Navy parka and thermal pants blended into the tower. *I'm wearing neon pink next time*, she thought and pulled off her fur headband. She waved in wide arcs, shouting even when she knew it was useless.

Waves crashed against the rig and that horrible groan came again. Her position dipped, and panic shot through her blood. Water ran off the platform. It was twenty-two below zero in the ocean. She'd never survive. The tower tilted, and she held on to a rung no wider than a drawer pull. She waved harder, losing the wet headband, and glimpsed the wind taking it away. She wiped at her goggle lens, trying not to cry, and thought *please, somebody see me.*

"I'm sorry, man."

"Jesus." Sebastian glanced at Esposito, Reckers, Collins, and Lewis. He read the sympathy in their eyes and it crushed him again.

"Drone gone. Battle group is on its way to block the shipping lanes."

Helicopters flew toward the ships the satellite had tracked. Until the battle group arrived, the U.S. and Norwegian Navy were making sure they didn't escape. Sebastian didn't care. He suddenly didn't give a damn about anything except losing Olivia. Regrets spilled through him and he heard the pilot say they had been ordered to search for survivors. Sebastian pulled his helmet on and reached for the harness, needing to focus. He rigged up, prepared to haul anyone out of the water. Through burning eyes, he studied the churning surface and saw debris, and two bodies. Male. He couldn't help imagining Olivia gruesomely torn apart and a deep misery gripped him to his soul. *Livi.*

Suddenly Max came to his knees. Grabbing binoculars, he sighted out the window. He checked the TDS again, then looked at him. "Unless she's got a GPS in heaven, she's above sea level."

Sebastian grabbed the TDS. The GPS beacon was clear. *Olivia.* He sighted on the horizon. "Its about eighty meters. South." He swung left, sighting in. "The abandoned oil rig." Sebastian grabbed the pilot's shoulder. "Go to the rig."

"The Northern Lion *wasn't anywhere near it."*

"But Nevolin had a four-man submarine."

The chopper turned, and he heard the pilot radio command. Sebastian's heart pounded with expectation. *Please be alive*. He shifted to the door, impatient as they approached the rig. It was deserted, the undercarriage broken, debris floating around it and bashing the weak structure.

"That sucker is swaying badly," Max said. "It's not going to last long." Debris from the *Northern Lion* hit the rig so hard he could hear the deep tone of metal to metal. At the waterline, the steel was bending. Sleet pelted his face and suit, misty clouds swirled with the beat of the chopper blades. He sighted above sea level, but the rig was empty. He looked at Max.

"GPS stopped moving. I can't tell how high up, but it's there. Coonass, I hate to say it, but it could be just her boot."

His stomach rolled at the thought and he was impatient for speed, to get near enough to tell steel girders from icicles. He signaled the pilot to take a spin around the top and he nodded, then banked the Huey. Sebastian scanned the oil rig.

"Lock and load. If she's there, so are Nevolin and Kolbash!"

Marines cocked weapons, perched on the edge of the deck. He caught the flash of something rolling on the platform and through the binoculars, he narrowed his view. A drowned rat? Quickly, he scanned the rig. The steel scaffolding was webbed around the building, the battering wind tearing off the aluminum sides. He jerked his attention to the tower.

His heart screamed with joy when he spotted a banner of dark red hair kicking in the wind. "Target acquired! She's on the tower." Barely, he thought, smiling when Max grabbed his shoulder, shaking it hard. The chopper sped toward the rig.

"Harness up. Pass north." He adjusted into the harness, then clipped to the zip line.

"The rig's big enough to land but if that tower falls and hits the rotors, we're all going down."

"Get above the tower. Use the loudspeakers. Let her know we see her." She was hanging on, waving frantically, her hair saturated to dark as the helicopter rose, and put them in position to drop.

"*Incoming!*" The chopper suddenly banked right sharply and Sebastian gripped the metal edge as the Russian jet screamed toward them, already sending a track of bullets across the water to the rig. He saw them spark off the rig. The tower and metal started to tear. The pilot radioed they were under attack as the Marines unleashed the fifty-caliber machine guns. Danish jets shot across the sky and drew the dogfight above the clouds. As the Huey swept back toward the tower, Sebastian hung on the edge, ready to bail.

"Hold! Hold there!"

The pilot called her name. She looked up. Sebastian knew he'd never seen anything more beautiful in his life. He leapt from the chopper, diving toward her.

Olivia's world narrowed to one goal; not letting go. She gripped the rungs, and thought, *one of your dumber ideas.* She was only delaying the inevitable and for a moment, she whined that her life came down to hanging on to some metal rods in a storm. Then she swore she heard her name and looked up. *Oh thank you, thank you!* The helicopter lowered toward her, growing larger by the second. Then a man jumped off the edge, sliding down the cable line.

Suddenly, the platform was tilted sharply, pulling the weight of the building. Above the hammer of the helicopter, the screech of tearing metal dropped her in sharp jolts. *Don't let go, don't let go.* Icy water churned beneath her. Massive waves crashed on the tilted platform. Dangling like an ornament on the tower, she tried to shift her weight, get her boots on the rung. Then it tore from the supports, and the frozen sea came rushing closer.

The tower broke away and he let loose the zip line, reaching for her. He caught her parka hood as she hit the platform and he yanked on her jacket to stop her slide into the sea. Hand over hand, he pulled her out. Sebastian secured the line, then tried to rouse her. She was unconscious, limp, and he slipped the rescue harness over her head and under her arms, then wrapped his arms and legs around her. "Take us up! I have her!"

The winch lifted them away from the sea as the chopper rose higher, beyond the rig. Suspended over whitecaps, the wind spun them and a few seconds later, the building slid off the platform and crashed into the black ocean. Sebastian clutched her tightly, shielding her face from the storm, and called to her. She didn't respond. He couldn't see any wounds, and into his communications said, "Prep for CPR. She's not responding!"

Sebastian grabbed the skid, and Max grasped her parka, and with the Marines pulled her inside. Esposito hauled him over the edge. Sebastian unclipped from the cable, and turned to Olivia, the Navy medic working over her. She lay on a backboard.

He looked at Max on the other side, the defibrillator charging. He met his gaze. "She's not breathing."

Oh God.

The medic yanked open her parka and three more layers and started CPR. Sebastian held the oxygen over her nose and mouth and squeezed. He counted the reps of the corpsman, and breathed for her, willing her to come back. He leaned close to her ear.

"Don't check out now, baby, please." He heard the fracture in his own voice, felt the raw sting. He'd made promises to himself, and he needed her to help keep them. He'd already lost her once today and suddenly he could barely breathe. "Jesus, Livi. Come on. Breathe, baby. We're not done yet."

Olivia was in a gentle, warm place till she felt the incessant pressure in her chest. Instantly, she felt the biting cold, and arched, drawing in cold air. She coughed and didn't move, couldn't, her body numb. Someone called her name, peeled her eyes open, and flashed a light. She turned her face away and felt hands fussing with her, removing her wet boots. Her breathing shivered with chills and she opened her eyes.

Sebastian hovered. "Hello, *cherie*. I'm glad you came back to the party."

She frowned and it dawned on her. "Oh God."

"—was looking out for you. What hurts?"

"My butt." Those great lips curved in a smile.

"Anything else? Can you move your feet? Arms?"

She knocked her feet together, then lifted her arm and cupped the back of his head, bringing him down to her. "That was some really bad timing, huh?"

"We'll get better at it," he whispered before he covered her mouth with his.

Oh, she would have missed this, she thought, drinking him in, hungry just for the feel of his skin on hers. She met his gaze. "That was just crazy." Tears burned her eyes. Her lip quivered. "I was smelling fried onions for a second there."

He moaned, palmed her hair, then pressed his forehead to hers. "I thought I was going to lose you, Livi. I thought I *had*."

The *Northern Lion* explosion, she realized, gripping his hand. "I'm so sorry I did that."

He scoffed. "No, you're not. I would have done the same thing." He pulled another thermal blanket over her, then fastened straps over it. His hands were shaking a little.

"Probably with a little more finesse, though."

"Armed, at least."

"That's what I forgot." She stammered, chills wracking her. "And my ChapStick."

For a deep breath, he just stared. "You're making me crazy, you know that."

"I didn't plan on it going that badly."

He muttered something in that Cajun she could never understand, then leaned down in her face so she could hear him above the engines. "Why'd you even try to work a deal with that maniac?"

Her teeth chattered. "Because you were there."

His features tightened. It was a trust he'd never had from her, and she saw what it meant to him in his dark eyes. He kissed the top of her head, and murmured, "You sure have a lot of faith in me, baby."

She gripped his arm hard, squeezing, making him listen. "I'm here, aren't I?"

His shoulders worked with a deep chuckle and his big hands swallowed hers, warming them. And for the ride to safety, he never let her go.

SEVENTEEN

Sebastian learned of Nevolin's graphic broadcast en route to the LPH, but his only concern was Olivia and making her warmer. Her shivering was near violent. The instant the helicopter doors slid open, he was beside her, lifting the backboard with Max and the Marines. The corpsman, Cintuk, ran alongside her with his bag. Wind beat them across the flight deck till they were inside the lift, a medical team waiting for them. They put oxygen over her mouth and Olivia squeezed his hand tightly, looking a little scared as they entered the lift. Cintuk checked her vital signs again and she tried to sit up.

Sebastian stopped her. "I know you're ready to fight more Russians, but take it easy."

She propped on her elbows, her eyes going wide when the medic held a syringe. "Whoa. Is that necessary?" Her voice was muffled behind the mask.

Cintuk met her gaze. "Your heart stopped. Yes, it is." He didn't wait for a concession, pushed away clothing till he found bare skin, and injected her hip.

"Just like a sailor, trying to take liberties. Don't try that again, swabby."

"Then don't fall out of the sky again . . . ma'am." He flashed her a grin, then turned to his supplies. Another corpsman crammed heat packs around her feet and a third with scissors cut off her clothes.

Olivia sat up and pulled off the mask. "Whoa, no no!" She pointed at the young man. "NSA is going to be really upset if you cut their twenty-thousand-dollar prototype." The young man backed away, eyes wide. "I can get out of them on my own. You"—she pointed to Cintuk trying to start an IV—"stop sticking me while we're moving. I'm not dying, obviously there's no rush."

"Olivia, honey, they're only trying to help you."

"I know, and thank you." She glanced around at the corpsmen anxious to do their job, then to him. "But Nevolin is getting away in a minisubmarine. With Kolbash and ugly Stefan." She pointed the blame for her swollen lip. "That sub has a five-hundred-foot crush depth. Double hatches, and the woman is very skilled at driving it or we'd all be dead. We were underwater when the *Northern Lion* was hit."

The aftershock of the impact could have destroyed them, he thought, and she grabbed his hand, glancing between him and Max.

"She has the *Siofra*."

His eyes widened.

"Only half of it." As the corpsmen wrapped her in blankets, she didn't break eye contact. "You guys shot Kolbash in the shoulder, a through and through. A couple hours later, he looked like he could run a marathon."

An awakening shifted over his skin. "It works?" A new spin on things again, he thought as Max pulled out a radio.

She arched a brow. "And how fast was that?"

Medical pushed him back and brought her into the infirmary. A pulled curtain and she was shielded so she could get out of the wet thermal suit. That this relic of jade actually existed wasn't his main concern, but what Nevolin planned to do with it. He pushed his fingers through his hair. He needed to broaden his thinking. Then he looked at Max. He was on the satellite phone and he held it out. Sebastian smiled when he heard the cheers coming from Ice Harvest as he put it to his ear. His gaze shot to Olivia's silhouette against the curtain as he assured everyone she was alive and well. Nevolin's escape to the old oil rig clarified when Riley reported on a video broadcast spread across the airwaves in several countries.

"If they weren't hunting for Nevolin before, they are now," Max said quietly, handing over his TDS Recon.

Sebastian watched the video broadcast on the small screen. The crimes of Moscow were in the open for the world to see. He almost felt sorry for the FSB.

"She plays dirty." He didn't try to factor the video into their SSU mission. "McGill know of the escape sub?" He kept his voice low, glancing at the curtain.

"Yeah, we're dropping sonar buoys. It has to surface sometime."

"The tanks won't last long with three people breathing off them after traveling with four from the *Northern Lion*. She can hide inside commercial traffic, but needs GPS navigation." He handed back the Recon. "I want to be there when she surfaces."

"Same here. This is one crazy bitch. She does all this for revenge, but killed her way to get it?" Max shook his head, looking disgusted. "She'll go after the rest of the jade. I'd bet my new dive suit on it."

"She has to know where to look first."

Max's expression soured. "Her daddy already found one piece, and last I checked, that was more than we had."

"But we have the Viking's ship, and Nevolin isn't her father. The scientists Olivia saw on the *Northern Lion* are dead. Her odds just went down and we need to get ahead of her. Fill Noble in on the jade. Olivia will be itching to talk to him. Demanding it," he said with a small smile. The scrape of the curtain drawn back made him turn and a ribbon of pure delight galloped through his heart, erasing the last of his fears.

Dressed in thick olive drab military long johns, Olivia held an ice pack to her swollen jaw and lip and wiggled her sock-covered feet deeper into the blankets. The corpsman sandwiched heat packs around her legs and feet. At least her hair was drying and braided down her shoulder, but Sebastian thought she looked small in the bed, the IV running under the covers. No frostbite, but she was going to be sore. Her hip had to be bruised from hitting the platform, and the doctor felt she'd had the wind knocked out of her long enough to stop her heart. He didn't want to live through that again, he thought, and leaned back against the bulkhead. From her bed, she made faces at him, rolling her eyes at all the fussing. The youngest with four older brothers who dragged her around like their favorite pet, she wasn't comfortable with the attention. *Behave*, he mouthed, and she crossed her eyes.

In his earpiece, he heard the transmission traffic and glanced at Max. He pointed to his watch, then held up five fingers. Navy SEALs were dropping onto the ships right now and would have control A-sap. He planned on interrogating the crew, though he was good with just sinking the suckers. Ground Zero thought otherwise, yet from inside the LPH, he heard the jets zipping in an aerial fight. Russia wasn't backing down, and wanted the evidence destroyed. Moscow hadn't got the message that dropping ordnance on U.S. Navy ships would get them the booby prize. Since the *Trident* was in Danish territory, a treaty violation to the third power, the Danish Air Force was duking it out a half mile above them.

The doctor backed away, smiling as he crossed to him. "She'll be sore for a few days from the impact," he said. "But nothing is broken. She needs to eat some food and stay warm, but she'll be fine."

"Hey! I'm right here, ya know," Olivia said, and the doc laughed to himself, leaving with a chart in his hand. She raised the bed up, wincing as the cushions straightened. "Heat on my feet and ice on my butt, I feel like a baked Alaska."

Cintuk snickered to himself. "I'm going to get you some chow," he said, and before he backed away, she grabbed the young man's hand.

"Thank you for saving my life, Wade." He blushed, nodding, then mumbled, "You're welcome, ma'am," before he headed to the mess hall. Olivia's gaze followed Cintuk out, then shot to his. "Get over here."

He laughed shortly. "Now I know you'll be fine." He crossed to her.

"Dropping out of the sky apparently does little for attitude adjustment." She smiled, unrepentant, then made room on the mattress. He sat.

A few seconds passed without a word, her gaze ripping over him with the power of touch.

"But it does wonders for not wasting time." She grasped his load-bearing vest and pulled him closer. "Ever again." She brushed her mouth over his. "Are you ready for this? For me?" Her brows wiggled, the dare in her eyes.

God. He was coming apart at the seams just thinking about being with her. "In a big way."

Her gaze lowered meaningfully to his lap and Sebastian swore he felt that like a stroke of heat. She met his gaze. "Oh goody." She didn't let go of his vest. "Now don't do anything stupid."

"Hello, pot? You're black." Her soft laugh tickled up his spine. He'd never get tired of hearing that and leaned in, staking his claim. "Mine. Mine. Mine."

"You just wait till I get this ice off my booty." Her smile melted as she crushed her mouth over his, igniting him all over again, and he'd have stayed right there if the loading tone hadn't sounded through the ship. She leaned back, her eyes sparkling. "Go get those bad guys, baby."

He stole a quick kiss, then left the cabin, stopping at the threshold and looking back. He'd nearly lost her, again, and her ashen skin and the curl of her swollen lip was like a knife to his heart. Nevolin and Kolbash left her on the crumbling rig to die. Sebastian understood that fate better than anyone, and the thought of her suffering that horrific hopelessness drove rage through his blood.

Interrogation would barely take the edge off—for now.

* * *

"She's alive and, for the most part, unharmed." The voice of the LPH commander sent a sigh through the room.

McGill collapsed deeper into his chair, and Mitch didn't think he'd ever seen anyone so relieved. So was he. Aside that it had been damn unpleasant in here thinking she was dead, Corrigan didn't deserve getting snagged in this. Her archaeology dig had little to do with the missiles, and more with Nevolin's psychotic quest for justice.

"Doctor Corrigan witnessed the broadcast, sir. From a field laptop. A Norwegian salvage company was dismantling it for the metal, and the last crew left it in a weakened state ten days ago."

McGill set up a time to speak with Dr. Corrigan and signed off, focusing his attention on kicking some Russian ass. The man wasn't holding much back when it came to the *Trident,* and really didn't have to explain himself. Three years ago, Russia planned to attack the United States with chemical weapons. But what enraged McGill more was that they got that close and were only detected *after* the *Trident* got trapped on the ice shelf. Nevolin's broadcast had everything the United States needed to remove Russia from the Security Council. Already the UN was calling a meeting. Shit was rolling downhill fast.

Gerardo was abusing his Russian contacts and agents were hunting down Nevolin's money trail. Her accounts were low and analysts thought the missiles were payment, but Mitch felt, she didn't give a damn. She had what she wanted and had accomplished the impossible, effectively gutting the Russian government. Putin hadn't made a statement and absolutely nothing was coming out of Russia. Mitch didn't think even a cell phone was working.

He watched the screen, the ships in the water that looked like bugs in a bucket. Half the battle group was backing off and had surrounded the vessels. South, the *Bowman* kept alert for the escape sub. The radio frequency on the minisub wasn't operating and the nearer to a shoreline, the more fishing and commercial traffic got in the way. His brain felt scrambled trying to keep tabs on it. McGill sent AWACS to the area, and David was checking each craft in the hundred-mile radius, narrowing the field around the rig for the mini-sub. If Corrigan hadn't survived, they'd have never known about Nevolin's sub. But Nevolin and Kolbash were escaping. They had minutes, not hours, to find them. The battle group was running at full speed toward the Greenland Sea. Only the LPH was able to get ahead because of the helos.

"SEALs have launched, sir." He tapped the keyboard and on McGill's screen the video of the assault showed. From helicopters, the SEALs zipped onto the deck without a shot fired. One missile was visible and Mitch thought, small, fast, and accurate. Nothing pissed off the brass more than being outsmarted, and with the *Trident*, Russia succeeded. A political embarrassment, but not irrecoverable. Price deserved the blame, yet never in the press. Her under-the-table deals hurt the United States, and Mitch wasn't looking forward to digging for more. This had been his first dive into her past.

He took a step closer to the big screen. "Four missiles total, we believe. Dragon One sunk one. I count two on two ships." He gestured to the satellite imagery from the AWACs jet thirty-five thousand feet up. "There's number four." He felt his first bit of relief as the crews were disarmed, and the teams took control. Satisfied, he turned to the tracking console and the feed from about twenty technicians hunting for Nevolin's ride. Maybe Dr. Corrigan could tell him something useful about the electronics.

About an hour later, David gestured him closer. "Dragon One is calling you, sir."

Mitch frowned. "Put them through." He crossed to a terminal and slid the headphone back on. The video link played and a glance at the label said it was the viewpoint of Tango One, Max Renfield.

A man in his fifties sat in what looked like the tanker's captain's quarters. He was secured to a chair, and Fontenòt cut him loose, then yanked the man's arm out straight. A butterfly switchblade flickered as he cut away the clothing. Tattoos decorated the man's arms and hands.

Fontenòt looked at the lens. *"Look familiar?"*

Mitch felt his insides tighten, and Fontenòt pulled the man's head back, exposing his throat.

"That is Cheslav Agar. Former KGB. Krasnaya boss." He touched the yellow bruises still decorating his face. "If he's there, then Vlad Dovyestoff isn't far behind. I met with them in Chechnya. They're the reason it went sour. Both knew enough about the German technology that they probably stole it, and it's no surprise that both were Price's Moscow contacts."

"You're just all connected, aren't you?" Fontenòt asked the man. He responded in Russian and Renfield opted not to translate the obscenities.

"He's the one who gave me over to Kolbash. He probably killed the guards we saw outside my prison. His own men."

Mitch watched. Fontenòt barely touched the man, circling him and manipulating the butterfly knife so close to his face, he had the guy flinching in seconds. The prisoner didn't realize he was bleeding from a couple dozen tiny nicks.

"Tango Leader, I'd take it as a personal favor if you left something for me to interrogate."

Sebastian looked directly at the lens, his expression barely controlled and savage. He didn't respond and simply cut the feed.

Yeah, Mitch thought, it was stupid to even ask.

Noble almost sobbed like a child when he heard Corporal Esposito's voice. *"Very much alive and with Agent Fontenòt."*

Riley gripped his shoulder, grinning. "Good call, Noble."

Safia did a little jiggle in the middle of the room. "God, Olivia rocks. Score one for the good guys!"

"Thank God Max has some OCD about tracking devices," Riley said, dropping into a chair for the first time since the *Northern Lion* was hit.

Olivia didn't know Max had inserted them. The team ribbed Max about it, but more than once, his obsession had saved the day. Then it got quiet as the background noise lessened.

"The Doc says to tell Noble that Nevolin has half of the jade."

The room went instantly quiet. He exchanged a wide-eyed look with Cruz. *"And she says it works."*

How did she know for certain, he wondered, then said, "Nevolin took it off the *Trident*."

"If it works, God that's just amazing—then it's giving off some energy," Cruz said. "The vibrations in the ice have stopped." He worked his keyboard, then looked up. "Last significant tremor was around the time Olivia was giving up the translation."

"This isn't good news. Nevolin has the *Siofra*," Noble stressed. "Gregor found it. How? Where? Learning how he did that will get us closer to its mate." He was anxious to speak to Olivia, but wasn't getting the chance till she was off the LPH. He was about to find a secluded spot to work when Safia declared a cappuccino celebration—the best they could do out here—and they toasted Olivia's good fortune and Max's OCD.

"I can't believe the Russian found it. With all this." Cruz waved at his surroundings. "You'd think we'd be ahead of them."

"Then we're not doing our job," Noble said. "We have the last days of the Viking here. There is proof of his travels in here."

"Sure, lots of it, but it doesn't pinpoint—"

Noble shook his head, refusing to give in. "It does, it has to. Gregor had been looking far longer than we have and he didn't have a damn ship to peel apart." He looked at Riley. "We need everyone back here. If half of it heals, then whole, it's dangerous." When they looked to argue, he put up a hand. "The princess sent away her only family, the only people who loved her, to get rid of it. Make no mistake, the jade is dangerous. A legend is formed—"

"—when the truth is too frightening to understand," Cruz finished, smiling.

Noble patted his shoulder, then looked at Riley, waiting for his help. He nodded and he and Safia turned to the computers. The last days of the Viking's life were on this excavation site, or under analysis by scientists far smarter than he. Something would turn up, he thought, and made a mental note to go back through his e-mail and online posts with Gregor. The man had implied it was in two pieces before Noble had found proof in the monk's words, but the diary hadn't been discovered till *after* Gregor died.

Noble looked toward the hole in the ice as if he could see through the metal alloy walls. Gregor had followed the Viking, not the legend.

Olivia opened her eyes and saw soft light spilling over Sebastian. He was slumped in a chair beside the bed, his hand on the bedcovers. She shifted to her side and simply watched him sleep. He wore the gray and white cold-weather uniform, and like before, it was stripped of any insignia. Looks new, she thought as her gaze traveled over the swarthy skin any woman would envy and the sexy five o'clock shadow dusting his jaw. Her gaze traveled down his body, remembering every muscle, his big hands and the familiar feel of them on her skin, yet it wasn't just her body that recognized him, it was her soul.

As if sensing her, he opened his eyes. The smoky darkness sent a dagger of something delicious through her. *Never waste a moment* sailed through her brain. "I love you."

For a second, he looked stunned, then his lips curved in a slow smile.

"I don't think I ever fell completely out of love with you."

"I know I didn't."

That struck her with hurt, and the pain she'd caused

rushed back like a slap. "I'm sorry, my greatest shame was leaving you when you needed me most. It was selfish."

He moaned, looking crestfallen as he sat on the bed. "You need to stop beating yourself up over that. We survived just fine."

She held onto his hand. "I wanted to be your one and only, and I knew I wasn't. Your oath came first."

"Now there you're wrong. You were my world. I'd have left the Marines for you."

Her eyes flared and she reared back. "I wouldn't have asked that, not out of pride, but because I didn't marry the Marine Corps, Sebastian, I married *you.*"

He was quiet for a second, his gaze sweeping over her face. "Even though you weren't there, you brought me home."

A little cry escaped her and she cradled his face in her hands and kissed him. Desire and a sumptuous heat spiraled through her as he scooped her off the bed and onto his lap. His kiss was never-ending, his cool hands sculpting over her body, leaving her breathless, and wishing there were locks on the door.

"I loved you then, Livi," he said between kisses. "More now and I didn't think that was possible."

Her eyes burned with tears, her smile making them tumble down her cheeks. "So it wasn't just the great sex?"

He grinned. "There is that, but I don't think it would have been as exciting without it."

"Want to take a test drive? To be sure?"

He laughed against her mouth as she fell back, pulling him with her. His warm hands slid under her top and he was damn near in the bed with her when a soft knock interrupted them. He dropped his head forward for a second, then eased back, rubbing his face. He was breathing harder than her and she slid her hand over his thigh. He flinched, grabbed it, trying to glare at her and failing.

"Jesus, I'll look like a walking Viagra ad if you don't quit."

"Ooo, porn star mode. I love it."

He chuckled, folding her hands on her lap before he called, "Enter."

Cintuk stepped inside with a stack of clothing Olivia recognized as her own. "Clean, dry, no harm to the thermal suit, which is very cool, by the way, and probably saved you from hypothermia."

She accepted the stack. They were still warm, her parka fluffy, and she barely had time to thank him before he was out the door again. She smoothed her hand over a tear in her sleeve, the memory so fresh, she felt her stomach twist. She looked at Sebastian. "Any survivors from the *Northern Lion?*"

"No." He rubbed the back of his neck, a sure sign it stressed him. That could have been her. "They're recovering bodies now. McGill wants you away from this and I agree."

She eyed him, nodding. "This isn't about the relic, it's about Moscow and the FSB."

He shook his head. "Diplomats will have to handle that, but it could escalate. A Russian drone dropped the cruise missile on the *Northern Lion,* and they're not happy anyone has the evidence, especially the U.S."

"And Nevolin?"

"I want her ass in a cell and me with a rubber hose, but until she surfaces, we wait. They'll find the sub, if they haven't already." He looked confused for a second. "Ross is tracking all vessels and believes she'll try some maneuver he saw in a movie."

Clearly, he didn't get it. "*Down Periscope*—a diesel sub travels under a freighter, outsmarts a nuclear sub fleet, wins the war game." She glanced, shrugged. "Yes, I still love silly movies." Sitting in the bed, she grabbed the clothes, wiggling into them. "Nevolin will go where her father found the half, she said in Benzù. I need to know how he did that. If I were Jal I'd have pitched them over the side of the ship and said forgettaboutit. We need a hookup with Cruz and to talk to

Noble. Nevolin knows where to go, we don't." She started to get out of bed, but he stopped her.

"Slow down, woman. You can't do it on this boat. There are ten ships in these waters. The air traffic here can't be spared for ship to shore, and Ice Harvest is classified. I called in favors to get here, and I'm fresh out. SSU is out of it. The U.S. Navy is in charge now."

She wondered about the favors, then said, "So no more intel either, huh?" She rolled up socks and pulled on her boots, then started lacing them.

"We have our own." He winked. "They don't need to know it."

She yanked the laces so hard she had to loosen them twice. "I'd rather see all three of them captured than find the relic. Kolbash . . . he just needs to die." She tied the laces, tucked them in, then smoothed her pant leg, trying to push down that totally mind-numbing fear lurking just below the surface. The moment Kolbash fired at her and she knew she'd never get off the rig replayed in her mind. She felt her heart pound again, the clarity of panic making her mouth dry. Her hand trembled as she rubbed her temple. *Never so scared in all my life,* she thought and lifted her gaze to Sebastian. He must have read something in her expression because his big hand swept over her hair, cupped her jaw.

"You're safe now, baby."

She turned her face into his palm, an ache in her throat. It magnified in seconds, and she tried to smother it, hating the weakness, but then he said, "You thought you were going to die out there, alone."

Olivia nodded and couldn't stop the tears. She clung to him, her fingers digging as her throat choked with sobs. He held her tightly, rubbing her spine, patiently letting her cry all over his clean uniform.

"I understand, *cherie,*" he whispered, then he told her about Singapore, the bomb meant to kill Safia and what it was like being trapped in the aftermath of the blast. That's

328 / Amy J. Fetzer

why Noble disappeared so suddenly last year, she realized, and when he described his injuries, his life slipping away, she tipped her head back.

"You know when it's ending, you can feel it, and you bargain with God. I don't care who you are, you bargain. I swore I'd find you." He laughed to himself. "But you didn't have a past, and honestly, I stalled the last couple months because a part of me was terrified you were married with children."

She sniffled. "And if I was?"

He eyed her. "Making you a widow wasn't out of the question."

She laughed, giving him a little shove, and he offered a wad of tissues, then pressed his lips to her forehead. "Get your jacket, Livi." She met his gaze. "The intel officer needs to debrief you first, then I'll get us off the ship."

She grabbed her parka, following him out. "God, I hope it's to someplace that involves sandals."

The minute she was near, he whispered, "It involves getting naked and prone."

She met his gaze, her smile sly. "Oh, honey, I *know* we can do better than that."

Reykjavík, Iceland

McGill was sending a jet for them, but it would take at least five hours to arrive. The long flight from the Landing Platform to land made him anxious to locate Nevolin. The battle group had the sea blocked, the missiles confiscated, and there were nearly a thousand sonar buoys floating out there trying to locate the minisub. Nevolin had less than an hour to surface or die. He wished she'd save them all the trouble, but with the relic in her possession, he knew she'd want it all.

From the backseat of probably the only hired car in the city, Sebastian watched the scenery pass. Reykjavík Airport was crowded with reporters and their equipment, and they filled every hotel. All they needed was a place to wait for contact with Deep Six, and he didn't wonder how Mac managed it, but Sebastian felt like the walking dead and needed some sleep.

Olivia's warm hand slid inside his jacket and his muscles jumped to attention.

It wasn't sleep he needed, really, and he should have known better than to give her an inch. She was the epitome of decorum through the debrief and even on the helo ride with Max and the Ice Harvest squad. But that's what anyone could *see*. She was subtle, but she was armed. She knew his buttons to push. He relished every second of it.

Sebastian rubbed his hand down his pant leg to keep from grabbing her right now. He didn't think the driver would appreciate the erotic movie playing in his head and his eagerness to start the show. Tucked to his side, she tipped her face up.

"Camp Lejeune, on the riverbank, under that beautiful oak tree."

His gut clenched at the memory of making love at dusk, like Adam and Eve. The heat of the evening, sweat-slick skin, and some inventive positions tripped through his mind. "I remember the sounds you made." She inhaled sharply and close to her ear he said, "The whole world's gonna hear them again if you don't hush up." She'd been teasing him with little hints of their past escapades. She had a lot to chose from, and his memory was too damn sharp.

"Oh, so unwise to issue a challenge, Sebastian." Her smile softened, that sexy tilt of her eyes. Her hand slid dangerously low across his stomach.

As the car pulled in front of the Reykjavík Hilton, he was anxious to get out of the public eye. He could feel the blood pumping to his groin as he opened the door. She climbed out, brushing against him. She'd shopped for less than an hour and while her efficiency at it was a small mercy, her Cheshire Cat smile played on his imagination till he could barely sign the register. She made an effort not to touch him, and it turned him on more. Really, he needed to get a grip before her effect was noticeable. He waved off the bellman, then grabbed her hand. With her shopping bags and his duffel, he dragged her to the elevator. He punched the number, then snaked his arm around her waist.

"Stop teasing."

"Ahh, but teasing implies no follow-through. If you can't tell the difference, I'm gonna have to work on that."

Her hand slid down his chest and beyond his belt. He closed his eyes for a second as she molded him. He clamped her wrist. "We'll embarrass our country in a few minutes."

"That's only if someone's watching." Her brows wiggled, and the minute the door swooshed open, she scooped up the bags and left the elevator. Sebastian couldn't wipe the smile off his face if he wanted, and followed. The view was great, her short fur jacket showing off her perfect behind in leather pants. It was all the airport shops had to offer, and whatever was in those bags. He didn't care. She wouldn't be wearing it for long.

Swiping the card, she sailed into the room ahead of him, and inside he dropped his duffel, glanced around, and zeroed in on her. She tossed off her jacket, loosened her braid. The way she was looking at him punched his sex drive to Mach 1 and he barely noticed the fire in the stone hearth warming the suite. It was already hot enough and he threw his jacket aside.

Her gaze strolled over him and just the thought of starting this again twisted inside him, warning him it was a lot bigger than old lovers and monkey sex. He advanced, wanting more, yet knew the instant he touched her there would be nothing left of them in about fifteen minutes. The closer she stepped, the harder his chest hurt. He stopped inches from her, crowding her. "There's no turning back, Olivia. We cross this line, it's forever."

Her features tightened, her gaze searching. "All or nothing?"

"Yes. It's selfish, all on me, baby, but I don't think I could handle losing you twice in a lifetime."

Her pretty green eyes teared. "I love you, Sebastian. I haven't said that to another man in fourteen years."

His heart did a quick tumble at that. "A piece of paper won't make a difference. It didn't—"

She covered his mouth with her fingertips. "Don't doubt me, please." The glossy sheen in her eyes about killed him and he grasped her wrist, kissed her palm. "It's all, Sebastian. You know I can't do anything halfway." She tried to smile, the tremor in her voice wrenching through him. "You have every part of me there is. You always have. Forever." He bent and she stretched to kiss him, her arms sliding around his neck and holding on.

"Not all of it," he said, laying soft kisses at the curve of her neck, the hollow of her throat. "And if memory serves . . ." He stroked a finger just inside her hip and smiled when she curled into it.

"Go ahead, play me like a fiddle. My body is your temple and I'm ready for worship," she said, and he choked a laugh. Then her warm mouth tasted his throat, her hands busy pulling his shirt from his trousers. The instant her skin met his, his muscles contracted like obedient little soldiers. Something lit in her eyes and he knew he was in for fun. Years ago, they'd be on the floor by now, yet the raw sensuality moving between them begged for patience, the slow slide of lips and tongue, and he coaxed her closer, but she turned in to the bedroom. She kicked off her boots, then stripped off her sweater, letting it drop. Her blouse followed and like a hound, he scented after her. His gaze traveled her smooth back, her rock-climbing muscles flexing as she peeled the tan leather pants down over that fantastic rear.

"Oh God." A thong. The noose of all men, he thought, and couldn't wait to get it off her.

She glanced back and did a little booty roll. "Icelanders have good taste, huh?"

His gaze ripped over her ripe body barely covered in

ocean blue silk and lace. "Oh yeah, that will keep me warm in winter."

She laughed lightly, and Sebastian advanced, thinking there's nothing sexier than a confident woman. She plowed her hands under his shirt and cable sweater, pushing them off over his head. Her tongue snaked over his nipple, the cushion of her breasts against his skin making him harder. He palmed her waist, slid his finger along the edge of the lacy cup, then bent, pulling it down. Her nipple spilled into his mouth and she gasped, her head dropping back. A moment later, the lacy scrap was gone, and he filled his palms with warm skin and woman, thumbing circles around her nipples till she was squirming.

"You need to get naked right now." She fumbled with his belt, his zipper. "Right now." She opened his jeans, dove her hands inside. He flinched when she wrapped him and he clutched her, then swept her off the floor and pitched her on the bed. She laughed and rolled to her knees, brazen, bare except for the blue thong.

Her hand on her hip, she snapped her fingers, then patted the mattress. "Playtime."

Laughing, he stripped with record speed, then reached for her. She practically leapt into his arms, her mouth turning him mindless. But he knew what she liked, what made her wild, and her sassy smile melted into a sigh as his lips closed over her taut nipple. His tongue snaked and she arched into him, offered more, watching him draw her nipple deep into the heat of his mouth. He gave it up slowly and dragged his tongue down the center of her stomach, nipped at her hip and felt her muscles jump. Then he hooked the thong, following the line of silk to her center, and she squirmed. He tugged the thong lower, teasing her flesh, then covered her center. She was damp and warm, and she held his gaze as he pushed a finger inside her, intimate, invading. Her breath shuddered, her eyes drifting closed. He toyed with the soft flesh, slicking her.

She whimpered, "Unfair," then gasped when he plunged

two fingers inside. She stiffened, panting as he stroked her, her hips rocking with him, and energy thrummed through her so thick he could taste it on his mouth. Then she crawled onto his lap, straddled his thighs, whispering how she wanted him, that she remembered the feel of him inside her and he better not hold back.

Slick skin to skin, they held still for a second. Eyes locked.

"I've missed you." Tears choked her voice.

Olivia was desperate for him. For the love she once threw away, for the man who wanted only to love her. Her hand trailed down his muscled torso, and lower, and she wrapped her hand around his hardness. His eyes darkened, and she watched his handsome face as she pushed his erection down, inching her body closer. The moist tip of him touched her slick folds and his grip on her waist tightened mercilessly.

"Jesus."

She rocked in a teasing slide, guiding him, but he was having none of that. He held her and thrust, filling her in one smooth stroke. Her gasp tumbled into his mouth, her body quivering in his arms. "Oh God, Sebastian."

"I know, *cherie.*" He ravaged her mouth. "I know."

It wasn't enough. He wanted her screaming, wanted her weak and panting and vulnerable—only for him. He moved, and drank her in—her wild red hair, the ripe round curves of her body—and she shoved back. Her breathing trembled and he held her gaze, loving the way she inhaled as he withdrew, the erotic smile in her eyes. Nothing was the same between them, each touch and whisper solidifying what they already knew, and when her hand slid down his chest to feel him plunge into her, he saw a different woman, exotic, exquisite.

"Olivia."

He drove his fingers into her hair, tipping her head back, and laid claim with his mouth, but her possession imprinted him. His kiss deepened as he slowly lowered her to the bed, whispering his love, his desperate need of her as he slid free and plunged again. The air in the room pulsed, flavored with her gasps, the snap of the hearth flames casting a glow over

334 / Amy J. Fetzer

her skin. Dampness pearled on her throat. He gripped the
headboard, his palm under her hips as he lifted her to him in
a slow piston of smooth flesh and woman.

Her body pawed his, drew him back, and his pace quickened. He slammed his eyes shut, the tight fist of her gripping his erection like a glove. Heat climbed up his spine, and he swore it split him in half. Tanned muscle and strength hovered over her, pleasured her. Her softness touched more than his skin, but his soul. She reached up and smoothed her fingers over his jaw, let them caress down his body to feel him plunge into her. It heightened his awareness, and her hips curled with each stroke, letting him feel every inch of his erection sliding in her. She never broke eye contact, her body undulating like a scarf in the wind.

She gripped his arms, her tempo increasing, and he recognized the glaze in her eyes, her rapid panting, and he surged harder, longer, adoring her little screams. Then he felt it, the ripple of pleasure, her hot tight center wrench and claw his erection. Sebastian thrust savagely and she begged for more, daring him to lose control with her. He felt the sharp edge of the moment, met her gaze, and sank deeper. Waves of pure ecstasy tore over his limbs, a great beast roaring up his spine, then his world sharpened, crashed, his climax rocketing through him and into her. Olivia arched, her back bending so deeply he thought she'd snap. She gripped his hips, grinding him into her. She cried out his name and he held her, suspended, eyes locked till the last tremors flexed through them. She smiled slowly, breathless, and they sank into the mattress, Icelandic down wrapping them in a cloud.

Her fingers skipped over his back. "You have not lost your touch, baby, I don't care what they say."

He chuckled, his face in the pillows, and had to gather the strength to lift his head. He kissed her, and he rolled to his back, taking her with him. He pushed strands of hair from her face, watching his moves.

She folded her arms on his chest, rested her chin there. "Marry me."

"Again," he whined.

She jabbed him.

He was hoping to do that, but . . . "With a priest. You're not getting quickie anything this time."

She grinned, lurched to kiss him. "No fat Elvis JP with a cape? Damn."

He tossed her on her back, hovered over her, then insinuated his knee between her thighs, pushing them apart. "But let's make sure you can't wear white."

She laughed, welcoming him, reminding him she wore red in Vegas, and he'd married a virgin.

EIGHTEEN

Sebastian closed the phone. The jet was on the tarmac, refueling. He couldn't stall any longer and crossed to the bedroom to wake Olivia. Inside the massive bed draped against the cold, she was sprawled across it, the downy covers pooled around her hips. Her hair masked her face, but her hip was bruised dark, and he thought, that's got to hurt. Made it worse last night, probably, though she didn't complain. He called to her as he crossed to the hearth, turning up the gas fireplace radiating warmth into the bedroom. She stirred on the bed and he got a strange satisfaction as she rolled over, moaned, and stretched.

She smiled up at him. "Hi."

Something wrenched in his chest. "Hi. It's seven A.M. Sore?"

"Incredibly. My butt is killing me." She poked it in the air. "Wanna massage it?" He didn't say anything, and she frowned. "I've lost my glow, haven't I?"

"Not unless you were aiming for black and blue."

She twisted, looking back at her hip. "Wow, it's going to take a lot of makeup to cover that up." Then she sniffed the air. "Is that food?"

"Nothing gets by you, huh?" She rolled her eyes. "I'm afraid there's not much beyond dried or pickled fish here, let me tell you. But you need to dress." He tapped his watch. "We have a plane to catch." She glanced at the clock, then pushed up off the bed, moving a little slower. She came toward him in her all naked glory. She never was shy about her body, and he wanted nothing more right now than to take her right back to that bed and love her till the land of the midnight sun went dark. But McGill wouldn't appreciate the delay. She leaned against him, every inch of her steaming through his clothes.

"As much as I wanna make up for lost time, my resistance is at an all-time low. Can you please behave?"

She scoffed. "You say that after . . ." She waved at the bed, the floor before the fireplace, "and especially that," pointing to the scoop chair. She grabbed her clothes as she passed him on her way to the bathroom.

He heard a little shriek and stuck his head in. "What?"

She pointed to her reflection. "I look awful."

She looked sexy as hell. Her hair was a wild cloud around her shoulders. He reached for her, laying his mouth over hers in way that told her it wasn't her appearance that drew him to her.

"Thirty minutes," he said. "McGill wants us at a secure location to transmit." She frowned. "With all the ships in the water, there are too many spies listening in." His gaze lowered over her body and he couldn't help copping a feel of everything she displayed. "Now you're down to twenty-eight minutes."

"Then stop touching me!" She pushed him out the door. "Find my panties, will you?"

He pulled them from his pocket, swinging the lacy scrap on his finger. "I think I'll keep the souvenir."

"You have *me*." She snatched them. "And going commando is not an option. Not in leather pants."

Sebastian grinned like an idiot as she closed the door in his face. He walked into the living area, glancing at the laptop as he crossed to the coffee service. Before he'd taken his first sip, the screen blinked to life. Incoming from Deep Six. Must be important for Mac to risk it, he thought, and nearly dropped the cup when he saw an aerial video stream. The minisub was caught in a fishing net and hanging off the side of a commercial trawler. SEALs crawled over the ropes, and he held his breath as the teams cracked it open like a can of peas. Two minutes later, he realized it was empty.

Ice Harvest

Noble sat inside a double cube used for conferences and adjusted the space heater, missing New Orleans and the fall temperatures that still warranted shorts. He glanced at the large laptop, the webcam blinking. He was anxious to find the pieces and laid out his paperwork in neat stacks, then started paging through jpegs of artifacts lifted from the dig. The general was sending out the materials to better repair the damage and get some of the analyzing equipment back here with the technicians. McGill wanted them operating now that the threat was elsewhere, and felt twenty-five scientists lurking in one area would compromise SSU. Noble agreed, especially with all the news reporters on Greenland covering the ships amassing in the Greenland Sea. Amazingly, their National Research Institute cover was still firmly in place.

He sat back and stared at the large flat-screen monitor, trying to understand how Gregor found the jade half somewhere west of Tangier by re-creating the notes Nevolin had shared on the *Northern Lion*. He had archive copies of the papers purchased by Gregor around the time they'd first discussed the legend online. Frowning, he opened the older e-mails and did a quick search of the date.

The Russian *had* mentioned visiting the *Khattara*—the ancient underground tunnel water system in Morocco. Portions were still bringing water inland, but the system was collapsing and the cavities stretched across the entire country. If the Viking hid it there, how on earth did Gregor locate it? According to the notes Nevolin shared, Gregor had been in Svalbard, Iceland, and the practically uninhabited Saint Josef Island. They were all once Viking strongholds.

He feared he may never know the entire path, and glanced at the maps positioned on the wall of the cube. The twelfth-century reproduction was overlaid with a transparency of the most current cartography, and typical of intelligence, the intelligence outposts were marked with yellow dots. Over that was another transparency mapping only Norse trade routes all the way to Turkey and into China. Each reference was substantiated with documented artifacts, local legends, trade records, and ships' pilot logs. Archaeologists were learning that the Vikings traveled great distances, the wide shallow draft of their ships allowing them to navigate rivers nearly effortlessly. They could travel where the galleon and clipper could not.

He poured more coffee, glancing at the time. He would never grow accustomed to the constant light and never knew for certain if it was morning or night.

He tried to imagine living with the long seasons, to think like a Viking, his task, and that the jade stone had, essentially, taken his daughter from him. He'd need to be rid of the jade pieces as quickly as possible. Buried and unmarked would have been his first choice. He considered that commerce was bursting because of the Crusades and the armies marching toward it. Scandinavians had fought in the holy wars, not for faith, but for plunder. The few coins collected by the Norseman showed he didn't venture far this trip. From Ireland south to Morocco were trade routes to Portugal Spain. He'd bypass England, he thought, because the commodities sold and traded bore a commonality with Ireland's goods. The Viking would be bringing necessary supplies back to his people. Analysis of the flora and fauna of the period and the small cask of honey implied he was in Morocco. Why honey, when the Viking Jal likely raised his own honeybees for mead? Perhaps a sampling to compare with his own, he thought, but couldn't ignore the science that said it was harvested on the North African coast.

He tipped a nod to Gregor for collecting the Portuguese, Moroccan, and Spanish merchants' papers, their financial records with several Scandinavian traders. Yet it was the personal mark of Jal, his signature, that lead Gregor to Benzù. A Rune spelling of his name. Sort of. Runes were more than representations of letters to Vikings, but tribal marks, signatures, and philosophy existed behind each one. Reading runes was as common a practice today as it was when Jal traveled the globe.

He enlarged a coin, wishing it had been cleaner when the photo was taken. Restoration was secondary to cataloging when the coming winter would make remaining on the ice a test of survival, not science. Dana was a few minutes from the dig, he thought eagerly, then paged back, enlarging a piece of sea glass. It looked like something found on any beach. The paragraph below it stated it was found with five other coins with the Viking, and he glanced as the photo of the small drawstring purse beside it. Traders rarely dealt in coins. Too many currencies and not all honored in all regions unless it was gold. The dinar was a currency match for Northern Morocco. The dated coin was exquisitely engraved. The piece of sea glass was meaningless, a token, and for giggles, he clicked on it, enlarging it a hundred times. He backed it up, his brows drawing tight.

What he thought were cracks in the glass were actually scratches. And intentionally made.

Four hours earlier

His air was spent when Dimitri saw the marker underwater and he let the propulsion torpedo drift away to grasp the red flag, then the rope line. Lizveta was right behind him with Stefan. He pulled to the surface, releasing his tanks and weight belt. They sank as the line hoisted them out of the water. He broke the surface, and saw the rope netting hanging from the ship. He released his hood and yanked off his face mask to grab on. He climbed, still surprised that the cold didn't affect him. His strength increased by the hour and he flung himself over the rail. He stood, then turned to Veta. She moved like a monkey, rapidly, and when she reached the rail, he gripped her under her arms and lifted her to the ship.

She smiled, wildly laughing, and he couldn't help returning it. It had been a long time since he'd seen her so carefree. Once Stefan was aboard, they shucked their dry suits, but his friend did not look well. Dimitri helped him out of it, but he was forced to wear the boots.

He looked at Veta and kissed her. She slipped a weapon from the holster at her leg. "I love you," she said, then turned away and strode toward the wheelhouse. Crewmen backed out of her path. The captain stepped out, sucking on a honey stick. He looked as if he hadn't bathed in a month.

"We go no farther." He sanded his fingers together.

Veta slapped them away. "Yes, we do." She pushed the gun in his face, against his eye. "Proceed to here. Quickly." She handed him a slip of paper. He took it, but didn't read it. "Now, Captain."

He didn't. "Money." He dragged out the word. "Or you go back in the sea."

Impossible, of course, Dimitri thought. The air tanks were empty, though according to Veta they should have run out long before now. The jade, he thought, and understood the relic was all she'd said it would be. Dimitri would not doubt her again. His gaze fell to the sack dangling from her belt. He felt incredibly drawn to it.

"You'll be paid when we reach our destination." She glanced around at the crew. "You could kill us and toss us overboard now, but Vlad wouldn't be happy, dah?"

The captain snickered, looking her over before he stepped into the wheelhouse. Vlad was likely dead or prisoner, he thought, staring over the bow to the ship waiting for the next leg.

Miles away, American warships and Danish fighter jets were hunting for them and it was a matter of hours before they sifted through the intelligence and found the sub. Dimitri didn't believe they had as much time as she calculated, but he could barely contain his energy. After months when he barely had the strength to dress, he relished life without the treatments and medications.

"Stefan, watch them." The scarred man faced the crew and aimed his assault rifle. It was still frosted from the cold, and Dimitri withdrew a weapon, racking the slide before he took position beside the culling tray with a perfect view of the crew. He waved the gun, and Veta walked the length disarming them, tossing the weapons overboard. The filthy crew stared at her, and he glared them into submission, his finger flexing on the trigger.

"Dimitri?" He met her gaze. She pushed the weapon down, smiling through her confusion. She touched his face, his lips. "We are almost free. Moscow is suffering and we have our justice."

He didn't agree, yet remained silent. She was swimming in euphoria. Her triumph, he admitted, was stupendous, but they weren't liberated from this mess yet. And may never be, he thought, glancing at the sack.

The sun was lower in the sky when they reached their rendezvous with a cannery ship. Like a dumping ground for fishermen, the ship was a floating factory, turning out a finished product before it docked. The fishing trawler sailed alongside and they had only a few moments to get aboard and continue. He wasn't interested in anything except the helicopter on the pad at the top. It belonged to her now. Her dirty money, he thought of it, though it had saved their lives often enough. He'd no one to thank for that—not that he would—the benefactor kept on the edge, sex and name undetectable.

It's best not to know these things, he'd learned. As the trawler's rubber tire bumpers scraped along the cannery hull, Dimitri had to tip his head back to see the railing. A metal and rope ladder rolled down and Veta was at the bow. She caught the rope line guide, drawing the end of the flexible ladder to her. She didn't wait for him and grabbed on, swinging for a moment before she climbed. He frowned at her agility and speed. Waves boiled around the ship and he waited till she was on deck before he started his climb. Stephan was slower to board and on the deck, he staggered, then fell to a keel of rope. Dimitri told him to rest, then grabbed the binoculars.

"Dimitri, come, quickly."

He sighted on the horizon. He could see vague shapes on the water. The Americans were surrounding the missile ships. He hadn't time to mourn his friends on the *Lion,* but they'd never intended to return after the video. It amused him that Veta got everything she wanted and her benefactor had, so far, nothing. He lowered the field glasses, an unfamiliar feeling spinning through his skin. His breathing increased, and his hand tightened on the binoculars. And tightened. He heard the pop of breaking glass and looked down. The lens was powder at his feet.

He inspected the binoculars, the dent in the casing, strangely amused. He was about to throw it in the sea when Stefan called to him, then gestured. He looked to the small helo pad on the upper deck and quickly overtook the ladders and stairs to the top. Wind unsteadied his footing as he joined them. He handed her the broken glasses and shrugged. She frowned at them, then him, her gaze inspecting.

"I am better than fine, do not worry so." He touched her cheek, a gentle move that melted the stiffness in her shoulders. He kissed her briefly, then climbed into the pilot's seat and performed the preflight. He turned over the engine. The blades beat against the air in slow pops of noise that echoed over the sea. Veta pulled on a helmet, Stefan behind her, booting up the notebook. The satellite was in range and if Stefan could track, so could anyone else. The storm was dissipating, the skies lightening to the never-ending dusk as he lifted off and turned toward the island.

Dimitri searched the helicopter deck for the sack, the shape of the jade stone feeling familiar now. He needed it near. She didn't have to tell him, he knew. Beside him, Veta tuned a radio, searching for chatter on the explosions, and her broadcast. He'd seen the confirmation when she loaded it to the Internet, but she wasn't certain it had reached Europe. She shook her head, looking scared that her efforts had failed.

It mattered little. It was done, and avoiding the authorities was their only priority now. The volcanic rock of the island crested the horizon, the cliffs to the north topped with snow. A ring of mist surrounded it and he glanced at his gauges, his fuel, then circled west to land at Keflavik. The Americans had abandoned the bases several years ago. They'd been untouched ever since. As he brought the aircraft to the small field, he called to Veta. She looked up and smiled. A jet sat near a hanger door, and he hoped there was food inside. And clean phones.

"It appears our friend's not upset that the Americans and Danes have the missiles."

"He does not know," she said lowly. "He would not get that close. Not with all of them monitoring communications."

Dimitri knew that it would only take a single word spoken over a phone to put the authorities on their trail, and now, they were looking. "Will I meet this man?"

"No. Never. And neither will I."

Somewhere over England

Their secure location was about twenty thousand feet above sea level. The jet was heading south. That's all Olivia knew. Landing anywhere didn't make a difference unless they knew where the second half was hidden. The pressure was on her.

She stared at the toes of her boots as she paced in the jet's short corridor. Her leather pants swished annoyingly, but she couldn't sit still. Nevolin was ahead of them, and she still couldn't believe the woman had left the minisub in those temperatures, even in a dry suit. One crazy woman, she thought, something niggling in the back of her mind. She'd been trying to drag it forward for the last hour, then rubbed her forehead and threw in the towel. Recalling the hours on the *Northern Lion* was a little more traumatic than she expected and when she looked around the cabin, five faces smiled back at her. She smiled back. The four Ice Harvest Marines were in civilian clothes and sitting in various seats, plowing through mounds of delicious looking baked goods like they hadn't eaten in a while.

"Better than Icelandic dried fish, ma'am," Recker managed between bites. And lots of lamb, she thought. Icelandic cuisine wasn't one of her favorites. Her gaze swung to Max sitting outside the cockpit. Despite the two computers built into the wall, his attention was locked on his TDS Recon. The little computer was slightly larger and thicker than a Blackberry, coated in black rubber and with a glow-in-the-dark keypad. He chomped into a muffin without taking his eyes off the screen.

Her gaze slid to Sebastian. He was tucked in the opposite wall, stretched out in the rust colored sofa, his boots hanging off the edge. His eyes closed, he listened to whatever was coming through his headphones. The cord stretched across the aisle to the computers. She envied their calm when she felt hyped. Nevolin was ahead of them by several hours at least. *What does she know that I don't?*

She grabbed the stacks of papers near his feet and thumbed through the first few. She'd read them twice already. They were copies of what Noble recalled from Gregor's notes. Nevolin shared because she wanted Noble's help, but he wasn't getting out alive after that. Not if she caught on that he'd done a damn fine job of leading her astray.

She felt watched, like a stroke down her body, and knew it was Sebastian. She looked in his direction. His lips curved with tender humor and it was all she needed for last night to flood back with amazing clarity. She hoped her blush didn't give her away, then gave up any pretense and shooed his feet off. He sat up, propping his arm on the back of the sofa.

She wiggled into the crook of his arm, leaned her head on his shoulder. "Do you believe in magic?" He blinked, looking confused. "On the *Northern Lion,* Nevolin showed off her lab, and a pile of fabric she said wrapped the jade. I got a brief look, and it was definitely wool, but I think it was more than just to protect it. I think it was to protect anyone who handled it." Sebastian's frown deepened. "I think the princess put a spell on it."

All attention was suddenly on her, the cabin gone silent. Even Max stopped eating. "Seriously? What made you think that?"

"The fabrics were embroidered with symbols and criss-crossed three times in three places. With chains, silver maybe. It's the rule of three."

They frowned at her, but Max spoke up. "Odd numbers are more powerful than even, to witches, at least, and let's face it, the Maguire's princess was one, in spades." He winked at her.

"Imagine knowing her, huh? She cut the jade in half, for pity's sake," Olivia said, thinking of the odds she was facing then. She was a witch who loved a man accused of murdering his future brides. "But the wrappings coincide with the monk's interpretation of her. But it's breaking the spell that really concerns me. In place for almost nine hundred years and suddenly ripped off? That can't be good."

"So you *do* believe in magic?" Sebastian said, his lips quirking.

She met his gaze. "With the Odd Squad, I've learned anything is possible, and after reading the monk's diary, yes, I do. The jade is a powerful object, we know that. I saw its results in Kolbash, and that was just half of it." She shook her head, still stunned by his transformation and the speed of it. "The protection the princess put on it is broken." In a big way, she thought, remembering how carelessly the wrappings were removed. "Whether Nevolin did it or her father, there's no way to tell, but Cruz said the vibrations inside Ice Harvest stopped when the *Northern Lion* left the area. That makes a good argument for the jade radiating something."

Max leaned back, swallowed. "You're thinking we could track the jade itself?" She nodded. "Electromagnetic pulse readings might get you something. Provided it's actually putting out something that can be tracked in the first place."

"Doesn't matter until we figure out where the Viking stashed it," Sebastian said.

Olivia sighed, settling into the sofa cushions. "Okay . . . Gregor was in Morocco. Nevolin said he'd made the trips more than once, and found it in Benzù. Soil samples from the ship confirm that. He planned on revealing the jade to his daughter when he returned from his last mission." She shrugged, unsympathetic that he didn't have the chance. If Gregor had succeeded, America would be a war zone. "The trade ports were numerous then. The Viking traded furs for sheep. Gregor found that out in Portuguese archives." From a fragment, but clear enough to see the last two items in Portuguese, and the Viking's mark. "I still don't get why Jal didn't hide it in the first place he could. The coastlines were overrun with Crusaders, and that area was Muslim ruled. It would have been dangerous and crowded."

"You're forgetting he was a warrior first." Sebastian leaned forward, picking up his coffee mug. She frowned. "And to a Viking, the jade was a weapon. A feared weapon. Wars were fought over it."

She understood his train of thought. "The monk wrote that the princess accepted it at Jal's encouraging. She'd refused it at first." Cat, as she thought of the princess, must have felt so alone to reveal the story to a Christian, let alone a monk. The Irish were probably fine with her pagan practices, but under English rule, even a hint of witchcraft meant her death.

"He'd hide it where he could retrieve it again," Sebastian said. "He'd want to be able to get it back and use it for his people." He shrugged. "I would."

The Marines agreed. Max swung the chair around and keyed up a map of the south of Spain. "Then it would have to be somewhere he could access without being seen in a very crowded place."

"And where he knew no one else would trespass either and find it too easily," Sebastian added.

A needle in a haystack, she thought. "Jal promised to hide it and tell no one. Maybe he took that to the extreme, and didn't even tell Zhu." She looked at the screen, impatient for Noble's help. She tried to make a mental list of everything pulled from the Viking ship and the most significant came to mind first. The sword, his Runic name beautifully engraved at the hilt, the jar, the embroidered stole on Zhu, the scrap of a Corrigan tartan. Suddenly, she looked up. "The coins, in his purse. It was lashed around his neck and beneath his armor breastplate and about five layers of leather, padding, and furs. That says to me he didn't share that with anyone."

"And they bathed so often then," Max said sourly, offering her a hunk of doughy bread spread with cream cheese. Right to my hips, she thought, taking a bite.

"You mean the collection of coins?"

She heard Noble's voice and turned. She touched his image on the screen, smiling so hard her cheeks hurt. Max got up and she took his seat. "Hi. Yes, there were several. A gold dinar, dirmahs, and three Roman coins. The area was Arab, Muslim ruled till the thirteen hundreds. Almohad somebody."

"Almohad, Sultan Abd al-Mu'min. He built the Tower of Homage."

It was still standing, she thought. "There was a piece of glass in the coin purse, Noble. Did you see it?"

His features tightened. *"I was just looking at it. Dana's here and she's restored it. I just sent you the jpegs."*

She scooted to the second computer and typed. The document file came up and she spread out the images. The glass was dull, the lines a dirty white. "The scratches aren't the least bit uniform, narrow and all short strokes."

Noble nodded approvingly. *"They're too crude to be something etched into the glass. Not by a sculptor. It's not an imprint. Dana says it doesn't go deep enough into the surface to be part of a mold. Glass was very expensive then, owned by the aristocracy, and this is a fragment with worn edges. That leads me to believe it was a memento."*

She agreed. "The scratches look like tally marks." She tipped her head, envisioning something in the two lines that formed a crooked V. "Or a bowl."

"A map?" Sebastian said, and she flinched as he leaned over the desk, pointing. "Hey, Noble. It's lopsided, depending on how you look at it."

"There is no up or down." She enlarged a portion, then reset it, frustrated. "Has the botanist learned anything on the plant?"

"He says it's a flowering plant, candytuft, and the soil analysis test results say it was from North Africa, some from southern Spain."

"So we have a location," she said. Sebastian left the chair and stuck his head in the cockpit for a minute. She felt the bank of the aircraft as she looked back to the photo of the piece on a lighted counter. "The marks were made from a knife, a narrow point. It had to be scraped several times to make a line." Two vertical lines, each with a flat top and bottom. Then beside it, a badly made triangle open at the bottom, and three horseshoe-shaped half circles filled the lower spaces. Two lines, she thought. Two. Lines. She inhaled.

"Two pillars." She looked at Noble. "It's two Greek pillars."

"Hercules?" Noble said, scowling down at his papers.

Sebastian glanced between the screen image of the glass and her. "I see it."

"Well, I don't," Recker said and she twisted to look at him.

"Two pillars is the Roman symbol for Hercules," Olivia said. "And he, or more precisely the fabled pillars, guard the entrance of the Mediterranean Sea. One pillar is Jebel Musa in North Africa. Near Benzù."

"Right where Gregor found it. In the old water system, I think."

The Viking and Gregor would have had to go cave diving to get in the water storage tunnels and they went on for miles. Jal would do it, she thought, not knowing why she was so certain. She looked down at the line drawing, and squinted, trying to see the shape without distraction. She flipped the image upside down, and leaned back in the chair. Her breath caught and she scooted over to look at Noble.

"I know where to look. The second pillar of Hercules."

"That's an awfully large area."

"You're going to love this," she said as she traced the shape of the etched lines to a sheet of paper, then faced the Marines. She held the paper up. "What's that look like to you?"

"Prudential Life," Max said, dusting his fingertips over a plate. "The insurance company logo."

"Yes," Sebastian said. "But the second pillar of Hercules *is* the Rock of Gibraltar."

She smiled, high-fiving him, then sat back, thinking Gibraltar was massive and they had to narrow down possible locations. Then she felt the blood drain from her face as that distant memory jumped to life. On the *Northern Lion*, the maps and diagrams. The two pillars.

Her gaze jerked to Sebastian's. "Nevolin. She knows it, too."

NINETEEN

Malaga, Spain

Veta pushed her hair off her shoulder, the dark shade startling her for a moment. She'd done everything she could to change her appearance and match it to the forged passport. Apprehension skated through her as she approached the customs agent. She was not here out of choice, but Gibraltar Airport was operated by the British military, and there were no nearby private airstrips to land their plane. Time was crucial. While a commercial flight was out of the question, the path here had been paved with bribes, she told herself as she stopped the tall desk.

The agent on the other side matched her prearranged description. He nodded ever so slightly, his hand out. She gave over the documents with a one-hundred-pound note tucked inside. Dimitri and Stefan went to different lines, and she made a casual glance, noticing large groups of travelers gathered around the television screens tuned to the BBC news channel.

The mood in the terminal was bleak and she focused on a screen. Her own face filled one side of the image, a photo she didn't remember on placards as people marched through the streets of Moscow. Another film showed a fiery ball hurled at the FSB headquarters in Lubyanka Square. It crashed through a lower window and ignited the drapes. Police formed a line, pushing protesters farther back. The mass of people had already stormed the barricades and she was surprised the police hadn't fired into the crowds, yet felt strangely proud and empowered by the people chanting her name.

The agent cleared his throat and she looked at him, took back her passport, then walked briskly toward the exit. She glimpsed Dimitri at another counter, waiting till his documents were stamped. Stefan wasn't far behind them and, spread apart, they walked quickly out of the terminal. Once outdoors, she breathed relief.

"It's good that your benefactor's clout has not run out."

"It will." She looked back at the terminal, thinking that was easier than she expected. Especially with her face in the news. She followed Dimitri as he crossed to the parking lot, staring down at a paper, then searching the rows of cars. He spied what he wanted and they rushed to the car. Behind her, Stefan walked more slowly and scanned the crowds of people, the cars, and the police checking everyone who exited.

Dimitri opened the door of a large sedan, and once inside, he lifted his pant leg to remove the relic strapped to his calf. Since she'd laid it beside him in the infirmary on the *Northern Lion,* he'd never let it out if his sight. Veta studied him, how he clutched the velvet sack and treated it like a favored pet. He insisted on carrying it. She did not care. She'd searched for it for him. He thought her obsession was to fill her father's quest, but all had been to save Dimitri. She loved him beyond all things and his cancer was taking him from her. The relic brought him back, and while his body healed, his features were changing. She couldn't say for certain with this skin growing tighter by the day—even his scars were fading—but his forehead seemed to be taller. Or was his hairline receding?

He laid it on the console between them, then started the engine, leaving the lot and stopping only to pay the fee. When she grasped the relic to store it safely, she instantly felt a humming sensation travel up her arm.

"Leave it alone."

"It must be concealed."

"Leave it!" he snapped, slapping his hand over it and drawing it closer.

She frowned at him, and the dark look he sent her gave her no comfort. Her gaze moved between him and the relic.

"I will die without it," he said and she believed him.

Then she noticed the hair on his hand that was not there two days ago before she faced front, vigilantly watching for a tail, for the police.

"You're certain where to find the rest?"

She nodded, touching it, then drawing her hand back and rubbing the tingling sensation. "Father found that in Benzú at the foot of the pillar of Hercules. Logic says the second pillar holds the second half."

"It's a big rock with tunnels. Be more specific."

"The tunnels, but I'll know more when I read the rest of his research notes."

"Then do it! We have authorities looking for us all. Our troops are dead. How long do you think your benefactor will help you? You lost his missiles."

"His crews did. He cannot blame me."

"After giving you twenty million? He will." She stared, wondering what was happening to him. He never spoke to her so harshly. "Now, Veta!" he barked and she flinched. His gaze slid to hers and she recoiled from it. Savage, she thought, and when he made a turn, his hand pawing the steering wheel, she heard it crack.

She felt the need to take it from him, to touch it and feel its energy. Her hand slid closer, but she didn't need to hold it. Energy practically arced into her hand. Then she closed her palm over it and felt the sudden rush of warmth slide through her body, into her blood. She felt it flowing though her veins, pumping through her heart.

Awareness of her surroundings amplified. Not like the scent of the air but its movement against her skin. Not the speed of the car but the wheels on the road.

She turned her gaze on Dimitri.

He didn't look at her when he said, "You feel it, da? Now see it."

He flipped down the passenger visor. She stared in shock at her reflection. Her skin was smooth and bright as it was before her father's death, before her life turned to vengeance. Capturing the second piece would renew more than their bodies. It would wipe away an ugly past and give her and Dimitri a chance for a new life.

RAF, Gibraltar

Sebastian smiled widely as he crossed the flight deck, his hand out to greet an old friend. Edward Granlen was a Royal Marine who'd dragged his ass out of a couple firefights. "Christ, it's a sin to look that young when I know you're old."

Eddie grinned, showing off perfect white teeth. "Wine, women, and more women," he said, then looked past him to the G5 jet. "That's some ride and you don't look like you're hurting for company."

Sebastian glanced between the two. Olivia's attention was on the Rock dominating the landscape, and he knew she was racking her brain to figure out where the relic was hidden in there. He introduced them.

Eddie's gaze slid to his. "Doctor? You've come up in the world." He went still, frowning at her.

"Yes, *that* Olivia," he said before he could embarrass himself, and she met his gaze. "Eddie and I served together. He saved my life."

"And God has never forgiven me," he said winking, then inclined his head to the staff cars waiting for them. He tossed Esposito a set of keys and pointed to the second car. "I don't know who is running your team, but they have some stones. Sorry, ma'am."

Olivia just smiled to herself. With four brothers, she'd

heard it all before she was ten. "McGill. The mess in the arctic."

Eddie's brows shot up as he held the door open for Olivia. "Bugger me, no kidding. Bloody damn Russians, just like Serbia, they want everyone suffering under their version of socialism." His gaze followed her as she gingerly climbed inside and he whistled to himself, shaking his head. "American women. God, I love them."

Olivia in leather pants was a feast for any man within a hundred yards, but Sebastian felt a little pinch of jealousy and eyed Eddie. "Off limits, pal," he said climbing in beside her. She grasped his hand, yet was strangely silent. "You okay? How's your hip?"

"Sore as hell, but I'll live. I need to get out there." She ducked to see the Rock, frowning. She'd seemed uneasy since they landed.

Max climbed in the front, then looked back between the seats. "Gibraltar is locked down and has been searched. Tourists aren't happy about that, apparently. Nevolin could have landed at any airstrip. We have alerts across the wire, but her broadcast should put her face across the world. Someone will spot her."

"A woman with two Russian men can't be that hard. The accents were pretty heavy, but I promise you, she's changed her appearance. She's already here."

Sebastian looked at her.

"She's had her father's notes and he found the first half. It's reasonable to think he knew where the rest was located." She sighed hard. "This thing was never meant to be found."

Eddie turned over the engine and drove off the flight deck, then maneuvered through the streets to the Devil's Tower Camp. The British Royal Regiment there was offering assistance but since the missile capture and the hit on the *Northern Lion*—his heart skipped with the memory—it was dicey politics. The UK declared the abandoning of the seventy-three men an abomination and the broadcast proved the harsh reality of the Russian FSB. With MiGs dropped inside Danish waters, the Danes were going for blood along with the United States. Deep Six was trying to draw out her benefactor. Someone paid her millions. They'd expect a return. Sebastian hoped Nevolin's backer did them all a favor, but with her moving through three countries easily—it was a sure thing that she had some heavy-duty help. He suspected it came from inside the FSB. And the Russian mafia, a given, but there weren't too many with the ability to move money, equipment, and MiGs that quickly. Infiltrating either organization wasn't healthy. Beckham had already tried it.

In less than fifteen minutes, they were walking into the NSA SIGINT listening post. They waited for the Marines and security checks. Sebastian was amused when Olivia flashed her ID and the agents aboard couldn't bow and scrape fast enough. She seemed oblivious as Eddie led the way into a conference room set up for their use. They were prepared.

Safia and Riley were already there, looking a little tired from the long flight hops to get here, but that didn't stop Safia. She leapt from her chair before a computer, rushing to Olivia. Sebastian smiled as they exchanged hugs, and Riley brushed a kiss to her cheek. "Welcome back from the dead, lass."

"Nice to be here, and thanks for keeping Ice Harvest together. I'd be really pissed if Nevolin had destroyed that, too." Her staff were all back on the dig, finishing the excavation while Noble and Cruz tried to narrow the jade's location.

"I'm linked with Deep Six," Safia said, "and Sam and Viva should be arriving at Ice Harvest by now. I'm really glad you're alive."

"Me, too." Olivia's gaze slid to Sebastian's and her lips twitched with a sexy smile.

"I brought you a couple changes of clothes," Safia said, nudging a travel case across the floor. "I didn't trust Cruz, but that's from him, with a message, don't be like China."

Olivia thanked her, then went to the box, ripping through

the tape. She lifted out a leotard-like suit, a zipper up the front from thigh to throat. "Dragon Skin. Aww, he's worried again."

Safia laughed. "Hey, don't knock it. It's a good worry, and that suit works great, but it almost drowned me." Safia glanced at Riley.

"And every woman needs to feel thirty pounds heavier, huh?" She dropped it into the box, nosing through the rest, and Sebastian frowned at the devices to register thermals and electrical current. Sebastian plucked it out, held it up, and Olivia shrugged. "Cruz thinks we can use it to track the jade's energy." She went to the computers, keying in the codes to reach Ice Harvest and waiting for the connection.

"You can't explore in the dark," he said, tapping his watch.

"I'm ready. I just need to check with Noble. Maybe he has more, because we sure as hell don't have time to search the entire Rock for eight inches of jade."

Behind her along one wall two TVs were tuned to BBC and CNN. Sebastian moved closer, glancing between them. The protests and violence covered Russia like a blanket. No statements were coming out and he spotted a film clip of Putin leaving his country estate, where he'd been showing off his body for the press. Protesters filled the streets and police were fighting them back with hoses. "Nevolin has her revenge and she's gaining sympathy." People marched through the streets with her picture on a post. "Christ. They're hailing her as a hero."

"I don't give a damn." He looked at her. "That sub was made for war, nothing else, and they almost succeeded." When Nevolin's photo flashed on the screen, Olivia tensed. Sebastian felt her outrage as if he wore it, and touched her arm. She snapped a look at him. "That woman needs to go straight to hell."

"When I see her, I'll be happy to oblige."

She kissed him. "I'll hold you to that." A ping sounded and she turned to the laptop, sliding into the chair. He joined her, waving at Noble. Cruz was behind him at a desk in the communications hut.

"It has a pulse. The jade. Cruz feels that since the vibrations stopped after your adventure on the *Northern Lion,* that it's giving off energy."

"That explains the extra equipment in the box. Thank you. But what do you mean a pulse? It's inanimate. EMP maybe, but I was within two feet of it and didn't get anything except a pretty play of light and a bit of awe."

Noble smiled patiently. "The monk wrote that the princess buried it in the mountains full of copper and silver ore. If it doesn't give off some kind of effect," he said, "then how did the wolves find it to dig it up?"

The Prudential logo was the Rock alone in the water.

The reality of Gibraltar was another view entirely, especially at dusk.

Olivia stood on the top and turned full circle. The city spread out like a skirt around three sides, the tallest point of the rock open to the Mediterranean Sea. She spotted the twelfth-century Tower of Homage from here. Like most of Europe, Gibraltar was an ancient city coated with everything modern in a cramped space. Thirteen hundred feet below, police and Royal Marines kept surveillance. Traffic had to be stopped for landing aircraft because the only runway bisected Churchill Avenue, a major highway and the only road to Spain. Even the tunnel construction to change that had been stopped.

But up here, the only sound was the warm breeze. She tipped her head back and tried to imagine it eight hundred years ago and Jal sailing between the straits of Gibraltar: the unblemished coastline, nations of ships scattered in the bay. Was he here first before Benzù? She envisioned the ships on the sea, the noise of the open markets, the stream of goods unloaded. There would have been Crusader knights with their entourages, as well as peasants, farmers, and slave markets.

A few feet from her, Sebastian was rigged with PRRs and the Marines were spread out like a fence farther down the Rock at the cable car landing. Olivia wanted to climb the rock face, but at this hour, it wasn't wise. The Rock itself stretched for three miles with a seven-mile coastline. The Straits of Gibraltar had been the hub of trade for centuries, but Olivia wanted only a clue where to look for the Viking's hiding place. Three miles was a lot of land to cover. Through the binoculars, she sighted on the land below. The beach was empty except for a couple people fishing, and she studied the shoreline. Cruz had gathered weather patterns and climatology to estimate the twelfth-century shoreline, about fifty yards wider than present day, but near the Rock the erosion proved that at least on this side of the peninsula water hit the rocks.

She swung her attention right, to the east and a lone figure sitting on a large boulder on the edge of the sand. She narrowed the view and the old man looked over his shoulder up at the top. His face filled the lens, and he looked right at her. Chance, she told herself, lowering the glasses. Just coincidence. Then she looked again. He was still staring. She stepped back from the edge, glanced around. She was the only one standing on the very top, she reasoned as Sebastian moved up beside her.

"Something's up, I can tell."

She felt silly for even mentioning it, but told him about the man. He scowled, immediately sighted with the single scope. "The one on the shore with the stick?"

"Yes, but forget about it. Let's go. This isn't useful. If there was a Norse marking or anything remotely like it here, it would have been found by now. The Rock was used as a defense post during three wars. There were holes bored through it for gun batteries as early as World War Two. Surely someone would have seen *something?*"

"I agree, so what do you want to try next?"

She let out a sigh. "The shore. Maybe Saint Michael's cave?"

His glance held doubt. "It wasn't discovered till the eighteen forties." They headed back down.

"All the more reason to think he hid it there." He arched a brow. "Okay, fine, I don't know."

The answer was like a word lingering on the tip of her tongue, just out of her reach. She tried thinking like a Viking with a secret to bury as she stepped carefully down the stone path of the overlook. The café and gift shop were closed up, an officer outside it. An iron fence surrounded the cable landing and while it was a habitat for macaque monkeys that usually crawled over everything, the place was empty. The police probably scared them off, she thought, though Recker and Lewis were doing a great job at looking mean and deadly. Even the guards gave them a wide berth.

"I feel like I'm really reaching here," she said softly. "And it's ticking me off."

"Try this." He handed over the EMP device. "Can't hurt."

She turned it on, working the controls. The device made a high tone and the meter dial shot right—to the electrical box on the cable car. "Oh yeah, that's helpful," she said, stuffing it in her jacket pocket.

A few minutes later, they left the cable car, passing the entrance to the World War II and Great Siege tunnels. Men in plainclothes with radios watched the streets, the crowds. It was an impressive show of force. Near the turnstile, one man in a guard's uniform tossed food to several dogs lingering around the hillside. At the base, she jogged across the parking lot and down to the shore. Behind her, the trot of footsteps made her turn. Sebastian did not look happy.

"Uh-oh, what'd I do?"

"Made yourself a target," he growled. "You're the brains of this outfit, honey. If Nevolin wanted to stop us, all she has to do is take you out."

She felt her skin creep up her arms. "Thank you for that visual."

His expression softened and he moved in close. "I have plans for you. Don't screw it up."

She smiled and was more than willing when he leaned down to kiss her. Her gaze shot to the troops, expecting she didn't know what, but all she got were big smiles. Recker gave her a thumbs-up and she laughed quietly, walking toward the shore. The tide was out, the sand a powdery pale gray. She tried positioning herself at the same angle of the Viking's etched glass, with the highest peak on her left. It was a view from the sea, she realized, yet beyond the familiar Rock shape, the land was just as craggy, a huge portion cut smooth for rainwater runoff to the water catchments. It flowed to a reservoir supplying the British territory with fresh water. On the north side was the port and city.

She studied every shadow on the stones and while she couldn't be certain the lines on the glass represented the two pillars, Noble was researching any known artifacts recovered from the Rock to see if Norse symbols had been collected over the years. But it felt right.

She looked at Sebastian. He was turning slowly, watching the terrain. Armed and dangerous, she thought, glancing at the Marines. His carbon copies were inspecting people, passing cars, blades of grass. She walked farther onto the sand pebbled with boulders she assumed broke off the Rock. Usually pictured dark, the Rock of Gibraltar was actually white limestone with great patches of green near the long buildings on the cuff of the formation.

She was surprised to see the old man walking on the shore. She thought he'd left and felt compelled to meet him. Old man of the sea would offer what? she thought sarcastically. She started walking to him, then stopped a local guy gathering mussels into a bucket.

"Do you know that man?" She gestured.

He looked up, then swung his gaze in the old man's direction. "No, sorry," he said in accented English. "But he's been here every day for a week now. He just sits right there, sunup to sundown." He frowned. "In fact, I've never seen him leave." He went back to collecting.

She thanked him and walked with Sebastian. He slung his

arm around her waist, tucked her close. "You look . . . I don't know, like you've seen a long-lost friend."

She leaned back, eyes wide. "That's exactly what it feels like. Like I'm waiting to be shocked. I've felt . . . just weird ever since we arrived." She sighed into his shoulder. "It's like I'm missing something really obvious, and I'll hate myself when I figure it out."

"Gibraltar in the eleven hundreds was one of the biggest trade ports of the Med. A Norse trader wouldn't raise attention, except for their large size, so what's different about him that he could get around here without notice?"

"That's provided I'm reading everything correctly." She hated to think Nevolin had some piece she didn't. She went back to eliminating the obvious, counting off on her fingers. "Not his looks, for sure, his height, no, his Chinese partner couldn't go far without getting snatched for slavery. Furs, cattle, horses." She shook her head, then looked at him suddenly. "It's his ship. It had a shallow draft, but wide. That's what enabled the Norseman to travel through China by river." She looked at the mass of limestone. "There were battlements up there for the protection of the port."

"But the men at the battlements were looking out at approaching ships, not down."

He was warming to the game of supposition, the staple of archaeology. "Up that way"—she flicked a hand north along the shore—"is the Moorish fortress, the Tower of Homage lookout. So if he wanted to get anywhere near the Rock he'd have to pass the battlements of Sultan Aloumed what's his face, all the traders in the city, ships docking near where Devil's Camp is now."

He shook his head. "The cliff face makes it impossible to see the base of the Rock and centuries earlier—"

"He could get right up close to it." He smiled, gave her a squeeze, and she said, "It has to be on this side. He could climb, but that risked being seen from the water."

Several buildings were built on the rock face; the city was literally growing up the side of it. On the land side were the entrances to the tunnels and her gaze lowered to the caves. They'd been investigated by archaeologists for decades. At the base of the Rock were several cavities eroded by the sea that looked like a giant's fingerprints in the limestone. The first two were on the tours, St. Michael's and Gorham's. From this distance across the water, they looked like hobbit holes, yet the entrances were nearly fifty feet high and just as wide. Neanderthal bones had been found inside in the late 1800s—there were diorama exhibits in one, she recalled from tour flyers—and during World War II, it had been blasted for ventilation for the maze of tunnels, and New St. Michael's was found halfway up the western slope. Heck, old St. Michael's was large enough to hold concerts inside.

Then the old man sitting on the rock twisted around and looked directly at her. Her breath caught. His pale gaze pinned her for a moment, and she walked across the sand. Sebastian called softly to her. She discreetly waved to stay close. Perched on the rock, the old man was hidden in the shadows of Gibraltar and small enough that his feet didn't touch the ground. His head was covered with a tan knit cap pulled over his ears, and his entire body appeared drawn inside his ragged clothes. His skin was the color of pecans, his face and hands mapped with wrinkles.

She didn't hesitate a step, feeling somehow forced to meet him. He smoked a hand-rolled cigarette like it was a joint, and in the other hand, he gripped a walking staff jammed in the sand. From the top of the twisted wood hung strips of frayed ribbon, the ends tipped with charms of twigs, metal— she recognized a Coke bottle cap—and shells.

The old man smoked, staring out over the water.

Olivia climbed up a few stones and sat on the rock beside him. He looked a little offended, but she just smiled, motioned for him to share the smoke. She took a short drag and blew it out. She'd smoked for years and the urge never really went away. But that tasted like goat crap, she thought, handing it back. He seemed impressed, and for a long moment she said nothing, just enjoying the view with him. Sebastian was nearby in her line of vision, eyeballing the man with a look that was just scary.

"You have finally come."

She inhaled, staring at his profile. He had an Irish accent. "You were expecting me?" Impossible, of course. Even she didn't know she'd been here till now.

But he only nodded.

She met Sebastian's gaze, his scowl darkening. "How could you know that?" he asked.

"It calls."

"What calls? To who?"

He simply patted her hand, his expression patient, almost serene. "It calls to its mate." His lips curved a fraction. "And its master."

Okay, this was just too weird, she thought, and frowned to herself, mulling over the legend, then took a wild leap. "The *Siofra*?" He stared blankly. "*Di nèny ér,*" she said in Chinese.

He smiled, a little proudly, and patted her hand again. Holy shit. How could he possibly know that? Her gaze shot to Sebastian. He looked just as stunned. His dark stare on the man, he made a rolling motion to keep pressing. She searched her pockets for a pen, but knew she didn't have any paper. On her palm, she drew the rune symbol she'd found on the Viking's breastplate and sword. It looked like an arrow pointing down, and she prayed he understood. "Have you seen something like this?"

The old man stared down at it for so long she was tempted to nudge him.

"*Mjöllnir,*" he said.

A chill moved over her skin. "Yes. Thor's Hammer. Yes!"

He drew his staff closer, the ribbons fluttering, and his gaze narrowed on one in particular. He pinched a red ribbon, then yanked it off and held it out. From the end, a piece of dull gray metal twisted in the breeze. Then he dropped it in her lap.

Olivia grabbed it, tipping it toward the setting sun. Her

heart pounded when she recognized the rune of protection. The frail piece was cut from something else, or rusted away, yet she smoothed her fingers over the metal and felt the indentations. "Where did you find this?"

He pressed his palms to his thighs and with a great effort, pushed upright, then picked his way over the limestone rocks toward the water's edge. Her gaze climbed up the flat stone cliff. Was it somewhere inside the Rock? In the tunnels? Then he looked back over his shoulder. His watery gaze fell on her. He pointed west.

Okay, she got that, but it was a big rock and the labyrinth of caves and tunnels was only reachable about three hundred feet up. He wasn't pointing anywhere near that area, but to the sea, to the smallest cavern in the stone at the farthest point. The tide was rising, nearly obliterating it from sight. Then in her mind, she saw the Viking's glass, the scratches mirroring the shape. Then the half-moon cuts at the bottom were the caves. Oh crap, it was a map.

Glancing at Sebastian, she worked her way to the old man. His lips curved in a knowing smile. He pointed again to the sea. Ya know, a little conversation would help, she thought, but instead she lifted the EMP meter toward St. Michaels cave, frowning when it did nothing. She waded into the water. Waves splashed her ankles.

Sebastian stopped beside her. "Too far away to get a reading, especially with the metal in the water catchments, whatever's powering those buildings, the cable car, and the supports."

"Then we have to get inside that cave." They turned back, and Sebastian waved the troops closer. The man was already walking the path back to the road. Dogs followed him. "Got really twilight zone for a second, huh?"

"Definitely. He knew the Chinese name for the jade," Sebastian said. "That's more than enough proof for me."

Walking, she glanced back at the Rock, watching the monkeys climb down the steep cliff face near the point. From here, the macaques looked like ants crawling over a crust of bread. Suddenly, she looked at the street, the path to the tour entrance. Dogs sniffed the ground, converged. And as they approached the street, she heard their whining.

She stopped and grabbed Sebastian's arm. "The vibration isn't energy or EMP. It's sound. Like how sound bounces back on your eardrum when you put a shell to your ear. Sound vibration. The old man said it calls. Look." She pointed to the cliff. The macaques were converged in one spot far above the point like a choir waiting for the conductor. "The monk said the wolves dug it up."

"Christ. The relic is a freakin' dog whistle?"

TWENTY

The local cops didn't know what discreet meant, Max thought, his gaze strolling over the cruisers blocking traffic when they didn't need to be. The whole idea was to keep people out of the Rock tourist section, not their homes. But the Royal Gibraltar police were under the Ministry of Defense, and unlike in England, they were armed. Which was good, but they really needed to rethink those covers. The checkerboard band above the rim had to go. He frowned at the dogs weaving around the cars, sniffing, and looked toward the Rock lit from lampposts.

On the opposite side on the sea, the far point of the Rock was the thing of pictures and logos. The rest spread in a slope into the peninsula. Beautiful city, he thought, then brought his hand to his ear, pushing his fingers through his hair. The Base radio was in his sleeve, separate from the earwig that let him hear the police chatter. There wasn't much. Brits weren't keen on breaking the rules.

He walked, crossing the street, then onto the parking lot. Instead of moving closer, he walked farther away for a better view of the entrance, heading toward a trash can wired to a wood post at the end of a fence. He caught static and, like a dork, looked at the sky as if he could see the satellite working its thing up there. He moved away from the trash can and heard it again.

"—still at the entra—"

It was Russian.

He spoke into his sleeve. "Drac to Base, get Granlen's people to check the guards. I just heard Russian."

"Which area? I'll see if I can pick it up."

"Zero in on my position. It's shortwave frequency. I'm not getting more than pieces." This was not good.

Someone was on the inside.

General McGill stood at the elevators, prepared to take his SSU out of the light and back undercover. He hit the button and eyed him so long Mitch grew uncomfortable.

"Agar is your money trail, and this Vlad Dovyestof, Dragon One has offered you his personal phone number." With two fingers, he held out a slip of paper. "You'll get your time with Agar, Major."

Mitch felt humbled for a moment, then frowned. "How'd Dragon One get it?"

"Viva Wyatt. She's Salvatore Fiori's daughter."

Mitch remembered the news reports on the Sicilian Mafia boss sent to prison by his daughter after her mother was gunned down in front of her. Xaviera Fiori—not a name you'd forget—was a teenager when she testified, then disappeared. He looked from the paper to the general.

"Thank them for me, since I know Fontenòt wouldn't offer it."

The general stared. "Then you don't know Sebastian."

"I'm learning, sir."

"See, for those guys, they've had the bullshit of politics and the Company screw them out of their careers and damn near their lives, but they still do it."

Mitch knew Kincade's bomb for Safia nearly killed Sebastian.

"They don't always obey the rules, but they don't hurt anyone either, and let's be honest"—he waved—"they get the job done. One person matters more than any of this." He glanced around at Deep Six. "Protecting We the People isn't worth much when that one countryman is left behind." He wasn't speaking of him, Mitch thought, but Mills.

The elevator door slid open and he stepped inside. He faced him.

"You were a dead man before Dragon One went into Chechnya."

The skin on Mitch's neck tightened.

"To them, you're square. In my book? Not hardly."

Great, he was on the general's shit list, too.

"Next time they offer you help," the door started to close. "Don't ignore it."

Gibraltar Bay

Keeping SSU under the wire meant not involving anyone they didn't absolutely need and doing this during the daylight would destroy their cover and bring attention. But time wasn't their friend. They hadn't been on the ground that long. But Nevolin had. Marines watched the water, but Sebastian's attention was on the Rock. The closer they drew to it, the stronger the feeling of doom grabbed at him. He equated it to the dread of a root canal. Olivia looked at him, and by her clouded expression, he knew she felt the same.

"We have to go high inside. The lower levels are the pre-twelfth-century history."

Sebastian adjusted her load-bearing vest when it wasn't necessary. He'd rather she wasn't involved, but he didn't know enough about historic markings to know what to look for, and she wasn't going to be left behind. He watched her check her gear, and his confidence grew when she did it right, methodically.

Eight hundred years ago, the shore was about fifteen hundred feet out. Now the caves were underwater with tunnels leading deep into the center of the Rock. He wasn't looking forward to it. His aversion to closed spaces was a leftover from Singapore. He hated the weakness but accepted it.

The rigid inflatable boat drove across the waves, a loan from the Royal Marines.

"From everything Noble said the tunnels are higher," Olivia said over the Personal Role Radio. "There isn't any data on the caves except the three big ones on the tours."

In the dark, Sebastian met her gaze. "None?"

"Other than the Neanderthal bones, and some pottery, no. A couple dive photos, but it's off limits and is reputed to go on for miles." That made Lewis pale a little. "The Great Siege tunnels bisect the ones blasted in the forties during the war."

Or were just made wider, he thought. It was a defense post. Everything from arms to food was stored in the tunnels; the older sections were viewable through barred windows, but no access. He knew she wasn't confident about the location. But it was the old man that convinced Sebastian. Something about the way he looked at her, as if they were familiar somehow. It calls to its mate and master, he'd said. The mate of the half of stone, he assumed, but the master? He had him there. The boat slowed, the half-moon casting the Rock in silver light. He stared up at the mountain honeycombed with caves and tunnels, the cutouts for the cannon battery like gouged shadows in the dark.

Esposito slowed the RIB to an idle. Sebastian checked the PRR and waterproof hand radios, then gave the go-ahead. Olivia put her regulator in her mouth, tested it, then adjusted her mask. She waved to him and went over the side.

Lewis looked wide-eyed from the water to him. "Gutsy lady, sir. I hate night diving."

That's my girl, he thought, dropping over the side. A moment later, he was beside her, gripping her arm and turning on the Sea Scooter's light. The underwater propulsion device pulled them along.

Shining his light around, his visibility was good till they reached near the caves. Sebastian slowed. Behind her, he spotted the churn of bubbles of the Marines. They were having the time of their life, he thought. Diving had to be better than a perch on top of Ice Harvest and thirty-mile-an-hour winds. As Sebastian shined the light, the silt and algae illuminated the water like dust in sunlight. He slowed the scooter, then spied the dark hollow of the cave. A school of fish scattered, and he felt the stone walls, the surf dying, and he inflated his buoyancy converter. He broke the surface, then speared his light inside the cavern before dunking it in the water and waving it. A moment later, Olivia popped up beside him. He tossed the light onto a ledge, then pulled himself out. He turned to help her, but she was already hoisting herself up.

She spit out her regulator. "When the tide's out, this is open, walkable." She tried to stand, then opened the clasp and dropped her tanks. She shut off the air, then hooked her mask and fins on the tank. As she creeped ahead, crouching, her light illuminated the interior.

Reckers and Lewis surfaced, and Reckers popped out his regulator long enough to say, "Max says there is trouble. He heard Russian on his radio, a cross frequency, he thinks."

Sebastian cursed, then looked as Olivia and recognized her fear. "Keep going, keep looking. Our time just ran out." He looked at Recker. "Radio base. Get the cops doing a house to house." The Marine nodded, then sank under the water. Sebastian stood, dropping his tanks on the ledge, then moved them both into easy position to get them back on. "Lewis, my six. Esposito, guard the entrance, anyone approaches, shoot first because Nevolin will." He tested comms and she nodded, then moved ahead.

"There's a hollow up here." Beyond the light, the darkness was inky black.

"Careful, watch the ground. It's limestone. It breaks."

He followed her, then grabbed her arm, wedging past her. "You're not behaving, honey."

"I know. But I keep thinking about the old guy. The stone's master. What the heck is that about? How does he even know about it?"

"I got a guardian kind of feel from him. Like he was waiting to pass the torch to you." He couldn't explain, it just was.

"Me? What the hell for?"

"You are a Corrigan, Olivia."

Her wet features pulled taut, and she swung her gaze to the tunnel, then back to him. "Get outta town, no."

"Never ignore the obvious because it's obvious."

"Okay, I'll play." Olivia moved ahead, working her way around a ledge. Forced to go slow, she examined the walls, the path farther in, and considered what it looked like eight hundred years ago. How much had worn away?

"Up that way," she said, and gripped the rock, pulling herself up the slope. She could see it widening ahead and waited for Sebastian. When he touched her shoulder, she moved on. She felt the climb in her muscles, though it didn't look steep. She paused, adjusted her stance, shining her flashlight.

He glanced around. "I don't see a single place to conceal it for this long without the water washing away the rock and sending it to the bottom."

"Me either and we're a hundred feet above sea level." She pressed on, crawling over the jagged rock. She felt the air change, become less stale. A breeze ghosted over her cheek. She went still, gripping the wall and filling the cavern with light. Holy Hannah, she thought. Sebastian appeared beside her, Lewis pulling up the rear and looking like he didn't want to be here.

"Amazing, isn't it?" Giant stalagtites hung like misshapen fingers. The walls gleamed with bits of crystal, and the refracting light turned everything an iridescent blue green. Water pooled in the center, and she grabbed a loose stone and tossed it. The plop was short, the ripple fanning out.

"Shallow. The ground would have been higher here then. Look at the erosion, see how smooth. High tide would have pushed the water, maybe even created an air pocket. But that means water reaches here. We have to go higher."

"Do the World War II tunnels reach this far?"

Lewis unfolded a map encased in plastic. "No, but the siege tunnels do."

"Any way to access them?"

"Not on this map. I don't think anyone's tried coming this way."

She worked her way across the rocks, staring at the openings. She took the right one.

"Olivia?"

"It's right. Don't ask me how though. Odd Squad vibe, I guess."

She kept going, each step positioned before moving on. She'd gone about forty feet when she said, "It's flatter here. Another cavern."

She straightened and when Sebastian moved up behind her, he said, "You're now about a hundred fifty feet above sea level."

She jerked a look at him. "Really. This one twists to the right toward the sea." She took it, hunched, and had to crawl for a few feet. She went still, frowning deeply. "Did you hear that?" A hollow, tinny sound.

Lewis muttered something about if God wanted you in caves, he would have made them safer, but Sebastian was looking back toward the tunnels. He met her gaze and she knew he'd heard it.

"Keep going." He unlatched his weapon. She wedged through the opening, slipped, and Sebastian grabbed her vest.

She braced herself, then shined the light downward. "Oh, jeez, that would have left a mark."

It looked fathomless, and she felt around for another stone, then tossed it. It was a few seconds before it hit water. Her eyes widened. "Let's not go that way." She speared her light. "Up here."

Max eyed a striking woman about fifty walking by, then slid his gaze to Eddie Granlen. He sat at a outdoor café table, nursed a beer. They exchanged a nod. Eddie stood, threw down some cash, then walked in the opposite direction and stopped.

Street traffic putted along but most people were on foot. It was a beautiful cool night and he was soaking up the warmth, listening to the chatter on his PRR. Each exit of the Rock was covered by a few Royal Marines in plainclothes. The road into Gibraltar was stationed with more.

Moving into the shadows, Max sighted through his single scope, turning it to night vision and scanning the nearby windows. He squeezed the button, changing it to thermal. The area was bright with street light and he shifted from window to window, the doorways, the pedestrians beyond the barricades outside a café. He passed over the window above a restaurant, then came back to it. He spotted a figure near the window, then saw the shape of binoculars. As he walked nearer, he caught a couple words over his PRR. *Russian*. He motioned to Granlen, pointed to the second floor.

At the building, he drew his weapon, then overtook the side staircase, waiting the half minute till the officers were in position. "All in!" He pushed through the door, aiming, Eddie behind him. He heard the men tell their positions as he hurried up the cement stairwell to the second floor. Outside the door, they converged. Max kicked in the lock. The door burst open and they entered two by two, aiming. A big man with black hair sat in a corner, in the dark, a pistol in his hand. He hadn't moved, his chin on his chest.

Max could see the wire to the radio in his ear.

"Drop it." He entered, Eddie moving to his left, the team spreading out behind him.

There was a bottle of vodka on the floor between his feet. "Drop the weapon." The man lifted his head. His mouth curved in a sick smile.

"She has won and we have nothing," he said in Russian. "No country, no money. For some fuckin' rock!" His eyes shifted back and forth, deranged.

Max saw hopelessness. "It's over. Drop the weapon! Don't do it—"

The man lifted the gun to his temple and fired. The side of his head exploded like a pumpkin.

Max sighed, lowered his weapon. "Coward."

Then a woman in a towel rushed into the room and froze. She screamed. She saw the guns and put her hands up. The towel dropped. The men were caught for a second, but Max had seen better bodies. He aimed. "On your knees." She dropped, everything she owned jiggling. The troops fanned out to search the rooms.

"Who the hell are you?"

"Stacy. He's payin' me to be his friend."

I'll bet, he thought. She had her hands up, naked as a newborn, and Max holstered his weapon, then pulled her to her feet. He shoved the towel at her and pushed her into a chair. "Someone find her some clothes." He brought the radio to his mouth. "Esposito, come back." He checked the time. "Shit, they're already in the water."

"Go. I got it," Eddie said and Max looked back. A Brit came back into the room gripping a gray blue shirt. He recognized the embroidered insignia.

Like the tattoos.

Impatience clawed him. Dimitri felt a hunger like never before. It scraped him down to his bones, pulled at the marrow. He wasn't oblivious to the changes in himself, but he did not care. The cancer had cost him his career, the only job he knew. Now he had strength, the dexterity he'd lost over the last two years. He wanted a cigarette but the urge came too strong, as if he needed to eat it, not smoke it.

He felt the jade against his skin, the power of it tearing through his illness, thickening his muscles. His need for it scored under his skin. The tight confines of the locker were hot, and while he could not see Veta, he could feel her. Sensed everything about her. Her breasts cushioned against him, her hips to his hips. His groin thickened and he wanted to fuck her, badly, but his hunger was more for the stone than her.

It was here. The brother of it in a sack around his neck. He'd read the diary, knew what it was doing, but he had no control. He must have it to survive.

"I hear nothing," Veta said and he hushed her.

He'd been tucked in the rock face since before closing, waiting beyond an hour of silence and certainty that the British agents were all gone. Stefan told him they were outside, waiting for them, and as he pushed open the door, he couldn't tell if the sun was setting. He stepped out and turned to pull Veta from the locker. She breathed and stretched, then looked around. He crossed the siege battery lookout, then motioned her to walk ahead.

The corridors of stone were wide, the floor smooth from centuries of walking. But it's not where he wanted to be, and he opened his jacket, pulling out the jade and unwrapping it. It vibrated in his palms. He felt it travel upward, wrap him. He strode the corridor, suddenly knowing where to go, feeling it calling to him. Deeper into the darkness, he flicked on his small flashlight, suddenly amused they'd outsmarted them all. Stefan would watch and warn them, lead them on a chase if necessary.

Veta's hand closed over it. "Give it to me."

He shoved her away. "No. It leads the way."

She reared, staring at him with a look that bordered on revulsion. His eyes narrowed and yet she didn't back down. Her attention was on his face, his body. She sniffed at him like he was a fresh meal. "You want me, I smell it."

He dismissed her, striding to the section where an oblong cut in the rock was blocked with the two-inch-wide steel bars. He removed the bottle from his small waist pack. It was all he could get into the storage locker with him. He unscrewed the top and splashed the acid on the stone. It ate the metal, smoldering with a foul odor. Veta backed away. The smell had no effect on him. He gripped the bar. It came off in his hand. He glanced at her, scowling at how she took a step back from him.

"You fear me now?" It did not bother him. The energy rushing through his blood was like a drug.

"Nyet. But I can do this, too." She grabbed a bar and yanked it from its base. Then she bent it. "We don't need the other half. Stefan has not answered. We must stop."

He rounded on her, brandishing a bar of steel. "Never! You must pay for it all now, Lizveta. It is left for you and me." He pulled another steel rod, then another, and did not wait for her as he crawled through the opening and into the ancient hive of tunnels. "The legend is all truth. It gives back your youth."

"It gives us more," she said almost giddy, petting the stone. It glowed softly.

"This way." He ducked to the tunnel, sniffed the air, his light and the soft glow of the jade leading him deeper into the caverns.

As Sebastian searched the rock formations, he kept a watch on Olivia climbing the wall. She was experienced, but he knew she struggled wearing the Dragon Skin. It was her weight belt for the dive and climbing couldn't be easy. His light followed her. She left nothing to chance and searched every hole and crack. So far, nothing. Then she went still and sprayed a million candles' worth of power over the cavern. Sebastian crawled through and stood beside her.

"Something else, isn't it?"

"I'll say." The cavern was monstrous, its ceiling probably thirty feet high. Massive stalactites hung like teeth, meeting their mates on the ground piled with broken stone. A lot of broken stone. Not a good sign, he thought, then spotted another feeder tunnel. His light revealed two more black holes leading off into nothing. His weapon drawn, he inspected the shadows.

"We're above sea level by three hundred feet, Dr. Corrigan."

Hanging on the rock, she swung a look at Lewis. "Seriously?"

"Yes, ma'am. Water doesn't even come close to reaching up here. Creepy, huh? Almost like it drew the water in."

She shined her light at the formations dripping to the pool below, then to the ceiling again. "Then it's run off from the top, through cracks and fissures. But I've been known to be wrong."

"What are you going for?" Sebastian said as she climbed toward the uppermost corner.

"There's a cavity, deeper than the others. Looks unnatural. Too straight. Over this way," she said. "Give me some light above me so I can climb." He gave her what she wanted, but she was like a monkey up there, and he moved nearer when she disappeared behind a stalactite.

Olivia felt for a grip in the stone, then pulled herself higher. She braced her foot on the rock, twisted her Maglite, then held it between her teeth. She leaned into the hole. The walls were chiseled. She glanced back at Sebastian, but couldn't see him, the hole blocked by the giant stalactite. She worked a little higher, her forearms braced as her light flashed off something in the shadows. She leaned on her stomach, wiggling, and touched something smooth. She tipped her head to shine the light. She shrieked around the Mag-lite.

His shield. A piece of it, at least, but her light gave enough shadow that she recognized the similarities to the Viking's sword. Protection and power, the runes read. She reached for it, but had to get a little farther in to do it. A sliver of panic shot through her when one foot left the ground. Sebastian directed her, and she braced, then grabbed for it. As if made of grain, the shield disintegrated into pieces. She made a sound around the Maglite when she saw the small pile of wrappings behind it. Burlap, she thought, and snagged a few threads, carefully drawing it closer. It had weight. She adjusted the light in her mouth, then grabbed it. "Sebastian, oh God, it's here!" She braced her back and hip so she would use two hands and checked the wrappings for the spell, the chains. But there was nothing except the sack covering.

"You are one smart woman, Livi," came softly through the PRR.

She smiled to herself, feeling that skip right across her heart. "But he broke her spell." She looked at his shield, similar to the fragment the old man had given her. Olivia inhaled, then let it out in a long slow breath. *We did it,* she thought, then frowned when the stone suddenly grew a little brighter. "Ohhh boy, it's changing. Oh no, no, the mate is near!" She stuffed it down her dive suit, zipping it snuggly. "Did you hear me?"

"Climb down. We have company."

"What?" She flinched and grappled to keep from falling.

"I heard something. Take cover," he said softly.

Olivia worked slowly down.

The woman never behaves. Sebastian tucked his light under the pistol and followed the sound in the dark. "Lewis, no talking, shoot first."

"Roger that."

Then he spotted the figure and fired. The spark of return fire sprayed the cavern. Rocks burst in a shower of stone, plopping in the endless pool, on him, on Lewis.

"Give me the stone!" came like a burst from a bullhorn.

"Now you know that's not happening." They must have come through the war tunnels. "Lewis, use your light." The Marine turned the million-watt candlepower on the honeycombed walls. Shock pushed through him. "Will you look at that. Holy shit."

Kolbash was on the edge of the left tunnel, his hand gripping the rock above him, hunched when the ceiling was high. His arms looked long, swinging loosely from his shoulders like those of an ape. Nevolin was behind him, a little hunched and pawing his back. She wasn't in any better shape. Her face was broader, her nose sloping into her mouth.

"It is the fountain of youth," Olivia said, her whisper carrying. "But it turned back the clock too far. Biologically. He's going Cro-Magnon."

"Get your ass down here, woman!" Sebastian motioned for Lewis to move to his left, and kept his eyes on the target about twenty yards on the other side of the cavern.

Then Kolbash brought the weapon up.

Sebastian fired. "Livi, down!" But Kolbash held his trigger and waved his arm. Bullets ricocheted over the cavern walls. Chunks of stalagmites broke and tumbled. Olivia was an easy target as she worked her way down.

Sebastian put two more in Kolbash's chest. He staggered back. Kevlar, Sebastian realized, and a second later, Lewis fired. Clothing and flesh burst from Kolbash's kneecap and thigh. Kolbash went down, then, with an echoing roar, pushed to his feet.

"Okay, that's not supposed to happen."

Kolbash looked at the weapon in his hand, then threw it aside.

Nevolin appeared behind him, and Lewis put a round in her shoulder. She fell on her rear, but Kolbash didn't even look at her before he jumped. Far. Fifteen feet away, he landed in a squat, then straightened, yet he didn't quite make it to his full height.

"Give it to me!" came in a low growl. He gripped the half of stone, and went for Olivia.

Sebastian lurched from behind the stalagmite and threw himself at him. They collided midair and fell to the ground. The jade tumbled, bouncing twice. Sebastian pounded on Kolbash and Olivia dove for the stone.

With a savage scream, Nevolin scrabbled like an animal toward the jade. Lewis's shots followed her.

"Doc . . ?" Lewis warned.

"She's mine, Lewis!" Olivia let her come and punched, once, twice, her knuckles burning. Her mind filled with Noble and his bloody finger and she hit Nevolin again. The concierge and bellman. The NSA agent who was only watching their back. *This bitch needs to die.* Nevolin's nose bled, and Olivia shot out her leg, the sidekick hitting Nevolin's stomach. Nevolin flew back, uncoordinated and sloppy, but she had the strength to kill. She grabbed a piece of stalagmite, her face hideously twisted, and bolted for Olivia. Olivia prepared for the impact, but Nevolin never made it. A bullet impacted her forehead and threw her to the ground. Nevolin didn't move. Olivia looked at Lewis.

"He said shoot first, ma'am." She waved her thanks, then went for the stone.

Sebastian staggered back from Kolbash, but when Kolbash saw Olivia, the beast of a man lunged for the stones. She grabbed them first.

"Don't put it together!" Sebastian shouted.

"I'm not trying to!"

As if magnetized, the two pieces clapped together. For a second, nothing happened. Then the seam between the jade glowed, cool in her hands even with gloves, and she held it tight, thinking of the monk, of the princess and the life she'd led, the family she'd lost and the man she'd loved. She could almost see her and felt the power of the jade; it was like holding a spinning top in her hands. The core of it brightened, and she lifted her gaze to Sebastian, then to Kolbash. She gasped.

His features were demonic, his forehead thick and protruding, his nose flat across his face. He stared at her with watery red eyes. His skin was covered in hair, even his ears. Sebastian aimed at him, but Kolbash was mesmerized by the jade, its radiance. Like an animal, he sniffed the air, advancing. His features grew more distorted, his mouth protruding beyond his nose. His shoulders dropped. His posture curved.

"He's morphing," Lewis said. "Jesus H!"

Sebastian pushed Olivia behind a stalagmite, then saw the strange glow in her green eyes. "Olivia?"

"It turns on evil," she said, her gaze on Kolbash. "It turns only them."

Then he saw her lips move, words he didn't recognize spilling from her mouth. He felt a chill when he realized it was Gaelic. She repeated it, holding the jade skull, its aura intensifying. Her words enraged Kolbash and, like an ape, he scaled the walls, demanding the stone. His eyes held a wild crazed sheen and Sebastian's pistol followed him.

"Don't shoot. It won't do any good."

"It can't hurt." He fired.

Kolbash jumped out of the path, grabbing Nevolin by the arm and pulling her. Her body bounced on the stone and he held her at his side like a rag doll. The ground beneath his feet shifted, stalactites broke and fell. Olivia stumbled forward and Sebastian lurched, grabbed her vest, stopping her fall. The jade slipped from her hands and rolled down the incline.

The stone dazzled Kolbash and he grabbed it, immediately darting into a darkened tunnel.

"No!" She tried to go for it, but Sebastian blocked her.

"It's coming down." A massive crack separated the stone wall. Powder dusted the air. He pushed her toward the Marine. "Lewis! Get her out of here."

Lewis grabbed her shoulder. "Ma'am, we have to go."

Sebastian followed Kolbash and the blood trail.

"Sebastian, don't!" The ground rolled, chunks breaking off, separating them.

"Now Doc. It's caving," Lewis pulled her back. "We'll be trapped!"

"No! Sebastian, don't. It's not worth it. Let it go!"

But she couldn't see him, the cave-in filling the void. She tried her PRR, heard him beg her to get out. *"Please Livi, go."*

"Not without you!"

"I'm coming back to love you, baby, don't forget that. Lewis!" he demanded.

Lewis latched onto her BC vest, dragging her until she had no choice, till she was forced to crawl backward down the sloping rock. She kept looking back, hoping to see Sebastian. She found a spot to turn around and the downhill climb went faster, but the shaking rock made her grab for purchase. *The jade's doing this. My fault.* She slid down the short incline to the ledge and the tanks. Sebastian's were beside hers. Lewis helped her lift her tanks and her heart shattered. *He's coming,* she thought, *he is.* She wanted to scream, to cry, but all she did was pray and pull on her mask. She inflated her buoyancy converter. Rock tumbled, plopped in the water.

"Down, now." She tapped Lewis and hugging the Sea Scooter, they jumped. They grabbed on to the propulsion to bring them out of the cave and into the open sea. Several yards later, they surfaced. Esposito grabbed her tanks and pulled her aboard. Olivia immediately shed them and demanded the infrared scope.

Someone handed it over and she focused on the cave. The boat rocked.

"Where's Agent Fontenòt?"

"In there. With Kolbash. They're in the tunnels."

Lewis grabbed a hand radio. "Fox One to Drac. You there?" Max came on the line and Lewis spoke to him.

Olivia didn't hear, her throat so tight she could barely breathe. *Come on, honey, come on.* He didn't show.

She stared at the cave entrance, waiting. Stones tumbled from the passageway and into the water. Then like a yawning monster, dust and rock belched from the cave.

Oh, Sebastian. "Get me on the shore. Now."

No one spoke as the boat swiftly turned on a curl of waves.

Sebastian checked his pistol, then slapped in another magazine. He prayed Olivia made it out and glanced back. More rocks fell, the way behind him closing off as he pushed ahead. The confines brought memories he didn't want as he crawled through. He heard Kolbash's heavy breathing, like the grunts of a wild beast. He could see the glow of the jade, the trail of blood splashed on the rocks. He neared.

In the hollow, Kolbash stopped, clutching Nevolin in his

arms. She was a limp bloody rag, and he pawed her face, lifting the jade as if she could see his gift. Then suddenly he rounded, his eyes red as he gripped the stone.

A monster, Sebastian thought, aiming for his eyes. Kolbash's expression changed from twisted rage to helpless pleading, as if he knew what the jade was doing to him and wanted to end it. Sebastian thought of the lives he'd taken, the destruction this man left behind, and obliged. He fired. The bullet penetrated Kolbash's eye, the back of his head splattering the stone.

A moment later, the ceiling caved.

Olivia jumped out of the car and ran past the police and Royal Marines. Emergency crews arrived. Talk was furious, and she caught a few morose looks. She ran faster into the tunnels, passing British troops. They didn't look hopeful.

She rushed into the tunnel, the corridors wide and uneven. "Sebastian." She ran to the right, trying to put their position in the caves with the tunnel and batteries. She saw several men at the torn wall, pulling rocks from the twisted metal. She slowed.

"Oh God, please." Her throat burned, tears swelling.

Max threw aside rocks with a wild fury, his expression killing her.

"No, no!" She grabbed rocks, flinging them. "I did *not* reach this point in my life to lose him again. I wasn't stupid this time, I wasn't." The weight of her grief sent her to her knees, sobbing and frantically tearing at the stones. Max came to her, pulling her from the ground, and she clutched him, sobbing. "He didn't have to go after him."

"Yes, I did."

She looked up, banging her head with Max's chin. She turned. The dark corridor was shadowed with searchlights, but she recognized his walk and ran to him. He opened his arms, taking her against his chest like an incoming round. She clung to him, crying.

"Don't do that again!" She punched his back.

"Aww, jeez, don't cry, honey."

"Yeah, sure. Give me a minute." She buried her face in his chest, sniffled, and he tipped her face up, brushing his thumb across her tears.

"I almost screwed it up. Sorry."

"I forgive you."

He smiled. "Be tough to love you if you didn't."

"Good thing I'm so magnanimous." He grinned and she touched his face, his lips.

She loved him in her soul, down to her bones. Every cell of her body beckoned for his love, for a life with him and she was just feeling her relief when he said, "Missing this?"

She twisted, refusing to let him go, and saw the jade in his palm. "Oh my God." It was one piece and cold. "We need to cover this somehow."

"I don't think it's dangerous anymore." He pressed it into her hands. She frowned at it, agreeing, then met his gaze. "You found your legend, *cherie*. You found the truth."

"Yeah," she said, thumbing the blood on his forehead. "I found more than that. I found my way back to you." Her lip quivered a bit, and he moaned, kissed her, his mouth rolling slowly over hers. She clung, her fingers digging in as if to pull him inside her, his passion locking everything else out. With Sebastian, there was little room for much else. He crushed her in his arms, and she wanted only more of him, of his sexy smiles and dark looks. More endless nights in his arms.

She was meant to be with him, she understood that now. She had an Irish princess to thank for that. Because as far as second chances go, this one was legendary.

TWENTY-ONE

Thirty miles outside Moscow

L eonid slipped into the old barn and backed up against the wall. He waited for his eyesight to adjust to the darkness.

He didn't know who he was meeting with, a danger in itself, but he was determined to learn who'd orchestrated Nevolin's capture of the sub and the buyers for the missiles. Someone close to his office had leaked classified material to the *krasnaya mafiya*. A call made from Vlad Dovyestoff's cell phone number brought him here. The number to trace had come from a source he could not confirm.

The nuclear warhead missiles were in Danish hands, inspected by the UN, the Americans, and Russia was paying the price for the renegade woman and her lover. The crimes of the *Trident* and the loss of a hundred family members of her crew on the *Northern Lion* had the people in an uproar. Russia had struck twice on her own people.

He felt the burden of his own blame.

The damage from protesters was more than a few buildings and parked cars. Russia's future was uncertain and the president did little to ease their outrage. His reelection to office again would prove that corruption still reached his door. Several of his FSB colleagues had vanished, sinking into the underworld rather than face charges. The Security Council met with officials and had determined to conduct a complete review. He would never learn the truth, he thought, wanting nothing to do with it while the burden of the truth fell in his lap.

He drew his weapon, moving to the far right, near the horse stalls that had not been used in a two decades. He pushed between the rotting slats that carried the stench of age.

A figure left a stall, opening the gated door.

He kept in the shadows.

Instantly he recognized Golubev. Overweight and slovenly, the man waddled near. His hand was inside his coat pocket. On a weapon, Leonid assumed. Golubev was never far from his own defense. "You are an embarrassment to the Politburo."

"I saved face for Russia. We were close and would have won if Commander Nevolin had not trapped the *Trident*. We could have annihilated the capitalists!"

Leonid thought it ironic that people like Golubev blamed capitalism. Corruption began with denying the people their livelihood and keeping it for themselves. If the government would leave the Russian people alone, Leonid knew in his bones, they would prosper. Russians didn't need the government in their personal lives. But it was the way, he thought.

"The Americans?" he said, no longer trying to hide his disgust. "No, Golubev. Never. They would have retaliated and Russia would be worse off than we are now. You involved Agar, the krasnaya. Surely, you did not believe they would let these deaths go unanswered."

"I did not bring them into it, she did!"

"Nevolin needed a connection to do that, someone to pave the way with Dovyestoff. Vlad has escaped, yet Agar is in the custody of the Americans." He would be dead soon. The mafia would not allow this failure to go unpunished.

Golubev's eyes widened and Leonid found a little pleasure in his panic.

He lifted the weapon.

"I did this for Russia!" Golubev pleaded.

"For your own pockets. Our president wishes it. And I obey orders."

"Whose? Who gave this order?"

"I did." He pulled the trigger two times. Each round met its target. Golubev could not move fast enough to avoid their strikes. His skull exploded first, the second bullet striking his chest, penetrating his heart. He fell forward like a slab of meat.

Leonid collected the shells, unscrewed the suppressor, then holstered the weapon. He crossed to the entrance and paused. His car sat alone, its warm hood still steaming against the frigid cold. His gaze never turned to the man tucked against the fir trees.

"It is done."

"That how you Russians answer every problem? With that?" He inclined his head to the barn, but Leonid knew he didn't want an answer. "It's not finished until we find the person who paid for this. We won't let it."

He turned his head to look at the man. He was younger and vital, and Leonid felt a measure of intimidation. He appeared prepared to kill him right now.

"Agar is talking."

It mattered little to Leonid. "I fear we will never find the person." The millions given, spent, led them to accounts in Switzerland and the Grand Cayman Islands. The man responsible was only a number.

"We'll find him." He met his gaze. "He's lost millions and the missiles, and I imagine he's a little upset. He'll strike again." His lips curved in a smile and Leonid noticed the hint of old bruises. "This was all orchestrated to bring down the FSB."

Leonid snapped a look at him.

"And to bring our countries to the brink of World War Three. He didn't care if it was Russia or the United States who made the first strike. Ask yourself who's powerful enough to destroy us all, Sodorov? Who wanted to sit back and watch us eat each other alive?"

The man didn't wait for an answer and turned away, slipping into the forest.

Leonid walked to his car, Golubev's beside it. From his trunk, he removed the parcel, then tossed it inside the old barn. He climbed into his own vehicle and drove away. A half mile from the barn, he hit the detonator. On the horizon, any evidence went up in flames.

New Orleans
Two months later

The sun was unrelenting in a cloudless sky. The breeze off the water cooled the New Orleans heat, taking the fragrance of flowers on the wind. Around them were nearly a hundred people, frothy decorations, and a half dozen bridesmaids, but his world centered only on the woman declaring her love for him. Sebastian felt unhinged till this moment, but it was tough to keep a straight face when Olivia was crossing her eyes as the priest spoke.

Life was certainly going to be interesting again, and he was looking forward to it. He glanced at the waterfront filled with family and friends. Last time, the ceremony was over in five minutes. This time, it was full throttle.

Olivia's mother was loving every second of it. Her dad didn't look too unhappy either. But it was her brothers who amused the hell out of him. The hippie, anti-establishment brothers who gave him hell were grinning from ear to ear, two of them in Navy uniforms. Yup, definitely fascinating, he thought, meeting her gaze.

She took his breath away, her gown a vision in soft pale gold, fitted, hauntingly medieval and showing off a body he hungered for. Across her shoulder, she wore a little sash of her Corrigan tartan, and he thought the Maguire's princess would be proud. Yet it was the look in her eyes that snagged him by the throat. Absolute love, faith, his trust. He could conquer anything if she just kept looking at him like that.

They exchanged rings and Olivia gasped when he slid on the rock. It was shaped like Ice Harvest, a smooth pale blue diamond he'd bought in Singapore and never knew why. She slipped on his band and he laced his fingers with hers, neither of them really listening till the priest declared them married. Again. He leaned in.

"Mine. Mine. Mine," he said and she laughed softly, and he kissed her, sealing a vow to the only woman he'd ever loved. Till he'd seen her hovering over him in the alley, he never realized how much he'd missed her. How incomplete he was without her. She was the missing piece of his life, part of his soul he'd lost, and though he'd never believed in past lives, Sebastian understood—he'd loved her for centuries.

Loud cheers surrounded them as she drew back, and he recognized that mischievous gleam in her green eyes. "Rut-roh. What are you planning?"

"To make you a very happy man tonight."

"Oh Livi, you already have." Her eyes teared, and she kissed him again before they turned down the aisle. Old memories faded, new ones filling every moment with her. Then the somber music suddenly changed, and he laughed, pure delight spilling through him. She was such a rebel. Sebastian spun Olivia into his arms, dancing down the aisle and into to their new life—the King's "Hunka Hunka Burning Love" leading the way.

AUTHOR'S NOTE

People often ask me where I get my ideas. It's fiction—anything can spark it. Part of this story came from a photo in the May 2007 U.S. Navy magazine, *All Hands*. I would have never seen it if I hadn't been in a Navy hospital waiting for an appointment. (Go Navy!) The picture was a cross section of a glacier with a submarine traveling beneath its jagged underside. It was Photoshopped, I'm sure, yet the image fascinated and scared the heck out of me. It was paired with a wonderful article, "Navigating the Frozen Sea," by U.S. Navy MC1 Steven Smith, about U.S. submarines traveling under the arctic circle during Operation Ice Exercise (ICEX) with the UK Navy. Submariners have my deepest respect. That tour of duty takes bravery many of us, including me, don't have.

Vikings invaded Ireland long before England. Kidnap, pillage, and plunder was the order of the day. Over the years, trading became more profitable, and hundreds of pieces of proof of Nordic tribes grace Ireland's museums and private collections. I even saw it on eBay, provenance doubtful. The Celt and Nordic tribes found in China are a reality. The discoveries change the way we look at migration long before there were borders. More are being discovered as the polar ice cap grows smaller.

For more information try these sites:

www.giftofireland.com/Articlethree.htm
www.barnesreview.org/html/julyaug2000lead.html

The Kilbarron castle ruins are real, yet the friary is ficti-tious, as is the entire legend. However, those of you who've read my historical PenDragon series might recognize a con-nection. Yes, the Maguire in the legend is Ian, the same clan leader who caused Siobhan and Fionna a great deal of trou-ble. The legend is part of his love story, as yet unwritten. To Ireland, forgive my license with a bit of history. My fondest wish is never to offend anyone and just write a story that will take you places. I hope you've enjoyed Sebastian and Olivia's story. Look for the final book in the Dragon One series soon.

Don't miss Mary Wine's BEDDING THE ENEMY,
in stores now!

He was staring at her.

Helena looked through her lowered eyelashes at him. He was a Scot and no mistake about it. Held in place around his waist was a great kilt. Folded into pleats that fell longer in the back, his plaid was made up in heather, tan, and green. She knew little of the different clans and their tartans but she could see how proud he was. The nobles she passed among scoffed at him, but she didn't think he would even cringe if he were to hear their mutters. She didn't think the gossip would make an impact. He looked impenetrable. Strength radiated from him. There was nothing pompous about him, only pure brawn.

Her attention was captivated by him. She had seen other Scots wearing their kilts, but there was something more about him. A warm ripple moved across her skin. His doublet had sleeves that were closed, making him look formal, in truth more formal than the brocade-clad men standing near her brother. There wasn't a single gold or silver bead sewn to that doublet, but he looked ready to meet his king. It was the slant of his chin, the way he stood.

"You appear to have an admirer, Helena."

Edmund sounded conceited, and his friends chuckled. Her brother's words surfaced in her mind and she shifted her gaze to the men standing near her brother. They were poised in perfect poses that showed off their new clothing. One even had a lace-edged handkerchief dangling from one hand.

She suddenly noticed how much of a fiction it was. Edmund didn't believe them to be his friends, but he stood jesting with them. Each one of them would sell the other out for the right amount. It was so very sad. Like a sickness you knew would claim their lives but could do nothing about.

"A Scot, no less."

Edmund eyed her. She stared back, unwilling to allow him to see into her thoughts. Annoyance flickered in his eyes when she remained calm. He waved his hands, dismissing her.

She turned quickly before he heard the soft sound of a gasp. She hadn't realized she was holding her breath. It was such a curious reaction. Peeking back across the hall, she found the man responsible for invading her thoughts completely. He had a rugged look to him, his cheekbones high and defined. No paint decorated his face. His skin was a healthy tone she hadn't realized she missed so much. He was clean-shaven, in contrast to the rumors she'd heard of Scotland's men. Of course, many Englishmen wore beards. But his hair was longer, touching his shoulders and full of curl. It was dark as midnight, and she found it quite rakish.

He caught her staring at him. She froze, her heartbeat accelerating. His dark eyes seemed alive even from across the room. His lips twitched up, flashing her a glimpse of strong teeth. He reached up to tug lightly on the corner of his knitted bonnet. She felt connected to him, her body strangely aware of his, even from so great a distance. Sensations rippled down her spine and into her belly. She sank into a tiny curtsy without thought or consideration. It was a response, pure and simple.

And try THE FALCON PRINCE by Karen Kelley . . .

She needed to clear her head. Nothing in life mattered when she was out running. This was her time. She didn't have to worry that people thought she was a little mentally off-balanced. She didn't have to . . .

A hawk swooped down, landing on the trail in front of her.

She came to a grinding halt, feet still running in place, and then stopping altogether.

What the hell? Hawks didn't just land in front of people. And it should have taken off as soon as it spotted her.

Ria stared at the bird as she tried to catch her breath, bending over and resting her sweaty palms on her knees.

The hawk was magnificent, with a creamy white breast and speckled, dark brown wings that blended into black tips. The bird was so close she could see its sharp talons. Talons that were made for catching and holding prey. Something about this wasn't good. Probably because the hawk still hadn't moved. It stared at her as though it were silently trying to communicate. This was weird. No, it was more than weird.

Almost as weird as the thick fog rolling in. She straightened, her gaze flitting from tree to tree until she could no longer make them out. An icy chill raced down her back as if someone had run an ice cube over her spine.

Fog wasn't that unusual. Right? It was early morning, and the trail behind her house was in a low spot. Except this fog wasn't like any fog she'd ever seen. Kind of *Friday the 13th* creepy.

Alrighty, maybe this was her cue to leave.

Someone groaned, but the fog was so thick now she couldn't see a thing. Ria hesitated. What if the hawk had been trying to tell her that his owner was hurt? That . . . that . . .

It had finally happened. She had completely lost her freakin' mind.

But the fog began to dissipate enough that she could make out a man's face. A very tall man. At least six-two. With short dark hair. Strong chin. Green eyes that studied her. Tanned skin. Muscular chest . . .

Her assessment came to a screeching halt.

Muscular *bare* chest.

The man stepped forward. "I'm Prince Kristor, from New Symtaria. I'm here to take you back to my planet," he said in a deep commanding voice.

The fog vanished.

The man was totally naked.

Keep an eye out for THE DEADLIEST SIN
by Caroline Richards, coming next month!

The air was like a heavy linen sheet pressed against Julia's face, yet a cold sweat plastered her chemise and dress to her body. It was peculiar, this ability to retreat into herself, away from the pain numbing her leg and away from the threat that lay outside this suffocating room.

A few moments, an hour, or a day passed. She found herself sitting, her limbs trembling against the effort. Guilt choked her, a tide of nausea threatening to sweep away the tattered edges of her self-regard. Why had she ignored Meredith's warnings and accepted Wadsworth's invitation to photograph his country estate? Julia felt for the ground beneath her, flexing stiff fingers, a film of dust gathering under her nails. If she could push herself higher, lean against a wall, allow the blood to flow . . .

The pain in her leg was a strange solace. As were thoughts of Montfort, her refuge, the splendid seclusion where her life with her sister and her aunt had begun. She could remember nothing else, her early childhood an empty canvas, bleached of memories. Lady Meredith Woolcott had offered a universe onto itself. Protected, guarded, secure—for a reason.

Julia's mouth was dry. She longed for water to wash away her remorse. New images crowded her thoughts, taking over the darkness in bright bursts of light. Meredith and Rowena waving to her from the green expanse of lawn at Montfort. The sun dancing on the tranquil pond in the east gardens.

Meredith's eyes, clouded with worry, that last afternoon in the library. Wise counsel from her aunt that Julia had chosen, in her defiance, to ignore, warnings that were meant to be heeded. Secrets that were meant to be kept.

She ran a shaking hand through the shambles of her hair, her bonnet long discarded somewhere in the dark. She pieced together her shattered thoughts. When had she arrived? Last evening or days ago? A picture began to form. Her carriage had clattered up to a house, a daunting silhouette, all crenellations and peaks, chandeliers glittering coldly into the gathering dusk. The entryway had been brightly lit, the air infused with the perfume of decadence, sultry and heavy. That much she could remember before her mind clamped shut.

The world tilted and she ground her nails into the stone beneath her palms for balance. She should be sobbing by now but her eyes were sandpaper dry. Voices echoed in the dark, or were they footsteps, corporal and real? Her ears strained and she craned her neck upward, peering into the thick darkness. There was a sense of vibration more than sounds themselves, hearing as the deaf hear. Footsteps, actual or imagined, would do her no good. She felt the floor around her, imagining a prison of rotted wood and broken stone, even though logic told her there had to be an entranceway. Taking a deep breath, she twisted onto her left hip, arms flailing to find purchase, to heave herself into a standing position. Not for the first time in her life, she cursed the heavy skirts, entangled now with her legs, the painful fire burning higher.

No wall. Nothing to lean upon. If she could at least stand—She pushed herself up on her right elbow, wrestling aside her skirts with an impatient hand. The fabric tore, the sound muffled in the darkness. The white-hot pain no longer mattered, nor did the bile flooding her throat. Pulling her legs beneath her, she dragged herself up, swaying like a mad marionette without the security of strings.

The silence was complete because she'd stopped breathing. Arms outstretched, her hands clutched at air. Just one small step, one after the other, and she would encounter a wall, a door, something. She bit back a silent plea. Hadn't Meredith taught them long ago about the uselessness of prayer?

And then it happened. Her palms were halted by the sensation of solid stone. Instinctively, she stilled, convinced that she was losing her mind. The sensation of breath, the barely perceptible rise and fall of a chest beneath her opened palms. Where there had been black there was now a shower of stars in front of her eyes, a humming in her head.

And then she saw him, without the benefit of light or the quick trace of her fingers, but behind her unseeing eyes.

She took a step back in the darkness, away from him. The man who wanted her dead.